D0742622

NOBODY'S GIRL

Abandoned when just hours old and clutching the object which was to give her her name, Pearl Button had a hard start to life. Now 16, she's finally managed to escape. Finding work at a nearby cafe, Pearl is thrilled to start earning her own money, even if she must contend with sharp tongued owner Dolly Dolby and her menacing son Kevin. Soon, though, Pearl's life is thrown into jeopardy when she becomes tangled up in the murky South London underworld, while at the orphanage where she spent her wretched childhood, a terrible secret is about to be unleashed.

NOBODY'S GIRL

NOBODY'S GIRL

by

Kitty Neale

Magna Large Print Books
Long Preston, North Yorkshire,
BD23 4ND, England.

British Library Cataloguing in Publication Data.

Neale, Kitty
    Nobody's girl.

        A catalogue record of this book is
        available from the British Library

        ISBN   978-0-7505-2863-4

First published in Great Britain in 2007 by HarperCollins Publishers

Copyright © Kitty Neale 2007

Cover illustration © Rod Ashford

Published in Large Print 2008 by arrangement with HarperCollins Publishers

Magna Large Print is an imprint of Library Magna Books Ltd.

Printed and bound in Great Britain by
T.J. (International) Ltd., Cornwall, PL28 8RW

With thanks to Maxine Hitchcock, Keshini Naidoo, and all the team at Avon for their much appreciated kindness and help in bringing this novel to print.

For Rita McAneny.

We have worked together, laughed together, shared sadness and tears, my precious friend for over twenty years.

Author's Note

Many places and street names mentioned in this book are real. However, others, and some of the topography, along with all of the characters, are just figments of my imagination.

Prologue

The moon was in its first quarter as the man climbed out of his car. A high wind wailed through the skeletal branches of trees, the sound echoing that of the tiny bundle clutched in his arms. He ignored the cries, uncaring, feeling only disgust as he held the bundle away from his body.

His face was grim. He was going to make his daughter pay for almost ruining the family name, and her bastard would pay too. It would cost him dearly, yet worth it to watch her suffer, not once, but twice. My God, he had thought her perfect, his only child, but she had turned out to be a slut.

He reached the end of the lane, his eyes flicking from side to side as he turned onto a small, built-up road. He had chosen well. There were no houses, and with a wartime blackout in force, no streetlights pierced the dense blanket of darkness.

The building loomed, but still he was cautious, looking swiftly over his shoulder before roughly laying the bundle on its concrete steps. The wrapping fell to one side, the infant mewling, but the man was heedless of the cold night air.

At first he had wanted the bastard dead, but then decided it would be too easy for her, the slut's suffering short. No, he'd bide his time, watch her grieve, and then one day, when the time was right, he'd tell her the truth. And when he did, he'd watch as she suffered all over again.

His smile thin, he swung on his heels now, swiftly walking away.

He was only just out of sight when a door swung open. A woman emerged, running swiftly down the steps and, taking up the baby, she carried it inside.

1

Battersea, South London, 1956
Dolly Dolby picked up a thick white plate from the stack and scowled. 'Gertie, get in here!'

Up to the elbows in hot water, Gertrude Wilson sighed and, grabbing a tea towel, she hurriedly dried her hands before leaving the small, cramped washing-up area. She was used to Dolly's moods and met her ferocious gaze with equilibrium.

'What do you want now?'

Dolly stiffened with annoyance. She was a woman at odds with her name: there was nothing doll-like in her appearance. Tall, formidable, and big-boned, with a broad flat face above wide shoulders, her only saving grace was long, thick, chestnut-brown hair. However, the only person likely to see it was her husband when she let it down at night. In the kitchen she wore it pulled back tightly and covered with a thick hairnet.

Scowling again, she indicated the remnant of dried egg on the rim of the plate. 'What do you call this?'

'I do me best, but I ain't feeling too good today.'

'What, again? Mrs Neverwell, that's you. If it ain't your bleeding varicose veins, it's your arthritis. Maybe I should think about replacing you with someone who can wash up properly.'

It was an empty threat, but one Dolly enjoyed. Gertie had been working in the café for over ten years, and in her own way Dolly was fond of the woman. There weren't many who would put up with the conditions in the small washing-up room, which contained just two deep Belfast sinks with wooden draining boards. There was a tiny window looking out onto the yard, and now, in July, it was like working in a hothouse.

'After all the years I've worked for you, you're threatening to sack me over one dirty plate,' Gertie whined, her small brown eyes filling with tears.

'All right,' Dolly placated, 'don't start with the waterworks. I'm just spouting wind and you know that. Just make sure that in future you wash up properly.'

'Two full breakfasts with black pudding and fried bread,' Rita Marriner shouted as she hurried into the kitchen, slapping an order slip onto the table.

Dolly glared at the young waitress. 'Didn't you hear the bell? Those two breakfasts have been standing there for nearly five minutes.'

Rita's eyes blazed as she picked up the standard meal of sausages, bacon, fried eggs and beans. 'No, I didn't hear the bell. I've only got one pair

17

of hands and it's a bit much expecting me to cope with all the tables. It's about time you found another waitress.'

'Don't give me any lip, young lady. You're getting paid extra so you ain't got much to complain about. Now get those breakfasts out of here and make sure you ask them if they want bread and butter with it.'

Clutching the two plates, Rita pushed the swing doors with her bottom, saying as she reversed out of the kitchen, 'Why don't you stick a bloody broom up me arse and I'll sweep the floor at the same time!'

Dolly's mouth opened and shut like a fish floundering out of water. She turned her eyes on Gertie, taking her anger out on the thin, middle-aged woman as she yelled, 'What are you looking at? Get on with the washing-up.'

As Gertie scurried off, Dolly slapped four rashers of bacon into a frying pan, her shoulders rigid. Rita had been working in the café for only about two months, but the young madam would have to go. It was always the same with youngsters nowadays: they gave you lip, and she wasn't putting up with it. Mind you, with only one waitress at the moment she'd have to stay her hand until she found a replacement.

'Two eggs on toast, and one full breakfast,' Rita yelled again, the door abruptly swinging shut.

The pace was picking up, costermongers from the market ready for their breakfasts. Two more rashers joined the pan, all Dolly's concentration now focused on the morning rush.

Bernard Dolby stood behind the counter, a large stainless-steel pot in his hand as he poured tea into thick, white china cups. The antithesis of his wife, Bernard was quite short and thin, except for a slightly protruding beer belly. He had light brown hair that was thinning, and most of the time his grey eyes carried a mild expression.

Rita came running up, looking harassed as she picked up the cups of tea, calling out as she hurried away again, 'Two slices of bread and butter please, Bernie.'

He turned to the work surface behind him, spreading butter on the bread before cutting the slices into neat triangles. 'Who are they for, Rita?'

'Table two.'

'Morning, Derek,' Bernie said as he took the plate across the room and placed it beside the man.

Derek Lewis looked up, his pug-nosed face breaking into a grin. 'Watcha, mate. I won me fight last night.'

Bernie smiled, wondering what the other amateur boxer looked like. One of Derek's pale blue eyes was swollen, the start of a nice black eye visible. 'How many rounds did you go?'

'Only six, then I knocked him out just before the bell.'

'Well done,' Bernie said, but seeing two customers waiting to pay for their meals, he went back to his post.

'Right,' he said, taking the first slip, 'that'll be one and six, please.'

Bernie picked up the two shillings proffered. 'There you are, a tanner change. Dolly's doing

19

her steak-and-kidney pie for lunch.'

The man licked his lips. 'That'll do us. Save a couple of slices, Bernie.'

'Will do.' And taking the other man's slip he added, 'Egg and Bacon, plus bread and tea – that'll be a shilling.'

The two young men left and, as the café filled with more customers, Bernie refilled the large teapot, ready for the rush.

It was nine thirty before Bernie drew breath, a sheen of sweat on his forehead as the last customer paid his bill.

'Rita, when you've finished clearing the tables, you can have your break.'

'I'm dying for a fag. Can't I have a breather now?'

'If my wife comes out of the kitchen and sees the state of the place, she'll have your guts for garters.'

'It ain't my fault. It's impossible to do double my tables *and* clear them at the same time.'

Bernie exhaled loudly. He sympathised with the girl, but knew what Dolly would say if she saw the mess. He came out from behind the counter, saying with a placatory note in his voice, 'Come on, if I give you a hand they'll be cleared in no time.'

The girl heaved a sigh, but began stacking the plates on table two as Bernie started on the next one.

Dolly stuck her head out of the kitchen door. 'Rita, get me a cup of tea.'

'I'm busy,' she replied shortly.

Bernie held his breath, but knew what was coming as his wife marched into the room.

'What did you say?'

'You heard me. I've been rushed off my feet since six thirty this morning. These tables need clearing and I ain't had a break yet. If you want a cup of tea, I don't see why you can't get it for yourself.'

Dolly's face suffused with colour as she glared at the girl. 'You, miss, are on a week's notice.'

'Huh, is that a fact? Well, sod your week's notice. I'm going now and you can stick your bleedin' job.'

Dolly's jaw dropped as Rita ripped off her apron, threw it on a table and then marched out of the café, only to reappear moments later to grab her handbag from under the counter. Briefly she glowered at them both, but then as a parting shot, before slamming the door behind her, she spat, 'Do you know something, Dolly Dolby? You're a miserable old cow and I ain't surprised you can't keep a waitress for more than five minutes.'

For a moment there was a shocked silence, but then Bernie sighed heavily, turning to his wife. 'Now you've gone and done it. How are we supposed to manage the lunches?'

'I'll get Kevin down here to do the counter. You'll have to do the serving.'

Bernie, knowing what a lazy young bugger their son was, said with a doubtful shake of his head, 'I don't think he'll take kindly to that. And anyway, he's probably still in bed.'

The bell pinged and both glanced towards the

door again as a young woman came in, her head low as she looked at them shyly from under her lashes. She was a small, mousy-looking creature, wearing a shapeless, grey cotton dress that hung on her tiny frame. Straight, light brown hair sat on her shoulders, parted at the side and fastened with a slide.

For a moment they gazed at her. Then, gathering his thoughts, Bernard asked, 'What can I get you, love?'

'I ... I saw the notice in the window for a waitress.'

'Oh, right, then you'd best speak to my wife.'

Dolly took in a great gulp of air, her eyes momentarily looking heavenward before she spoke. 'I've just lost a waitress so your timing is perfect. Sit down,' she offered, her voice unusually soft.

Bernie listened as his wife began to question the girl. She had arrived at an opportune moment, but she looked so slight that a puff of wind could blow her over.

'Right, what's your name?'

'Pearl Button.'

'Blimey, your parents must have a sense of humour.'

The girl's voice was quiet, barely above a whisper. 'I ... I'm an orphan. When I was left on the orphanage steps, they found a tiny button clutched in my hand. That's how I got the name.'

'Gawd, if it wasn't so tragic, it'd be funny. Anyway, how old are you?'

'I'm sixteen, but I'll be seventeen in October.'

'Speak up, girl, I can hardly hear you. How old

22

did you say you are?'

'I said I'm sixteen.'

'Christ, you're just a kid. Have you been a waitress before?'

'Er ... no, but I can start straight away, and I'm quick at picking things up,' she said, for a moment her expression animated.

Dolly brushed some crumbs from the table, obviously thinking it over as Bernie urged, 'Give her a try, love.'

He watched as his wife continued to ponder, but it seemed that need overcame her doubts. With a small nod she said, 'All right, the job's yours. It's Tuesday, but if you really are willing to start straight away, we'll give you a full week's wage on Saturday.'

'Oh, thank you,' Pearl said, and as she smiled for the first time Bernie saw a flash of beauty. The girl had an elfin face with a pointed chin. Huge brown eyes seemed to take up most of her face, but they were hidden again as she lowered her head.

'You don't know what the hours are, so don't thank me yet. Your shift will start at six thirty in the morning, ending at three thirty in the afternoon. You'll get an hour for lunch between eleven and twelve.'

'That's all right. And ... and the pay?'

'You're only sixteen so it's two quid a week. Until we get another waitress I'll give you a bit extra, and you should pick up some tips too.'

'That's fine.'

'Hearing you speak it's obvious that you don't come from these parts. Where do you live?'

'I have a bedsit over an empty shop further along the High Street.'

'Don't tell me you're renting one of Nobby Clark's rooms?'

'Well, yes, my landlord is Mr Clark.'

Bernie and Dolly exchanged glances, both knowing what a dodgy character the young man was. The premises had been left to him by an aunt, but he had run the grocery shop into the ground. He had a reputation for shady deals, and some said that letting the upstairs rooms was just a front for his other activities.

Sixteen, Bernie thought, the kid is only sixteen and living alone in one of Nobby's grotty bedsits. As he coughed she looked up at him, her vulnerability making him swallow. God, once Dolly showed her true character the girl wouldn't last five minutes. He forced a smile, saying kindly, 'Well, love, if you can start straight away I'll show you the ropes, but first, how about a nice cup of tea?'

'Make it a quick one,' Dolly said sharply. 'This place looks like a bomb's hit it and I want it cleared ready for the lunchtime rush. While you're at it, Bernie, you can pour a cup of tea for me and Gertie. Pearl can bring it through to the kitchen and I'll introduce her to Gertie before I start on the lunches.'

Bernie moved behind the counter, and when his wife was out of earshot he decided that if they wanted to keep this waitress, it wouldn't hurt to put her in the picture. He beckoned Pearl forward, handing her a tray with three cups on it. 'Now listen, love. Before you take these through to the kitchen I should warn you that my wife can be a bit sharp at times. It's just her way, but it's lost us a few waitresses in the past. My best advice is to ignore her if she's in a bad mood, and for Gawd's sake, don't answer her back.'

For a moment Pearl appeared disconcerted, whilst Bernie hoped he hadn't put his foot in it. They needed a new waitress desperately, but now he might have scared her off.

Her amazing eyes were wide as she looked at him, but then with a faint smile she said, 'Thanks for warning me.'

Bernie watched her as she walked to the kitchen, thinking it was like seeing Daniel going into the lions' den. Yet there wasn't only Dolly to contend with, there were the costermongers too. Rita, with her dyed blonde hair, thick make-up and hardened appearance, had given as good as she got, enjoying their ribald jokes. Pearl, on the other hand, looked as innocent as a lamb and he doubted she'd cope. They were a good crowd really, who looked after their own, and maybe he could tip them the wink, asking them to lay off the girl. He'd start with Derek Lewis. The man might look like a hard nut, but underneath Bernie knew he had a soft spot for waifs and strays – a category that Pearl Button certainly fitted into.

2

Pearl had been introduced to Gertie, drunk her tea and, now doing her utmost to take in what Mr Dolby was saying, she was back in the dining room.

'Right, Pearl, give me a hand to clear these tables. I'll explain what you have to do as we go along, though it ain't hard. Take the customer's order and write it on a slip, along with the table number.'

'Table number?'

'Yes,' Bernie said, pointing to a block of wood next to a cruet set on which a number was painted boldly in red. 'Leave the top copy with the customer, and the carbon copy goes to the kitchen. Always ask if they want tea and bread and butter with their meal because we make a good profit on those. Dolly will ring a bell when the order is ready so make sure you listen for it. Have you got that?'

'Yes, I think so.'

'Good. Now as soon as a customer leaves, make sure you clear the table ready for the next one. Take the dirty plates to the kitchen and give the table a quick wipe down.'

Pearl already felt bemused.

'Don't look so worried. Once you get the hang of it you'll be fine. Oh, yes, I forgot to mention cutlery. You'll find knives and forks over there on that trolley,' Bernie pointed.

The door opened and two elderly ladies bustled in, pausing as they took in the scene. 'Blimey, don't tell me you've lost yet another waitress.'

'I'm afraid so, Ena.'

'It's just as well you keep your wife out the back or you'd lose all yer customers too,' the other lady chuckled.

'Yeah, I think you're right. Now what can I get you?'

'Just two cups of tea, please.'

'Pearl, take those plates to the kitchen,' Bernie said, with a wave of his arm, 'and then finish the rest of the tables.'

Pearl picked up the stack, hurrying away. Nerves made her hands shake, the cutlery on top rattling and sliding in an alarming manner. With relief she placed them on the large wooden table at the entrance to the washing-up room, glancing through to see Gertie giving her a wide grin. The woman's sparse, reddish hair was moist from the steam rising from the sink, her face shiny with perspiration.

'Is that the lot?' she asked.

'I've only got two more tables to clear.'

'Thank gawd for that. I'll just about finish the washing-up before the lunchtime rush starts.'

'Yeah, so stop talking and get on with it!' Dolly snapped.

Pearl had just cleared the last two tables, taking the crockery through to the kitchen, when the back door to the yard opened.

'Sorry I took so long, Dolly,' a short stocky

woman said as she rushed in. 'The waiting room was packed and it was ages before I saw the doctor. Mind you, it was a waste of time. He reckons I'm just a bit run down and said I should take a tonic. Tonic indeed! I tried to tell him that it's more than that, but he wouldn't listen.'

'Christ, another Mrs Neverwell. I don't know why I put up with you and Gertie.'

'Hello, love,' the woman said as she spotted Pearl.

Dolly heaved a sigh. 'Pearl, this is Mo, or Maureen Price, and she's my vegetable cook. Now enough chat and let's get on. Mo, you've been out for over an hour, so get on with the potatoes.'

With a smile at the harassed-looking woman, Pearl left the kitchen. 'What do I do now?' she asked Bernard.

'It'll be quiet until lunchtime and it'll give me a chance to show you how things work behind the counter, but first you can refill the cruets.'

A couple of young women came in. 'Two teas, please,' one of them said, and turning to her companion she added, 'Grab a table by the window so we can keep an eye on our prams.'

Pearl started on the first table, checking the condiments and filling those she found empty. It was hot, the sun blazing through the windows. Her throat was dry, but, too shy to ask for another drink, she carried on.

She had finished half of the tables when a door she had seen to the side of the counter opened, a tall, dark-haired young man appearing.

'Any chance of a cup of tea, Dad?'

Bernie's face darkened, but his voice was level

28

as he said, 'We're still a waitress short and I could do with a hand later.'

'Sorry, no can do. I've made other arrangements,' and, picking up the cup of tea that his father had poured, he headed for the kitchen, pausing for a moment as he passed Pearl.

She kept her head down, moving to the front of the dining room, and couldn't fail to hear the remarks made by the two young women sitting at a window table.

'Cor, that Kevin Dolby's a bit of all right.'

'Yeah, and he certainly ain't a chip off the old block. He looks nothing like Dolly or Bernard.'

'If I wasn't a married woman, I might be tempted.'

'Leave it out. Your old man would skin you alive.'

'Yeah, you're right.' Glancing out of the window, she added, 'Sod it, we'd best be off. My baby's waking up.'

As they hurried out, Pearl only had one table left to check and it was where the two elderly ladies sat. Smiling shyly at them, she picked up the salt pot, carefully removing the lid.

'How are you getting on, dearie?' one asked.

'Fine,' Pearl told her.

'Just keep your head down and you'll be all right. What's your name?'

'Pearl Button.'

'Blimey,' she said, unable to keep a straight face and echoing Dolly Dolby as she added, 'Your parents must have a sense of humour.'

Pearl just nodded, and as she made to move away Kevin Dolby reappeared, taking a seat in

29

the dining room. The old lady put a hand on her arm, whispering urgently, 'Dolly Dolby can be a dragon, but she's as soft as shit when it comes to her son. If you want to stay in her good books, take my advice and stay away from Kevin.'

Puzzled, Pearl now went to the counter, but she had hardly reached it when the kitchen bell rang. When she hurried to answer it, Dolly said, 'Give that breakfast to my son.'

Pearl picked up the huge fry-up and carried it through to the dining room, her mouth salivating. It was nearly eleven, and with no breakfast that morning her stomach growled with hunger.

Nervously she placed the plate in front of Dolly's son, relieved when, after giving her a cursory glance from hazel eyes, he went back to reading his newspaper, only murmuring, 'Get me a couple of slices of bread.'

She went to the counter to find Bernard chalking a list of lunchtime meals onto a blackboard. There was steak-and-kidney pie, sausages and mash, pork chops, or liver and bacon. Apple or Bakewell tarts were added for pudding, along with custard. Once again Pearl's mouth salivated, her stomach growling as she buttered the bread.

With more important things on his mind, Kevin hardly noticed the new waitress. He finished his breakfast, stood up and, leaving his empty plate on the table, went back to the kitchen.

'Mum, can I have a word?'

'What is it, love?'

'Most of me mates have got cars, but I'm still riding a scooter.'

'Blimey, Kevin, that Lambretta was a lot of money and you've only had it for a year.'

'Yeah, I know, but I've been offered a lovely Vauxhall Wyvern for two hundred quid.'

'Two hun–'

'Listen, Mum,' Kevin interrupted, 'a new one would be five hundred and fifty, not forgetting the purchase tax. This one's only a couple of years old and it's a bargain.'

'It's still a lot of money, son.'

'Please, Mum,' Kevin wheedled. 'All me mates have got cars now. Scooters are for kids.'

'Kevin, I threw a big party for your twenty-first birthday and it cost me a pretty penny. Now you want money for a car. It doesn't grow on trees, love.'

Kevin pouted, his expression for a moment that of a small boy. 'Pleeease, Mum.'

'I'll think about it.'

He smiled secretly, knowing that with a bit more persuasion he'd get his own way. He could pull the asthmatic trick again, say it was due to the dust he breathed in when riding his scooter. That would give her a fright and with any luck she'd give in.

'We could do with a hand at lunchtime.'

The smile left Kevin's face. 'I've got things to do, Mum. Can't you manage without me?'

'We're a bit pushed. Rita walked out and the new girl's inexperienced. I doubt she'll cope with the lunchtime rush.'

Kevin knew what buttons to push. 'From what I saw she's doing all right, and I must say she ain't bad-looking.'

'She's just a kid and far too young for you,' Dolly snapped.

Pearl came in carrying Kevin's empty plate, and as she placed it on the table he moved to her side, throwing an arm around her shoulder. 'Hello, we haven't been introduced.'

The girl flushed, looking up at him with wide, brown eyes, her words sounding breathless as she said, 'Er ... hello.'

'Kevin, we can manage without you,' Dolly said hurriedly.

He smiled inwardly. 'Thanks, Mum. I'll see you around tea time.'

'Don't stand there gawking, Pearl. Get back to your work!'

'Yes. Sorry, Mrs Dolby.'

Dolly's face softened almost imperceptibly as the girl ran back to the dining room. At last, a youngster who showed a bit of respect. Mind you, she'd have to keep an eye on her when Kevin was around. Pearl was just a bit of a kid, and as she was an orphan there was no knowing what sort of background she came from. There might be bad blood in her family and she was therefore totally unsuitable for her son.

'Mo,' Dolly shouted, 'have you finished the spuds?'

'Not yet, but I won't be much longer.'

'We're all behind 'cos of your bleedin' trip to the doctor's. When you've finished, get on with the onions. There's liver and bacon on the menu today so make sure you do enough.'

'Yeah, all right, Dolly.'

It was quiet for a while as the women worked, Dolly placing the pork chops in the oven before laying out the pies ready for warming. Next she part-fried the liver, ready to be finished off with bacon when she got an order. There were only the sausages to get on now. So after vigorously forking them, Dolly placed them on a tray to cook later.

She glanced up at the clock. 'Gertie, you'd better have your break, and you, Mo, get the spuds on.'

Mo placed the large pans on her cooker, added a generous amount of salt and lit the gas. 'There, done, and once I've finished the onions I'll get on with the cabbage and carrots.'

The Bakewell and apple pies had been delivered yesterday, and the custard already mixed, so after giving Gertie a bacon sandwich, the woman's usual fare, Dolly took this opportunity to have a break too.

In the dining room there were only a few customers, but Dolly knew it was the calm before the storm. At lunchtime the place would be heaving and she hoped the new girl would cope. After a quick look at the tables, she sat down near the counter, her eyes now on Pearl.

Bernie was showing her how to make the tea, water pouring into the pot from the hot-water urn, a cloud of steam momentarily obscuring Pearl's face. As it cleared, Dolly saw that the girl's cheeks were pink from the heat, and she frowned, noticing for the first time how pretty she was. She hadn't seen it when interviewing her, and wondered why.

As though suddenly aware that she was being observed, Pearl quickly lowered her head. That's it, Dolly thought. It was her mouse-like demeanour, the way she kept her eyes down and her shoulders hunched.

'As that tea is freshly made, you can pour me a cup and take a couple through to the kitchen for Mo and Gertie,' she said, thankful that at least the girl wasn't plastered with make-up. Kevin usually went for the obvious types, and had made a play for several of her previous waitresses. Of course, as soon as this happened she got rid of them, vowing never to employ a girl with looks again.

Had she made a mistake with Pearl? Yet as the girl came from behind the counter and carefully placed a cup of tea on the table, she doubted it. Once again she looked like a mouse, with a slim figure that was almost boyish. No, she definitely wasn't Kevin's type.

3

As the first lunchtime customers entered the café, Pearl took a deep breath in an effort to steady her nerves. She waited until they had sat down before approaching their table, trying to sound more confident than she felt. Her pad was poised.

'What can I get you?'

'Hello, who's this?' the costermonger asked his companion.

'I dunno. Rita served me for breakfast. Has she left, darlin'?'

'Yes, this morning. Now, what can I get you?' Pearl asked again.

'Blimey, she talks well, Charlie.'

'Yeah, I'll grant you that.'

The door opened again, four men walking to a nearby table and, seeing them, Pearl's hands shook. She hadn't taken this order yet, but already had to take another. 'Please, what would you like?'

'You on toast will do. Mind you, with the amount of meat on you I wouldn't get much of a mouthful.'

Pearl reddened, relieved when the one called Charlie placed his order. 'I'll 'ave the steak-and-kidney pie, love.'

'Yeah, I'll 'ave the same.'

She scribbled it down, dashing to the kitchen, but as she laid the order on the table, Dolly spoke sharply. 'What do you call this?'

'It ... it's an order.'

'There's no table number on this slip, and this copy goes to the customer. If they're paying separately they have a slip each. I have the bottom copy.'

'I ... I'm sorry. I'll write it out again, but I don't know if they're paying separately.'

'Make sure you ask next time.'

'Yes, sorry.' Then hurriedly leaving the kitchen, Pearl approached the table again, her head bowed.

'I'm sorry, I forgot to ask if you're paying separately for your meals.'

35

'Yeah, but don't worry, love. We'll split the bill between us.'

'Oh, thank you.'

'Here, miss, are we getting served today?'

'Yes, sorry,' Pearl said as she went over to the other table, her head once again low and feeling that she had said nothing but 'sorry' since she started. She flushed as one of the men at the table began to sing.

'"Pussycat, Pussycat, what did you there? I frightened a little mouse under her chair."'

Bernard Dolby wandered over. 'Give Pearl a chance, Frank. It's her first day and she hasn't done the job before.'

The man slowly scrutinised her and she held her breath, thankful when he finally said, 'Liver and bacon for me.'

The other three men gave their orders and this time, asking if they were paying separately, she had to make out four slips. As she tore them off and handed them out, it seemed a daft idea to her. Why write separate orders for each customer? Surely there was a more efficient way? However, as the café began to fill she dismissed it from her mind, and after dashing to the kitchen with the orders she almost ran to the next table.

Having finished their meal, the four men on table five stood up. As they walked towards the counter, one beckoned to Pearl, saying, 'Do you want a tip, love?'

She didn't know what to say. Yes, she needed tips, but hadn't expected to be asked.

'Here's a good tip for you. Have a bet on Imperial Lad running in the three thirty at Newmarket.'

All the men burst into laughter. 'Gawd, that's a good one, Frank.'

Humiliated but determined to hide it, Pearl went to clear their table. It was only as she picked up the last plate that she saw the threepenny bit underneath. Pearl looked up quickly, just in time to see Frank giving her a wink as he went out of the door. Oh, he was nice really, and somehow she would have to get used to these rough men's humour.

It was chaos by one thirty and Pearl could hardly keep up, her brow beaded with perspiration as she carried yet more plates out of the kitchen. She glanced at the clock, praying the lunchtime rush was almost over. Her lips were parched, throat dry, and she felt weak with hunger, legs wobbling beneath her.

Bernie was standing at table one, talking to a huge, fair-haired, craggy-faced man who looked like he'd been in a fight. She shuddered, hating violence, but when she finished giving the customers on table seven their order, Bernie beckoned her over.

'Pearl, this is Derek Lewis. He's an amateur boxer and a good one. Take his order next, will you?'

'Yes, sir.'

'Blimey, girl, there's no need to call me sir. Bernie will do.'

'Is there any steak-and-kidney pie left?' Derek asked.

'No, I'm afraid not, but the liver and bacon is

very tasty.'

Pearl saw that Bernie was looking at her with approval, and when Derek agreed to have the liver, Bernie positively beamed.

'Well done, love,' he whispered as she hurried past, slip in hand and heading for the kitchen.

When she had cleared three more tables and taken another order, the bell rang in the kitchen. Pearl went to get the order, which was the liver and bacon for table one.

'Don't worry, love,' said Derek Lewis, when she brought it over. 'Bernie tipped me the wink and I'll have a word with the other costermongers. They'll leave you alone in future.'

'Oh, no, don't do that. I don't want them to think I've been complaining,' Pearl's eyes were wide with appeal, but then she suddenly swayed. The room dimmed, voices came as though from a distance, her knees buckled, and she knew no more.

When Pearl opened her eyes, she saw unusually pale blue ones looking back at her and it took her a moment to realise she was in Derek Lewis's arms.

She struggled, but became still when he said softly, 'It's all right, pet. I'm just taking you through to the kitchen.'

'Wh ... what happened?'

'You fainted.'

Pearl was placed on a chair and, dizzy again, she leaned forward.

'What's going on?' Dolly asked sharply.

'She passed out, Mrs D. Your old man told me

38

to bring her in here.'

'Yeah, well, you can go now.'

When Derek left the kitchen, Gertie hurried over. She gave Pearl a glass of water, and then asked, ''Ave you been sick in the mornings, love?'

'Sick ... no.'

'So you ain't up the duff then?'

'Up the duff?' Pearl parroted, her head still swimming.

'She's asking if you're in the family way,' Dolly snapped.

'No, of course I'm not.'

'Why did you faint? Are you ill?'

'Oh, no. It's just that I didn't have any breakfast this morning and–'

Bernie stuck his head around the door. 'How is she?'

'She's just hungry. Can you manage without her for a while?'

'No, not really. There's customers waiting to be served.'

'I can give him a hand for a little while,' Gertie offered.

Dolly exhaled loudly. 'All right, go on then, but just while I give this daft cow something to eat, and then she can get back to work.'

Gertie scampered out, and as Dolly shoved a pork chop onto a plate, Pearl sat watching, mouth salivating. Her head was clearer now, but her stomach rumbled.

A dollop of mash was added, then some vegetables and thick gravy, Dolly's voice gruff as she plonked it in front of her. 'Right, get that down you.'

'Thank you,' Pearl said, and though she tried not to scoff, in a very short time the food disappeared.

'I don't think going without breakfast is reason enough to faint. When was the last time you had anything to eat?'

'I ... I had some soup yesterday lunchtime.'

'Christ, will you speak up, girl?'

'I said I had some soup yesterday.'

'Is that all? No wonder you passed out. Why didn't you tell me you were hungry?'

'I didn't like to, and as I started after ten, I didn't think I was entitled to a break.'

'For goodness' sake! We aren't bad employers and you only had to say.'

'There's something else, Mrs Dolby...'

Pearl paused and Dolly snapped, 'Well, spit it out.'

'I don't think I've got enough tips to pay for this meal.'

'Pay for it? You don't have to pay for it! Lunch is a perk of the job.'

Pearl's eyes lit up and, having gulped down the glass of water, she rose to her feet. A free lunch every day would make all the difference. She would be able to manage on the wages and wouldn't have to look for an evening job after all. Things were looking up.

'Thank you for the meal. It was wonderful, but I'd best get back to work.'

'Are you sure you're feeling all right now?'

'Oh, yes, I'm fine,' Pearl said, still smiling as she hurried out of the kitchen. She'd been warned about Mrs Dolby, but the woman wasn't so bad. The job was hard, but she was sure it would become easier once she got the hang of it, and if they found another waitress it could be a doddle. She would be finished at three thirty, leaving her lots of time to study, her goal now becoming a little closer.

'Are you all right now?'

'Yes, I'm fine thanks, Gertie.'

'Right, I'll get back to the kitchen. There's only one more customer waiting to be served on table eight, and a few more to clear.'

'Thanks,' Pearl said again.

She glanced around the café, but there was no sign of Derek Lewis. Determined to thank him for his help on her way home, she later asked Bernie where she could find him.

'He's a costermonger selling china about half-way down the market.'

'Why are they called costermongers?' Pearl asked.

'It's an ancient name for men selling stuff from barrows or stalls, especially fruit and vegetables. I know it isn't used much nowadays, but I like to keep up the old traditions. Most of the men working in the market have had their pitches handed down from father to son, and though they may sound a bit rough at times, they're a good crowd.'

Pearl listened with interest, and then glanced at the clock. It was after two thirty. All the unoccupied tables were cleared, and apart from one or two late customers, the café was nearly empty. Pearl's feet were throbbing, but at least her tummy was full, and despite the constant ribbing from some of the male customers, she'd enjoyed her first day.

Bernie gave her a tray of tea to take to the kitchen, saying he would pour one for her when she returned.

'I don't want any more fainting fits, girl,' Dolly said. 'See that you eat something before you start work in the morning.'

Pearl agreed, about to leave the kitchen when her employer spoke again. 'You did well for your first day. Keep it up.'

Pearl smiled, unused to praise, and was still smiling as she returned to the dining room.

'Blimey, Dolly, what's come over you?' Gertie asked.

'What's that supposed to mean?'

'If I'm not mistaken, you actually praised the new waitress.'

'Yeah, well, this one's a bit different. She shows me some respect, which is more than I could say for Rita.'

'Things 'ave certainly changed since the war,' Mo said as she came over to take a cup from the tray. 'Kids ain't got any respect nowadays. My Emma came down this morning dressed in something she called Capri pants. They looked daft, if you ask me, and I told her they were too short, but she just laughed. She said it's the Brigitte Bardot look. I ask you, who's Brigitte Bardot? She's got herself a bleedin' record player too, a Dansette, and it cost twelve quid. Now all I hear day and night is flaming rock-and-roll music.'

'Twelve quid! Where did she get that sort of money?'

'She got it off the club, and I just hope she keeps up the payments. Gawd, I wish her father was still alive. He'd 'ave sorted her out.'

'Yeah,' Gertie agreed. 'And as for that Brigitte Bardot, she's a French actress, and from what I've heard she's a right sexy piece.'

'It's disgusting, that's what it is,' Dolly said. 'The way young girls flaunt themselves nowadays they're just asking for trouble. Still, as I said, Pearl seems different, and she doesn't wear make-up plastered all over her face.'

'She seems a nice enough kid,' Gertie agreed.

'Right,' Dolly said, putting her cup back on the tray, 'let's get finished up. I don't know about you two, but I'm fair worn out.'

The back door opened and Kevin appeared, his look furtive as he clutched a bag behind his back.

'Hello, love. What have you been up to today?'

'Not now, Mum,' he said, hurrying through the kitchen without stopping.

Dolly frowned, wondering what was wrong with the boy. She went back to her tasks, rushing to get them finished so she could go upstairs to their flat. Kevin looked upset, and she wanted to know why.

As she walked along the market, Pearl's eyes were peeled for Derek Lewis. When he saw her approaching him he quickly finished a sale, moving to the front of his stall.

'Are you feeling better now?'

'I'm fine and wanted to thank you for helping me.'

'Leave it out. It's the first time I've had a girl

43

swooning at me feet and it won't do me reputation any harm.'

'Here, Derek, got yourself a bit of stuff, 'ave
you?' a voice called from the next stall. 'Hang on,
ain't that the little mouse from the café? Well, at
least you'll only 'ave to leave her out a bit of
cheese.'

Derek laughed, shouting back to the stallholder, 'Shut up, Frank! You're just jealous.'

'Not me, mate. I like a bit of meat to get hold
of, and you've seen the size of my wife.'

'Yeah, nobody could miss Lucy when she's in
full sail.'

'You cheeky bugger,' Frank Hanwell called, but
then had to serve a customer. 'What's that, missus?
Of course me lettuce is fresh. Hand-picked from
Covent Garden this morning.'

Derek chuckled and then turned his attention
back to Pearl. 'You could have knocked me down
with a feather when you passed out. What
brought it on?'

'Oh, nothing really. It's just that I hadn't eaten.'

She saw Derek frown, his soft voice at odds
with his build as he said, 'Are you all right for
money, love?'

'Yes, I'm fine, but I must go now. Thank you
again for your help.'

As Pearl walked away she kept her head low,
but as she passed Frank's stall he started to sing
again. '"Pussycat, Pussycat, where have you
been? I've been up to London to visit the Queen.
Pussycat, Pussycat, what did you there? I frightened a little mouse under her chair."'

She picked up her pace, and with the raucous

voices of the other traders calling their wares, she didn't see or hear Derek Lewis approaching Frank Hanwell, his fists clenched threateningly.

When Pearl walked into her bedsit she sighed with appreciation. The room was small, with just a built-in cupboard and chest of drawers, but to her it was heaven, a place of her own.

In one corner there was a curtained-off area, behind which was a sink and a single gas ring. In a tiny cupboard there were a few pieces of crockery, a small saucepan and a frying pan.

After kicking off her shoes, Pearl went to the tiny kitchen, placing the kettle on the gas ring. She wasn't hungry after that wonderful meal in the café and was counting her blessings, especially as she was down to her last tin of soup.

Who'd have thought she'd get a job with a meal thrown in? She turned on the gas tap, frowning when she realised she'd have to feed the meter. Her precious few tips were just enough to cover the shilling needed, so feeding the coin into the slot, she hoped there would be more tips forthcoming in the morning.

There were used tea leaves in her small strainer and, carefully pouring boiling water over them, she frowned at the weak brew. Still, things were looking up and soon she'd be able to get a bit of shopping. Not only that, now that she was earning again her dream of taking art classes felt a little bit closer.

After drinking the tea, Pearl had a strip wash, carefully hung up her one and only decent dress, then threw on an old pair of pyjamas. Sitting cross-legged on her bed, she picked up her sketch pad and pencil.

Everything had looked dire that morning, and she had been in despair when she'd seen the advert for a waitress. Her elfin face lit up with a smile and she began to draw a face from memory. Dolly Dolby slowly emerged on the page, but when the sketch was finished Pearl flung it aside, wishing she could afford paint and brushes.

Painting was all Pearl lived for, and never a day went by when she didn't try to create something. With no money for paint she would sketch, burying herself in the task of perfecting whatever she was drawing. In the orphanage it had been her refuge, a way of blanking out all that went on around her.

She was constantly picked on by the other children, all laughing at her because she was never chosen for fostering or adoption. From the day she had been found on the steps until the day she left, the only home Pearl had known was the grey and forbidding orphanage, her bed one among twenty that lined the dormitory. She had plucked up courage once to ask why she couldn't be put forward for a foster home, only to be told by grim-faced Miss Unsworth that she wasn't suitable. When she dared to ask why, she had received a slap, Miss Unsworth telling her that she should count herself lucky that she had a home in the orphanage.

The face of Derek Lewis swam into her mind so, taking up her pad again, Pearl began to sketch. In the orphanage, picked on and helpless against the teasing, she had quickly realised that

46

she needed someone to look out for her – someone to hide behind. She had chosen an older girl, one who, like her, was a loner, and it had worked.

Of course, eventually the girl went into foster care, and Pearl was left alone again. It was the first time she'd faced such a traumatic parting, but Pearl had learned another hard lesson. To survive she couldn't get attached to anyone. If she hardened her heart, she couldn't get hurt.

From then on, through the years, she found other girls to hide behind, girls who would stand up for her, but though they didn't know it, her feelings remained detached.

As Derek's pug-nosed face took shape on her sketch pad, Pearl smiled. He had already offered her some sort of protection, volunteering to make sure that the other costermongers laid off the teasing. Of course she had protested, but a warm feeling now spread through her body. Yes, Derek Lewis was someone she could hide behind, and it would be a good idea to make him a friend.

4

As he cashed up the till, Bernard Dolby's mouth was set in a scowl, his thoughts on his son instead of the task at hand. Kevin had walked through the dining room earlier, going upstairs without a word. The lazy git should get another job, but after leaving the engineering factory three months ago, wasting years of training, he wasn't making much of an effort to find other employment.

The young tyke had avoided National Service by becoming an apprentice, deferring his call-up until he was twenty-one. Then he'd avoided it again by failing the medical, much to Dolly's delight. Asthma. Huh, in Bernie's opinion a bit of physical training would have sorted that out, turning Kevin into a man instead of a mummy's boy.

Dolly wouldn't hear a word against her precious son and had mollycoddled him from childhood. *He's your son too*, a small voice said at the back of Bernie's mind, and once again he scowled. Yes, Kevin *was* his son, but other than his conception, he'd had no hand in the boy's upbringing since Kevin was a toddler. If he so much as raised his voice to Kevin, Dolly went mad.

Bernie hunched his shoulders. It was his own fault, he knew that, but for a quiet life he always gave in to Dolly. His wife had a temper, one that he feared, and he'd felt the lash of her hand from almost the first day of their marriage.

Yes, he'd married her, but she was three months gone with Kevin and he hadn't been given a choice. When Dolly's father had marched round from the house next door, his pregnant daughter in tow, Bernie's own parents had forced him to the registry office.

It had been drink, of course – a party that got out of hand – and somehow, though he had no recollection of it, he'd taken Dolly amongst a pile of coats left by the guests in an upstairs bedroom.

48

'Have you finished cashing up?' Dolly asked as she came through from the kitchen.

'Yeah,' he said, entering part of the takings in the cash book.

'Well,' she said pointedly, holding out her hand.

Bernie gave her some notes and she clasped them avidly. 'I'm going upstairs. I think Kevin is upset about something.'

'I'll wait for Nora to turn up and then I'm off to the bank to pay in the rest of the takings.'

Dolly hurried upstairs and, putting the bags of coins and notes into a small sack, Bernie waited impatiently for their cleaner. Nora was a nice woman, but slow-witted. She'd been cleaning the café for the past twelve months and was surprisingly good at the job, the best they'd had. He smiled now as she came in, a headscarf tied turban-style around her head as usual.

'Hello, love.'

'Hello, Mr Dolby,' she said, her round face breaking into a smile.

'I'm off to the bank. If you need anything, my wife is upstairs.'

'Righto,' and without preamble she went to fetch the broom, bucket and mop. Nora might be slow, but she was thorough, and Bernie knew that the floor and the kitchen would be sparkling by the time she'd finished.

As he stepped outside, Bernie took in a great gulp of air, feeling as though he'd been released from his chain. His eyes roamed the market. It was quiet, many of the stallholders packing up for the day, and he envied them, envied their camaraderie, and their freedom.

Shortly after Kevin was born, Dolly's gran died, leaving her the café. Dolly had been working for her gran since she left school, and with her mother roped in to look after Kevin, she had carried on. Like a fool Bernie had agreed to work with her, but soon realised his mistake. She ruled absolutely, dismissing any suggestions he made and keeping a firm hand on the purse strings.

A few years later, when war had been declared, he'd gone eagerly to join up, only to be declared unfit with a heart murmur he didn't know he had. He'd looked forward to getting away from Dolly, her violence *and* the café. Instead he'd seen his friends going off to fight, and several were killed in action. He'd eventually volunteered to be an air-raid warden, but in truth it wasn't out of patriotism – it was for the same reason as he'd tried to enlist in the army: to get away from Dolly for a while.

Of course the bloody café had survived the air raids and, despite rationing, they had made a living. Nowadays the place was a little gold mine, but what did he see of it? Huh, just the pocket money that his wife gave him.

'What's up, Bernie? Has Dolly been giving you what for again?'

Yes, that's how they saw him, Bernie thought: as a downtrodden and henpecked husband. He forced a smile, turning to face the costermonger.

'Well, you know Dolly.'

'Not as well as you, mate, thank God. Do you fancy a game of darts tonight?'

'Yes, thanks.' As he walked away, Bernie knew

that as he threw each dart he would picture his wife's face etched on the board.

'What's the matter, sweetheart?' Dolly asked when she saw her son slumped in a chair.

'Nothing, Mum.'

She sat on the arm of the chair, stroking his hair. 'Don't give me that. I can see you're upset about something.'

Kevin pushed her hand away. 'Leave it, Mum.'

'Don't be silly, son. If you're upset about something, maybe I can help.'

'If I tell you what's wrong, it won't do any good.'

'Tell me anyway.'

'My friends are going to Brighton on Sunday, but I can't go with them.'

'Why not?'

''Cos they're all driving down by car, and can you see me keeping up on my scooter?'

'Surely one of them could give you a lift?'

'Yeah, I suppose so, but you don't know how it feels to be the odd one out. From now on I'll have to scrounge a lift every time we go somewhere.'

Dolly stood up, exhaling loudly. 'Kevin, I know how much you want to buy that car, but it's an awful lot of money, son.'

'See, I knew you'd say that! I told you to leave it, but you insisted I tell you! What good has it done?' he cried, bending forward then as though gasping for air. After forcing a wheezing sound and hearing his mother murmuring worriedly, he straightened. 'It's that bloody scooter and the

51

dust I inhale that causes these attacks, but forget it, Mum. You can't afford to buy me the car so that's that.' And on that note Kevin reared from the chair, stomping to his bedroom, the door slamming behind him.

Dolly paced back and forth but then, casting a glance behind her, she went into her bedroom and to the dressing table. Tucked in the bottom drawer, from under her underwear she took out her cash box. This was her hidden hoard, money the tax man had no knowledge of, and carefully added to over the years. Taking the notes that Bernie had given her and the key, she opened it, her eyes mentally assessing the contents. Why not? she thought. They weren't hard up, and if riding that scooter was making Kevin ill, he'd have to have a car.

'Here you are, love,' Dolly said, knocking before going into Kevin's room. Her son had become a stickler for privacy, but it was probably normal at his age.

'Thanks,' Kevin cried, jumping up and throwing his arms around her. 'You're the best mum in the world.'

Dolly smiled, and touched his face. 'And you're the best son.'

'I'd better get a move on before he sells the car to someone else.'

Kevin released his mother, leaving the room without a backward glance, his face alive with excitement. Good old Mum, she had coughed up, as he knew she would. The radio he'd nicked and stashed in the bottom of his wardrobe wouldn't have raised more than a pittance, but now he had all the cash he needed.

He rushed through the dining room, totally ignoring Nora as she vigorously swept the floor. In the yard he hopped on his scooter and in no time he was at Larry Mason's house, relieved to see the Vauxhall parked outside.

'Is the car still for sale?' he asked, hiding his anxiety when the man came to the door.

'Yeah, do you want to have another look at it?'

'I've just been to see a Morris, but I can't make up my mind between the two. Mind you, the Morris is cheaper.'

'Huh, you can't compare a Morris to a Vauxhall Wyvern.'

'Maybe not, but I ain't made of money.'

'Come on, I'll take you for a spin. It might help you to make up your mind.'

Kevin hid a smile. He knew he was going to buy the Wyvern, but there was no need to let Larry know that. He wasn't ready to part with two hundred quid and intended to haggle.

'It runs like a dream,' the man said as they drove along Falcon Road.

'The engine sounds all right, but I think I'll go for the Morris. It's fifty quid cheaper and I ain't got money to burn.'

'How about I knock off twenty-five quid? It's still a better car, and I can't go any lower.'

Kevin pursed his lips, pretending to consider the offer, and then said, 'All right, Larry. I'll take it off your hands.'

In another hour Kevin was on his way to see some important contacts, his heart thumping.

They'd have to take him seriously now. They needed a car, and he had one. And without it, the job would be impossible.

5

On Saturday, Pearl took her first week's wages, pleased to find an extra ten shillings. With tips she had made two pounds, thirteen and sixpence. A guinea would have to go to her landlord, but now that she didn't have to buy much food, art classes were definitely on.

She hugged herself with excitement. Art classes! She could actually go to art classes! Her mind slid back to the orphanage and the one teacher she had liked. Miss Rosen had come to the orphanage during Pearl's final year, and she'd been inspirational, encouraging her to look at objects in a new way.

'See the texture of the bricks,' she would say, 'feel them, and there's the sky, Pearl. It isn't just one shade of blue with clouds like puffs of cotton wool. Look closely – there are far more colours.'

And she had looked, and she had learned, but not enough, not nearly enough. Only three months after Miss Rosen arrived came Pearl's release, and she was one of the first to leave that year. And that's how she saw it: release – as though she had spent her whole life up to that moment in prison. Miss Rosen was the only teacher she missed, but she would never forget her art lessons.

Before leaving she'd been told they had found her a job in a laundry, and a place in a hostel, both of which she hated from the first day. The work in the laundry sickened her, making her stomach turn. Her job was to sort out linen from great bags, and check that the laundry mark was in place before sending it on to the washroom. The sheets, from a local psychiatric hospital and an old folk's home, were often covered in blood, vomit or excrement. She had tried to distance her mind, but it was impossible, and then, after months and months, there came the final straw. A sheet she pulled out was so covered in filth that she had bent double, vomiting on the cold stone floor.

With little money saved, she had left both the job and the hostel. She moved to an area a long way from the orphanage, alighting from the train at Clapham Junction station. Maybe it was luck, maybe she had a guardian angel, but almost immediately she'd seen a card in a newsagent's window offering a cheap room to let. After asking directions she had made her way to Battersea High Street, enthralled by the busy, bustling market. She had taken the room, and then when almost down to her last penny, providence stepped in again when she found the job in the café.

Pearl jumped as she heard a sudden knock on her door and opened it to see her landlord.

'Your rent's due, Miss Button,' Nobby Clark said.

'Yes, I'll get it for you,' she agreed, hiding her distaste. Her landlord was a greasy-looking young man, with dark, slicked-back hair and a small moustache. But it was his eyes that she hated most; button black and hard, they made her shiver.

He marked the rent book, handed it back, and Pearl was glad to close the door on him. For the rest of the evening she sketched. She attempted Kevin Dolby, but couldn't get his handsome face right. With a sigh she scrunched the paper into a ball before throwing it in the bin. God, Kevin was so good-looking. Despite knowing that he would never be interested in her, she still felt her heart skip a beat every time she saw him.

At ten thirty Pearl climbed into bed and was just drifting off to sleep when she heard noises coming from the empty shop below. She sat up nervously. Men's voices, the scraping of what sounded like chairs, a soft laugh. She strained her ears, but the voices were indistinct, muffled. Who was down there?

Pearl wished there were other tenants, someone she could run to, but hers was the only room occupied.

Laughter again, loud this time, and Pearl relaxed a little. Perhaps it was her landlord showing someone the premises, but at this time of night? Despite her trepidation, curiosity had Pearl rising to her feet and, slipping on a thin cotton dressing gown, she padded softly downstairs.

The internal door creaked as she opened it a little, and for a moment she froze, but then the handle was snatched from her hand as it was flung wide by her landlord.

Nobby Clark glared angrily, pushing her rapidly back into the hall and slamming the door shut behind him. 'Have you heard the saying that curiosity killed the cat?'

Wide-eyed, Pearl looked back at the man, but her throat was too constricted with nerves to answer.

'What did you see? Answer me, you silly cow! I said, *what did you see?*'

'N ... nothing,' she managed to gasp.

'Are you sure about that?'

'Y ... yes,' she stammered, finding her voice at last. 'I ... I heard noises and thought it might be burglars.'

'What – in an empty shop?'

'I ... I didn't think.'

'That's obvious. Now listen, and listen well. What goes on in my shop is none of your business and in future keep your nose out.'

'Yes, Mr Clark.'

He stepped back a pace, took a cigarette out of a packet and lit it, blowing smoke into the air as his shrewd eyes bored into hers. 'Get back upstairs,' he snapped.

Pearl scampered away, her heart thumping. When she reached her bedsit she hurriedly shut the door, leaning against it as she drew in great gulps of air. She *had* seen something. Before Nobby Clark shut the door she'd had a brief glimpse of three men sitting around a table, and piled beside them were stacks of cartons. She had seen the markings. Cigarettes – they were cartons of cigarettes.

'Did she see anything?' Kevin Dolby asked anxiously.

'Nah, she didn't have a chance.'

'Christ, you should've locked the internal door.'

'I know that!'

'Are you *sure* she didn't see anything?'

'I've told you, ain't I? Now shut up and I'll give Vince a ring. If you'd had the sense to buy a van we'd have a lot more stuff to offer him. I'm not sure he'll be interested in this little hoard.'

Kevin glared at Nobby. Bloody hell, they wouldn't have any transport if it wasn't for him, and there was no way he was going to be seen driving a flippin' van. The Vauxhall gave him a bit of kudos and he enjoyed the envy he saw in his mates' eyes.

Nobby returned from making the call, a satisfied smile on his face. 'Yeah, Vince is gonna take them, but he wants delivery now.'

'Christ, it'll take us over an hour to get to Streatham and back.'

'Look, the sooner we get shot of the stuff, the sooner we'll get our dosh, and it's better than stashing it here overnight.'

'I'm not happy about using my car again.'

'We can hardly get a bus.'

Kevin hung his head. That bloody girl had unnerved him. She had almost walked in on them and if she'd seen the stash, what then? Pearl worked for his mother, for Christ's sake – she knew his face!

'Come on, Kevin,' Dick Smedley said as he picked up one of the cartons. 'Let's get a move on.'

Kevin pinched his bottom lip between his fingers, but then nodded. Pearl bloody Button hadn't seen anything, so why was he worrying? The warehouse job had been easy, and they'd got clean away. All right, it wasn't a big haul, but even so, they were on a nice little earner. For once he wouldn't have to cadge money from his mother. He'd have plenty to spend on his favourite hobby. If you could call it a hobby, he thought with a smile. Soho beckoned ... the girls ... the things they let him do.

When Kevin reached Soho, walking the narrow streets, neon lights announced the clubs. Kevin frowned. It had been a hard lesson, money leaving his pocket like water, for drinks that cost an arm and a leg, but he knew better now and wouldn't frequent those dives again. It had taken a few trips, but he'd finally found what he was looking for. Now he turned down an alley, his excitement beginning to mount. When he reached the last door on the left it bore no indication of the delights inside, but he just hoped that Eva was available.

She was, and following her into the bedroom he licked his lips in anticipation. Eva knew just what to do and stood waiting, but as he stepped forward she held up a hand in warning.

'No bruises this time or I won't entertain you again.'

His eyes narrowed. She was out of role and he didn't like it, his erection dying. He wanted her submissive, frightened. 'All right, I'll be careful.'

She switched into the act, her eyes becoming wide with fear. That was better, the trigger he needed, and now he walked towards her again.

'No, please!' she begged.

He grabbed Eva, ripping the clothes from her body before throwing her on the bed. He wanted to pummel her, punch her, but had to hold back, yet even so, her cries of mock pain drove him to ecstasy.

It was quick, too bloody quick, and annoyed, Kevin threw money onto the bed. If he got his needs regularly, maybe he'd be able to last longer, but at least he had a few bob now and would be back. Without saying a word to Eva he left.

It was one o'clock in the morning when he drove down the side entrance, parking in the large yard at the back of the café. He was quiet as he made his way upstairs, but despite that, his mother appeared in her bedroom doorway.

'Kevin, where on earth have you been? I've been worried sick.'

'Don't start, Mum. I got held up, that's all.'

'Held up. Where?'

'Er ... the car had a flat tyre.'

'But surely it didn't take long to change it?'

'For Christ's sake, leave it out, will you! I ain't a kid, you know,' Kevin shouted as he stomped off to his bedroom.

Only a few minutes later he heard raised voices. His mother was berating his father again, taking her angst out on the old man. He despised him, despised his weakness. What sort of a man let a woman rule him – hit him – belittle him? Why didn't his father stand up to her?

As a kid he'd thought it normal, but as he got older it became apparent that in other households it was the man who ruled, not the woman.

His home was different and he hated it, hated seeing the way his father kowtowed to his mother. With this hate came fear. Was he the same? Was he less than a man, like his father?

Yes, his first trip to Soho had introduced him to sex, but it hadn't really taken away his fear. The tart was paid to do as he asked; paid to be submissive.

In between trips to Soho he'd taken a few girls out, usually the obvious types, and had played the big man. Yet deep down he was still nervous, especially if they showed a bit of spunk and stood up to him. When that happened he dropped them like hot potatoes, and so girls came and went, giving him the reputation of a ladies' man, one that he enjoyed.

His mother's voice rang out again and, hearing it, Kevin's determination was renewed. Not for him someone like his mother. Not for him a woman with a forceful personality. If the day ever came, and he doubted it, that he got married, he would make sure his wife was a pretty little thing. Someone meek and mild, who would have no chance of dominating him.

6

'I'm home, Gran!' Derek Lewis called as he stepped into the small terraced house. It was Monday and he'd been delayed, but now hurried upstairs. 'Are you all right?'

'I'm fine,' she said.

Derek gazed down at his beloved gran, and frowned worriedly. She still looked frail, despite the doctor saying she had only a touch of bronchitis. Connie Lewis was a tiny woman, grey-haired and thin, but she was wiry and rarely ill. 'Sorry I'm late but I had a bit of stock to pick up. Have you had your medicine?'

'Yes, and stop looking so worried. I think I'll be well enough to come downstairs tomorrow.'

'We'll see.'

'We won't. If I have to stare at these four bloody walls for much longer, I'll go batty.'

'All right, keep your hair on. I'm off to make us something to eat. What do you fancy?'

'Something light. Perhaps a boiled egg, with bread and butter.'

'You need more that that. How about a pork chop with mashed potatoes?'

'No, thanks, but you have a chop. Is it your night for the gym?'

'Yes, but I don't want to leave you if you still feel rough.'

'I told you, I feel fine, and a fraud for laying here.'

'Are you sure you'll be all right on your own?'

'Gawd, Derek, will you stop treating me like a bleedin' invalid? I ain't ready for the knacker's yard yet.'

There was a spark in her eyes now and Derek grinned. When his mother had been killed during the war, he'd come to live with his gran. At the time he'd been ten years old, a lost and frightened little boy, but she had taken him under her wing, showering more love on him than he'd ever received from his flighty mother.

He'd questioned Gran about his father, but she fobbed him off so many times that he'd given up asking. It was only as an adult that he found out why. On his birth certificate, the space for listing the father's name was blank.

Derek bent forward, planting a kiss on his gran's papery cheek. 'I'm off to put your egg on.'

'It wouldn't suit you, love.'

'Very funny, and if you're cracking jokes you must be feeling better.'

'I am, and put plenty of butter on me bread.'

As Derek went downstairs he found his thoughts turning to the café and the new waitress. Pearl looked such a frail little thing, too frail to be working for Dolly Dolby. When she fainted and he'd carried her to the kitchen, she was as light as a bird, her huge eyes full of fear as she looked at him. Well, she had no need to fear him. In fact, he was determined to look out for the girl.

In no time his gran's egg was ready, and having spread the butter thickly on the bread, he carried the tray, complete with a cup of tea, upstairs. 'There, get that down you.'

'Thanks, pet, and what are you having?'

'I think I'll pop into the chippy on me way back from the gym. It ain't good to spar on a full stomach.'

'Derek, you've had fish and chips three times this week!'

'It won't kill me, Gran. You'll be up soon and no doubt shoving vegetables down me throat again.'

'I will, and I'll make sure you eat the lot.'

They smiled at each other. Then Connie tapped the top of her egg, and Derek went to the bathroom for a wash. He stood looking at his face in the mirror over the basin. For a moment a frown creased his forehead. Boxing had certainly taken its toll, and was that the start of a cauliflower ear? Yes, maybe, but what did it matter? He'd never been much to look at in the first place.

An hour later he'd given his gran another cup of tea, and was ready to leave. 'Are you sure you'll be all right on your own?'

'Derek, for goodness' sake just go. Those kids you're helping along will be waiting for you.'

'All right, I'll see you later,' he called, clattering back downstairs and out of the house.

In no time he reached the gym, a few kids crowding round him as soon as he walked in. His eyes flicked round the large room, noting a few other nippers having a go on the punch bags, their thin arms making little impact. A couple of blokes were sparring in the ring, a trainer watching them avidly, but other than that the place was empty.

Derek tousled the nearest boy's head. 'Right, let's get you lot sorted. Jimmy and Bill, you do some skipping, and, Ricky, get your gloves on ready for a spar when the ring is clear.'

They all ran to do his bidding and he smiled. They were good kids, better off in the gym than running the streets.

Jimmy, though he wouldn't admit it to anyone, was Derek's favourite, a kid he was sure he had turned round. The lad had hesitantly entered the gym six months ago, and it hadn't taken Derek long to learn that the boy was regularly beaten by his drunken father. He'd been running wild on the streets, rebelling, nicking stuff off stalls, but coming to the gym had changed all that. At first he'd seen the boy taking his anger out on the punch bag, but gradually he had grown in confidence.

Yes, Jimmy was a lot happier now, especially since Derek had taken it upon himself to have a quiet word in his father's ear.

The following morning, Pearl was dashing along the High Street. Some costermongers were already setting up, and as she passed Derek Lewis he raised his hand to wave.

His stall was half ready, piled with china, and Pearl looked at some of the sets with interest. Maybe in another couple of weeks she could buy cups and saucers to replace the old chipped ones she'd inherited with the room.

She reached the café, rushing inside to see Bernie behind the counter as usual. 'Hello, love,' he said cheerfully. 'I've just made a pot so do you want a cuppa before you start?'

'Yes, please,' she said, taking her apron from the hook and tying it around her waist.

'Here you are then, and take this one through to Dolly.'

Pearl took the cup, careful not to slop any tea in the saucers. It was something she knew Dolly Dolby hated, and had felt the sting of her tongue the first time the tea had over-spilled.

Gertie didn't start work until seven, and Mo

nine, so there was only her employer in the kitchen.

'Good morning, Mrs Dolby,' she said, hoping that the woman was in a good mood.

'Morning,' Dolly said shortly, adding, 'I thought I told you to tie your hair back.'

'I'm just about to do it,' Pearl said, hurriedly fishing for the elastic band in her apron pocket.

'Get it done and go back to the dining room. It won't be long before the breakfast rush starts.'

Pearl scraped her hair back, hopes dashed. Mrs Dolby was obviously in a foul humour, and she dreaded the rest of the day. When her employer was in a good mood – if any of her moods could be called good – the job was easier, but when bad-tempered, like today, she would build mountains out of molehills, making all their lives a misery.

She went back to the dining room, and as she swiftly drank her tea, Bernie gave her a sympathetic smile.

'I can see by your face that you've found Dolly with the hump. It's Kevin's fault. He didn't come home until one in the morning on Saturday and he was out all hours last night too. Dolly was out of her mind with worry.'

'One o'clock in the morning! My goodness.'

'Yeah, and God knows what the young tyke was up to.'

Pearl wondered too, but then the café began to fill with costermongers, all ready for large breakfasts. They took it in turns, watching each other's pitches, but even so, the café was soon packed.

Derek Lewis came in at eight, but ordered only

two bacon sandwiches to take away.

'No breakfast this morning?' Pearl asked.

'My gran's a bit under the weather so I'm popping home to give her one of these. Frank's keeping an eye on my stall.'

Pearl watched him leave, wondering if she could tell him about her landlord and his threat on Saturday night. She was frightened of Nobby Clark, needed someone to protect her, but didn't feel she knew Derek well enough yet. This was a tight-knit community and she knew she had a long way to go before she was accepted. Until then, it might be more prudent to keep her mouth shut.

Pearl was taking her break, tucking into her meal, when Kevin came down from the upstairs flat.

His eyes flicked around the dining room, but then he walked towards her table. Pearl's stomach fluttered and she quickly lowered her head.

'Hello. Pearl, isn't it? How are you getting on?'

'F ... fine, thanks,' she said, amazed and gratified that he had spoken to her.

Her eyes rose, and as they fastened momentarily on his, she flushed. God, he was gorgeous, yet why did he look so anxious?

'Do you live around here?'

'Er ... yes, I live over the empty shop further along the High Street.'

'All right, is it?'

'Yes, it's fine.'

'Who's your landlord?'

'Mr Clark. Nobby Clark. Do you know him?'

He smiled, perfectly even, white teeth flashing.

67

'No, not really. See you,' he said abruptly, walking away.

Pearl was thrilled that Kevin had spoken to her, but puzzled by the strange conversation.

Gertie then dashed out of the kitchen, looking harassed. 'One of the ovens isn't working and Dolly's doing her nut,' she told Bernie.

'All right, I'm coming,' he said. 'Keep an eye on things out here, Pearl.'

She rose to her feet, unable now to think about Kevin's strange behaviour as three young women came in, asking for teas.

Kevin was still smiling as he strolled along the High Street. Christ, he'd been shit scared that the new waitress had clocked him on Saturday night, but a short conversation had allayed his fears. When Pearl had asked if he knew Nobby Clark, it was obvious that she hadn't seen him in the shop. If she had, she wouldn't have asked the question.

'Watcha, Kevin. With that smile on your face you must've got your leg over last night.'

'Morning, Frank, and yes, I did,' he lied.

'You jammy young git. My old woman had a headache as usual.'

'So much for marriage,' Kevin quipped back.

'It's got its compensations, and she ain't always under the weather.'

Kevin pictured Frank's wife and shuddered. Like his mother, she looked a right battle-axe and he wouldn't fancy waking up alongside her every morning.

'Morning, Derek,' he called as he reached the

next stall.

'Watcha, Kevin. How's the new waitress? She ain't fainted again, has she?'

Kevin frowned. Fainted? It was the first he'd heard of it. 'I don't know what you're on about and as far as I know she's fine.'

'She passed out cold on her first day and I had to carry her through to the kitchen. Ain't she a pretty little thing?'

Kevin's eyes widened. Pretty! Blimey, Derek must need his eyes tested. Pearl was thin, pale and insipid, without an ounce of femininity. 'Can't say I think much of your taste, mate. Still, if you like her, as far as I'm concerned, she's all yours.'

For a moment Derek's face saddened. 'She wouldn't want me, Kevin.'

'You don't know that. Give it a go, mate.'

'Nah, it'd be a waste of time.'

Kevin called goodbye, sauntering along the High Street, his arm lifting to acknowledge other stallholders. He was still smiling happily, thinking about the money in his pocket. Yeah, he had plenty of dosh now, and would take another trip to Soho tonight.

7

During the next couple of weeks Pearl made a point of chatting to Derek Lewis whenever she got the chance, and this had certainly done the trick. The other costermongers still ribbed her, but in a friendly way, and their jokes were no longer smutty. On the whole she enjoyed the waitressing job. As long as she kept her head down and showed Mrs Dolby respect, the woman wasn't too bad.

Pearl still felt like an outsider, but had learned a lot. There seemed to be unwritten rules in this little community. There was a strict code that no matter what you saw, or heard, you didn't speak to the police. People round here took care of any problems in their own special way, but how they did it was still a mystery to Pearl. She had heard snippets of conversation – talk of keeping to your own patch and not treading on anyone's toes – but had no idea what it meant.

It was a busy morning, about a month after Pearl had started working at the café. She wiped a hand across her forehead. 'Can I have my break now, Bernie?'

He was about to answer when a tall, buxom woman walked into the café. As she approached the counter Pearl's ears pricked up.

'Are you still looking for a waitress?'

'Yes, we are. Take a seat and I'll get my wife.'

Bernie winked as he passed her, but Pearl frowned. It was hard work managing all the tables on her own, but if Mrs Dolby took this woman on, she'd miss the extra ten shillings a week in her wage packet.

When Dolly came out of the kitchen, wiping her hands on her large white apron, Bernie followed behind. 'Right,' she said brusquely, as she sat opposite the woman, 'my husband tells me you've come about the job.'

'That's right.'

'Have you had any experience?'

'I've been a waitress in the Trafalgar Café at Clapham Junction for three years, but now they've sold the place to Greeks and they're turning it into an omelette bar.'

'An omelette bar? That's a new one on me.'

'Me too. I could stay on, but don't fancy it somehow.'

'I can't believe the old Trafalgar Café has been sold. It's been in the same family for years.'

'I know, but old Mrs Watson wanted to retire and none of her lads would take it on.'

'Tell me a bit about yourself.'

'My name is Alice Freeman. I'm thirty-two and live just off Falcon Road. I'm married, with one daughter.'

'How old is she?'

'Yvonne's eleven.'

Dolly pursed her lips. 'The hours are six thirty to three thirty. How are you going to manage that with a kid of eleven?'

'It isn't a problem. My mother lives next door and already looks after Yvonne while I'm at work.'

71

'Right, so I suppose it's down to pay. What are you earning now?'

'I'm on three pounds a week.'

Once again Dolly pursed her lips. 'All right, we can match that. When can you start?'

'On Monday.'

'Right then, the job's yours.'

'Thank you,' Alice said, smiling widely.

Pearl picked up the plates, her thoughts racing as she took them through to the kitchen. It didn't seem fair that Dolly had offered Alice three pounds a week when she, Pearl, was earning only two. They'd be doing the same hours, the same amount of work, but because the woman was older, she'd be paid more.

Gertie turned to give Pearl a grin. 'If someone's applied for the waitress job, things will be a lot easier for you. You've been running around like a blue-arsed fly since you started and must be fair worn out.'

'I don't mind.'

'What's she like?'

Before Pearl could answer, the door swung open, Mrs Dolby walking in with Alice Freeman behind her. 'Gertie, Mo, this is Alice. She's starting work with us on Monday.'

'Hello,' Gertie said, Mo following suit, both looking at the woman appraisingly. Alice was a strong-looking young woman, with fair hair pulled back in one long plait that hung down her back.

'And this is Pearl, our other waitress.'

'Hello,' Alice said. 'Have you been managing the tables on your own?'

'Yes, but I've coped.'

'She has,' Dolly agreed, 'for a new girl she's done remarkably well. Mind you, a lot of our customers ain't got time to hang about and they've been getting a bit impatient at the slow service.'

Pearl flushed. She'd heard the complaints, and on occasions a few costermongers walked out, saying they'd go across the road to the pie-and-mash shop. She hadn't realised that Mrs Dolby knew, and hung her head.

'Now then, girl, I ain't criticising. As I said, you've done well. Now go on back to the dining room and fetch us all a cup of tea.'

'Yes, Mrs Dolby.'

'Well, Pearl,' Bernie said as she walked up to the counter, 'we've got another waitress at last, and an experienced one at that. Things will be easier all round now.'

Pearl managed a small smile, watching as Bernie poured the tea. She took the cups through to the kitchen, finding Alice chatting to Mrs Dolby, the two women obviously getting on well.

'Don't worry, Mrs Dolby,' Alice was saying, 'I'll be able to show Pearl the ropes and her speed will pick up in no time.'

'Did you hear that, Pearl? You'll learn a lot from Alice, so take note of what she tells you.'

With a small nod, Pearl placed the tray on the table. Alice was looking at her, a strange look in her eyes, one almost of triumph. But why?

Pearl found out on Monday. When she arrived at the café, Alice was already there, standing behind the counter and making a pot of tea.

'Right, Pearl, once I've poured this you can take

one through to Mrs Dolby. I've sorted out our tables. You can have the ones at this end, and I'll take the others.'

Alice had chosen the easiest tables to work, those nearest the kitchen, and Pearl looked at Bernie for his reaction.

He was emptying bags of coins into the till, and just smiled, saying, 'Good morning, love. It's good that you won't have to manage on your own now. There'll be no complaints about the service today.'

Pearl had a bad feeling about Alice. She was already asserting herself, but since her days in the orphanage Pearl had never had the courage to speak up for herself. Now, taking a cup of tea through to Mrs Dolby, she had a sinking feeling in the pit of her tummy.

'Good morning, Pearl,' Dolly said. 'Now that Alice has started, watch and learn from her. It was rough on you starting with no one to show you the ropes, but you ain't done bad.'

'Thank you, Mrs Dolby.'

Dolly's broad, flat face broke into a smile, her voice unusually soft. 'Go on, get on with your work.'

As Pearl went back to the dining room she saw both Bernie and Alice chatting as they drank their tea.

'Come on, Pearl, I've poured a cup for you too,' Alice called.

It was a friendly gesture and Pearl responded, chatting to the woman whilst Bernie popped out to the kitchen.

Alice glanced around the café. 'I expect it's the

same routine as the Trafalgar and I'll soon settle in.'

'I'm sure you will, but I think there must be an easier way to take the orders.'

'What do you mean, love?'

'We have to write out a separate chit for each customer, and sometimes if there are four on a table it takes ages.'

'That sounds a bit daft to me and not very efficient.'

'I think it would be easier to write out one slip per table, listing the order with the customers initial beside it. Most come from the market, they know each other, and nine times out of ten sit with the same crowd each day. Of course, if strangers sit at the same table it wouldn't work, but that doesn't happen very often.'

'It sounds like a good idea to me.' The bell pinged, and as customers came in, Alice said, 'Right, Pearl, shake a leg.'

Pearl frowned. Alice made it sound like a command, but the first four men took a seat at one of her tables so she went to take their order. 'Good morning, and what can I get you?'

'Morning, love,' Frank said. 'I'll 'ave me usual.'

'Me too,' another man said, adding, 'Is that another new waitress?'

'Yes, she's starting today.'

'She looks like a battle-axe, Frank.'

'Yeah, a bit of a Boadicea, if you ask me.'

Pearl was smiling as she wrote out their chit. It was obvious these men liked to find nicknames for people. During her first week, Frank had started to call her Minnie Mouse, but she didn't mind. It was just their way, and she was getting used to them now.

The smile left her face when she went into the kitchen. The new waitress was talking to Mrs Dolby and she looked as pleased as punch at what she was hearing.

'Blimey, Alice, that's a great idea and I don't know why I didn't think of it myself. My old gran set up the present system, and as it worked we just carried on. Now though, if we do things your way, not only will it speed up service, it'll also save us a fortune on order pads. Well done, Alice, and it's lovely to have someone who takes an interest in the business.'

'Thanks, Mrs Dolby,' Alice said.

'Pearl, our new waitress has just come up with a marvellous idea for taking orders and we'll start using it straight away. I'd best get these breakfasts on so I'll leave Alice to put you in the picture.'

With a smile of satisfaction, Alice beckoned Pearl to the dining room. 'Mrs Dolby was dead chuffed when I suggested writing out one order chit for each table and it's certainly got me into her good books.'

'But ... but it was my idea.'

'Well, yes, but does it matter who came up with it? As long as it makes things easier for us, that's all that matters. Oops, better get a move on, customers are waiting.'

Pearl stood rooted to the spot for a moment, unable to believe that Alice had pinched her idea. It was her own fault, she should have plucked up the courage to speak to Dolly herself, but now it was too late. She heaved a sigh. Maybe Alice was right – after all, it would make things easier for them – but she still had a bad feeling about the woman.

By eight thirty the café was heaving, and when Derek Lewis came in he took a table at the far end of the café, surprised when Alice came to serve him.

'Hello, where's Pearl? She hasn't left, has she?'

'No, she's in the kitchen. I'm doing the tables down this end. Now then, what can I get you?'

'Just a couple of eggs on toast.'

Carrying two plates, Pearl came backwards through the swing door, and as she rushed past she didn't see Derek. He watched her, his face showing his disappointment. He'd decided to pluck up the courage to ask her out today, and now felt deflated. He'd been rehearsing what he was going to say, his stomach knotted as he came in the café, but now he wouldn't have the chance. Maybe he'd be able to catch her on her way home.

Derek kept his eyes on Pearl as she worked, and when Alice put his breakfast in front of him he hardly looked at it as he picked up his knife and fork. Would Pearl say yes? Christ, he hoped so. She always seemed pleased to see him, and sometimes stopped for a chat. He'd never had attention from a girl before, and hoped he hadn't misread the signs.

Pearl was rushing to the kitchen again, but this time she saw him. Her elfin face broke into a smile. 'Hello, Derek,' she called, but sailed on past.

Derek finished his breakfast, drank his tea, and then went to pay at the counter, pleased when Pearl came to his side.

'Hello, how are you?' he asked.

'I'm fine thanks. How's your gran?'

'She's back to normal, and bossing me around as usual.'

'That's good.'

'Er ... Pearl, I was wondering...'

As Bernie filled two cups of tea, Pearl grabbed them, and Derek was left staring at her back as she hurried away. His heart sank. She hadn't even let him finish his sentence. Maybe he'd imagined it and she didn't like him after all. Sadly he watched her running around for a moment. Then, with his shoulders slumped, he left the café.

It was eleven o'clock when Derek saw Kevin Dolby strolling through the market, and he lifted his arm to catch his attention.

'Watcha, Derek, how's things?'

'Fine, but I wanted to ask your advice.'

'Fire away.'

'It's that waitress, Pearl. She seems to like me, but how can I know for sure?'

'You can't, mate. Sometimes you just have to take a chance. Anyway, I don't know what you're worried about. She can only say no, and there's plenty more fish in the sea.'

'Yeah, I suppose so,' Derek murmured as Kevin walked away. It was all right for him – he was a good-looking bloke and obviously had no trouble finding women. Derek thought back to the one time he'd asked a girl out, and she'd made her distaste plain. Would Pearl be the same? Would she tell him to bugger off too?

A customer came to the stall and, pushing his worries to one side, Derek went to serve her, pleased when she purchased a tea set.

Pearl was relieved when her shift finished and was just preparing to leave when Dolly came out of the kitchen. As she walked the length of the café, her eyes inspected each and every table, but thankfully they were all clean and tidy.

Pearl's ears pricked up when Alice said, 'Mrs Dolby, can I have a word about our tips?'

'What about them?'

'It's a bit frantic in here, both for the breakfast and lunch servings, and I've noticed that Pearl ain't quite got the hang of it yet. To help out I've cleared a few of her tables, but some customers leave tips and in the rush I might have put hers in with mine by mistake. I wonder if it might be better if we have a jar on the counter to pool them in, sharing the money out at the end of the week.'

'Surely mixing Pearl's tips with your own won't happen very often?'

'That's just it. I don't know. As I said, there'll be times when I'll have to clear Pearl's tables, and it's easy to get in a muddle.'

'What do you think about this, Pearl?'

'I ... I'm not sure. Maybe it would be better to keep them separate.'

'You should think yourself lucky that Alice has helped you out, and by clearing your tables she takes on extra work. If you ask me she should keep any tips she finds.'

'Oh, no, Mrs Dolby,' Alice protested. 'That wouldn't be right. I'd rather we share them.'

'Very well then, until Pearl gets up to speed you can put a jar on the counter. If and when she improves, we'll discuss it again.'

Pearl wanted to protest, to tell Mrs Dolby that she didn't need Alice's help. With only half the tables to do now she could easily manage, but seeing impatience on her employer's face, she was held back by fear.

Both she and Alice took their handbags out from under the counter, saying goodbye as the left together, but when the door closed behind them, Alice turned to Pearl, her smile ingratiating. 'I hope you don't mind my suggestion, love. After all, we don't want to get our tips mixed up, do we? See you tomorrow.' With this she walked off in the opposite direction to Pearl.

For a moment Pearl watched her, unhappy but helpless. Alice had made her look bad in front of Mrs Dolby, and she should have had the courage to speak up for herself. Yet both women were dominant, assertive and she just didn't have the nerve. Kevin was walking towards her, heading for the café, and once again her heart skipped. It wasn't often that he spoke to her, but just a rare smile in her direction was enough to bring the colour flooding to her cheeks. Would he speak to her now?

'Watcha, Pearl.'

'Er ... hello,' she stuttered, but he walked straight into the café without breaking his stride. Disconsolately she started to stroll along the market, berating herself for being silly. Kevin Dolby would never look at her twice. He had the pick of the girls and she could never compete.

Derek was looking out for Pearl and at three forty-five he saw her meandering down the market. Fingers crossed, he went to the front of his stall, smiling when she drew near.

'Hello, love. Off home, are you?'

'Yes, I've finished my shift.'

'Er ... Pearl. I ... I was wondering if you fancy going to the pictures one night?'

Her huge eyes rose to meet his and he gulped. Christ, she was such a lovely little thing. She looked so innocent, so frail, and he held his breath for her answer.

'The pictures? Well, yes, I suppose so.'

'That's great. How about tonight?'

'Yes, all right. Can we go to the Granada? There's a Marlene Dietrich film on that I'd love to see.'

'Fine with me. How about I pick you up at seven?'

'Yes, do that.' And smiling shyly, Pearl walked away.

Bloody hell, he'd done it! With a little skip, Derek was grinning as he returned to the back of his stall, and was busy for the rest of the afternoon.

As Derek walked in the door that evening, Connie Lewis assessed him shrewdly. 'What are you looking so happy about?'

'I've got a date, Gran.'

'Have you now? And who with? I hope she's a

nice girl and not one of these painted tarts you see nowadays. Does she live around here?'

'Now then, Gran, I'm twenty-six, not sixteen, and don't need an inquisition. But yes, she's a nice girl and I think you'd like her. Now, I'm off upstairs to have a bath.'

Connie frowned as her grandson left the room. Derek wasn't one for the girls so she was surprised to hear he had a date. She was under no illusions. Derek couldn't be described as handsome. He'd been a plain little boy when he'd come to live with her, and was plain now, but of course boxing hadn't helped.

Yet he was a lovely lad, kind and caring, in fact, sometimes too caring. She smiled, remembering all the lost and wounded animals he'd brought home over the years, from wild birds to cats. In fact they still had one of the cats now, a fat and lazy creature that spent all day asleep on a chair.

As if knowing she was thinking about him, Marmalade opened one eye, yawned and stretched, rousing himself enough to settle in another position before closing his eye again. Connie smiled. Yes, Marmalade was a good name for the ginger cat, and she was quite fond of the old thing really.

She rose to her feet, walking across the kitchen to feed cabbage into the pan of boiling water on the stove. Unbidden, Connie found herself thinking about her daughter, an expression of sadness crossing her face. Mary had got herself pregnant and had never revealed the name of Derek's father, but she didn't deserve to die that way – trapped under the rubble of a pub when it had been bombed during the war.

'What's for dinner, Gran?' Derek asked as he returned downstairs, towelling his hair dry.

'Stewed steak.'

'Smashing.'

'Where are you taking this girl tonight?'

'We're going to the flicks.'

'Well, just make sure you behave yourself!'

'What's that supposed to mean?'

'Oh, sorry, love. Take no notice of me. I know you'll be a perfect gentleman.'

'What's up, Gran? You not only sound snappy, you look a bit down too.'

'I was just thinking about your mother. It's her birthday tomorrow.'

'We'll take some flowers up to the cemetery as usual.'

'She seems to fill my mind more than ever around this time. I don't know why. It's almost as though she draws close to me on her birthday. I know she wasn't much of a mother to you, but I'll never forgive myself for the way I treated her.'

'Gran, it was a long time ago and about time you forgave yourself. And, well, to be honest, I can hardly remember her now.'

Connie checked the vegetables and, seeing they were ready, she drained them before dishing up their dinner. As she placed the plates on the table and sat opposite Derek, her eyes flicked to an old black-and-white photograph of her daughter on the mantelpiece. Mary had been such a pretty girl, with dark hair and eyes, and Connie couldn't help the comparison. Derek bore no resemblance to his mother at all. In fact he didn't look like anyone in the family. He was big, lumbering, with wide shoulders and a large head. There was something Slavic-looking about his features – Polish, maybe? She heaved a sigh, knowing full well that Derek's origins were something they would never know. And now as she began to eat, she was just praying that this girl he was taking out wouldn't hurt him.

8

Pearl went into her room and slumped onto the side of the bed. She'd been taken by surprise when Derek asked her out, saying yes without really thinking about it.

At first it had been nice to have her own place, but now had to admit that she was growing lonely. Art classes didn't start until September, and sitting alone in her bedsit every evening had lost its appeal.

Derek was a nice man and she pictured his face, his misshapen nose, thick lips, and heavy brows, softened by his lovely, kind smile. She had only coveted his friendship, but his invitation sounded like a date. What if he tried to kiss her? She had never been out with a man before, and had no idea what to expect, but surely there must be a way to make Derek understand that it really was only friendship she sought.

Pearl rose to make herself a drink. If Kevin Dolby had asked her out it would have been different. She'd have jumped at the chance, and shivered at the thought of being held in his arms. Don't be silly, she told herself, smiling wryly. Kevin would never look at her twice and it was just a silly dream. When the kettle boiled she made the tea, pleased that nowadays she had milk and sugar. Nevertheless she only put a small amount of each into her cup. She had only half the tables in the café now, and that meant half the tips. Yes, it was silly to dream about Kevin, but art classes were a different matter and still within reach if she was extra careful with her money.

At six o'clock Pearl stood at her sink having a strip wash, after which she surveyed her frugal wardrobe. There wasn't much to choose from and she would love some new clothes, but more important was saving for paint and brushes. She pulled on a navy cotton skirt that had faded with so many washes, adding a blue striped blouse with a Peter Pan collar. Without navy shoes to match, she would have to wear her usual black, low-heel court shoes, and after flicking a brush through her hair she was ready.

Derek rang the bell on the dot of seven and, stomach fluttering with nerves, Pearl picked up her rather old-fashioned clip-top handbag before going downstairs.

He grinned when he saw her. 'Hello. You look nice.'

Pearl took in his appearance. He was wearing a grey striped suit with wide lapels, the material straining across his huge shoulders. His shirt was white and his tie a bit loud, but she returned the compliment. 'You look nice too.'

85

Derek's face suffused with colour, the red flush rising from his neck to his hairline. 'Thanks,' he spluttered, and gaining some equilibrium added, 'Right, are you ready to go?'

They jumped on a bus that took them along Falcon Road and up St John's Hill to the cinema. The queue at the ticket office was short, and then Pearl smiled when Derek went to the kiosk to buy her a box of chocolates.

'Here you are,' he said, his smile a little shy as he handed them to her.

Pearl thanked him and then he took her arm, walking up to an usherette, who clipped their tickets before they went in to see the film.

It was pitch-black as they pushed through the double doors, but another usherette came forward, shining her torch along a row of seats about three down from the back. Pearl shuffled past a few people, whispering apologies, and then pulled down the folding seat, sitting hurriedly. Derek sat down heavily beside her just as the *Pathé News* began, and they settled back to watch.

Halfway through the B movie, Pearl opened her chocolates, offering the box to Derek and finding that as the flickering, bluish light from the screen playing across his face, it emphasised his pug nose and craggy cheeks. He turned to smile at her, the effect softening, but she quickly looked away. His bulk filled the seat, Pearl feeling tiny beside him, and moments later he was groping for her hand. She surreptitiously moved it, taking another sweet from the box and offering one to Derek, the moment thankfully passing.

The main film was on, Marlene Dietrich looking beautiful and sultry, when Pearl stiffened. Derek's arm was moving slowly around her shoulders. God, what should she do? She didn't want to encourage him, but didn't want to lose his friendship either.

Hastily she whispered, 'Sorry, Derek, I need to go to the powder room.'

Pearl spent a long time in the ladies, staring at herself in the mirror and dreading going back to sit beside Derek. He was a lovely man, she knew that, but at the thought of being in his arms and kissed by him, she quaked.

'Well, Pearl, what did you think of the movie?' Derek asked as they made their way home.

'It was good, and thanks for taking me.'

'We'll have to do it again soon.'

'Yes,' she said quietly.

'I tell you what. How do you feel about coming round one night to meet my gran? She's a lovely old girl and I know you'd like her.'

Pearl sucked in her breath. If she didn't say something now, she'd lose her nerve. 'I'd like that Derek, and I'm glad that we've become friends. I'm too young to think about having a boyfriend, so this is lovely.'

'Yeah, right,' Derek said.

She caught the note of disappointment in his voice. 'I know you live with your gran, but what about your parents?' she asked softly. 'I haven't heard you mention them.'

'My mother was killed during the war, and I don't know who my father is.'

Pearl smiled at him with sympathy. 'I don't

know anything about either of my parents.'

'We've got something in common then.'

Pearl rapidly changed the subject. 'Did I tell you I'm starting art classes in September?'

'No,' Derek said, and for the rest of the journey back to Battersea High Street, she spoke of her ambitions.

It was as they drew level with her bedsit that the door to the shop opened, Nobby Clark coming out, with Kevin Dolby behind him.

'Watcha, Nobby ... Kevin,' Derek said. 'Me and Pearl have just been to the flicks.'

Kevin's smile was tight. 'Is that right? Sorry, mate, we can't stop to chat.'

Pearl frowned as they walked away. 'Kevin once told me that he didn't know Nobby Clark, but now they seem very friendly.'

'I think you must have got the wrong end of the stick. They go back years; we all do. Kevin is about five years younger than us, but as a nipper he was always hanging around us older lads. Nobby used to be the ringleader and I ain't proud of the things we got up to but, unlike Nobby, I grew out of it.'

'What do you mean?'

'You know what young lads are like. We were always up to mischief.'

Pearl shook her head, unable to make sense of it all. She was sure that Kevin had said he didn't know Nobby Clark. He had lied. But why?

Kevin climbed into his car and, leaning over, he opened the passenger door for Nobby, his mind on Pearl Button. Shit! The bloody girl had seen him with Nobby and that was the last thing he wanted.

'Bloody hell, Derek and Pearl Button. Talk about beauty and the beast,' Nobby chuckled as he climbed into the passenger seat.

'Beauty? Pearl ain't a beauty.'

'Take a closer look, mate. Her clothes aren't up to much, and she doesn't wear a scrap of make-up, but when you get a good gander at her face, she's a bit of all right.'

'Don't tell me you fancy her too?'

'Nah, she's too scrawny for me, but I can see the attraction for Derek. He always was a soft bugger and I think the girl brings out his protective instinct.' He chuckled again. 'When we were kids, do you remember that dog? Derek went mad when we chucked stones at it.'

'Yeah, I remember. He nearly blew his top. When Derek's got his pepper up he can be a nasty sod.'

Kevin revved the car, but before driving off he paused. 'Look, mate, I ain't sure about casing this joint. It's a bit too soon after the last job and I thought we were going to lay low for a bit.'

'We only got peanuts for those fags and I need more dosh. Dick Smedley said this job would be a doddle. Come on, it won't hurt to take a look.'

In half an hour they were sitting outside the storage depot. It was in total darkness and there was little to be seen, but even so, Nobby peered through the windscreen. 'Dick's right, it looks a piece of cake. It's still in Vince's manor so we'll have to clear it with him, but as long as we offer him the gear, I reckon he'll be OK.'

'What makes Dick so sure they store booze?'

''Cos he went there pretending to apply for a job.'

'What about the alarm system?'

'According to Dick it'll be easy to nobble.'

'Huh, and he's an expert, is he?' Kevin's voice dripped with sarcasm.

'What's the matter? Turning chicken, are you?'

'You know me better than that. Anyway, it'd be a waste of time using my car. We'd only get a few cases in the boot.'

'Like I said, you should've got a van, you daft sod. Still, it shouldn't be a problem. We can nick a van and dump it afterwards.'

Kevin chewed his bottom lip. Up to now, Nobby and Dick had only attempted petty thieving, low risk, but small returns. Now they were looking for bigger jobs, bringing him on board as the driver. There was no doubt this one could make them a lot of money, and at *that* thought he grinned. 'All right. I'm in.'

'Good boy. Right, let's get back to Battersea.'

Kevin drove home, dropped Nobby off outside his house, and then parked at the back of the café.

His thoughts turned to Pearl Button again, and he scowled. On occasions, until they could shift it, they stored a bit of stolen gear in the back room of Nobby's empty shop. What if Pearl got nosy again? What if she found it? And if she did, would she link it to him? He was frowning as he quietly went up to the flat, holding his breath as he tiptoed past his mother's room. Maybe he should have a quiet word in Pearl's ear. The girl

90

needed a hint that if she was going to live around her, no matter what she saw, or heard, if she wanted to stay in one piece the best policy was to keep her lips zipped.

9

Pricilla Unsworth sat behind her desk at the orphanage, relieved that she had finally sorted the records in preparation for her retirement. They were all in order, but one remained, one that had been carefully guarded from prying eyes. It was Pearl Button's, the child who had provided her nest egg, and taking out all but the barest details, she was going to destroy it, leaving no trace behind.

When she'd been approached all those years ago, she'd agreed to the ruse, and made sure that she was the one to find the new-born baby on the steps.

Everything had been done by letter; unsigned, with a box number as the return address. With so much to gain, Pricilla had diligently followed the instructions. The person who'd abandoned Pearl wanted no risks, and certainly no questions asked. To that end he, or she, had insisted that Pearl Button was never fostered out, or put up for adoption. Pricilla had thought this over-cautious in the extreme, but financially the arrangement suited her well. For each year that Pearl Button remained in the orphanage, Pricilla had been paid, the money building up to a nice little nest egg.

She picked up the thin file. No doubt the child had been born out of wedlock, perhaps another victim of a wartime romance, but it was almost as if this person wanted to punish the baby along with the mother. Many times she had wondered who she'd dealt with, and had decided it was a man. Of course she couldn't be certain, but surely only a man could act so callously.

There had been just one sticky moment that occurred during Pearl's last year, but thankfully it had passed. Pricilla had been surprised when she'd received a letter from a woman enquiring about an abandoned baby, giving only the date of birth. When Pricilla realised it was Pearl's, her heart had missed a beat. She'd replied, denying any knowledge of the child, and to be on the safe side had arranged for Pearl to leave the orphanage earlier than anticipated. Thankfully there had been no further enquiries.

It was over now, the girl no longer under her care. Pearl Button had left the orphanage, she had been found employment, a place in a hostel, but that was as far as Pricilla's authority went. She had no idea where the girl was now, and didn't care. It was done, finished with, and Pricilla smiled. The money she'd received for Pearl Button had provided a decent retirement fund, and now a nice little cottage in the country beckoned.

About to tear the letter to pieces, she was annoyed to hear a knock on the door. 'Yes, what is it?'

The art teacher came into the office, her eyes puzzled as she gazed at Pricilla's poised fingers.

Quickly stuffing the letter back in the file, she saw Emily Rosen placing an envelope on her desk.

'What's that?'

'I've come to tender my resignation.'

'Really?' Pricilla said. 'And may I ask why?'

'There is no longer any reason for me to stay.'

Pricilla shook her head impatiently. The woman wasn't making any sense, but what did it matter? She was leaving too and wouldn't have the task of finding a replacement. In truth, she had never liked the woman, finding her too inquisitive about the children, asking to see records that were none of her business. There was another knock on her door, and heaving a sigh of exasperation she called, 'Come in.'

'Oh, Miss Unsworth, can you come quickly?' the harassed teacher begged. 'A serious fight has broken out in the playground and I can't break it up.'

Pricilla tutted with impatience. 'I can't deal with it now.'

'But, Miss Unsworth, it's the older girls and I can't get through them to the poor child they're picking on. She's on the ground and looks to be in a dreadful state.'

Pricilla rose hastily to her feet. 'I'll have to sort this out,' she told Miss Rosen.

The woman nodded, saying quietly, 'Very well.'

Pricilla hurried from her office, but had she looked back, she would have seen the art teacher surveying the file she'd mistakenly left on her desk. Emily Rosen reached to pick it up, flicking it open. As she scanned the contents, a gasp escaped her lips. Her face lit up with joy and for a moment she hugged the file to her chest. Then, carefully replacing it in the exact position she had found it, Emily Rosen scurried out.

In Battersea, Pearl was looking at her sketches. Of all of them, the drawing of Derek stood out as best. His kind eyes looked incongruous against his craggy features, but Pearl thought she had captured the essence of the man. She picked up the sketch of Nora and frowned. She didn't see much of the cleaner, and the sketch was one she wasn't happy with. Nora had a round face that was somehow featureless, making it difficult to capture on paper. There was something missing, and as she tried to picture the woman in her mind, she realised it was Nora's childlike innocence. Placing Nora's picture to one side, Pearl lifted one of her favourites, a sketch of Frank Hanwell's son.

She had seen the lad a couple of times hanging around his dad's stall and was taken by the eight-year-old's features. He had dark, unruly hair, a tiny nose sprinkled with freckles, but it was his cheeky, gap-toothed smile that Pearl had wanted to capture. She gazed critically at the sketch. It wasn't perfect, and without paint she had been unable to capture the boy's wonderful emerald-green eyes.

Placing the drawing back inside the folder, her thoughts returned to Derek Lewis. He'd looked disappointed when she told him they could only be friends, but had still invited her to meet his gran. Thinking of that, her eyes widened. He'd be here soon and she wasn't ready!

As she dashed around, Pearl knew why she had agreed to go to Derek's house. She was curious – curious to see what a normal home looked like. All she had known was the orphanage and then the hostel, family life a mystery to her. She'd heard talk, of course. When girls came back to the orphanage after being fostered for a while, they spoke of the families they had stayed with and she had listened to their stories with avid interest. Of course, not all of the tales were good ones, and some were horrible. One girl of thirteen had been used as a servant, forced to do housework from early morning to night, and had slept in a small, cold room under the eaves of the house.

When she heard a knock on the street door, Pearl shook her thoughts away as she hurried downstairs. The orphanage held mostly bad memories, ones she wanted to forget.

'Hello, love,' Derek said. 'I've told Gran I'm bringing you round and she's looking forward to it.'

'Is she?' Pearl found she was suddenly nervous and as they walked along the High Street she clung to Derek's arm. He looked down at her, smiling with pleasure and she managed a small smile back. Oh, he was a nice man. Would his gran be the same?

It didn't take them long to reach Derek's house. As they walked in Connie Lewis stepped forward.

'Hello, ducks, nice to meet you,' she said, leading them into a small room at the front.

'It's nice to meet you too,' Pearl said, smiling shyly. Derek's gran was a surprise. She was a tiny, thin woman with sharp features, but like Derek, her eyes were kind.

'Take a seat, love,' she invited.

'Thank you,' Pearl said, doing so.

'Derek tells me you're an orphan.'

'Yes, that's right.'

'How old were you when you were put in the orphanage?'

'From what I've been told, I was a new-born baby and left on the steps.'

'Oh, that's awful. Your mother must have been desperate to do that.'

Pearl looked down at the threadbare rug under her feet. Yes, her mother must have been desperate, perhaps unmarried, but Pearl would never know the answers. Over the years she had thought about her. Did they look alike? She had read a novel once in which a servant had been taken by the master and then thrown on to the streets. Was that what had happened to her mother? Scenario after scenario filled her mind. Had her mother been ill – too ill to look after her – and, as she had never come back to claim her, had she died?

'I'm sorry, love. Me and my big mouth, and now I've upset you,' Connie cried.

'No, please, I'm all right.'

'I'll go and make us all a cup of tea,' she said, bustling from the room.

'Sorry about that, Pearl. My gran does have a tendency to put her foot in it, but she doesn't mean any harm.'

'It's all right. There's no need to apologise.'

Pearl gazed around the room with interest. There was a three-piece suite, and she was sitting on one of the rather lumpy chairs. Under the window she saw a highly polished sideboard, with a lace runner across the top on which sat a few china ornaments. The fireplace was small, and covering the grate there was a little painted paper screen in the shape of a fan. There was a carved fender, and in one alcove a small table on which sat a rather ugly plant. Even with so little furniture the room was crowded, and there was the faint scent of lavender in the air. Pearl found it cosy and wondered what the rest of the house was like.

'Here we are,' Connie said as she came back into the room.

Derek took the rather laden tray from her, admonishing, 'You should have called me, Gran. This weighs a ton.'

Pearl saw pretty china cups and saucers, a teapot, and a plate piled with slices of cherry cake. Connie moved the plant from the small table, and as Derek laid the tray down she bustled out again, calling, 'I'll just get the milk and sugar.'

Derek grinned. 'To tell you the truth, Pearl, we hardly use this room. We live and eat in the kitchen.'

'Oh, I wouldn't have minded the kitchen.'

'Well, tell Gran that.'

'Tell me what?' Connie asked as she came back into the room.

'That Pearl would've been happy to sit in the kitchen.'

'Blimey, and there's me trying to make an impression. Well, we're in here now, and here we'll stay. Do you take milk and sugar, love?'

'Yes, please.'

Connie handed her a cup of tea, followed by a plate with a slice of cake on it. Pearl floundered; with both hands full she couldn't drink her tea or eat the cake. Maybe she could balance one on her lap?

Connie followed the same procedure with Derek, but instead of consternation, he roared with laughter. 'I've only got two hands, Gran. Am I supposed to eat the cake with me toes?'

Connie laughed too, her eyes bright as she looked at Pearl. 'As you can see, we ain't used to airs and graces. All right, I give in, let's go to the kitchen and at least we can sit around the table.'

'Thank Gawd for that,' Derek said.

Pearl stood up and followed Connie through to the kitchen, Derek behind them with the tray. The room was larger with a well-scrubbed table in the centre.

'Sit down, love,' the old lady said.

From then on it was more relaxed, the ice broken, and soon Connie was asking Pearl questions again, this time about her job in the café, and Dolly Dolby.

'I hear the woman's a bit of a battle-axe. Is that right?'

'She isn't too bad. Well, unless she's in a bad mood.'

'And that's every other day,' Derek said with a chuckle.

'Derek tells me you live in a bedsit.'

'Yes, I'm renting it from Nobby Clark.'

'Is he that tyke you used to knock around with, Derek?'

'Yeah, that's the one.'

'Huh, he's nothing but trouble. When he was left the shop he could have done all right, but from what I heard he got hooked on gambling. It's a mug's game and the shop went under, all the profits going to the bookies. All right, he was only nineteen at the time, but that's no excuse. You were running the stall on your own, and you've done well. What's Nobby up to these days?'

'Nothing honest, that's for sure.'

Pearl thought about the cartons of cigarettes she had seen, wondering if she should mention them, but then Derek stood up.

'I'm just going out back for a Jimmy Riddle.'

'A what?'

'You explain, Gran.'

'Jimmy Riddle – piddle, it's cockney rhyming slang. He's gone to the outside toilet,' Connie said, and as the door closed behind him she leaned forward, her eyes now hardening. 'How old are you, Pearl?'

'I'm sixteen, nearly seventeen.'

'Christ, you're just a kid. Look, I know you've become friends with my Derek, but I don't want him hurt. He likes you, I can tell, but you're a bit young for him.'

'We ... we're not courting. We're just friends.'

'That's as maybe, but I still think he's looking for more than that. I don't want to cross-examine you, but I can't see why you've latched on to Derek. Surely you'd prefer friends, girls of your

99

own age?'

'I don't know any girls, and those that come into the café seem to be a bit stand-offish.'

'Yeah, well, that's probably because you talk like you've got a plum in your mouth. You stand out as different, an outsider, and they're bound to be suspicious.' Connie leaned back and sighed heavily. 'All right, I'll say no more, but if you don't want things to go any further with Derek, it might be better if you stop seeing him.'

'Gran!'

Connie's head shot round. 'Derek, I didn't know you were there.'

'That's pretty obvious. Now what's going on? I only heard the tail end of what you were saying, but why are you telling Pearl to stop seeing me?'

Connie hung her head. 'I don't want you hurt.'

'Gran, I'm a grown man. I like Pearl, and she likes me, but I know she's only looking for friendship. Now if you don't mind, I think you should keep your nose out. Come on, Pearl, I'll take you home.'

'Oh, please, don't fall out over me.'

'It's all right, dear. Derek's right and I had no business interfering.' Connie stood up, going to her grandson's side and laying a hand on his arm. 'I'm sorry. Pearl's a nice girl, and I like her. I was just trying to protect you, that's all.'

Derek's face softened as he looked down at the tiny woman. 'Do I look like I need protection? Now come on, let's start again, and how about cutting me another slice of cake?'

Pearl heaved a sigh of relief. Seeing the loving look that Connie Lewis was giving her grandson, she felt a twinge of envy. It must be wonderful to have someone to love you like that, unconditionally. Maybe she *could* think of Derek as more than a friend – maybe she could become part of this small family. She would have a home, Derek would always be there to look out for her, and she would never have to be afraid again. Yet even as she considered it, Kevin Dolby's face flew into her mind. Stop it, stop dreaming, she berated herself.

10

Nobby Clark threw open the door of the empty bedsit with a flourish. 'There you are, and it's a guinea a week rent.'

The balding, flabby man looked around before testing the bed. 'Yes, it's all right. Is there a bathroom?'

'There's one further along the landing.'

'How many tenants will I have to share it with?'

'Only one. A young woman lives on the floor below, but she's a nice quiet girl.'

'What about my car? With the market set up every day, I can't see anywhere to park outside.'

'This is one of the few premises with a side entrance. You can drive round the back and park in the yard, but don't come in through my shop. There's another door that leads into the downstairs hall. You can use that.'

'Right, I'll take it and I'll pay a month's rent in advance.'

Nobby grinned, pleased to have a bit of extra money coming in. They were still planning the next job and things were a bit tight. 'What do you do for a living?'

'I work in insurance.'

'And what's your name?'

'Trevor – Trevor Bardington.'

There was something about this bloke that gave Nobby the creeps, but with a month's rent in his pocket he wasn't one to look a gift horse in the mouth. He'd put a bet on, one that was heavily tipped, and maybe the bad luck that dogged him would change. Yeah, perhaps he'd be on to a big winner.

'Thanks,' the man said as Nobby handed him a rent book and keys. 'I'll pick up my things and be back later.'

As both men left the room to go downstairs, Pearl Button was on her way up. They waited until she reached the landing, Nobby saying, 'Hello, Pearl, you're just in time to meet Mr Bardington. He's moving in to the room above yours.'

'Hello,' she said shyly.

The man nodded, saying nothing and, once again thinking he was a strange one, Nobby led him down to the street door, showing him out before going through to his shop.

It wasn't long before Kevin Dolby and Dick Smedley turned up, looking furtively behind them as they walked in.

'Are we nearly set to do the job?' Nobby asked.

Dick answered, 'I've seen a van and have been watching the driver's movements for several days. He parks it up in the same spot every night, and as he's got a ladder stashed on the top it solves another problem. I doubt he'll notice the van's gone until the following morning, so we'll have done the job and dumped it before it's reported missing.'

'Sounds good,' Kevin said. 'And is it the usual buyer, Nobby?'

'Of course it is. I daren't offer it to anyone else – you know that. Anything that isn't small time is always fenced through Vince.'

'He must be raking it in.'

'Yeah, but he ain't one to cross. He's got the borough sewn up, and if we offered it to anyone else his boys would turn us into mincemeat. I don't fancy storing the booze overnight, so we're to take it straight to his club. He's gonna wait for us, and after unloading we can get rid of the van. Now it's just a matter of deciding when we hit the warehouse.'

Dick pursed his lips. 'I reckon tomorrow night. They get a delivery today, and nothing gets sent out again until Monday morning.'

'That's fine with me. What about you, Kevin?'

'Yeah, I'm in.'

The three men went over the plans again. When they were satisfied, Kevin rose to his feet. 'Right, how do you fancy a drink before we go to see the match?'

'Good idea.'

Kevin felt a thrill of anticipation as they left the shop. After the job he'd be able to take a trip to Soho, and if the haul was a big one more trips would follow.

Pearl was pleased that another tenant was moving in, but had hoped it would be someone young, ideally a girl she could make friends with.

Mr Bardington looked to be in his forties. He was a big man, overweight, with a grey unhealthy appearance, and cold blue eyes. She had looked forward to having someone else in the house, especially at night, but wasn't sure she liked the look of the older man.

Her bedsit was like an oven, stuffy, and even with the window open it felt airless. She wiped a hand across her brow as she perched on her bed. It was the third week in August, and with art classes starting soon, she wanted to check her savings.

She'd been frugal, and with any luck there would be enough to buy paint and brushes. She checked her tips, a frown creasing her forehead. With fewer tables to work, her tips had gone down, but surely not this much.

Mentally Pearl assessed the day. She had regulars who sat at her tables, and most tipped her once a week. Frank Hanwell always left her three-pence on a Saturday, along with the other costermongers who sat with him. Derek too was generous and he mostly left her sixpence.

An awful suspicion began to fill her mind, one she wanted to dismiss but couldn't. It was over three weeks since Alice had started work in the café, and despite her earlier trepidations, they were getting on well together. She'd assured Alice that she could manage, but the woman still thought nothing of clearing Pearl's tables along with her own, and also took over behind the counter to give

Bernie a break.

Alice seemed to have boundless energy, and though the weather was blazing hot, she was rarely still. Yes, Alice cleared her tables for her, but what about the tips she found? Was she putting them in her own pocket?

Pearl stood up and moved across to the window. Oh, surely she was imagining things. It was wrong to be suspicious, yet it had happened so many times at the orphanage. They had little, but still had to guard their tiny treasures from thieving hands. Pearl remembered a ribbon she'd been given by a departing teacher. It had been pink and she'd treasured it, but one day it had gone. She had never found out who took it, but suspected an older girl, a bully whom she'd never had the courage to confront.

Now there was Alice, and if the woman was stealing her tips, what could she do? She daren't accuse her – Alice would go mad – but was there another way? Derek!

She could ask him to have a word with her, or maybe she could tell Bernard Dolby... Round and round her thoughts went until at last her mind calmed. Take one step at a time. Watch Alice, and if she really was pinching her tips, then maybe their employer would sort it out.

At seven o'clock, Pearl was ready. Derek was boxing tonight and had invited her to the match. She had hesitated, hating the thought of the brutality, but Connie Lewis wanted to go, and had urged Pearl to join her.

She still hadn't made up her mind about taking

the friendship with Derek any further, but as a regular visitor to his house she was growing close to his gran. Now, picking up her handbag, she went to collect Connie.

By eight o'clock they were in one of the large function rooms at Battersea Town Hall, sitting in the front row and watching a match between two young men.

Pearl found the atmosphere gladiatorial: the smell of sweat; the baying of the crowd; the boxers dancing around each other in the ring, exchanging flurries of punches that had the crowd rising to their feet yelling for more.

A bell clanged, the round coming to an end, and as one of the boxers sat in his corner, Pearl's stomach turned as he removed his gum shield, took a mouthful of water and then spat it into a bucket. Another man took a soaking sponge, running it over the young man's puffy, red face, blood now visible and oozing from his nose. Oh God, it was awful, but as she glanced around, Pearl could see that she was the only one affected.

'There's only one more round to go and then Derek's match is next,' Connie said, gripping Pearl's arm with excitement.

Pearl fought nausea and the need to flee. A hand tapped her on the shoulder and she spun around.

'Watcha, Pearl,' Kevin Dolby said. 'Enjoying it, are you?'

'Er ... it's all right.'

'Your boyfriend is on next.'

Pearl didn't bother to correct him. Derek was just a friend, but in the crowded room it was

106

impossible to speak without shouting. Instead she just nodded.

'It'll be a good match and I've got a few bob on Derek.'

Pearl forced a smile before turning to face the front again. She looked up at the ring, wondering why it was called a ring when it was, in fact, square, but then the bell signalled the start of the last round.

Both young boxers began the dance again, circling around each other, until one lunged forward. A gloved fist connected with a chin, a boxer bouncing off the ropes in front of Pearl before falling with a crash onto the canvas.

The referee rushed over, his arm slicing the air as he counted the boxer out. '...Eight – nine – ten,' he yelled.

The boxer didn't move, and signalling that he was out for the count the referee bounded over to the other man, grabbed his arm and raised it into the air to show who was the victor.

By then, Pearl and the defeated boxer were the only ones who weren't on their feet, the cheers for the local lad deafening.

A couple of men scrambled under the ropes, kneeling beside the young boxer as they tried to bring him round. Pearl found she was holding her breath. Oh God, he still wasn't moving. Was he dead? With a groan he finally sat up, eyes glazed as he was helped to his feet and led from the ring.

Pearl saw the winner dancing round, his body slick with sweat and his arms punching the air with delight. When the accolades of the crowd gradually diminished he too ducked under the ropes and left the arena, a satin gown covering his body and a towel draped over his head.

'That was a good match,' Connie said as she sat down. 'Here, what's the matter? You look as white as a sheet.'

'I ... I feel a bit sick.'

'Gawd, you're a soft one.'

'I ... I think I'll have to leave.'

'Don't do that, love. Derek will be ever so disappointed. Look, go outside and get a bit of fresh air. His match won't start just yet.'

Pearl rose to her feet, stumbling for the door. The air felt heavy as she stepped outside, and she could hear distant rumbles of thunder, a summer storm threatening. She leaned against a wall, startled when she heard a voice.

'What's up, Pearl? Don't you like the sight of a bit of blood?' Kevin asked as he nonchalantly lit a cigarette.

'I ... I think it's awful.'

'You've got Derek's match to watch yet. It's a heavyweight bout and more my cup of tea.'

'I don't think I can go back in.'

'If you ask me, you ain't the right type to live around here. You don't fit in. Things go on – things you have to keep your nose out of, if you know what I mean.'

Pearl's eyes widened, and with a menacing smile Kevin continued, 'This is just a little warning. No matter what you see, or hear, keep your mouth shut. It's safer that way.'

She couldn't speak, managing only a small nod.

Kevin threw his cigarette onto the pavement,

grinding it out with the sole of his shoe, his manner changing again as he said softly, 'Are you coming back in?'

'In ... in a minute.'

Pearl gulped as Kevin walked away. She was seeing him in a new light and her mind was reeling. Instead of her heart skipping a beat when she saw him, it was now jumping with fear. He had threatened her, but why?

The noise inside the function room rose again and, pushing herself from the wall, Pearl went inside, deciding that now, more than ever, she needed to stay close to Derek Lewis.

As they watched Derek's match, Kevin found his eyes drawn to Pearl. When Derek or his opponent took a punch, instead of jumping up and baying with the crowd, the girl covered her face with horror.

When he'd followed her outside and issued the veiled threat, she had looked at him like a frightened rabbit caught in headlights. Her eyes were amazing and as she stared up at him, he enjoyed seeing her fear. She was a timid little creature who seemed incapable of standing up for herself. In fact, she was the complete antithesis of his mother, and for the first time he could see why Derek was attracted to her.

Kevin continued to watch Pearl, seeing her growing distress when Derek sustained a nasty cut above his eye. Christ, what on earth did she see in him?

The two heavyweights continued to lumber around the ring, sweat pouring from their bodies, and with only one round to go, both men looked exhausted. They came together, clinging to each other like two bulls locked in an embrace, the referee once again shouting, 'Break!'

Dick Smedley hissed, 'I think our bets are safe. I reckon Derek will win on points.'

'Yeah, he'd better,' Nobby said. 'I stuck four quid on him instead of a horse.'

The round came to an end, and as a small stool was quickly put in Derek's corner, he slumped onto it. His face was sponged, the cut attended to, and after the referee took a quick look at it, he signalled for the match to continue.

Aware that this was the last round, both boxers put in a bit more effort, and there were flurries of punches. Derek was obviously trying to protect his cut, his gloved hands high over his face and body leaning forward as he stalked his prey. He managed to land a good few punches, but the other boxer remained on his feet until at last the bell rang.

Both boxers went to their corners, but remained standing, and a hush descended on the crowd as the points were counted.

'I wish they'd get a bloody move on,' Nobby hissed.

The result! And as the referee raised Derek's arm in victory, cheers rang out.

Kevin found himself watching Pearl again, and as she stood up he saw tears running down her cheeks. She looked up at Derek as he came to the ropes to grin down at her, blood now oozing from the cut.

Kevin scowled, surprised to find himself suddenly jealous. But why? The skinny cow wasn't his type. He liked his women to have a bit of shape.

'Come on, let's go. We'll collect our winnings and then have another drink,' Nobby urged.

Kevin nodded, but his thoughts were still distracted as he followed his two mates. What would sex be like with Pearl Button? Would she let him dominate? Of course she would – the timid little cow would be too scared to put up a fight. He found himself hardening at the thought. He wouldn't have to pay her either. Pearl was one he could have for free, and maybe, just maybe, he might sample the goods.

11

On Sunday evening, Pearl looked up at her ceiling, puzzled. Mr Bardington seemed to be pacing back and forth, and had been doing so for over an hour. At first she tried to ignore it, but now it was driving her mad. Thump, thump, thump, his heavy footsteps unrelenting.

She couldn't sketch, it was impossible, and throwing her pad aside she decided to have a bath. She rarely used the room, preferring a strip wash to the brown, stained, roll-top bath, but maybe soaking in nice deep water might relax her.

Pearl had a lot on her mind. There was the anxiety that Alice Freeman might be taking her tips, but worse, the veiled threat Kevin Dolby had issued. It had forced her hand, making her decide to take things further with Derek. Though she didn't like his looks, she felt safe with him and knew she would have no need to fear Kevin Dolby, or anyone else, whilst he was around.

She crept upstairs, clutching her towel and wash things. The bathroom didn't look inviting, the distempered walls grey and flaking, but she locked the door behind her and turned on the taps.

With her eyes closed, shutting out the ugly room, it was nice to lie back in the water, letting it trickle over her shoulders. At last she couldn't hear Mr Bardington pacing. There was a faint sound of music now, something classical, and Pearl luxuriated in the peaceful solitude.

The water was tepid, refreshing, but finally Pearl climbed out, towelling herself vigorously. She was perching on the edge of the bath, drying her feet, when the door handle turned. She froze as it rattled again, but finding her voice she called, 'Who's there?'

'It's Trevor Bardington. Sorry, I didn't realise someone was in there.'

'I've nearly finished and it'll be free in a few minutes.'

'Right, thanks,' and as she heard his footsteps retreating, Pearl dressed quickly.

She scooted out, but as her eyes flicked along the landing there was no sign of the man. Soon she was back in her room and, throwing on pyjamas, scrambled into bed. Yet why was she frightened? Mr Bardington had only tried the door – he hadn't forced his way in. Pearl turned, clutching her pillow. It was Kevin's threat that was making her jumpy and more than ever she felt alone, vulnerable, in these almost empty premises.

It was after midnight when Kevin, Nobby and Dick walked quietly to a nearby street, pleased to see the van parked in the usual spot.

'There's nobody about,' Nobby said.

Dick scratched his chin. 'It won't take long to open that door.'

'Come on then, let's get on with it,' Kevin said impatiently. He didn't like standing around and was nervous of being seen. The sooner they got into the van and drove off, the better.

Dick, skilled at the task, soon had the door open, and in another few minutes Kevin had hot-wired the van, the engine coming to life.

'Jump in the back, Dick,' he hissed as Nobby climbed hurriedly into the passenger seat.

Kevin took as many backstreets as possible, finding his mouth dry as they drew up outside the warehouse. The premises were in darkness and Kevin twisted round in his seat to speak to Dick.

'Are you sure about the alarm?'

'As sure as I can be.'

Nobby climbed out. 'Come on, Dick. We'll cut the padlock and open the gates. When that's done, Kevin, you can drive in.'

Kevin waited, finding his hands sweating as he gripped the steering wheel. The two men made light of the lock, and soon the metal gates were swinging open. With a look in his rearview mirror, Kevin drove into the grounds, pulling up in front of the loading bay.

Dick walked up the ramp, inspecting the alarm box high on the wall. 'I hope that bleedin' ladder's long enough,' he mumbled before bending down to his bag of tools.

Nobby struggled to get the ladder off the van. 'Give me a hand, Kevin.'

As soon as they'd placed it up against the wall, Kevin returned to the van, ready for a quick getaway if anything went wrong.

Dick climbed the ladder and then Kevin watched as he placed a small torch between his teeth, leaving his hands free to work on the alarm box.

Kevin's tension eased. Dick seemed to know what he was doing. He removed the cover, carefully handing it down to Nobby before reaching inside the box. Then suddenly a deafening, clanging racket pierced the silence.

Kevin froze momentarily, but then in panic he gunned the engine to life, eyes on stalks as he screamed, 'Come on, let's get out of here!'

Dick slid down the ladder, grabbed his tools, and then both men scrambled for the van.

Nobby just about managed to leap into the passenger seat as Kevin screeched off. 'Shit!' he yelled, holding on to the dashboard for dear life.

Dick had almost shot into the back of the van and, with tyres screaming, Kevin was out of the gate, driving with his foot hard on the accelerator.

'For fuck's sake,' Dick yelled, 'give me a chance to shut the back doors!'

Kevin slowed almost imperceptibly before turning a corner, his ears peeled for the sound of police sirens. Dick managed to pull the doors closed, and soon they were streets away.

'Slow down, you stupid bastard! You're drawing attention to us,' Nobby shouted.

'Watch your mouth,' Kevin spat, his eyes now flicking to the back of the van and to Dick Smedley. 'So much for the alarm being a fucking doddle! Christ, it serves me right for getting mixed up with amateurs.'

Nobby's voice was dangerously low: 'We ain't amateurs. It was just bad luck. Now find somewhere to dump this van, and soon.'

Kevin turned left towards the industrial arches under Clapham Junction station. In the pitch-darkness his headlights pierced the gloom and, parking in front of the first unit, he scrambled out of the van.

'Come on, this'll do. We can make our way home through the backstreets.'

The three men walked quickly, constantly looking behind them and relieved when they reached Battersea High Street.

'That was a bloody fiasco,' Kevin said, breaking the silence.

'I'll admit it was a cock-up, but we got clean away.'

'Yeah, but empty-handed.'

'There's always another job, and we'll make better plans next time.'

'Next time! You must be kidding!'

Nobby shrugged. 'You'll be looking for easy money again soon, and I'll be in touch.'

'Don't bother,' Kevin spat as he marched away.

Trevor Bardington still couldn't sleep. Standing in the darkness of his room, he looked out of the window on to the three young men below him in the street. He recognised his landlord, Nobby Clark, and though the men seemed to be arguing, he wasn't interested. His appetite was rising again, and try as he might he couldn't fight it. How many times had he moved? How many different areas had he lived in? He'd lost count. So far he'd been lucky, very lucky, and had never been caught.

He turned away from the window and threw himself onto his bed. Once he had seen that face it was impossible to get it out of his mind – impossible to fight the desire. Now, as he had done so many times in the past, he began to plan.

Other than the young girl downstairs, this place was ideal, and if he used drugs again, there would be no noise. Of course, the time and place would be crucial, and it wouldn't be easy. His brain turned. There had to be a way, there was always a way, and as an idea began to form, Trevor Bardington smiled. He'd love it, he knew he would. They all did, despite their protests.

12

When Pearl awoke on Monday morning, she knuckled her eyes before climbing tiredly out of bed. She hadn't slept well. Trevor Bardington had started pacing again and it had been after one in the morning before he'd stopped.

Why did he spend hours walking back and forth across his room? Was he an insomniac? God, she hoped not. If she got a good night's sleep, getting up at five forty-five in the morning wasn't a problem, but if the noise continued it would be impossible.

She'd have to wait and see, but if the worst came to the worst, perhaps she could ask Nobby Clark for a different room. There were two empty ones on this landing and one above. She didn't fancy being on the same floor as Mr Bardington, but the one further along on this level would be fine and not directly underneath the man. The only downside was that it looked over the rear of the building, with nothing but a yard and the back of a factory wall in view. With this room she enjoyed being able to look on to the High Street, seeing the hustle and bustle of the market. Tired of drawing faces, she had begun to sketch the scene. Of course, she still craved colour. How else could she bring the pictures alive? The colourful stalls with their brightly striped awnings, the fruit and vegetables piled high, the crowds bustling, red-faced from the heat. They needed colour, and she just *had* to buy some paint.

The breakfast rush was in full swing and, though tired from lack of sleep, Pearl was doing her best to keep an eye on Alice. So far she hadn't cleared any of Pearl's tables, but as they were so busy it was impossible to watch her all the time.

Frank Hanwell came in, his son, Eric, with him, and Pearl smiled as she went to serve them.

'Hello, and what can I get you?'

'My usual, and beans on toast for Eric.'

The boy grinned at Pearl and once again she was captivated by his face. If he'd been a girl, Eric would have been described as beautiful. Somehow, handsome didn't fit, and seemed an inadequate description. With lovely emerald-green eyes, slightly slanted like a cat's, flawless skin, with a dash of freckles, he had to Pearl, perfect features.

She grinned back at him. 'One slice of toast, or two?'

'Two, please, miss. I'm helping my dad on his stall today.'

'Are you? That's nice.'

'Lucy's a bit under the weather, and school doesn't start again until September,' Frank said by way of explanation. 'I don't know about help, though. Somehow I think Eric might be more of a hindrance.' He leaned forward, the sting taken out of his words as he ruffled the boy's dark hair.

Pearl wrote out the order and hurried to the kitchen, her tables now full, but as she returned to the dining room she was just in time to see a couple of her customers leaving. Alice left what she was doing and hurried to clear their table. Pearl kept her head low, but was watching from under her lashes when she saw Alice slip something into her apron pocket.

As if suddenly aware that she was being observed, Alice's head spun around. Their eyes locked, but it was Alice who looked away first, her face slightly flushed as she picked up the rest of the plates, brushing past her to the kitchen.

Pearl waited until Alice returned to the dining room, surreptitiously watching her movements. Alice passed the counter, but didn't put any money into the jar, and Pearl was sure then that Alice was taking her tips. But what could she do? She was too scared to confront Alice, and anyway, she'd deny it. Yet how could she offer proof?

'What's up, Pearl?' Derek Lewis called.

She went to his table, her mind still turning. If someone else saw what Alice was up to, there was no way the girl could deny it. 'Derek, can I talk to you later?'

He frowned. 'You're not going to tell me you can't see me tonight, are you?'

'No, of course not. It's just something I may need a bit of help with.'

'Oh, right. Well, anything I can do, you only have to say the word.'

'Thanks, Derek.'

The rest of the day seemed to drag by. Pearl kept an eye on Alice, but she kept to her own tables. Then, at three fifteen, near the end of her shift, Kevin came down from the upstairs flat. He walked towards her, but instead of a threatening look, he was smiling.

'Hello, love, how are you doing?'

Pearl stared at him in confusion. He had issued veiled threats at the boxing match, but now he was being pleasant. 'I ... I'm fine thanks.'

'How's it going with Derek?'

'Er ... we're still good friends.'

'If you were my girl, we'd be more than friends by now.'

'Kevin!'

They both spun round to see Dolly's head poking out of the kitchen door. 'I suggest you let Pearl get on with her work.'

'Yeah, all right, Mum,' he said, but not before throwing Pearl a wink and whispering, 'Would you like to be my girl, Pearl?'

He sauntered off, the café door closing behind him, Pearl left red-faced. His girl! Surely he didn't mean it? No, of course he didn't. Her mind was still grappling with the change in Kevin's character when Dolly came marching out of the kitchen, heading towards her.

'Your job is to wait on tables, Pearl, and not to flirt with my son.'

'I ... I wasn't flirting with him. Honest,' she protested, hands shaking.

'I don't want to see you chatting with Kevin again. You're here to work and I suggest you remember that.'

'Yes, Mrs Dolby.'

The woman threw her a dark look. 'Finish clearing that table and you can go.'

Pearl vigorously rubbed the surface, relieved when Dolly went back to the kitchen. She rinsed out the cloth, took off her apron and, taking her bag from its usual place under the counter, murmured, 'I'm off, Bernie. See you tomorrow.'

'Bye, love, and take no notice of Dolly. Mind you, it might be safer to stay away from Kevin.'

'Your son's a bit of all right, Bernie,' Alice chuckled, 'and you can't blame Pearl for having her eye on him.'

'I ... I haven't got my eye on him,' Pearl protested.

'Oh, yeah, and pigs might fly,' Alice said. 'You fancy him, and it's as plain as the nose on your face.'

A blush stained Pearl's cheeks and she lowered her head.

'Leave the girl alone, Alice,' Bernie admonished.

Pearl threw him a grateful smile, saying a hurried goodbye as she left the café. Why did Alice have to stir it, and what if she said the same things to Dolly? God, she could get the sack. It was bad enough worrying that Alice was pinching her tips, but now she had to worry about losing her job.

Pearl stopped by Derek's stall, watching as he served a customer, amazed that with hands so large and chunky he was able to handle the most delicate china without breaking it.

As the customer walked away he came straight to her side. 'What did you want to talk to me about?'

'It doesn't matter now.'

'Tell me anyway.'

Pearl couldn't confide in him about Kevin, instead saying only, 'I think Alice is pinching some

121

of my tips.'

'Are you sure?'

'I could be wrong, but I doubt it. You see, I don't get many tips now, even from my regulars. Sometimes Alice clears my tables and I think I saw her pocket a tip. I waited to see if she put in the jar, but she didn't.'

'The bitch! What did you say to her?'

'How can I say anything until I'm a hundred per cent sure? And anyway, it's my word against hers and she's sure to deny it.'

'Yeah, I see what you mean.' He paused for a moment, but then smiled. 'When I'm in the café, I'll keep an eye out too. If we both catch her out, she won't have a leg to stand on.'

'Oh, thanks, Derek. I don't know what I'd do without you.'

Kevin passed, lifting his hand to wave at them both, but Pearl lowered her head. She had to prevent Dolly from thinking that she was flirting with Kevin, but how?

'Is there something else worrying you?' Derek asked. 'You still look a bit down in the mouth.'

She raised her eyes, saw his concern, and in that moment, made up her mind. If she had a boyfriend, Dolly would know she wasn't after Kevin and her job would be safe. Taking a deep breath, Pearl forced a smile. 'I'm fine. It ... it's just that I was wondering if you'd still like me to be your girlfriend.'

'Of course I would.'

'Good, because I'd like that too.'

'Pearl, are you sure?'

'I'm sure.'

He grinned with delight. 'Cor, wait till I tell Gran.'

'She might not approve, Derek. She'll think I'm too young for you.'

'You'll be seventeen soon, and I'm twenty-six. That makes only nine years between us. Anyway, Gran likes you and I think she'll be dead chuffed.'

Another customer came to the stall, Derek saying hurriedly, 'I'll pick you up at seven. We'll go for a nice meal to celebrate.'

'All right, 'bye,' Pearl said, wondering as she walked to her bedsit if she'd made the right decision. She was going to be Derek Lewis's girlfriend, protected and safe, but what if one day he proposed? Could she face becoming his wife? She pictured his cosy terraced house, his lovely gran, and smiled. Yes, surely she could. They would be a family, and if a baby came along? At that thought Pearl's steps faltered. When she worked in the laundry the women had often talked and joked about sex. Innocent though she was, she had soon found out from their ribald remarks how a baby was made, but could she bear to do *that* with Derek?

When Derek told Pearl that his gran wanted to see her, she went round to the house straight from work the next day, shaking with nerves.

At first Connie Lewis was a bit frosty, and deeply suspicious of Pearl's motives. 'I thought we agreed that you're far too young for Derek,' she said as they sat in her cosy kitchen.

'I know, but I've grown very fond of him.'

'Huh, you can be fond of a cat,' she said, her

eyes flicking to Marmalade. The huge ginger cat opened one eye, but seeing there was no food being offered, he closed it again. 'Just what do you see in Derek? It ain't his looks, that's for sure.'

'I know he isn't handsome, but that doesn't matter. There's more to a man than looks. Derek is so kind, so caring, and I feel safe with him.'

'Safe! What's that supposed to mean? It sounds like you only want him for protection, but protection from what? Are you in trouble?'

'No,' Pearl said hurriedly. 'Oh dear, I seem to be saying all the wrong things. Please, Connie, I'm just trying to explain that I don't care what Derek looks like, it's his ways that count. I just want to be with him, to become part of this family, and and maybe one day there'll be children.'

At last the ice began to melt, and a small smile played around the corners of Connie's mouth. 'Kids – that'd be nice, but you're far too young to think about marriage yet.'

'Yes, I know I'm jumping the gun, but I just wanted you to know how serious I am about Derek.'

Connie sat quietly for a moment, but then her eyes locked with Pearl's. 'All right, I'll say no more. At the end of the day I just want Derek to be happy. I know I shouldn't cross-examine you, but he's never had a girlfriend before, his looks saw to that. You're a pretty girl, and could probably do better, so you can't blame me for being suspicious.'

'I could never do better than Derek. He's wonderful.'

124

At last it seemed that Pearl had said the right thing. Connie suddenly relaxed, a wide grin now on her face. 'You're right there. My Derek's a diamond. He'll be home soon so you might as well stay for dinner.'

'Thanks, I'd love to,' Pearl said, heaving a sigh of relief.

13

When art classes started in September, Pearl and Derek settled into a routine. She went for lessons one night a week, and Derek went to the gym on Tuesdays and Thursdays. On the other evenings, she visited his house, sharing the family meal, growing closer to Connie and feeling part of the family. For Pearl, it was wonderful, Connie becoming like the mother she'd never had.

Pearl stood at her easel on Thursday evening, critically gazing at her effort before mixing more watercolours. Like Miss Rosen, this teacher was pleased with her work, and one day Pearl hoped to progress to oils. She had done a wash for the sky, satisfied with the stormy effect, and now raising her brush she attempted a tree. As this was an autumnal scene, in her mind's eye she imagined a high wind blowing, so she bent the tree, making it skeletal with few leaves clinging to the branches. As she stepped back a pace, the woman at the next easel spoke.

'I wish I could get the hang of doing that. Mine

never seems to turn out right.'

Pearl wandered across, seeing that the woman had fashioned her tree with a huge trunk and a mushroom of bright green growth sprouting from the top. All right, it wasn't very good, but what did it matter? She had seen that the elderly lady loved the classes.

'It looks nice,' Pearl smiled.

'Leave it out, love, it's rubbish.'

The teacher came to their side, her head cocked as she surveyed the old lady's attempt. 'Not bad, Mrs Fox, and you're coming along nicely.'

'Do you think so? Well, thanks very much, but I wish I could paint like this young lady.'

'Keep up the good work and you will.'

She then wandered on to the next easel, the old lady winking at Pearl. 'Yeah, and pigs might fly too.'

Pearl grinned as she went back to her own work. She loved the mixed ability classes, finding everyone so friendly. Picking up her paintbrush again, she buried herself in the countryside scene.

The time flew past and to Pearl her painting wasn't quite finished. She was still daubing, still endeavouring to get it just right when the teacher came to her side.

'Well done, my dear,' the woman said softly, 'but know when to stop. You'll spoil the effect if you overwork it, and anyway, it's time to go home.'

'Is it?' Pearl said, becoming aware of the noise in the room as people prepared to leave. She hurriedly packed up too, and as she left the class, there was a smile on her face. She was following her dream at last, a dream that one day her painting would be good enough to exhibit.

Pearl stepped outside to find Derek waiting for her. 'Watcha, love,' he said, leaning down to plant a kiss on her cheek before taking her things to carry. 'I finished early at the gym so thought I'd come to walk you home.'

She clutched Derek's arm as they walked along, pleased to see him, and glad that she had learned to relax when held in his arms. She still didn't enjoy his kisses, finding it hard to respond, and so far, fearing being alone with him, she hadn't invited him up to her room.

There was only one person who marred her contentment, and that was Kevin Dolby. For some reason he had taken to chatting to her, often asking her how things were going with Derek, but she couldn't understand why. He'd teased her once, asking if she wanted to be his girl, but she knew he was just making fun of her. He was so good-looking and there was no way he'd be interested in her, but still her stomach filled with fluttering butterflies every time she saw him. Oh, she didn't want to think about Kevin; it only made her unsettled.

'How did your class go?' Derek asked.

'It was fine, and I'm learning so much.'

They continued to chat, Pearl enthusing about her art teacher, and when they arrived at Battersea High Street, Pearl unlocked her street door. She took her things from Derek, smiling up at him. 'Thanks for walking me home, but there's really no need.'

'I don't mind,' he said, eyes soft as he leaned down to kiss her, lips soft and moist as they settled on hers. ''Night, Pearl. I'll see you tomorrow.'

'Yes. 'Night, Derek,' Pearl said, relieved that he didn't expect more.

She watched him walk away, his arm lifting in a small wave, before she went inside and climbed the stairs to her bedsit. The house was quiet as Pearl flopped onto the side of the bed, eyes looking up to the ceiling. Mr Bardington had stopped his pacing and she rarely saw the man. In fact, he had become so quiet that she often forgot he was in the building. Like her, he was an outsider. Still, now that she was courting Derek, the locals were coming round and warming to her.

Pearl kicked off her shoes and went to make herself a drink, but soon after drinking it, she heard noises from the street, people shouting. Puzzled, she went over to the window to see a crowd of about twenty people. In the dim light from a street-lamp she spotted Derek amongst them and threw up the window.

'Derek. What's going on?'

He looked up. 'Come down, Pearl.'

She threw on her shoes and dashed downstairs, Derek coming straight to her side. 'I was on my way home when I met up with this lot. Eric's missing. Have you seen him?'

'No. Oh, Derek, it's after ten o'clock. Where can he be?'

'I dunno. He didn't come home from school and, as you can see, a lot of people have rallied round to search for him. They've looked everywhere but are running out of options.'

'Have they tried Battersea Park?'

'I dunno, but we couldn't cover an area of that size. What makes you think he'd go there?'

'There's a lot to attract kids, but it was just a suggestion. Anyway, if the police have been told, they'll probably cover it.'

'Yeah, they've been told, but not until after eight o'clock. Frank was hoping he'd turn up before then.'

Pearl saw Frank Hanwell, his face drawn with worry. 'Eric! Eric!' he shouted, his eyes frantically searching the dim High Street. 'Where are you, you little bugger?'

'Frank looks awful. Is there anything I can do to help?'

'You can join us on the search. Apparently he's not at any of his friends' houses, and to be honest, I don't know where we're trying next.'

Pearl walked with Derek to Frank's side, the man's eyes wild as he looked at them. 'I can't understand it, Derek. He's never done this before.'

'Don't worry, Frank. The police are sure to find him, even if we don't. Pearl has suggested Battersea Park and she could be right.'

'Eric wouldn't go to the park on his own. Lucy would kill him and he knows that.'

'He's just a kid. Think about what you got up to as a nipper.'

Frank's shoulders slumped. 'All right, we'll try there.'

It was after one in the morning before they gave up, footsore and weary as they trudged home.

Derek once again walked Pearl to her door, and after giving her a swift hug he said, 'Try to get

129

some sleep, love. The police are still looking, and maybe there'll be good news in the morning.'

Pearl was so tired that she could barely respond. 'Oh, I hope so, Derek.'

They said good night, Pearl almost staggering up to her room, but despite her exhaustion it was some time before she was able to sleep. The police would find Eric – they just had to. Behind closed eyes, tears gathered as she pictured the boy's beautiful face.

Nearly a week passed and there was still no sign of Eric. Frank's stall stood empty, the man incapable of running it and, trying to rally round as much as possible, the other costermongers set it up for him, working it between them to make sure the man had an income.

Frank's wife, Lucy, hadn't been seen, and rumour had it that she was in a terrible state. Eric was their only child, the love of their lives, and amongst the gossip in the café there was a lot of sympathy for the couple.

Gertie was also badly affected. She lived next door to the Hanwells and knew them well. Though she still washed the dishes, her tears were often seen dripping into the washing-up water, her bright smile gone.

When Pearl finished work on Wednesday she stopped off at Derek's stall. 'There's still no news,' she said sadly.

'I know, love, and I feel so helpless. It's been six days since Eric went missing and police seem to have exhausted all their enquiries. Now everyone's back is up about the way they're treating the Hanwells.'

'What do you mean?'

'They keep questioning them, and have talked to the neighbours. They've asked what sort of parents they are, if there were any signs of mistreatment, and have spoken to the teachers at Eric's school. Pearl, surely they don't think that Frank and Lucy had anything to do with his disappearance?'

Pearl placed her hand on his arm. 'I've only lived around here a short time, but I've seen Frank with Eric and it's obvious how much he loves his son.'

'Yeah, and as far as I'm concerned the police are barking up the wrong tree.'

'Oh, Derek, where can Eric be?'

'I dunno, love, but I hope to God some nonce ain't got hold of him.'

'A nonce. I don't understand.'

'Christ, I keep forgetting what an innocent you are. It's another word for a paedophile.'

Pearl shook her head. 'I still don't understand.'

'They're sick bastards who like sex with children.'

'No!' she cried, but then something she remembered from the orphanage fell into place. When she'd been about ten, a girl of the same age had been fostered out, but after only a month she came back, a sad, pale shadow of the pretty girl who had left. She hardly spoke and lay curled on her bed for hours, but whispers went around the dormitory. The older girls said she'd been interfered with by the foster parent, a man who liked children. Pearl hadn't understood, but now it all made sense. 'Oh, Derek, that's terrible.'

'Look, don't get upset. I'm probably wrong.'

'Oh, I hope so.'

A customer came to the stall, and with a small, sad smile, Derek said to Pearl, 'I'll see you later, love.'

Pearl walked away with a sick feeling in her stomach. With her head down she didn't see Kevin until she walked into him. 'Oh, sorry,' she blurted.

His hands gripped her arms. 'What do you expect when you walk around looking at the pavement?'

'Yes, sorry, I'm afraid I was thinking about Eric Hanwell.'

'Everyone is talking about his disappearance. I wonder what happened to the poor little tyke.'

'I don't know. I just wish the police would find him.'

'Yeah, but he'll probably turn up dead.'

The colour drained from Pearl's face. 'Oh, don't say that!'

'Look, he ain't the sort of kid that would run away, so what other option is there?'

'Derek said that a nonce might have got hold of him.'

'If that's the case, the poor little sod would be better off dead.'

Pearl found herself gawking at Kevin, and then with a small sob she ran to her bedsit. Eric was such a beautiful boy with the face of an angel. Surely nobody would harm him?

As Pearl got ready to go round to Derek's that

evening, she suddenly paused as a noise came from upstairs. Unused to hearing anything these days from Mr Bardington, her ears pricked. What was that faint sound she had heard? Was it a cry? Was the man ill?

She stood absolutely still, but there were no further sounds and, relaxing again, she continued to dress. It seemed strange to see so little of someone who lived on the same premises – in fact she saw more of his mail. Pearl never received any letters, but there were often large brown envelopes delivered for Mr Bardington. If Pearl saw them she would pick them up and place them on the bottom stair, and they always disappeared. If it wasn't for that she wouldn't know the man lived there.

Ready now, she picked up her handbag and was soon on her way to Derek's. She had become very fond of Connie's cooking, and with the extra meals she was having Pearl was putting on weight. Her few outfits were getting tight, but thankfully Mo had told her about a shop that sold second-hand clothes. Paint, brushes and paper were always top of Pearl's wish list, but realising there was no choice but to buy new clothes, she decided to take a look at the shop the next day.

The evening soon passed, and after a huge dinner of steak-and-kidney pudding, they sat playing cards.

Derek suddenly smiled across at Connie. 'I've got a nice surprise for you.'

'Have you now. And what's that?'

'I'm going to buy a television.'

'And where is the money coming from?'

'Don't worry, Gran, it ain't new, but it's in good working order.'

'A television. My, ain't we coming up in the world, Pearl?'

'We certainly are,' Pearl agreed, loving being included as part of the family.

'That'll be one in the eye for her next door. She's always bragging about her television. If I hear one more word about some geezer called Dixon of Dock Green, I think I'll go mad.'

'Who's he?' Derek asked.

'Oh, it's some sort of programme about a copper. Someone called Jack Warner plays him, and her next door is mad about it.'

'Well, Gran, now you'll be able to watch it too.'

'Yeah, I will, won't I?' she said, smiling widely.

'I'd best be off,' Pearl said as the game of rummy came to an end, Connie winning as usual. Pearl leaned down to kiss the old lady on the cheek. 'I think you cheat.'

With a look of indignation she said, 'No I don't, you cheeky mare.' Connie then smiled, patting Pearl's arm. 'Go on, get yourself home and we'll see you tomorrow.'

Derek walked her to the High Street as usual. As they stopped outside Pearl's street door, he took her into his arms, neither seeing Kevin Dolby watching them from a doorway on the other side of the road, a scowl on his face.

Kevin waited until the coast was clear before he moved. He'd been looking out for Nobby Clark, but there was no sign of him. Money was really tight and he was growing frustrated, so much so that despite the last cock-up, he was ready to do another job.

Once again he scowled. That Derek was a jammy git. Pearl had blossomed lately, her figure filling out, but it was Derek who tasted the goods. Blimey, what was wrong with the girl? How could she fancy that ugly bugger?

He looked up at her window and, seeing the light go on, he crossed the road. Without money in his pocket there was no chance of a trip to Soho. Maybe it was time to give Pearl Button a try.

Kevin looked up and down the High Street. Seeing nobody about, he rang her bell, a smile plastered on his face when she opened the door. 'Hello, Pearl. I was just wondering if you've seen Nobby Clark.'

'Er ... no.'

'I was supposed to meet him here at the shop,' Kevin lied, 'but so far he ain't turned up. Do you mind if I come in and wait?'

'But it's after ten o'clock. Why would you be meeting him at this time of night?'

'Now then, Pearl, you know better than to ask questions. Come on, girl, let me in,' Kevin insisted as he pushed his way past her.

Pearl's eyes were rounded as she stared at him, but Kevin made for the stairs. 'Your room is on the first floor, ain't it?'

He didn't wait for her answer, or look over his shoulder, convinced that she would follow him.

Kevin wasn't wrong, and as he walked into her room his face stretched with surprise as he looked around the walls. 'Well, well, did you draw these?'

'Yes,' Pearl said, her face reddening.

'They're good – in fact, very good. It seems you've got hidden talents.'

'Thank you,' she said, obviously pleased.

Kevin hid a smile. So, the way to this girl was through her sketches. He made the most of it. 'That's a brilliant one of my mother. You could sell these, Pearl.'

'Sell them? Oh, no, I don't think they're good enough.'

'Leave it out, of course they are. Blimey, look at that one of Derek. It's as good as a photograph.' Kevin sat on the edge of her bed. 'Have you got any more?'

'Yes, but you won't want to see them.'

'Why not? I've got nothing else to do until Nobby shows up.'

Pearl picked up a large folder and without thinking about what she was doing, sat beside him on the bed. 'Here's one of Gertie.'

'Blimey, that's marvellous,' and careful not to touch her, he looked at all the drawings in her portfolio. 'Has anyone else seen these?'

'No, you're the first.'

'Well, love, I feel privileged, but I don't see one of me.'

'I ... I haven't got one.'

As she turned, their eyes met, and as though Pearl suddenly realised their close proximity she became agitated, quickly stuffing the drawings back into the folder. He gently touched her arm, saying softly, 'Any chance of a drink?'

'I ... I've only got tea or lemonade.'

'Lemonade will do me.'

He watched her as she went to the small kitchenette. She was such a meek little thing and he didn't want to frighten her off, but Christ, he was as hard as a rock and couldn't wait much longer. When she returned he took the glass, his smile teasing.

'I still think that drawing of Derek is good, but I don't know what you see in him.'

'Derek is lovely, kind and caring.'

'I could be kind and caring too.'

She flushed and Kevin loved it. God, what an innocent, the daft cow like putty in his hands. She fancied him, there was no doubt about that. Placing the glass on the floor, he made his move. Taking her hand, he pulled her down beside him on the bed, enfolding her in his arms.

'Pearl,' he whispered, one of his hands brushing her breast.

'No, stop it!' she protested, pulling away.

'Come on, Pearl, you know you like me. I only want a little cuddle, and there's no harm in that.'

'I ... I'm going out with Derek and it wouldn't be right.'

For a moment Kevin wanted to slap her, but resisted, instead planting a sad expression on his face. 'Yeah, sorry, but I've fancied you for ages.'

'Fancy me! You ... you fancy me?'

'Of course I do. Look, I'll come clean. I'm not really waiting for Nobby. I came round here to see you.'

Pearl's eyes were wide. 'But ... but Derek...'

'Don't worry about him.' And on those words Kevin pulled her into his arms again. For a moment she stiffened, but then he raised her chin with one finger, his lips meeting hers. She

137

groaned, and he smiled. His kisses grew deeper, his hands wandering over her body, touching her in places that he knew she'd love.

'No, don't,' she protested as he began to unbutton her blouse.

He stopped, whispering, 'Sorry', as he released her.

Pearl clutched her blouse together, gasping, her eyes dark with desire as they met his. As he hoped, she made the move this time, leaning into his arms. He struggled to take his time, almost bursting, but at last he could sense that she was ready. Once again she resisted a little as he began to remove her clothes, but as he gently coaxed, she suddenly melted.

Unable to wait any longer, he pushed Pearl onto her back, and as he entered her she cried out, stiffening beneath him. There was some resistance, but unsurprised to find Pearl a virgin, her cries of pain heightened his passion. He was the first!

Kevin took Pearl quickly, ignoring her pain. She was innocent, acquiescent, and he felt like a man, conquering, dominant and in control. Of course, there was an element missing, one that he had to pay for in Soho, but it was still good and for a while he was able to lose himself in her body.

All too soon it was over and, annoyed that he hadn't lasted longer, Kevin rolled away to light a cigarette, ignoring Pearl's sniffles until she spoke.

'You .. . you shouldn't have done that, and ... and it hurt.'

'You didn't put up much of a fight, and anyway, it always hurts the first time,' he said dismissively, thinking that at least that's what he'd heard.

When he had finished his cigarette, he turned to look at Pearl again. She looked vulnerable, innocent, her huge eyes tear-filled as they met his. 'I'm sorry I hurt you, but it'll be better next time. Come on, give me a cuddle.'

She shook her head, but he settled himself beside her, wrapping her in his arms. For a moment she stiffened, but when he didn't do anything other than hold her, she relaxed, snuggling against him. They lay like that for a while, but then reliving the moment that confirmed to him that Pearl was a virgin, Kevin found himself hardening again.

Slowly and gently he began to stroke her. She resisted a little, but then became compliant. Kevin smiled. He'd let her enjoy it this time, but in future he'd teach her a trick or two, show her what *he* liked. He entered her, moving slowly, teasingly. She groaned, this time with pleasure.

'Well, you certainly enjoyed it that time,' he leered when it was over.

Pearl lay quietly for a moment but then threw her arms around him. 'Oh, Kevin, I didn't realise love could be like this.'

'Love! It ain't love, you daft cow. It was just sex, and don't go reading anything else into it. I ain't looking for a steady girlfriend.'

Pearl's eyes were rounded with shock as she stared at him. 'But–'

Kevin rose to his feet. 'No buts, Pearl. As I said, it was nothing, and by the way, there's no need for Derek to find out.' With a dismissive wave of his hand he added, 'See ya,' before walking out.

14

When Kevin left, Pearl was in tears, going over and over what had happened. He was so handsome, so kind about her sketches, and she'd been flattered by his attention. When he started to fondle her she found her body reacting in ways she'd never felt before. His hands had been gentle, touching her, arousing delicious feelings, and though she had protested at first, in truth she didn't want him to stop. Despite the initial pain she had never felt so close to anyone before, their bodies fused, as one, and she found herself reaching out for something, a longing. Was this it? Was this how it felt to be loved and in love?

A small sob escaped her lips, remembering how her feelings had been dashed. Kevin had dismissed it as nothing. Oh, what an idiot she'd been. He didn't love her, didn't want her, the sex meaningless. He had just used her, and she'd let him.

She felt dirty, soiled, and now dashed to the sink, washing all traces of Kevin from her body.

It was some time before Pearl returned to her bed, tossing and turning all night. She hated herself, hated her treacherous body, at last drifting off to sleep in the early hours of the morning.

It was the doorbell that woke her at nine in the morning but, unable to face the thought of seeing anyone, she curled into a ball. The ringing persisted. Crawling out of bed, Pearl went to the window to see Derek below. Oh God, she couldn't see him. He would know – he would look at her and know.

He waved frantically, and it was obvious he wouldn't go away unless she spoke to him. She lifted the window, leaning out a little. 'Derek, I'm not well. I can't come down.'

'When I went into the café, Bernie asked me if I'd seen you. What's wrong, love?'

As Derek shouted up at her, several heads lifted, and Pearl cringed. They were all staring at her. Could they tell? Did it show?

'I've got an upset tummy,' she called desperately. 'Will you tell Bernie? I ... I may see you tomorrow, but it depends how I'm feeling.'

'Is there anything I can get you?'

'No, but thanks.' Pearl lifted her hand to give Derek a small wave, anxious to shut the window and get away from the prying eyes.

She crawled back into bed, just wanting to hide away, and soon, exhausted, she escaped into sleep.

It was half an hour later when Trevor Bardington parked his car, smiling as he pulled out a bag of shopping. He'd bought cereals, some fruit, a bar of chocolate, and with the girl downstairs at work, he had the place to himself.

It had been a pain keeping him quiet when Pearl Button was in, but the drugs had done the trick. Now, though, he would make sure the boy was fully awake.

Trevor went up to his room, smiling fondly at

the child tied to his bed. The boy had been in a drug-induced sleep, but as his eyelids fluttered, Trevor could see that he was waking up.

Those wonderful emerald-green eyes flickered open, looking glazed at first, but seeing Trevor, they rounded with fear.

'So, you're awake, and as a treat I've got you some chocolate,' Trevor said as he untied the bindings. 'Now, if you're really good, I'll take the gag off. You will be quiet, won't you?'

The boy nodded, but his eyes filled with tears. Trevor knew that, tempting as it was, he couldn't keep him much longer. He tousled the boy's hair, annoyed when he flinched. Why did they have to pretend?

He heaved a sigh. Yes, the lad would have to go soon, but he'd get a good price when he passed him on.

When Pearl awoke again it was after ten o'clock. Something had disturbed her, a sound, and she sat up groggily. Had somebody rung the doorbell? She rubbed her eyes, becoming still when she heard a cry.

Another cry, muffled, and her eyes went to the ceiling. Surely it wasn't Mr Bardington making that noise?

For a moment the house was silent, the only sound street noises outside. Another faint cry, a yell, and suddenly Pearl flew out of bed. Please God, no, she thought frantically as she pulled on some clothes.

Barefoot, she tiptoed upstairs, struggling to stay calm. Surely she was wrong? Surely she was imagining things? It couldn't be – it just couldn't!

Softly Pearl crept along the landing, and reaching Mr Bardington's door she pressed her ear against it.

At first she heard nothing, but then, as the cry came again, Pearl's stomach turned a somersault.

For a moment she froze, stiff with panic. She had to do something, had to find help. Derek, she'd get Derek! Without coherent thought, Pearl flew back downstairs, her bare feet making little sound. She dashed outside, leaving the street door wide open behind her, eyes wild as she made for Derek's stall.

The pavement was sharp underfoot, but Pearl was hardly aware of it. 'Derek!' she screamed.

'What is it? What's the matter?'

'Eric ... I think I know who's got Eric! Quick, you've got to come!'

'Come where? Who's got him?'

'It's the man living in the room upstairs. I think Eric's in there with him. I ... I heard a child crying.'

'Charlie! Denis! Rick! Bob!' Derek yelled. 'Quick, come with me.'

'What's going on?' one called.

'Pearl thinks she knows where Eric is!'

Abandoning customers, the men ran to his side, other costermongers alerted and joining them.

Derek quickly explained, their faces darkening with fury as they all ran to the open door, Pearl behind as they thudded upstairs.

Everything happened so quickly that Pearl could barely take it in. Derek's shoulder crashed into

143

Mr Bardington's door, wood splintering, and still in momentum he almost fell into the room, the other men followed in his wake. Mr Bardington yelled, and as all hell let loose, she craned to see over their heads. There was a scream of fear, and then the man was on the floor, a sea of heavy boots kicking him again and again, each one landing with a sickening crunch. He shrieked, and as Pearl ducked low she had a brief glimpse of him, his nose shattered and his face running with blood. She swallowed, wanting to protest, but then Derek appeared with Eric in his arms and bile rose in her throat. Oh, no! Oh God!

All thought of protest died on Pearl's lips as anger threatened to overwhelm her. She wanted to join the men, to kick Trevor Bardington, to punch him, beat him, to make him suffer for what he had done to an innocent child. He was an animal, a monster! A wall of redness formed in front of her eyes, but then Derek yelled in her ear.

'Pearl, come on, we've got to get Eric out of here! We'll take him to the café and someone can run for Frank and Lucy.'

Derek's voice somehow penetrated her fury and she reacted quickly. 'Yes, of course. I'll get something to cover him.'

As they went down to the next landing, Pearl dashed into her room, grabbing a blanket from her bed to cover Eric's naked body. The small crowd that had gathered hushed as they stepped outside, but then a cry went up. 'Good on yer, Derek.'

'It was Pearl who found him, not me. Now let

144

me pass. This child needs his mother. Madge, will you run and get her?'

The woman nodded, hurrying away.

As the crowd parted, Derek carried Eric to the café. Dolly must have been alerted, and as they walked in she motioned them upstairs to her flat. 'Take him to my bedroom.'

As soon as Eric saw Dolly's bed he went into a panic, fighting to get out of Derek's arms.

'It's all right, darling,' Pearl said, and as Eric held out his arms in appeal, she took him, holding him closely.

The blanket slipped and there was a gasp. Dolly held a hand over her mouth in horror. 'Oh my God,' she whispered. 'His ... his little bottom is covered in blood.'

Pearl sat on the edge of the bed, but as she lowered Eric onto her lap he cried out in pain. Tears flowed then, rolling unchecked down her cheeks as she managed to lay the child gently on his side. She had barely covered him with the blanket when Lucy and Frank Hanwell flew into the room.

'Eric! Eric!' Lucy sobbed, thrusting Pearl aside. For a moment she gazed down at her son, but then she lay beside him on the bed, pulling him into her arms.

Frank watched, his face drained of colour, and as Dolly whispered her concerns, his fists balled. 'Yeah, ring the doctor, but where is the bastard who did this? I'll kill him with my bare hands.'

'Don't worry. I think you'll find he's already been taken care of,' Derek murmured.

As Dolly left to make the telephone call, Frank

dropped to his knees by the bed, but Eric turned his head away, refusing to look at his father.

'Oh, son. Oh, son...' With a strangled sound in his throat, Frank rose to his feet.

For a while nobody spoke as Lucy continued to rock the boy in her arms.

Then Frank turned to Derek. 'You found my son and I don't know how to thank you.'

'It wasn't me, mate. As I told the others, it was Pearl who found him.'

Frank's eyes were moist as he looked at her. 'Well, love, I don't know how to thank you either, but I'm deeply indebted to you.'

The doctor arrived and asked all but Eric's parents to leave. Derek and Pearl went downstairs.

'Pearl, your feet are bare,' Dolly said brusquely, 'and you look awful. You'd best take her home again, Derek.'

'Yes, Mrs D.'

Pearl was led outside, but then shock set in and she was hardly aware of anything as Derek walked her home. Many stallholders and locals patted her back as they trod the short distance, but when Pearl winced as she stood on something sharp, Derek picked her up, carrying her to the still-open street door.

The house was silent as they went in and suddenly Pearl stiffened in Derek's arms. It felt like a house of horrors now, the thought of living there abhorrent.

'I ... can't stay here. I just can't.'

'All right, love, I'll take you round to my place. Connie will take care of you.'

146

Pearl didn't argue, but as Derek carried her outside again she saw Kevin Dolby amongst the crowd. As their eyes met his smile was like a leer and Pearl looked quickly away, feeling sick inside.

Her arms tightened around Derek's neck. Oh God, she had betrayed this lovely man. Instead of being cared for and treated like a hero, she should be stoned.

15

After staying at Derek's overnight and then all weekend, Pearl was able to return to work, but she was still full of self-loathing. Derek and Connie had been so kind. They had believed her lies about being ill and she'd been cosseted by both of them. Of course, this had made her feel worse and she felt torn in two. She had betrayed Derek. Should she break up with him?

Pearl baulked at the thought. Despite her feelings for Kevin, he didn't want her, he'd made that plain, and if she broke up with Derek she'd be alone again, unprotected. Not only that, she would lose Connie too, a woman she had grown deeply fond of.

A foretaste of what was to come happened as she walked through the market on her way to work. She was greeted with smiles, waves, and several stallholders stuffed bags of fruit into her arms. She was even given a bunch of flowers from the old lady who sat on the opposite corner to the café. The flower seller was known for being mean, her flowers often wired around the base of the blooms to make them look tight and fresh. Pearl took the carnations, the old crone patting her hand, and laden, she was greeted with more smiles from Bernie when he saw her.

'Hello, love,' he said. 'Are you feeling better now?'

'Yes, I'm fine, thanks.'

'I see the stallholders have been showing their appreciation. You'd better take that lot through to the kitchen.'

'Have you heard anything about Eric?'

Bernie's face straightened. 'He's in hospital, and may be there for some time. Go and have a word with Dolly. It'll be better coming from her.'

'Pearl!' Dolly exclaimed. 'It's good to see you, girl, but you still look a bit pale. Are you sure you're up to doing a full shift?'

'Yes, I'm fine. Bernie said that Eric's in hospital and you'd tell me why.'

Dolly exhaled loudly. 'This ain't gonna be easy for you to hear, but from what we've heard he has a lot of rectal damage needing surgery. The poor kid is badly traumatised too.'

'What about Mr Bardington? Has he been arrested?'

'Pearl, don't ever mention that man's name again, especially to the police. We have a way of looking after our own around here, and believe me, he got what he deserved. As far as the police are concerned, they were told that he ran off.'

'Oh, please, don't tell me that he got away?'

'No, love, there was no chance of that. That

148

bastard will never harm another child.'

'You ... you don't mean that he's–'

'Don't ask,' Dolly interrupted. 'All I'll say is that there are a couple of blokes who run this borough, and they sorted it out. That's all you need to know. Now go and get yourself a cup of tea before the rush starts.'

With a small nod, Pearl went back to the dining room. She had seen the beating, and from what Dolly had inferred, could guess what had happened to Trevor Bardington. If she wanted to remain in this area, like everyone else she would have to keep her mouth shut. But her stomach churned. If she had called the police instead of running to Derek, the man might still be alive, but instead she had caused his death.

'You look awful,' Bernie said. 'Are you sure you can manage today?'

'Yes,' Pearl told him. She saw Bernie's concerned expression, the kindness in his eyes, and blurted out, 'I feel awful about what happened to Trevor Bardington. He'd still be alive if I'd called the pol–'

Bernie held up his hand before she could finish the sentence, saying quickly, 'Who said he's dead?'

'Dolly said he'd never hurt another child again, and ... and I assumed that's what she meant.'

'Don't assume anything, Pearl. That bastard got the kicking he deserved and a good one at that, but it wasn't one of our lot that took a knife to him. When he was handed over, that came later. From what we've been told, he's been castrated, and that's why he'll never be able to hurt

149

a child again.'

'Castrated?'

'Christ, girl, I ain't about to explain the procedure. Sufficient to say that the man's alive and you have nothing to feel guilty about.'

'Oh, thank God,' Pearl said, relief making her collapse onto the nearest chair.

'Here, get that down you,' Bernie said as he placed a cup of tea in front of her.

Pearl gulped the hot, sweet brew and a few minutes later Alice Freeman arrived.

'Hello, Pearl, it's good to have you back. You still look a bit rough, but don't worry, I'll help you as much as I can until you're up to scratch again.'

'Thanks, Alice.'

'You're a bit of a hero around here now and it's nice to hear that Derek and his gran have been looking after you.'

Pearl hung her head. Yes, Derek and Connie had been wonderful, but after what had happened with Kevin she didn't feel like a hero. She felt more like a slut.

By the end of the morning rush, Pearl had been inundated with gifts. She had also been hugged, thanked and made a fuss of by every customer.

Derek came in at eight o'clock, his face showing concern. 'Are you all right, Pearl? Is your tummy still holding up?'

'It's fine, but I'm a bit overwhelmed by the way the customers are treating me.'

'You're the talk of the market. They've taken you to their hearts and you're one of us now.'

'But, Derek, all I did was hear a noise.'

'Yeah, but you acted on it. If you hadn't, we might never have found Eric. Or when we did, it might have been too late.' He reached out to take Pearl's hand. 'Listen, love, I know you can't face living in your bedsit, so I've had a word with Gran. She said you're to stay with us until you find somewhere else to live. When you finish work, give me a shout, and I'll come with you to pack up your stuff.'

Pearl hung her head with shame. She didn't deserve this kindness, yet at the thought of living in that room, knowing what had happened above her, she felt sick. Derek's offer was her only alternative, at least until she could find somewhere else.

'Thanks, Derek,' she murmured, unable to look him in the face.

It was midday before Pearl saw Kevin. She wanted to hate him, but couldn't, her heart skipping a beat as he passed. He walked through to the kitchen, ignoring her, and when he came out again, he barely glanced in her direction. Pearl's eyes blurred with tears. It didn't seem possible that he could ignore her after something so intimate had happened between them.

Kevin spoke to his father and then walked out of the café without a backward glance, leaving Pearl feeling sick inside. She'd been an idiot, a fool, but despite what he said, she had still clung to the hope that he loved her.

There was a knot of pain in Pearl's stomach, but then she dashed at her tears, shoulders stiffening with resolve. This was another lesson, one she would never forget. She had let down her barriers – barriers put up long ago in the orphanage. She had allowed someone into her heart, and was now suffering for it. Never again. She would never let her barriers down again.

She was fond of Derek – Connie too – but she wouldn't allow her feeling to go deeper than that. From now on, nobody would be able to hurt her.

For the rest of the shift Pearl did her work, but her smile was forced, and once or twice she saw Bernie looking at her worriedly. As soon as the lunchtime rush was over he called her to the counter.

'You still look a bit rough. Go on home and I'll help Alice to finish off the tables.'

Pearl thanked him, and though she wasn't ill, she was glad to leave. She had been fighting all day to bury her feelings and now felt emotionally drained. 'What about Mrs Dolby? Are you sure she won't mind?'

'You leave her to me. Now go on, get yourself home.'

Pearl pulled off her apron and was just leaving the café when she saw Kevin walking towards her. With her head down she made to walk past him, but this time he didn't ignore her.

'Well, Pearl. You're quite the little celebrity now.'

'Let me pass.'

'Now then, don't be hasty. I was just going to suggest that I pop up to see you again tonight.'

'Wh ... what?'

'I said I'd like to see you again.'

She looked up at his handsome face and her stomach fluttered. 'You ... you said you don't want a steady girlfriend.'

'Yeah, that's right, but we can still have a bit of fun on the side.'

Pearl's hand flew to her mouth as she shoved past Kevin, flaying herself for once more letting him get through her defences. One look at his handsome face and her resolve crumbled. It had to stop – it *had* to. She was nearing Derek's stall now and fought to pull herself together, forcing the mockery of a smile.

'You look awful,' Derek said. 'Maybe you went back to work too soon. I'll get someone to watch me stall and we'll collect your stuff.'

'I can't face going to my room now. Can we collect my things later?'

'Of course we can. Go on home and Connie will see you're all right. I'll pack up in about an hour.'

He leaned forward, giving her a peck on the cheek before she hurried away. Home, Derek had said. Oh, if only it could remain her home – a refuge where Kevin Dolby could never get near her again.

Pearl's steps faltered. There was a way. Instead of waiting, she could marry Derek as soon as possible. As Pearl continued her journey, the thought became more and more compelling.

At eight o'clock, Pearl and Derek had collected her things, and now they were back in his house. It had been hard to return to her bedsit, but with so few belongings it hadn't taken long to pack. Derek too had been impressed with her drawings, and was now urging her to show them to Connie.

She reluctantly pulled out her portfolio, and was amazed by Connie's reaction. 'Blimey, girl, this is a smashing one of Derek. It looks just like him.'

'See, Pearl, I told you they're good.'

'Why don't you sell them?' Connie suggested.

Pearl's stomach knotted. Kevin had said the same thing and she'd been so flattered, the memory of what happened afterwards making her flush with shame.

'Gawd, look at her, Derek. She's blushing. I ain't kidding, Pearl. I reckon you could sell these and make yourself a few bob.'

'Maybe. I ... I'll think about it.'

'Pearl's room wasn't up to much, Gran. I'm sure she'll be able to find something better.'

'Of course she will, and it's a shame we ain't got a spare bedroom. It can't be much fun sleeping on that sofa.'

'It's fine,' Pearl said, 'and it's good of you to have me. I'll find something else as soon as I can.'

'What did Nobby Clark say when you told him you were leaving?'

'He said he could see I wouldn't want to live there now, and even gave me back my week's deposit.'

'Huh, that's probably because Derek was with you. I wouldn't trust Nobby as far as I could throw him. Anyway, Derek, how about taking Pearl's stuff through to the front room, and then we'll have a nice cuppa?'

'I'll make it,' Pearl said, jumping to her feet, and as she began to prepare the brew, she felt at home in Connie's kitchen. Once again she hardened her resolve. She would marry Derek, stay in this haven, and now all she had to do was encourage him to ask her.

16

On Friday, Frank Hanwell set up his stall again, but he was a different man. There were no more jokes, no ribald exchanges with his customers, and when he went into the café the other costermongers became strangely quiet, most keeping their heads down as Frank headed for one of Pearl's tables.

'Hello, Frank,' she said quietly. 'What can I get you?'

'I'll just have an egg and a couple of rashers of bacon.'

'How's Eric?'

Frank reached out to grasp her hand, his eyes agonised and his voice barely above a whisper. 'He's coming home next week, but he won't let me near him. It's almost as if he blames me for what happened. He's so quiet, Pearl, but it's his eyes that get to me. They look blank, as though my son is dead inside.'

Pearl returned the pressure of Frank's hand, floundering for something to say. She felt so inadequate, so unworldly, and could find no words of wisdom to comfort the man.

'It's early days yet,' was all she could come up with, and after writing his order, she rushed to the kitchen. For a moment she stood just inside the door, reliving that awful moment when she first found Eric.

'What's the matter, girl?'

'Oh, I'm sorry, Mrs Dolby. I've just taken Frank Hanwell's order and–'

'Christ, no wonder you look upset. How is he?'

'He looks awful. He told me about Eric, and ... and I didn't know what to say to him.'

'I'm surprised he spoke to you about it,' Gertie said as she joined them. 'He's hardly said a word to anyone since it happened.'

'Maybe it's because Pearl found the lad,' Dolly said, rushing back to the stove to save some sausages before they blackened. 'We can't talk now,' she said impatiently. 'Pull yourself together, Pearl, and get on with your work.'

Gertie threw her a smile of sympathy before hurrying away and, taking a deep breath, Pearl picked up a couple of orders, carrying them through to the dining room. It was busy, the breakfast rush well underway, and when Derek came in he had no option but to sit at one of Alice Freeman's tables.

When Frank's breakfast was ready, Pearl placed it on the table, but the man said nothing as he picked up his knife and fork. He'd been joined by costermongers who always sat with him, but as Pearl took their orders the usual camaraderie and jokes were missing.

Awful though it was, when Frank left, it was as if everyone in the café sighed. The noise level picked up, and occasional subdued laughter could be heard.

Pearl went over to Derek, shaking her head sadly. 'Poor Frank, and now everyone seems relieved that he's gone.'

'It's human nature, love. It was a terrible thing that happened, and it touched all of us. A lot of people are probably thanking God that it wasn't their child, and they don't know how to comfort Frank.'

'I didn't know what to say to him either.'

'Nor me, and my stall is next to his. He's still very upset and is losing trade. I wish I could do something, anything, but feel helpless. I can't imagine what the family is going through, and rumour has it that Eric has been mentally affected. It may take years for him to recover, if he ever does. The poor little tyke.'

'Oh, Derek, why is the world so cruel?'

'I dunno, love, but lots of good things happen too. It's just that when something like this occurs, we forget them. Count your blessings, Gran says, and she's right. Come on, cheer up.'

Pearl forced a smile, leaving Derek to take an order. She turned to look briefly at him over her shoulder, glad that he had come into her life. No matter what, she felt that Derek would always look after her – and was comforted by the thought.

Kevin came downstairs at eleven o'clock and, seeing Pearl, he smiled. She could pretend all she liked, but he knew she still fancied him. It was a bit of a bugger that she'd left her bedsit. She was staying with Derek, and out of his reach, but once she found another place he intended to sample the goods again.

Since that first time he'd been unable to dismiss her from his mind. Pearl had been a virgin and for some reason she felt like his property now. It wasn't easy to get a girl into bed, most insisting on walking up the aisle a virgin, but it hadn't been hard with Pearl.

He went through to the kitchen, ordered his breakfast, and made a point of sitting at one of Pearl's tables. She'd run off last time he suggested seeing her again, so maybe he should change his tactics. She was timid, soft, and a bit of charm wouldn't hurt.

'Hello, Pearl,' he said, smiling as she put his breakfast on the table. 'You look nice. Would you mind getting me a couple of slices of bread and a cup of tea?'

She said nothing, her lips tight as she scurried off. Kevin eyed her as she went to the counter, admiring her now shapely figure. Maybe it wouldn't be so bad having her as a steady girlfriend. He wouldn't have to take her out much, and as he'd been the first one to have her, it would be nice if he remained the *only* one. She would be his own exclusive property and on hand whenever he got the urge.

Kevin waited until Pearl returned to the table, noticing that her hands were trembling, the cup rattling in the saucer as she placed it on the table. 'Thanks,' he said and, glancing around, saw no

158

one in earshot. 'Pearl, I really would like to see you again. Maybe I could take you out one night?'

He saw the hesitation in her eyes, but then she shook her head, saying curtly, 'No, thanks. Derek is my boyfriend and I don't want go out with you.'

Unused to girls turning him down, Kevin spat, 'Yeah, but you slept with me, not him. Perhaps he'd like to hear about it.'

'Oh, no! Please, you can't tell him.' She paused momentarily, then begged, 'Please, Kevin, don't say anything to Derek. You ... you see, we're getting married.'

'What? You're going to marry that ugly sod?'

'Derek may not be much to look at, but he isn't ugly. He's a good man, a nice man.'

'Nice! And that's reason enough to marry him?'

'I ... I think a lot of him.'

Kevin's fingers tightened around his cutlery in anger. So, she preferred that ugly sod to him. Huh, well, he'd see about that. Once Derek found out that he'd had her first, there'd be no marriage.

'Bugger off,' he growled, and finding that he'd lost his appetite he swallowed only his tea before marching out of the café.

It didn't take him long to reach Derek's stall and Kevin feigned friendliness as he went to his side. 'Watcha, mate. How's it going?'

'Hello, Kevin. It's a bit quiet today.'

'Pearl tells me that you two are getting married.'

'Did she?' Derek grinned widely. 'Blimey, that's great.'

159

So, Pearl had lied, and now Kevin forced a laugh.

'It sounds like you knew nothing about it.'

'Well, we're courting, but I haven't proposed yet. I thought Pearl would want to wait until she's a bit older.'

'Huh, she's old enough and, believe me, she knows how to make a man happy.'

Derek's face darkened. 'What's that supposed to mean?'

Self-preservation kicked in, and Kevin baulked. Christ, was he mad? If he told Derek he'd been there first, the man would kill him. He desperately sought for a way out. 'Well, mate, I can see how happy you are, and it's obvious that it's down to Pearl.'

Derek jaws were working, his tension obvious, but as Kevin's words sunk in, he relaxed. 'You're right. Pearl's a smashing girl, and now I know she wants to marry me, I'll do the proposing. Mind you, I'll have to save for a ring.'

Kevin's eyes narrowed. He wanted to punish Pearl for turning him down, to make her pay. Not only that, he wanted to sample the goods again. He needed time to work on her and had somehow to put a spoke in Derek's wheels. 'If you ask me, she's a bit young and I reckon you should hold off for a while before proposing.'

'No, I don't want to do that. Her birthday's a month away, in October, and I should have enough saved for a nice little solitaire by then.'

Kevin managed a smile, yet as he walked away it was quickly replaced by a scowl. Christ, despite his trying to put him off, Derek was still going to propose in October. Pearl was a bitch. He'd shown her a good time and she'd enjoyed it, yet she was going to marry Derek bloody Lewis. Well, if that's what she wanted, fuck her. There were plenty more fish in the sea and he wouldn't waste his time on her again.

Pearl was anxiously watching the door, but it was after three o'clock before Kevin returned. She had to speak to him – had to know if he'd told Derek. He was heading for the kitchen and she quickly stood in his path.

'Get out of my way.'

'Did ... did you say anything to Derek?'

He sneered. 'Worried, are you? Well, you can relax. I didn't tell him, and in fact he's welcome to you.'

Pearl's breath left her body in a rush, and seeing that Bernie was looking at them curiously, she quickly moved out of Kevin's way. He swept past, and her heart jumped when Bernie called her over.

'Is there a problem, Pearl?'

'No, I was just saying hello to Kevin.'

His eyes narrowed. 'Pearl, I'm saying this for your own good. If you've got any ideas about my son, forget them.'

'I ... I haven't got any ideas about him.'

'I'm glad to hear it. You stick with Derek and you won't go wrong.'

She gave a slight nod, busying herself with a bit of last-minute tidying before her shift came to an end. Yes, she would stay out of Kevin's way, but she hated how her treacherous body reacted every time he came near her. Kevin changed like quicksilver: one minute nice, the next horrible. Pearl hung her head. She both loved him, and feared him, yet now wondered if he was right. Had she mistaken sex for love? Was it just lust that she felt?

It was time to go and as Pearl put on her coat, Nora arrived, beaming widely, her face holding the innocence of a child. For a moment Pearl's fingers itched to sketch her again and she studied her features, trying to hold them in her mind, but was too worried about Derek to concentrate. Had Kevin told the truth? Had he really said nothing to Derek?

She called goodbye, leaving the café to walk slowly to his stall, the breath leaving her body with relief when he smiled warmly. Oh, he was such a lovely man, and though he didn't arouse any feelings in her, she was safe with him.

Once again Pearl's resolve hardened. Kevin was dangerous, unpredictable, and it was better to keep out of his way.

'Hello, love, I just saw Nutty Nora charging through the market. She looked like a rag bag.'

'Oh, don't call her that. She may be slow, but she isn't nutty.'

'It's a nickname she's had for years.'

'It seems so unkind.'

'Yeah, you're right, it is, and from now on I won't use it. Mind you, I still think she could do with smartening herself up a bit. Sometimes she lets off an awful whiff.'

Pearl looked down at her own clothes. She desperately needed some new ones, and as the

162

second-hand shop was at the end of the market she intended to see if she could find a couple of outfits.

Derek had the local paper and she picked it up. 'Did you see any bedsits to rent?'

'Yeah, a couple, but there's no hurry for you to move out.'

'I don't think your gran would agree. I'm taking up her front room.'

'It's not her house, love, it's mine. Gran had the tenancy transferred to my name years ago. She wanted to make sure that if anything happened to her, I wouldn't get chucked out.'

Pearl smiled faintly. The house might be in Derek's name, but it was obvious who ruled the roost. 'It's still time I found somewhere else to live.' She stood on tiptoe to give him a kiss on the cheek, Derek gripping her hand for a moment before she hurried away.

Her heart was lighter as she opened the door to the second-hand shop, but was greeted by a musty smell that made her nose wrinkle. There was a mishmash of stuff for sale: old books, bits of china, a few pieces of furniture, all covered in dust. She was about to turn tail when an elderly lady came out of a back room, her heavily lined face breaking into a smile.

'Hello, dear. Can I help you?'

'I ... I'm looking for a couple of outfits, but...'

'Well, you're in luck. I've just had some stuff in that's in good nick and looks about your size.' She shuffled over to a metal rack, her fingers gnarled and bent with arthritis. After riffling through the rail she pulled out a skirt and blouse.

163

'Here they are and, as you can see, there ain't a mark on them.'

Pearl reluctantly crossed the shop floor but when she got closer, she could see what the old lady meant. The blue skirt looked lovely, pleating from the waist into a flare, and the white blouse immaculate. When the old woman pulled out a dress, Pearl's eyes widened. It was patterned with pink roses on a cream background, the material heavy and of good quality. The skirt flared from the waist too and there was also a matching bolero with short sleeves.

'You can try them on, if you like.'

'Oh, yes, please.'

She was led to the back room, finding it piled high with more clothes and old furniture, but there was a full-length mirror. The old lady left, and after trying on the skirt and blouse, finding them an almost perfect fit, Pearl reached for the dress. She twirled in front of the mirror, amazed at how lovely it looked, and now crossed her fingers that she could afford them. Quickly dressing, she then carried the outfits through to the shop. 'How much are they?'

'Well, now, let me see. You can have the skirt and blouse for a shilling, but I want two bob for the dress.'

Pearl gasped, unable to believe her luck. Both outfits would have cost pounds new. Afraid the woman would change her mind, she quickly pulled out her purse.

The clothes were shoved in an old brown-paper carrier bag, and as the old lady handed it over she cocked her head to one side, her eyes narrowing.

'In the not too distant future, we'll see each other again.'

'Yes, I'll definitely come here again.'

'I know you will, but it may not be to buy clothes.'

'What do you mean?'

'Don't worry about it, duckie. It's just that I know our paths were meant to cross and one day you and I will need each other.'

There was something all-knowing in the old woman's dark eyes and Pearl shivered. 'I ... I don't understand.'

'You will when the time comes and–' The door opened, a stout women coming in clutching a bag, garments spilling out of the top. 'Hello, Maud. I can see you've got some stuff for me.'

'Yeah, and it's decent gear too. That fancy piece I clean for had a clear-out.'

'Right, fetch it over here.' And turning to Pearl she added, 'No rest for the wicked.'

Pearl knew it was a dismissal, her mind turning as she left the shop. She played the old woman's words over in her mind. Their paths were meant to cross. But what did that mean?

'What have you got there?' Connie asked as soon as Pearl arrived home.

'I went to the second-hand shop.'

Pearl pulled out her outfits, gratified by Connie's approval. 'You've done well there, girl. How much did you pay for them?'

'Only three shillings for both outfits.'

'Blimey, old Bessie must be losing her marbles. She could have asked for more than that.'

'Oh dear, do you think I should have offered more?'

'Don't be daft. Bessie Penfold has made a mint over the years. If she's undercharging for stuff, she still won't lose out. She buys it for next to nothing and, believe me, I should know. When my Derek was a nipper, things were really tight. My old man died and I had no choice but to flog his clothes. Bessie Penfold gave me a pittance for them, but I was desperate and had to take it. She was as tight as a duck's arse, and it was only enough to feed us for a couple of days. I've never forgiven her and if she's getting her come-uppance now, I'm glad.'

'She said some funny things too.'

Connie's eyebrows shot up. 'Like what?'

'She said our paths would cross and that we'd need each other.'

'There's people round here who think she's got second sight. They say she's from gypsy stock and can see into the future. Now me, I think it's a load of old tosh. If you ask me you shouldn't take any notice of anything she said.'

Pearl smiled with relief. 'I don't believe that anyone can foresee the future, but I must admit she unnerved me a bit.'

'Yeah, well, she's had years of practice. You're lucky she didn't ask you to cross her palm with silver. She's conned a good few people over the years with her so-called predictions.'

Pearl was surprised. Despite her strange words, she had liked Bessie Penfold, and though she was obviously in a lot of arthritic pain, the woman had been kind and cheerful. Yet Connie made her

166

sound mean and conniving, a woman who fooled people into parting with their money. Would their paths cross again, Pearl wondered, and if so, why?

17

Pearl scoured the local papers and looked at cards in newsagents' windows, but her attempts to find another bedsit were half-hearted. She loved staying at Derek's, and though the sofa was playing havoc with her back, she didn't want to leave.

On Tuesday evening, over a week later, and whilst Derek was at the gym, Connie flicked her eyes away from the television, clearing her throat before she spoke.

'Pearl, don't get upset about what I'm going to say, but I really think it's time that you found a place of your own again. Now don't look at me like that, love. I've enjoyed having you here, but you need a proper bed to sleep in. And, well, what with you and Derek courting…'

Pearl gulped, her voice a whisper: 'All right, I'll try harder to find a room. Maybe there'll be something in the local paper this week.'

'Oh, love, I'm sorry I've upset you, but you're welcome to come round here as often as you like. You've become like a daughter to me, but it just isn't right that you and Derek are sleeping under the same roof.'

'But why?'

167

'Gawd, girl, do I have to spell it out? My Derek may be a diamond, but he's still a man. It's too much of a temptation, love.'

'But he'd never take advantage of me.'

'Pearl, you should listen to yourself. You sound like some sort of old-fashioned heroine in a novel. Derek's bedroom is next to mine and I've heard him tossing and turning all night. He didn't do that before you came to stay. He loves you and, well, as I said, he's a man and he wants you. I know you're an innocent, but surely you understand what I'm getting at?'

Pearl lowered her eyes. An innocent. No, she wasn't an innocent now. Kevin Dolby had seen to that. He was leaving her alone, but despite her determination to harden her heart, it still leaped every time she saw him. She had thought about finding another job, but loved the café and was reluctant to leave. As long as Kevin didn't talk to her, as long as she kept out of his way, she could cope, and surely one day soon she would get over him. She sighed heavily. She didn't want to leave the safe haven of this house either, but had no choice.

'I'll find a bedsit as quickly as I can and ... and I'm sorry I've been so much trouble.'

'Don't be daft, love. You ain't been any trouble, and when Derek's out I enjoy your company. It's just ... well, as I said. Come on now, cheer up. I meant it when I said you can come round as often as you like.'

That was something, Pearl thought, and maybe, just maybe, she could find a bedsit in a family house this time.

Pearl found her prayers answered the following day.

During her break, Mo stuck her head around the kitchen door. 'Pearl, can I have a word?'

'Yes, of course.'

Mo bustled over. 'I told Dolly what I've got in mind and she said to talk to you out here. Mind you, I'd better make it quick. She might be in a good mood at the moment, but there's no guarantee it will last. Anyway, to get to the point, I've been thinking and it's like this. Since my old man died, there's only my daughter, Emma, and me. It's been a bit of a struggle bringing her up on me own and money's been tight.' She scratched her head before continuing. 'I'm daft really and I don't know why I didn't think of this before. You see, I've got a spare room. It ain't very big so I couldn't ask much in the way of rent, but if you're willing to pay me around fifteen bob a week, it's yours.'

'Oh, Mo.'

'It's only when I heard that you needed a bedsit that it came to me. I mean, I've got an empty room, you need a place, and I'd hate to have a stranger moving in. I had a word with my Emma, and she's all for it. We've done the room up between us, so, what do you say?'

Pearl grinned with delight. It sounded wonderful. She would be living in a family house, one with a girl of her own age, and who knew, they might become friends. 'I'd love to move in with you, Mo.'

'Blimey, girl, you ain't seen the room yet. Why

don't you pop round tonight? I live at number fourteen Pennington Street. It ain't far, and you'll be able to walk to work in five minutes.'

'Mo, it's about time you got back to the kitchen,' Dolly snapped, her face red as she marched into the dining room.

Mo pulled a face and then winked at Pearl.

'Tonight then?'

'Yes, and thanks.'

'There's no need for thanks. See you later, or as my Emma would say, "See you later, alligator."'

Pearl looked puzzled and Mo chuckled. 'Everyone says it. That Bill Haley and his rock-and-roll band have even turned it into a song. Emma is mad on him. "See You Later, Alligator" is one of his hit records. You're supposed to respond with, "In a while, crocodile." Yeah, I know, daft, ain't it?' she added, still chuckling as she bustled away.

See you later, alligator. It sounded silly to Pearl, but it brought a smile to her face. Rock and roll. Yes, she had heard the foot-tapping music, but without a wireless, she rarely heard the latest trends. Oh, it sounded like it was going to be fun living with Mo and her daughter.

Derek was disappointed when Pearl told him she'd like to go Mo's house on her own, but she felt it was best. It only took ten minutes to walk to Pennington Street from Derek's and, slightly nervous, she knocked on Mo's door.

'Hello, love, come on in,' the woman said, grinning as she stood to one side.

The small hall was immaculate, and at the

170

warm greeting, Pearl relaxed. She was taken immediately upstairs and, flinging open a door, Mo ushered her inside. The room *was* small, but Pearl fell in love with it at first sight. There were lemon flowered curtains at the window, toning with the lemon candlewick bedspread. The floor was covered in rather dull, brown lino, but a nice rug lay beside the bed. She saw a single wardrobe, a small dressing table, and a tiny wicker chair in one corner.

'I know you usually get a sink in a bedsit, Pearl, but the bathroom is only next door. You'll have to share it with me and Emma, of course, but I'm sure we'll all rub along nicely. If you want to cook, you can use the kitchen, and as long as you tidy up after yourself there won't be a problem.' With an anxious frown, Mo added, 'Well, love, what do you think?'

'I love it!' Pearl cried. 'It ... it's so pretty.'

'As soon as I decided to let the room, me and Emma done it up.'

'It's lovely, and the wallpaper is smashing too,' Pearl said, eyeing the tiny lavender and yellow flowers.

'You should have seen the state we got into hanging it. I think we got more paste on ourselves than the paper. Still, in the end we didn't make a bad job of it, and now we're going to tackle our bedrooms. They ain't been touched in donkey's years and it'll be nice to freshen them up. Anyway, Pearl, do you want the room?'

'Oh yes, and can I move in at the end of the week?'

'Of course you can. Emma ain't in tonight –

she's gone out with her mates – but I'm sure the pair of you will get along fine. She's a bit older than you, and a little wild at times, but she ain't got a bad bone in her body.'

'Wild?'

'Maybe that's the wrong word. It's just that things have changed so much since the war. When I was a young woman I dressed like my mum – well, there wasn't any choice. Now though, there are all these weird and wonderful fashions aimed at youngsters. Only the other day I saw a group of those teddy boys, and if you ask me they look bleedin' daft. Tight trousers, long jackets, and their hair! My God, with long sideburns and those daft quiff things hanging over their foreheads, it's a disgrace.' She sighed before continuing the tirade. 'My Emma has taken to wearing some very funny clothes too, and she loves to go out dancing. Still, she's a good girl really, and if you ask me it's this music from America that's causing it. Give me a nice crooner like Dickie Valentine, not this flaming rock-and-roll stuff.' Mo suddenly chuckled. 'Gawd, hark at me, I'm really on me soapbox. Come downstairs and I'll make you a nice cup of tea.'

Pearl glanced around the room again before following Mo. The kitchen was small, with a scullery leading to a back yard, and after making the tea, Mo led her into the living room. Like Connie's, it was stuffed with furniture, most looking faded and old, but again it was immaculately clean.

'I know you're courting Derek Lewis, but I'm afraid I can't allow him in your room. My Emma ain't allowed to bring boys home either, so the same rule applies to both of you.'

'That's fine with me.'

'Oh, that's good. I was a bit worried about laying down the law and my Emma says I'm old-fashioned. Old-fashioned! I let Emma stay out until ten thirty, but she still complains. My old dad would have skinned me alive if I wasn't home by nine thirty in the evening, and that was when I was engaged.'

'With having to get up so early in the morning, I'm mostly in bed by ten. Where does Emma work?'

'She's got a job in Prices, the candle factory. She's been there since she left school and seems to like it. Of course, with our surname being Price, she got a bit of ribbing at first, but that soon wore off.'

Pearl found herself totally at ease in Mo's company and they chatted for another half-hour. Then, glancing at the clock on the mantelpiece, she rose to her feet. 'I'd best be off, Mo, and thanks again for letting me have the room. I'll move in on Saturday night, if that's all right.'

'That's fine, and I'll see you at work in the morning.'

Pearl hurried along the road, pleased that she had found somewhere so nice to live. It would be easier to leave Derek and Connie now, and she would be living with a small family again. It was odd really. Both Connie and Mo were without husbands and had struggled to bring up a child on their own.

Pearl's mind shied away from her next thought.

If Mo and Connie could do it – why had her own mother left her on the orphanage steps?

On Friday, Derek was late coming into the café for his breakfast, and with a few minutes to spare Pearl was standing by his table chatting to him when Kevin appeared.

His eyes flicked round the room and, seeing them together, he strolled over. Pearl held her breath, but he smiled pleasantly.

'Are you fighting again on Saturday night, Derek?'

'No, not this time.'

'That's a shame. Nobby Clark says it's always safe to put a bet on you.'

'There's no such thing as a safe bet. Nobby should have learned that by now.'

'He loses most of his money on the horses, and it's a mug's game. He'll never learn and I think most of the nags he's bet on are still running.'

Pearl listened to the exchange, and as her heart thumped in her chest she cursed that Kevin still had this effect on her. He winked, and she flushed.

'I hear you're moving in with Mo Price and her daughter. I must say, that Emma's a bit of all right.'

'Have you been out with her?' Derek asked.

'No, but I might just sample the goods. What do you think, Pearl?'

Pearl felt a surge of jealousy, but managed a nonchalant shrug. 'Please yourself. Anyway, I'd best get on,' she said, hurrying away and hiding her feelings behind a bright smile as she approached a customer. The order taken, she cast a glance at Derek, glad to see that Kevin had left. He grinned and she couldn't help but return it. He was like a big, cuddly bear, warm, safe. Kevin was the opposite, a handsome sleek panther, dark, predatory. She shivered, at last realising that she didn't want to be his prey. Oh, if only Derek would propose soon.

Pearl was surprised at how hard it was to leave Derek's on Saturday evening. She had tried not to grow too fond of them, but still found the parting a wrench, particularly with Connie. It had been like having a mother: a woman who cared about her welfare, showed her affection, and greeted her with pleasure when she came home from work. Now she was moving out and there would be no quick hugs at bedtime, no lovely meals, and no cosy evenings sitting in front of the television.

'Well, 'bye then,' Pearl choked, picking up her bags, only for Derek to take them out of her hands.

''Bye, love. See you tomorrow,' Connie said, giving her a kiss on the cheek.

'Tomorrow?'

'Well, yes. You'll be round for dinner, won't you?'

'Oh, yes, I'd love to,' Pearl said, her heart lifting.

'Blimey, I thought we'd sorted this out. You're moving to Pennington Street, not Outer Mongolia, and can come round as often as you like. If you want to pop in to see me after work each day, that'd be lovely, and you can share our meals as usual.'

'Oh, Connie.'

'Well, let's face it; you'll become as skinny as a rake again if I don't feed you. Now off you go, and don't worry, you'll be fine with Mo. She's a good sort.'

Pearl nodded, following Derek outside. She was on the move again, but this time reluctantly. It hadn't been hard to leave the orphanage, the hostel, or her first bedsit, but leaving Derek's was like leaving home.

'You can always change your mind,' Derek said as if reading her thoughts. 'You're welcome to stay at my place.'

'No, Connie's right. It's time I moved out.'

'What do you mean? What's Gran got to do with it?'

'Well … er … she sort of said I should try harder to find a bedsit.'

'She what? When?'

'We had a chat when you were at the gym on Tuesday. She's right, though,' Pearl said hurriedly. 'I couldn't sleep on the sofa indefinitely.'

'She had no right to force you out without discussing it with me. Wait till I get back. I'll have a few words to say to her.'

'No, Derek, please don't fall out over me. She's only doing what she thinks is for the best.'

'Huh, best for who?'

Pearl glanced up at Derek's face, seeing anger, and decided that this might be the ideal opportunity to hint about marriage. 'Connie's concerned about you. We … we're courting and it

176

isn't right that we were living under the same roof. I don't know about you, but it kept me awake, knowing that you were in the bedroom above me.' Pearl's face reddened with shame as she told the lie, but consoled herself with the thought that it was only a little white one. If Derek loved her and proposed, she'd do her best to be a good wife. She couldn't love him in return, but she liked him, and surely that was a good basis for marriage?

'Bloody hell, I had no idea you were laying awake, and I must admit it was the same for me.'

'Yes, Connie told me that she heard you tossing and turning.'

Derek suddenly stopped walking and, dropping her bags on the pavement, he turned to face her. 'I ain't much good at fancy words, Pearl, but I think a lot of you. In fact, more than a lot.'

Pearl's breath caught in her throat. Was this it? Was he going to propose? 'I ... I think a lot of you too.'

His huge arms reached out, enfolding her, crushing her to his chest. 'You've made me a very happy man. I can't say I'm pleased that you're moving out, but if both of us aren't getting any kip, perhaps Gran's right. We'll still see each other every day, but if you ain't happy at Mo's, just say the word.'

No proposal, Pearl thought, disappointed as she pulled herself out of Derek's arms. 'I'm sure I'll be fine,' she whispered, and as he picked up the bags again, they continued their journey to Pennington Street.

18

It was Sunday morning before Pearl met Mo's daughter. She had gone down to the kitchen to get a drink but, seeing Emma, her jaw dropped. She had blonde, tousled hair, and was wearing Capri pants with a red, off-the-shoulder sweater. To Pearl she looked the ultimate in sophistication.

'Watcha, Pearl, it's nice to meet you at last.'

'Hello,' Pearl replied shyly.

'So, you work in the café? Rather you than me.'

'It's not too bad.'

'What, you must be kidding. That Dolly Dolby is a right old dragon.'

'Now then, Emma,' Mo admonished. 'Dolly might be hard, but she's fair.'

'Yeah, if you say so, Mum. Anyway, Pearl, what sort of music do you like?'

'Er ... I don't know really. I don't get the chance to listen to much music.'

'Well, we can soon sort that out. If you ain't got anything planned, come up to my room and we'll play some records.'

'Not now, Emma,' Mo protested. 'It's Sunday morning so let's listen to something soothing for a change. How about putting a few of *my* records on instead? Pearl might like Frank Sinatra, or maybe Doris Day singing "Secret Love." That one's got a smashing tune.'

'No, thanks, Mum, I don't want putting to sleep.' She turned to Pearl. 'I suppose we'd better keep the old girl happy. We can listen to Bill Haley later.'

'Old girl! Who are you calling an old girl? I'm only forty-three.'

'All right, keep your hair on.'

'Yours could do with a brush, my girl.'

'You must be kidding. It took me ages to get it like this.'

'You've wasted your time then. Why don't you have a nice perm like me?'

'Mum, it's nineteen fifty-six, not 'forty-six. Perm indeed. They're for old ladies.'

Pearl listened to this repartee, unable to help smiling. The banter between Mo and her daughter was all light-hearted, with smiles to take the sting out of the words.

'Why are you wearing those daft trousers again?' Mo asked her daughter.

'Daft! They ain't daft. They're the latest fashion.'

'Huh. What do you say, Pearl? Don't you think they look soppy?'

Pearl floundered. She didn't want to offend either of them. 'Er ... I think they're nice, and they suit Emma. I don't think I could wear them, though.'

'Of course you could,' Emma said, looking Pearl up and down. 'We'll still go up to my room but instead of playing records, we'll do something about your wardrobe.'

'My wardrobe?'

'Yeah, you need bringing up to date and I've

got just the thing.'

Pearl followed Emma upstairs, surprised when instead of going to Emma's bedroom, they went into hers.

'Right, let's have a look at your gear,' Emma said, sitting on the side of the bed.

'I haven't got many clothes,' Pearl told her and, going to her sparse wardrobe, she pulled out the lovely rose-patterned dress. 'I got this from the second-hand shop, but I haven't had the chance to wear it yet.'

'Gawd blimey, it looks like something a posh bird would wear to a royal garden party. It's way too old for you.'

'Is it? But I think it's lovely.'

'I can see you need teaching a thing or too. What else have you got?'

'Just a few skirts and blouses.'

'Come on, I'll show you some of the latest gear,' Emma said, going into her room. She pulled out a pair of trousers. 'I got these Capri pants in Petticoat Lane last week, but they're a bit too tight. Try them on.'

Pearl looked at the pale blue trousers doubtfully, but at Emma's insistence she slipped them on. 'Here, try this sweater with them,' Emma said, holding out a black polo neck.

Once again Pearl did as she was told, and when she turned to look at herself in the mirror her eyes widened.

'Sit down and I'll have a go at your hair. That style looks schoolgirly. You need to fluff it up a bit, like this,' Emma said, picking up a comb and vigorously backcombing Pearl's hair. 'Don't you wear make-up?'

'Er ... no.'

'Right, more to sort out. I'm gonna enjoy you living here, Pearl. It's sort of like having a kid sister. Here, try this,' she said, spitting on a block of mascara and rubbing it vigorously with the small brush. 'Put some of this on your eyelashes, and then try some lipstick. You need a bit of powder too, but my shade would be too pale for your skin.'

Bemused, Pearl applied the make-up, astounded at the result. Her eyes looked larger, her lips fuller, and though the backcombed hair looked strange, it did add height.

'Come on, let's go and show Mum your new look,' Emma urged. 'I can't wait to see her face.'

Pearl took one last look in the mirror before following Emma downstairs, and as they walked into the kitchen, Mo gaped. 'My God, what has my daughter done to you?'

'Leave it out, Mum. She looks great.'

'She looks like a clone of all your friends. If you ask me, these new teenage fashions are like a uniform. Teddy boys all dress alike and you girls are the same.'

'Take no notice of her, Pearl. In fact, next week I'll take you up to Petticoat Lane and you can buy a few things of your own.'

'Thanks, Emma, but I'm afraid I can't afford new clothes. Any spare money I have goes on painting material.'

'Painting! What do you mean?'

'I ... I go to art classes.'

'Do you?' Mo said, and turning to her daughter

she added, 'You could do with taking a leaf out of Pearl's book. Instead of spending all your time going dancing you could be learning something too.'

'Oh, yeah, like what?'

'Well, how about dressmaking? That would come in handy.'

'Mum, all my life I've had to wear clothes that you made for me, and jumpers that you knitted. It's the last thing that I want now and I'd sooner buy them off the rails.'

Mo's face saddened. 'I didn't know you felt like that. I ... I did the best I could.'

'Oh, Mum, please don't get upset. I didn't mind when I was a kid, honestly I didn't, but it's different now that I can afford to buy my own clothes. Look, I'll think about learning something, maybe typing and shorthand.' She turned to Pearl, an appeal in her eyes, 'Here, why don't you show us some of your paintings?'

Pearl took the cue. Emma had upset her mother and obviously wanted to divert the conversation. 'I haven't done many paintings yet. But I've got lots of sketches.'

'We'd still like to see them.'

Pearl hurried upstairs, grabbed her folder and riffled through it until she found the one of Mo. It was a good likeness, but unsure of how the woman would feel about it, she stuffed it into her dressing-table drawer before returning downstairs.

'Gawd, look at this one of Dolly Dolby,' Mo said as they went through the folder. 'And there's one of Gertie too. These are really good, Pearl.'

'Thank you,' Pearl said, gratified to see Mo

looking cheerful again.

'Oh, look, here's one of Nora.'

'It's not very good. She's a difficult subject.'

'The poor woman is a sandwich short of a picnic, but she's harmless.' Mo picked up another sketch. 'My goodness, this is a marvellous drawing of Derek.'

Emma looked over her mother's shoulder. 'Yeah, but it doesn't make him look any better. Oh Christ, sorry, Pearl, I forgot you were going out with him.'

'That's all right. I know he isn't much to look at, but he's a lovely man.'

Emma looked as if she was about to say something else, but then changed her mind as her mother found yet another drawing of someone she knew.

'It's young Eric Hanwell. He looks so happy in this picture. Did you draw it before, well ... you know?'

Pearl nodded, her face saddening. In the sketch Eric looked mischievous, impish, his gap-toothed grin wide. Would he ever look like that again? She looked up as Emma spoke.

'Mum told me that you found the kid. It must have been rotten for you.'

'Yes, it was terrible, but nothing compared to what poor Eric went through.'

'What was the bloke like who did it?'

'In his forties, flabby, but to be honest I hardly saw him.'

'I heard that he got done in.'

'He didn't. Bernie told me that he was castrated.'

'That's not what I heard, and anyway, he deserved more than having his balls cut off.'

'Emma, that's enough! I won't have you talking like that,' Mo admonished. 'What we heard were rumours, that's all and, if you ask me, nobody knows the truth.'

'Yeah, sorry.'

'I should think so too. What's done is done and it's best forgotten. Pearl was in an awful state when she found the boy and it isn't nice to make her go over it again.'

Pearl hung her head. They thought Trevor Bardington had been killed, but it had to be a rumour, it just had to be. Surely Bernie hadn't lied.

She picked up her portfolio. 'I'd best get ready to go round to Derek's. They're expecting me for dinner.'

'That's a shame. I was going to suggest taking you to meet a few of me mates,' Emma said.

'Oh, I'd have loved that. Maybe another time?'

'All right, perhaps tomorrow night. You can wear that gear again.'

'Thanks, I'd love to meet your friends.'

Pearl went back to her room. It had been a strange morning, but one she'd enjoyed until the conversation turned to Trevor Bardington. She liked Emma and maybe they really could become friends.

Pearl decided to leave the mascara and lipstick on, but when she sat across the table for dinner at Derek's, she could sense an atmosphere.

'Why are you wearing that muck on your face?'

184

Connie asked.

'It's only a bit of mascara and lipstick.'

'You don't need it, and if you ask me it makes you look like a tart.'

'Gran, don't say things like that. I think Pearl looks nice.'

'Rubbish. Nice girls shouldn't wear that stuff.'

'All young girls wear make-up nowadays,' Derek protested.

'In my day only tarts painted their faces. Pearl looks better without it.'

'I think she looks fine.'

As Connie scowled at her, Pearl felt like a naughty little girl. She lowered her eyes, but then Connie's voice softened.

'Take no notice of me, love. I saw my daughter painting all that muck on her face, and ... well ... has Derek told you what happened to her?'

Pearl lifted her head, seeing sadness in Connie's eyes. 'He told me that she was killed during the war.'

'Yes, that's right, but it was well before the war, in nineteen twenty-nine, when she met up with some rough characters and took to plastering her face with make-up. She started going to the West End, but wouldn't tell me what she was up to. Then one day she came home with a bun in the oven.'

'A bun in the oven?'

'She was pregnant, *and* unmarried. I can't tell you how ashamed I was. I mean, you can imagine what the neighbours would have said.' She exhaled loudly. 'I couldn't face the gossip, and though I'll regret it till the end of me days, I chucked her out. When Derek was born I still wouldn't have anything to do with her. In fact, I didn't even see him until my daughter was killed in nineteen forty, and by then he was ten years old.'

'I'm so sorry,' Pearl whispered.

'I don't deserve sympathy. If I could turn the clock back I'd have done things differently, and then perhaps my daughter would still be alive.'

'Leave it out, Gran. She was killed by a bloody bomb.'

'Yeah, but if I hadn't chucked her out, she wouldn't have been in a pub. She'd have been at home, looking after you instead of palming you off with neighbours while she was out having a good time.'

'Gran, you know that she was a bit wild, and I doubt you could have kept her in. Anyway, you can't spend the rest of your life living on what might have been.'

'Yeah, I expect you're right, but it's something I'll never know.' She turned to Pearl. 'I'm sorry for lecturing you about make-up. It was wrong of me to compare you with my daughter. You're a nice girl, a good and innocent girl, and I'm sorry if I've upset you.'

Pearl flushed. Innocent – Connie thought she was innocent. Oh God, if only that were true.

19

After only two weeks of living at Mo's, and the day before her birthday, Pearl was happier than she had ever been in her life. Emma had continued to take her under her wing, and now Pearl was transformed. Her hair had been restyled and, despite initially protesting, she had been unable to resist the young fashions for sale in Petticoat Lane.

Even the shopping trip had been a revelation. Emma thought nothing of bartering with the traders, returning their cheeky repartee, and managing to get a good few bob knocked off the prices. Pearl loved the wide flared skirt she had purchased, together with a sweater. They were the latest thing, Emma assured her, buying one too, but in a different colour.

It was Saturday night, and instead of going to the pictures with Derek, she was going dancing again with Emma. She loved the loud, foot-tapping music, and with Emma's help had learned to jive. She hadn't liked disappointing Derek again, but loved the company of Emma and her crowd, never before feeling so young, alive and carefree.

'Does this look all right?' she asked Emma, spinning around to show her the outfit.

'Yeah, but don't wear your sweater on the outside. Tuck it in, and clip that wide, elastic belt

I gave you around your waist.'

Pearl nodded, happy to take Emma's advice, and looking in the mirror she had to admit the outfit looked better. With a grimace she stuffed her feet into a pair of high-heeled shoes that Emma had lent her, wondering if she would ever get used to them.

'Right, I'm ready.'

'Me too, so let's get going.'

As both girls went downstairs, Emma broke into song.

Pearl smiled, recognising 'Be-Bop-a-Lula' by Gene Vincent. Emma was mad on it. Mo stood at the kitchen door, doing her best to look stern.

'Now, you two, I want you home by ten thirty and no later.'

'Keep your socks on, Mum. We won't be late.'

'You're wearing too much make-up, Emma. You're skin is lovely and doesn't need plastering with pan stick.'

'I ain't got that much on, and anyway, it covers up my spots.'

'You wouldn't have spots if you didn't wear that muck on your face.'

Pearl hid a smile, used to this nightly exchange. In some ways Mo was of the same opinion as Connie about make-up, but Emma would win the argument; she always did.

'All right, I won't put so much on next time, but we're meeting the girls and if we don't get going we'll be late. 'Bye, Mum, love you,' she added, planting a smacking kiss on Mo's cheek and leaving an imprint of pale pink lipstick.

Mo smiled with pleasure at her daughter's show

of affection. 'Go on then, off you go, but don't forget what I said. Ten thirty and no later. 'Bye, Pearl, have a nice time.'

''Bye, Mo,' Pearl called as she followed Emma outside and, linking arms, the two girls hurried along Pennington Street.

The dance hall was crowded, the music loud, and already two of the girls in their crowd had been asked to dance. Emma was next, and suddenly Pearl found she was alone. She stood a little self-consciously on the edge of the floor, jumping when she felt a tap on her shoulder.

'Hello, Pearl. I'm surprised to see you here. I didn't think this was Derek's scene.'

When Pearl saw it was Kevin, her first instinct was to walk away, but hiding her feelings, she answered, 'I didn't know this was your scene either. Derek's not here. I came with my friends.'

His eyebrows lifted and then he looked her up and down. 'You look a bit tasty tonight. Do you fancy a dance?'

'No, thanks.' She saw his face darken and shivered, hoping he wasn't going to turn nasty.

'I insist,' he said, pulling her on to the dance floor.

The tempo changed to a ballad and as he put his arms around her, she looked up into his handsome face. As they danced, there were many girls eyeing him and he had the pick of them all, but he didn't notice them, concentrating only on her. Despite her resolve, Pearl loved being in his arms, melting against him, but when he spoke softly in her ear, she stiffened.

189

'Do you still think about the night we had it off, Pearl?'

'No ... I don't.'

'Leave it out, you needn't pretend. You loved it, loved me fucking you, and if you ask me nicely, I'll do you again.'

Pearl felt her stomach turn. He made love-making sound so crude, animal-like and she'd been mad to let him get through her defences again. 'No, thanks,' she snapped, trying to break away.

He held her arm fast, now trying to pull her from the dance floor. 'Come on, you needn't play games. My car's outside and the back seat is roomy.'

'No,' she gasped, struggling again.

'Are you all right, Pearl?' Emma asked, rushing to her side.

'She's fine, and you can get lost,' Kevin snapped.

'Let her go,' Emma insisted loudly.

Several heads turned in their direction and with a snarl, Kevin released Pearl. 'Sod you then, it's your loss.' But as they made to walk away, he spat, 'I don't think your mum would want you knocking around with a tart, Emma. I've had Pearl and she was easy.'

Pearl felt the heat rise in her body and, unable to look Emma in the face, she made a dash for the door, her heels wobbling dangerously on the polished floor.

'Wait, Pearl! Wait,' Emma shouted.

As she reached the street, Pearl took in great gulps of air. Her face was still flaming, and she

190

dreaded facing Emma and her friends. She wanted to run, to flee, and jumped when a hand touched her arm.

'It's all right, love,' Emma said softly. 'I don't know what made Kevin Dolby say that about you but I know you're not a tart. He can be a nasty bugger and my mum warned me about him ages ago.'

'Did she?'

'She's worked in the café for years and has seen him grow up. She said he's turned into a nasty sod and blames Dolly. Apparently anything Kevin wants, he gets, so my guess is that he asked you out and you said no. Am I right?'

'Yes,' Pearl said, grabbing the excuse.

'He ain't used to being turned down, and that was his spiteful way of getting his own back. Come on, come inside and forget about Kevin Dolby. He ain't worth wasting your breath on.'

Unable to face going back into the dance hall, Pearl shook her head. 'I think I'd rather go home, but I need my coat and bag. Would you mind getting them for me?'

'All right, but are you sure you won't change your mind?'

'I'd rather go home.'

Pearl slumped against the wall, relieved when shortly after Emma returned with both their coats. 'Oh, you don't have to leave too.'

'You're upset, and my mother would skin me alive if I let you go home on your own. There'll be other nights for dancing and, anyway, I've already told my friends I'm leaving.'

'Did ... did they hear what Kevin said?'

'No, they were well out of earshot.'

Pearl sighed with relief. They spoke little on the way home, and when they arrived Mo looked at them with surprise. 'You're early, and what's the matter, Pearl? Your mascara's run and you look like you've been crying.'

It was Emma who answered. 'Kevin Dolby upset her. She turned him down so he called her a tart.'

Mo's lips tightened. 'I'll see that Dolly hears about this.'

'Please don't tell her,' Pearl cried. 'She'll sack me, you know she will.'

'Yeah, you're probably right. Kevin can do no wrong in Dolly's eyes. All right, I won't say anything, and as I've said to my Emma, keep away from Kevin. He's nothing but trouble.'

'I ... I think I'll look for another job.'

'You could do that, but if you like working in the café it doesn't seem fair. Why don't you hold your hand and if Kevin gets funny again, I can back you up?'

Pearl shook her head, unable to tell them the truth and instead blurting out, 'No, I don't want you to do that. Anyway, as you said, Dolly wouldn't believe us and she'd turn on you too.'

'Don't let that nasty sod chase you out of your job,' Emma said. 'If Mum can't back you up, then I will.'

Pearl's heart ached. Emma and Mo were being so nice. They were indignant with Kevin on her behalf, yet she didn't deserve their support. She *had* slept with Kevin Dolby and what would they think of her if they knew the truth? Would they label her a tart too? With a forced smile she said, 'Thank you, and I'll think about it, but I've got a bit of a headache and I'd like to go to bed now.'

Both Mo and Emma smiled at her sympathetically, but when Pearl climbed into bed she laid awake, gazing up at the ceiling. She was a fool, a complete and utter fool. She'd been determined to keep away from Kevin, yet one smile from his handsome face and, like an idiot, she had melted. Why? She knew what he was like: one minute charming, the next vicious and cruel, yet it hadn't stopped her from almost falling into his arms.

His words rang in her mind and she was unable to hide from the truth any longer. Yes, she *did* think about the night they made love, and he was right, she did want him. He had aroused such wonderful feelings, ones that she yearned to feel again.

Pearl flushed with shame, filled with self-disgust as she turned onto her side and pulled the blankets up to her chin.

The following morning Pearl awoke after a restless night, and as memories of the previous evening flooded her mind, she dressed despondently before making her way downstairs.

'Happy birthday,' Mo and Emma chorused as she walked into the kitchen.

'Oh, thank you. How did you know?'

'Derek told us, and here you are, love,' Mo said, handing her a package and envelope.

'And this is from me,' Emma added as she did the same.

Pearl felt overwhelmed, her heart lifting as she opened her cards. She blinked rapidly as she read the lovely words and, gulping, opened her packages. There was a smart wide black patent belt from Mo, and a make-up bag containing mascara, powder and lipstick from Emma. 'They're lovely. Thank you so much.'

'Emma chose the belt,' Mo said. 'With winter on its way I wanted to get you a nice warm scarf.'

'Leave it out, Mum. She'd rather have the belt. I'm right, ain't I?' Emma said, grinning widely at Pearl.

'Oh, yes, it's just what I wanted. And the make-up's wonderful too.'

'Right, let's have some breakfast,' Mo said, beginning to bustle around. 'It's my treat today so you'll be having more than cereals, Pearl. In fact, I was thinking about our eating arrangements last night. I wondered if you'd rather pay me a bit extra each week and then I'll do your breakfast every day. It seems daft cooking separately. What do you think?'

'Yes, I'd like that.'

'How about another five bob and for that I'll do your laundry too?'

'Oh, yes, please, that would be wonderful.'

Mo chuckled. 'I still can't get over how well spoken and polite you are. I must admit I was a bit worried that you wouldn't fit in at first, but in the short time you've been here you've become like part of the family.'

'Yeah, it's like having a kid sister,' Emma reiterated. 'It's a shame you're going round to Derek's today. We could have had another trip to Petticoat Lane.'

'Maybe next week,' Pearl said, wishing that she didn't have to see Derek. She would have preferred to spend the day with Emma, but couldn't let Derek down again.

'Well, Gran, what do you think?' Derek asked as he placed the ring on the table. 'I got it second-hand from the pawnshop.'

Connie gazed at the diamond in its old-fashioned setting. 'It's very nice, but I still think you should wait a while. Pearl's a nice girl, but you've only been courting since the end of August. She's also very young and might not be ready to settle down.'

'I think a lot of her and don't want to lose her. If she says yes, we could wait until she's eighteen, but at least she'll have my ring on her finger.'

'It'd be better to hold off for another year before proposing.'

'No, I ain't waiting. I've got the ring and I've made up my mind. Pearl's the girl for me and I'm gonna propose today.'

Connie sighed, wishing that Derek could see what was under his nose. Since moving in with Mo and her daughter, Pearl was changing. She was making friends of her own age and seeing less of Derek. She gazed worriedly at her grandson. He was going to be hurt, she could feel it in her bones, and despite liking the girl, she wished he had never met Pearl Button.

Pearl was on her way to Derek's when she saw Kevin Dolby walking towards her. She hurriedly

195

crossed the road, but he crossed too, stopping in front of her and barring the path. His eyes, she saw, were full of contrition. 'I owe you an apology, Pearl.'

The memory of the humiliation he'd caused her on the dance floor was fresh, and her mouth tightened. 'Leave me alone. Just go away and leave me alone.'

'Look, I know I was out of order last night and I'm sorry.'

'You told Emma that you'd slept with me, and you ... you called me a tart.'

'I know, but it's your own fault. You shouldn't have turned me down.'

'What did you expect? You know I'm going out with Derek and shouldn't have asked.'

'Yes, but as I said before, it was me you slept with. Admit it, Pearl. You'd rather go out with me.'

'I ... I wouldn't.'

He smiled, his voice soft. 'Why don't you come with me for a little drive out into the country? We need to talk and can find somewhere nice and secluded.'

'I'm on my way to Derek's.'

'Sod Derek.'

'I can't let him down, Kevin.'

His whole demeanor suddenly changed, his eyes hardening. 'I don't see why not.'

'I can't because he's expecting me, and not only that, his gran will have cooked dinner and–'

'Sod his gran too,' Kevin spat. 'Now I ain't asking you, I'm telling you. You're coming out with me.'

He reached out, viciously grasping her arm, and Pearl tensed. Last night she had admitted to herself that she still wanted him, still fancied him, but in this mood he was dangerous and all she felt was fear. With a quick jerk she pulled her arm out of Kevin's grasp, her shoulders hunched as she dashed past him.

Pearl didn't look back and ran the rest of the way to Derek's house. He opened the door to her knock and, seeing his huge bulk, she threw herself into his arms with relief, seeing them only as a refuge from her tangled emotions. She'd have to leave the café, it was the only way to avoid Kevin, but loving the job, her heart sank at the thought.

'Are you all right, love?' Derek asked.

'Yes, I'm fine,' she lied, forcing a smile as she stepped out of his arms.

With Derek she was safe, his home a haven, and with him her feelings were under control.

By three thirty they had enjoyed a delicious Sunday roast, but since she'd arrived Pearl could sense a strange atmosphere. Connie was un-usually quiet, and Derek seemed on edge. She had been thrilled when Connie handed her a card and present, and though she thought it appalling, she thanked her profusely for the long, old-fashioned flannelette nightdress.

'You'll be needing that with winter coming along,' Connie said.

'Yes, I'm sure I will, and thanks again. It ... it's lovely.'

'Here's my card, Pearl. Come into the front

room and I'll give you your present.'

There was a grunt of displeasure from Connie, and Pearl frowned, wondering what was wrong as she followed Derek out of the room.

'Sit down, love,' Derek said, his face flushed.

Pearl sat, and at the same time Derek kneeled in front of her. With her heart beginning to thump she saw him pull a small box out of his pocket. Pearl guessed what was coming and gulped, her breath caught in her throat. He was going to propose, but now that the moment had arrived, she found herself wanting to jump up and run. Since moving in with Mo and Emma, she was enjoying life. She loved going dancing, loved being with girls close to her own age, loved the music, the excitement. If she accepted Derek's proposal she would have to become a staid, married woman. Was she really ready for that?

'Will ... will you marry me?'

Pearl's eyes fixed on the ring. She thought about Kevin, how she was still attracted to him, but an attraction that was over-shadowed by fear. Derek, though, was offering her what, until now, she thought she wanted: a home where she would be part of a family, cherished and loved for the first time in her life. Still she hesitated, but then Derek spoke again.

'I don't expect you to marry me right away, love. I thought maybe in about a year, when you're eighteen.'

A year, they would wait a year, and she smiled with relief before saying, 'Yes, all right, I'll marry you.'

'Oh, Pearl, that's great.' And, leaning forward,

he pulled her into his arms. She closed her eyes tightly as he kissed her, but thankfully it was brief.

'There's only one thing, Pearl. It's me gran. I'm all she's got and I'd hate to leave her on her own. Would you mind moving in here with us when we get married?'

'Of course I wouldn't. It's what I expected and what I want.'

He jumped to his feet and, taking her hand, he dragged her back to the kitchen. 'She said yes, Gran,' he cried, 'and we're getting married in a year.'

Connie smiled thinly. 'Congratulations.'

There was a restraint in Connie's manner and Pearl frowned. Perhaps she was worried about being left on her own. 'I'm happy to move in here with you and Derek when we get married.'

Connie nodded, but she hardly spoke until Derek left the room half an hour later. After a quick look to ensure that the door was closed, she leaned forward. 'You've changed lately, Pearl, and you're not seeing much of Derek. You're out and about with Emma Price, no doubt meeting lads of your own age. Derek's a lot older than you, and the truth is I expected you to turn him down. A lot can happen in a year and I just hope you ain't gonna change your mind.'

'I won't change my mind.'

'I've told you before. I don't want my Derek hurt.'

'I won't hurt him.' As she said these words, Pearl really meant them. She would marry Derek and make him a good wife. She was just relieved that she had a year of freedom first.

Kevin banged on Nobby Clark's door, still in a foul mood. He was smarting that Pearl had turned him down again. Since that first time, she felt like his property and his fists clenched at the thought of her sleeping with Derek Lewis. His jaws ground. Right, sod her, if she wanted Derek she could have him and he'd never ask her out again. In fact, he really would make a play for Emma Price. She wasn't a bad-looking girl, but then again, she was a bit lippy. He remembered how she had intervened at the dance and he frowned. Emma wasn't like Pearl; she seemed fearless and not the sort of girl he could control. In fact, he thought, changing his mind, it might be better to give her a wide berth.

His trips to Soho were costing him a lot of money, and that was something he was short of at the moment. Once again his fists clenched in anger. With Pearl as his girlfriend he would've had what he wanted on hand, and could have taught her a few tricks.

Nobby Clark opened the door, forcing Kevin's thoughts to one side. 'Hello, mate, can I come in?'

'Yeah, I suppose so.'

As Kevin stepped inside he saw Dick Smedley, but the man offered no welcome.

'Watcha, Dick, how's things?'

'What do you want, Kevin?'

'I've come to see if you've got a job in the offing.'

'I thought you didn't want to work with

amateurs again.'

'Yeah, that's what you called us,' Nobby said as he sat at the table.

'Look, I've told you before, I didn't mean it. I was unnerved that night and you can't blame me for that.'

'Maybe, but you seem to forget that I'm the boss and I want a bit of respect.'

Kevin hid his feelings. If he wanted back in, he'd have to suck up to Nobby, but it went against the grain. The bloke was a loser and couldn't organise a piss-up in a brewery, but the need for money was paramount. 'I know you're the boss, Nobby, and we couldn't do the jobs without you. As I said, I lost it, but it won't happen again.'

'What do you think, Dick? Shall we let him back in?'

'I still ain't happy about that night. He was shit scared, and so keen to get away that he almost drove off without us.'

'I didn't. I'd never do that.'

'I only just managed to get into the back of the van before you shot off.'

'I admit I was keen to get away – that alarm was deafening – but I wouldn't have left you behind.'

Dick's eyes narrowed, but to Kevin's relief he said, 'All right, I suppose I'll have to take your word for it.'

Nobby smiled tightly. 'We'll give you the benefit of the doubt, Kevin. We need a driver so you're in. Take a seat and we'll tell you what we've got planned.'

20

When Pearl had shown her ring to Mo and Emma, their reactions hadn't been favourable. Both thought she was too young to think about marriage, but Emma was most vociferous in her opinions. She told Pearl in no uncertain terms that she was mad, that Derek was too old for her, and that she should go out with other men, not settle on the first one to propose.

The costermongers had reacted differently, all of them loud in their congratulations, and though they had ribbed Derek at first, some even saying he was a cradle snatcher, they seemed genuinely pleased. Pearl was one of their own now, and none had forgotten her hand in finding Frank Hanswell's son.

Three weeks had now passed since their engagement, and Pearl was enjoying life. She was still attending art classes, but going out and about with Emma for another couple of nights a week, it meant she was seeing less of Derek. He didn't seem to mind, content that she was now wearing his ring, and whilst she was out dancing with Emma, he spent extra time at the gym in preparation for his next fight.

Pearl still suspected that Alice Freeman was pinching her tips, but so far hadn't caught her. In her vigilance she noticed that Bernie was acting strangely too. He would leave the counter at odd times, Alice quickly stepping in to take his place, and though this put more work on to Pearl, she was coping well. Few customers had cause for complaint, but she still found it odd that Bernie chose to disappear at their busiest times.

Pearl was clearing a table when Kevin came downstairs. Since her engagement he hadn't spoken to her, and this had led to her job hunting taking a back seat. She still flicked through the local paper each week, seeing jobs on offer in shops and factories, but none offered the perks of the café with free lunch every day. As long as Kevin stayed away from her she was able to keep her feeling under control, but when her heart lurched every time she saw him, she wasn't sure if it was love she was feeling, or fear.

Before the lunchtime rush had started, Dolly marched out of the kitchen, followed by Bernie. Her stance was stiff, her face red with anger. 'Alice, come here,' she yelled. 'I want to talk to you.'

Bernie took Pearl's arm. 'Stay down this end for a while and out of the way.'

At first Pearl couldn't hear what Dolly was saying to Alice, but then her voice rose to a roar. 'Don't take me for a fool, girl! We've been in this business too long and know all the tricks.'

'It wasn't me,' Alice cried. 'It must have been Pearl.'

'No, lady, don't try to pass the buck. My husband knew that money was going missing and it didn't take him long to work out who was dipping in the till. We've a good mind to call the police and have you done for thieving.'

'No. Oh, please don't do that.'

Dolly's hands flapped, her temper high. 'Get your coat and get out. I don't know how you got references from your last job, but you certainly won't get any from me. In fact, I'll make sure that word passes in the area that you're a thief.'

White-faced, Alice grabbed her coat from the hook. She took her bag from under the counter, and then Pearl's mouth gaped as Alice almost flung her out of the way in her haste to leave.

She regained her footing as the door crashed shut, Bernie shaking his head. 'Alice thought she could take us for mugs, Pearl, but I knew what she was up to.'

'What do you mean?'

'She was fiddling the till. I noticed takings were down a bit weeks ago so I decided to keep an eye on her, and though I'm sorry to say it Pearl, I had to check up on you too. It didn't take me long to realise that Alice was always eager to take over the counter, and when I started to leave it more often, she got greedy.'

'Well, Bernie, that's got rid of her,' Dolly said as she joined them. 'You'd better stick a card in the window again and let's hope we don't have a long wait before someone applies for the job. It's a bloody shame. I liked the girl and still can't believe that she was robbing us.'

'She was at it, all right, and for a good few bob too.'

'Huh, well, at least you caught her out. The trouble is it ain't the first time and I doubt it'll be the last. Finding staff we can trust isn't easy.'

'We've got a good one in Pearl.'

'Yes, you're right,' Dolly said, her face softening, and touching Pearl's arm she added, 'Until we find another waitress, I'm afraid you'll have to cope on your own again.'

'I don't mind.'

'You're a good kid and I'll stick a bit extra in your wages again. In fact, we'll give you a rise too. I know you're only seventeen, but good staff are hard to find and we don't want to lose you.'

Pearl was happy and relieved. She hadn't really wanted to find another job and it would be awful to leave the Dolbys in the lurch. She liked working in the café, and as long as Kevin left her alone it would be fine, especially as she'd be earning more money.

When the costermongers began to arrive they showed no surprise that Pearl was covering the tables on her own. Waitresses came and went frequently in the café, but it was nice when some said they hoped she wouldn't be joining the exodus. She was coping with the rush, but only just, and wondered how long they would have to wait before finding a replacement for Alice.

'What happened to Boadicea?' Derek asked during a lull.

Pearl leaned forward, saying quietly, 'She got the sack for fiddling the till.'

'Huh, I ain't surprised. You must have been right about her pocketing your tips too.'

'Yes, and maybe I should have told Bernie.'

Neither noticed that Bernie had left the counter and Pearl jumped when he spoke from behind her. 'So, she was diddling you too, and yes, you should have told me.'

'I ... I'm sorry, but I was too frightened to accuse her without proof.'

'I tried to keep an eye on her too, but couldn't catch her at it,' Derek said.

'She was a fly one, that's for sure, but don't worry, the word's already going round.'

Derek chuckled. 'Talk about jungle drums. I doubt the girl will get another job in this area.'

'One of the factories might take her on.'

'Yeah, maybe.'

Pearl saw customers waiting and, leaving Derek and Bernie chatting, she went to take their orders. Soon after, Frank Hanwell came in, and as he took a seat their eyes met. She had another customer to serve before going to his table, but was soon by his side.

'Hello, Frank, what can I get you?'

'I'll have the sausages, onion and mash. I've got a bit of good news too. Eric seems to be coming round. He's talking to me again, and last night he let me tuck him into bed.'

'That's wonderful.'

'It's a step forward, but I wonder if we'll ever see him smile again. He's still unnaturally quiet, and he won't go to school. Not only that, my old woman wants us to move out of the area. Eric won't come near the market and she thinks it would help if we make a fresh start somewhere else.'

'Maybe she's right.'

'I've lived here all my life, and the stall was handed down to me from my father. It's all I know.'

'There are other markets, Frank.'

'Yeah, I suppose so, but it's still gonna be hard.'

'If it helps Eric, it'll be worth it.'

He nodded, but then three other costermongers sat at his table, bringing the conversation to an end. The pace slowed a little after that, but each time Pearl passed Frank's table, she couldn't help noticing how distant and distracted he looked. The other men were chatting, but Frank was picking at his food, his eyes faraway. Five minutes later he called Pearl over and, as though talking to her earlier had sealed his decision, his voice was lighter as he spoke.

'Bring us all a cup of tea, would you, love? I've got something to tell this lot.'

Pearl saw the puzzled glances that passed between the men but hurried to the counter, returning with the teas to hear Frank telling them that he was leaving the market. 'My stall's up for grabs. If you know anyone who might be interested in taking the pitch, let me know.'

'Blimey, Frank, what brought this on?' Charlie Slater asked.

'Her indoors thinks that Eric needs to get out of this area, and I reckon she's right.'

They all nodded in understanding, Charlie saying, 'I know a decent geezer who's after a pitch. How much do you want for it?'

Pearl moved away, her face showing her confusion as she went to the counter.

'What's up?' Bernie asked.

'Frank's moving out of the area and is giving up his stall. There's talk of someone buying the pitch, but I thought they rented them from the council.'

'You're right, they don't own their own pitches, but it's a busy market and a spot rarely becomes available. They're like gold dust, so when one comes up, someone who's willing to pay is tipped the wink.'

'But surely anyone can apply to the council for the empty spot?'

Bernie chuckled. 'Yeah, that might be how it's supposed to be, but the costermongers have got unwritten rules the council knows nothing about.'

Pearl shook her head, still bewildered as she walked away, but the lunchtime rush was almost over and it was time to finish clearing the tables.

Feeling tired and washed out, Pearl was glad when her shift ended. She had an art lesson that evening, but still hadn't managed to get a grip on seascapes. Her efforts at painting the ocean lacked depth, colour, movement, and though she had studied other paintings on the subject, her own attempts looked flat.

As she walked through the market she was frowning, hardly aware that she had reached Derek's stall.

'Cheer up, it might never happen,' he quipped. 'What are you looking so down in the mouth about?'

'It's nothing really. It's just that I've got art classes this evening and my attempts at painting the sea are dreadful.'

'I can't believe that.'

'It doesn't help that I've never seen the sea.'

'Blimey, we can soon fix that. I tell you what,

I'll take you down to Brighton on Sunday.'

Pearl's eyes lit up. 'Really? Oh, I'd love that.'

'You might not be so sure when we get there. It's nearly the end of November and it's bound to be a bit nippy.'

'I don't mind. In fact I hope the sea is rough and the waves huge.'

Derek grinned. 'You're a strange one, Pearl. Most people want sunshine when they go to the seaside.'

'Yes, but then the ocean would be boring. Oh, Derek, I can't wait to see it,' she cried, giving a little skip of delight.

He smiled again, and as a customer walked up to the stall, showing an interest in a rather large teapot, Pearl said a hurried goodbye, her steps lighter as she made for home.

Derek was lovely, he really was, and her heart warmed towards him. He might not be an oil painting, but he had a heart of gold, and though she had at first baulked at the idea of marrying him, it might not be so bad after all.

21

On Sunday, Pearl stood on Brighton beach, gazing at the scene in wonderment. Even the pebbles under her feet held fascination as she picked her way across them, stooping to pick up one after another as she studied the colours and strata, just as Miss Rosen had taught her to do at the orphanage.

Moving closer to the foaming waves, Pearl stood transfixed as they ebbed and flowed. She stepped forward, jumping back like a delighted child when the next wave tumbled in, almost soaking her shoes. She laughed, turning to look at Derek as he lumbered down to her side, face red from the whipping wind.

'Have you had enough now, love? We've been on the beach for an hour and I don't know about you, but I could do with some grub.'

'Just five more minutes,' she begged.

'All right, and I'm glad to see you're looking better.'

'It must have been something I ate, but my tummy's fine now.'

Pearl looked up at the sky, saw gulls soaring, wings silhouetted against the dark clouds, their plaintive cries echoing in the bleak seascape. Rain began to fall, and reluctantly she dragged her eyes away, trying to hold it all in her memory. Head down, she stooped again to pick up a shell, fascinated by the texture and colour. 'Oh, Derek, isn't this lovely?'

'Yeah, if you say so, but you're getting soaked. I think we should find some shelter.'

Pearl slipped the small shell into her pocket, her heart once again going out to this lovely man. He looked so wet, miserable, his expression hang-dog. All right, he wasn't much to look at, but nowadays she hardly noticed. Instead it was his personality that shone through, and suddenly she knew without a doubt that she really did want to marry him.

Pearl grabbed his hand, smiling widely. 'All right, come on then. Food it is.'

They scrambled across the beach, Pearl throwing a last look over her shoulder before they headed for the nearest café. She shivered as they entered the warmth, the smell of food suddenly making her stomach turn. Mo had insisted she have a huge breakfast before she left, but she'd been unable to eat more than a few mouthfuls before being sick. Now once again she felt queasy.

When the waitress came to their side, Derek ordered roast lamb, but Pearl shook her head. 'Just a cup of tea for me, please.'

'You need more than that,' Derek said, looking at her with concern.

'I had a big breakfast,' she lied. 'Honestly, I'm not hungry.'

He shook his head doubtfully, but said no more, and as his meal was put him front of him, Pearl looked away as he ate. The clouds thickened, rain teeming down and beating against the windows of the small café as though trying to gain admittance.

'I reckon we'll have to make our way home,' Derek said as he finished his meal and sipped his tea. 'I can't see the weather brightening up.'

Pearl didn't mind. She had seen the sea, it was etched into her memory and once again her fingers itched to paint. Derek paid for the meal and, head down against the driving rain and wind, they hurried to the railway station.

In the waiting room, a small fire burned in the hearth and they made for the nearest bench, hands in pockets as they huddled inside their coats. Fortunately they didn't have long to wait for a train back to London, the carriage empty as they climbed inside. As they sat down, Derek put his arm around her and Pearl sank against him, the smell of his damp clothes assailing her nostrils.

'Shame about the weather, but at least you've seen the sea now.'

'Yes, and it was wonderful,' Pearl said. She yawned, her eyes closed, and then she knew no more until they arrived at Clapham Junction.

'Wake up, sleepy head, we're home.'

Pearl opened her eyes, for a moment bewildered, and then realising that she had slept for the whole journey, she stumbled to her feet. 'Oh, Derek, I'm so sorry.'

'Don't be daft, love. I think working the tables on your own in the café must be wearing you out.'

Derek took her arm as she alighted from the carriage, but as her feet touched the platform, she swayed.

'I don't think this is just tiredness, Pearl. I think you've caught a chill or something. Come on, let's get you home.'

She knew Derek was right, but as the only waitress in the café they'd be in a terrible fix without her. Maybe Mo would have a couple of aspirins or something, and if she went straight to bed, she'd be all right in the morning.

Pearl did feel better the next morning, and though she couldn't face food, she felt strong enough to go to work.

The breakfast rush was almost over when a woman came into the café, Bernie greeting her. 'Hello, Madge, long time no see. How are you?'

'I'm fine, and I've come about the job.'

'Blimey, are you sure?'

'Yeah, I've had enough of working evenings and weekends.'

'Right, you'd better have a word with Dolly.'

Bernie went to the kitchen, whilst Pearl surreptitiously studied the woman. She looked to be in her mid-to-late forties, her eyes small, but bright. With short, coarse brown hair and a thin face, she reminded Pearl somewhat of a fierce terrier dog.

Dolly came bustling out of the kitchen, a smile on her face. 'Madge, nice to see you. Bernie tells me that you're looking for a job.'

'That's right.'

'After being a silver service waitress, it'll be a bit of a comedown.'

'All the functions are in the evening or at weekends. My boys are grown up now and I'd rather do day work.'

'What about the money? I can't pay you what you're used to.'

'With two of my lads at work, they're stumping up their keep. I don't mind taking a drop in wages.'

'Well, if you're sure, Madge, the job's yours. It'll be nice to have you working here.'

'Smashing, and if you like I'll start straight away.'

'With only one waitress, it'd be a godsend.'

Dolly turned, beckoning Pearl to her side. 'This

213

is Madge Harding, my cousin.'

'Hello,' Pearl said shyly.

'Nice to meet you, love. Perhaps you could show me the ropes?'

'I'd be pleased to.'

'Right, I'll leave you to it,' Dolly said brusquely. 'I've still got Gertie and Mo working for me, and once the tables are cleared we'll have a gossip over a cup of tea.'

As soon as Dolly was out of sight, Madge turned to Pearl again. 'How do we split the tables?'

'We split them in half, one section at this end, and the other nearest the kitchen.'

'Well, as I'm the last in, I suppose I'll be doing this end.'

'Er ... well, no, not if you don't want to.'

'Bless you, love, I don't mind. In fact it's only fair. Now, what else do I need to know?'

Pearl told Madge all she could think of, both women working happily together as they cleared the tables. Despite her fierce demeanour, Madge turned out to be a friendly soul, and when they took the stacks of crockery out to the kitchen, both Gertie and Mo greeted her with delight.

Dolly told Pearl to fetch them each a cup of tea, and when she returned it was to hear Madge saying, 'That Pearl seems a nice girl, but where on earth did you find her? She talks like she's got a plum in her mouth and certainly doesn't come from these parts.'

'As she's right behind you, why don't you ask her yourself?' Gertie chuckled.

'Gawd, sorry, ducks,' Madge said, her face red as she turned. 'Well, at least I wasn't running you down. I'm a nosy old biddy and must admit I'm curious about where you hail from.'

'I was brought up in an orphanage in Surrey.'

'You poor kid. Don't you know who your parents are?'

'No. I was left on the steps.'

'Christ, that's awful. So you haven't any family at all?'

'None that I know of.'

'Where do you live now?'

'I have a room in Mo's house.'

'Yeah, and she's fast becoming one of the family. Her and my Emma are now as thick as thieves.'

'That's nice,' Madge said. 'What about you, Gertie? How are you doing these days?'

'I ain't too bad, but my stomach still plays me up now and again.'

Dolly spoke, her voice sharp. 'You and Mo are both Mrs Neverwells. You're never out of that doctor's surgery and he must be sick of the sight of the pair of you.'

'Now then, Dolly, don't exaggerate,' Gertie protested.

'I ain't, but enough gossip for now. You can get on with that washing-up, and you, Mo, get back to the vegetables.'

Madge winked at Pearl, the two of them going back to the dining room. 'I see Dolly's as bossy as ever. I know we're related, but she still scares the shit out of me.'

'And me,' Bernie called, 'but if you don't want

215

her to hear you, you'd best keep your voice down, Madge.'

The woman's head shot round, eyeing the kitchen door with fear, whilst both Pearl and Bernie broke out into laughter.

'Only kidding,' Bernie spluttered.

'Oh, you bugger,' Madge said, but she soon joined in the laugher. 'Well,' she said, wiping eyes, which were wet with mirth, 'at least it's going to be all right working with you two.'

Pearl placed the tray of cups on the counter, deciding that she already liked Madge, and though she'd miss the extra money in her wage packet, she was glad that the woman had applied for the job.

Madge turned out to be a comic and often had Pearl helpless with laughter. As a local she knew many of the costermongers, giving them as good as she got in light-hearted fun.

Nearly two weeks had passed, and the only problem was Pearl's continuing ill health. It was becoming a real concern.

When she got up on Friday morning she was once again feeling nauseous, and as she sat opposite Mo at the breakfast table, her food uneaten, the woman eyed her thoughtfully. She then dropped the bombshell.

'Pearl, have you ... well ... have you been with Derek?'

'Been with him? What do you mean?'

'Er ... have you slept with him?'

'No, of course not.'

'Blimey, that's a relief, and I'm sorry for being

suspicious. I thought with you being sick in the mornings that you might be pregnant.'

Pearl's face stretched in surprise. 'Pregnant! You think I'm having a baby?'

'No, not now you've told me that haven't slept with Derek. I'm sorry, love, I should have known better. You're a good girl, but as I said, with you being sick and all...'

Pearl stared at Mo, her eyes transfixed with shock. She couldn't be – she just couldn't... Yes, she had missed once, but surely that didn't mean anything? Her mind tried to calculate dates, but so much had happened in such a short time that she'd lost track. She'd left her first bedsit, moved in with Connie and Derek for a while and then ended up here. Oh God ... and as realisation dawned, Pearl's face drained of colour. It wasn't just one period she had missed – it was two. With a gasp she stumbled to her feet and into the hall, taking the stairs two at a time as she fled to the sanctuary of her bedroom.

No! Oh, no! She was pregnant. But it wasn't Derek's baby she was carrying.

Pearl was lying on her bed when Mo tapped gently on the door but, unable to face her, she buried her head in the pillow. She heard the door open, and hunched her shoulders.

'Well, Pearl, from your reaction, I think I'm right after all. Come on, it ain't the end of the world. You're not the first girl to get herself pregnant before the wedding and I doubt you'll be the last. At least you're engaged to Derek and now you'll just have to get married as soon as possible. You ain't showing yet, so it won't be so bad.'

A sob rose in Pearl's chest. She had expected disgust, censure, but instead Mo was being so kind. What would her reaction be when she found out the truth?

'Try to pull yourself together, love, or you'll be late for work. Have a chat with Derek as soon as you get the chance, and don't worry, I reckon he'll be as pleased as punch. Anyone can see that he thinks the world of you.'

Pearl gasped, her whole body shaking and, obviously bewildered, Mo continued to pat her back. The door opened again, Emma coming into the room.

'What's going on?' she demanded. 'What's the matter with Pearl?'

'Shall I tell her, love?' Mo asked.

Pearl fought to bring herself under control, managing to nod her head in agreement, but couldn't look at Emma as Mo broke the news.

'Pregnant!' she gasped. 'Blimey, you soppy cow. Does Derek know?'

With another sob, Pearl shook her head. She would have to face Derek, but dreaded his reaction. She was carrying another man's child and there was no way he'd marry her now. Unable to put coherent thoughts in order, her mind raced. Connie would go mad too, and there was Dolly Dolby. What would she say when she found out that Kevin was the father?

Kevin! Kevin was the baby's father! Her stomach lurched. She had been denying her feelings for him for so long, but now that she was carrying his child they overwhelmed her. Despite the way he'd behaved – despite the flaws in his character – she was in love with him.

When Pearl finally dashed into the café she was half an hour late, but instead of giving her a reprimand, Bernie puffed out his cheeks in relief.

'I was worried that you weren't going to show up. Madge is late too, and Dolly's in a right old state.'

'I'm sorry,' Pearl told him, tying her apron hurriedly.

'You don't look too good, girl, and you look like you've been crying.'

'I ... I'm fine.'

'If you say so, but perhaps you're coming down with a cold.'

'Yes, maybe,' she said, thankful for the excuse.

The morning rush had just started and Madge still hadn't arrived. Pearl took her first order through to the kitchen.

'You look awful,' Dolly said.

'I think I'm coming down with a cold.' Pearl was glad to grasp at Bernie's comment. Mo wasn't due in yet, but she dreaded her arrival. She'd promised not to say anything, but Pearl knew how much the woman loved a good gossip. There wouldn't be a chance to talk to Derek until her break, but if Mo opened her mouth the news would spread like wildfire. Please, God, she prayed, let him hear it from me.

Madge came into the kitchen.

'Where have you been?' Dolly snapped.

'Sorry, but I ain't feeling well. I've got an

appointment at the doctor's but not until eleven thirty.'

'You look all right to me.'

'Have a heart, Dolly. When I woke up this morning I was in a terrible state, so wet with sweat that I had to have a bath. I may be a bit late, but I still turned up for work.'

'All right, don't go on about it, and get on with your work.' Dolly's eyes flicked to Pearl, 'and that goes for you too.'

As they scuttled back into the dining room, Madge threw Pearl a wink. 'Dolly missed her vocation. She should have been a bleeding sergeant major.'

Pearl managed a small smile but her heart wasn't in it. In truth, tears were just below the surface but she fought them as she tackled the breakfast rush. How had it happened? She'd only slept with Kevin once, yet she was pregnant. *Please let him want me. Please let him want our baby.*

Derek came in at eight thirty but she could hardly look at him, just murmuring that she needed to talk to him later. He looked puzzled, but seeing how pushed she was he didn't ask questions.

At last the café emptied, and at ten thirty Bernie called out, 'Pearl, you still look awful. Madge can manage now so why don't you have a break?'

Pearl picked up a stack of crockery and went to the kitchen. 'Dolly, I'm just about to take a break. Is it all right if I pop out for a while?'

'What for?'

'There ... there's something important I have to do.'

Dolly heaved a sigh. 'All right, but don't be long. Madge has to be at the doctor's for half-past eleven.'

'Good luck,' Mo called.

'Why does she need luck?' Dolly asked.

Mo and Pearl looked at each other, both stuck for words, Pearl's face now livid with colour. It was Mo who managed to stutter an answer, 'Er ... she's going to sort out the wedding date with Derek.'

Without giving Dolly a chance to speak again, Pearl swiftly left the kitchen, still wearing her apron as she made for Derek's stall.

He saw her coming and grinned. 'Watcha, love.'

'I ... I need to talk to you,' she stammered.

Frank's voice rose raucously from the next stall, 'Apples – Bramley apples. Come on, ladies, only sixpence a pound.'

Derek glanced at Frank and said sadly, 'I still can't believe that Frank's leaving the market. He's been pitched next to me for donkey's years. Anyway, love, what do you want to talk to me about?'

'Alone ... we need to be alone.'

'There ain't much chance of that. Can't it wait until tonight?'

'No ... it must be now.'

'Frank,' Derek called, 'can you watch me stall for a while?'

'Yeah, all right.'

'We'll go for a walk, will that do?' Derek asked as he took Pearl's arm.

She nodded, feeling sick inside. She may not be in love with Derek, but was very fond of him and if this hadn't happened she'd have married him. Unbidden, a thought popped into Pearl's mind. *Yes, but would you really have gone through with it?* Pearl shook her head against the question. She'd been enjoying life, loved living with Emma and Mo, and had been relieved when Derek offered a long engagement. A year was a long way off, and she had avoided thinking about marriage. Now everything was going to change and stark reality was staring her in the face. She was going to lose Derek, lose his friendship, his protection. Tears gathered, but she managed to hold them back. She had betrayed this lovely man, she was going to hurt him badly, and however bad his reaction, it would be no more than she deserved.

They walked to the end of the market, and along Shuttleworth Road, Pearl's head low. There was a pub ahead and as they drew alongside it, Derek stuck his head inside.

'The snug's empty. Come on, we can talk in there.'

With her head still low, Pearl sat at a table, and when Derek asked her what she wanted to drink her throat felt as if it was closing. She managed to speak, a croak, 'Nothing, thanks.'

He walked to the bar, soon returning with half a pint of beer to take the seat beside her. 'Now then, what's this all about?'

She couldn't look at him, she just couldn't, her voice still a strangled whisper when she finally was able to spit out the words. 'I ... I'm having a baby.'

There was a moment of silence, but then

Derek's voice was loud in protest. 'Don't be daft. Talk sense, Pearl. You can't be having a baby. We ain't ... well, done it, if you know what I mean.'

'Yes, I know, but I ... I'm definitely pregnant.'

There was another moment of silence and finally Pearl was able to glance at Derek, a swift look that showed his face white with shock.

'Who was it, Pearl? I'll bloody kill him.'

'I can't tell you. He ... he doesn't know yet.'

Derek seemed to slump in his seat, his head shaking in denial. 'I can't believe this. Here, wait a minute, did he force you?'

With all her heart, Pearl wished she could say yes. At least that might ease this lovely man's pain, but with a sigh she said, 'No, he didn't force me.'

'I'll still kill him.'

'No, Derek, please don't say that. I'm so sorry, I really am. It only happened once, that was all.'

'Huh, it only takes once. Bloody hell, Pearl, we're engaged. I was gonna marry you.'

Pearl looked at him at last and, unable to bear the hurt she could see in his eyes, tugged the ring from her finger. She then laid it on the table and rose to her feet, choking back tears as she ran out of the pub, leaving Derek slumped in his seat, looking like a whipped dog.

'Here, Pearl, where's Derek?' Frank called as she hurried through the market.

She couldn't answer him, couldn't speak. It had been awful, dreadful, Derek's pain terrible to see. He would never forgive her and she didn't blame him.

The café was almost empty when Pearl stumbled through the door and sank down at the nearest table. Head buried in her arms, a huge sob rose, a dam of tears bursting as she finally broke.

'Pearl, what's wrong?' Madge asked, hurrying to her side.

Unable to answer, she was aware only of Madge tugging her arm, urging her to the kitchen. 'Come on, girl, let's get you out of here.'

Somehow Pearl managed to drag herself up and as they entered the kitchen Madge said, 'Dolly, I've got to go now, but Pearl's in a right old state.'

'All right, get yourself off.'

Madge patted Pearl's back before hurrying out, Dolly then saying, 'Now then, what's all this? Mo's told us that you're pregnant and I must say I'm shocked. Still, it ain't the end of the world and I can't see why you're so upset. Surely Derek has said he'll marry you as soon as possible.'

Pearl knew there was no way out. She took a deep shuddering breath, struggling to bring herself under control. 'The ... the baby isn't his.'

They were all gawking, faces stretched with shock, but it was Dolly who voiced their thoughts. 'My God, you look such a little innocent, but now you're telling us that you're pregnant by another man. Who's the father then?'

'I ... I can't tell you.'

'Why not? Is he married?'

'No, he isn't, but he doesn't know yet.'

'Well, you'd better tell him, my girl, and as soon as possible.'

Yes, but how? Pearl thought. She hadn't seen Kevin for a couple of days, and when she did he ignored her. Worse was to come when Mo spoke.

'I thought you were a nice girl and that's why I offered you a room. You've only been around these parts for about five months, and in that short time you got yourself engaged to Derek Lewis. Now you've got the nerve to tell us you're pregnant, but it ain't his baby. Well, madam, after your shift you can pack your stuff and get out of my house. I don't want my Emma associating with the likes of you.'

With a sob Pearl fled the kitchen, and the café. She heard Bernie's shout, but nothing stopped her.

Tears blinded Pearl's eyes and she didn't see Bessie Penfold sweeping the pavement outside her shop until she collided with her.

'Blimey, girl, watch where you're going! Gawd, what's the matter? Has Dolly Dolby been on the warpath again? That woman can't keep wait-resses for more than five minutes.'

Without waiting for a reply, Bessie took Pearl's arm, ushering her into the shop and locking the door behind them. 'I've seen more girls leave that café than number nineteen buses. Mind you, I've never seen one leaving in a state like this. Hold on and I'll put the kettle on. You look like you could do with a cup of good strong tea.'

Bessie bustled out to the back room, but by the time she returned, Pearl had managed to calm down only a little. She was handed a cup of tea that looked almost black, but found her hands shaking so much that the cup rattled in the saucer.

'Now then. Do you want to talk about it?'

As she looked into the old woman's dark eyes, Pearl saw gentleness, wisdom, and with the need to unburden, the words spilled from her mouth, ending with, '...and I ... I've got to leave my room too. Mo is disgusted with me.'

'Don't take any notice of Mo Price. She's no better than she should be. I could tell you a few things about her that might shock you, but I ain't one to gossip. Right, let's take this one step at a time. First you need to have a word with Kevin Dolby, but if you ask me he'll try to squirm out of it.'

'But he can't – surely he can't? Oh God, what will I do?'

'You could get rid of it.'

Pearl stared at the woman in horror, her hand inadvertently touching her stomach. 'Oh, no, I couldn't do that.'

'Yeah, I suppose it could be a bit risky, but you could have it adopted.'

Pearl frantically shook her head. 'No, I'd never let my baby be adopted.'

'You can't support a kid on your own and, if you ask me, it would be the best thing for it.'

'No it wouldn't,' Pearl cried. 'I came from an orphanage and know what it's like. I've seen children fostered out and then returned, sometimes traumatised by what happened to them.'

'I said adopted, not fostered out.'

'I know, but some of the children put up for adoption were returned too. Can you imagine what it was like for them? They dreamed of being part of a proper family, but some people only want perfection, not a traumatised child who may wet the bed or find it difficult to settle into a normal home.'

'It wouldn't be like that for a baby.'

Pearl touched her stomach again. She knew what it was like to be without parents, without love, always wondering why she had been put in an orphanage. Always wondering who her mother was, her father was, and why they'd rejected her. She shook her head again. No matter what, she was determined that her baby wouldn't suffer the same fate. Her voice was strong as she said, 'Whether Kevin marries me or not, I'm keeping my baby.'

'All right, I can see why you feel like that, but it ain't gonna be easy for you.'

'I don't care. I'll manage somehow.'

'Yeah, I think you will,' Bessie said softly. 'Anyway, for the time being you need a place to stay. I've got a spare room and, though it ain't up to much, you're welcome to it. If you need a job for a while you can help me out in the shop. It's getting a bit much for me nowadays, but I won't be able to pay you much.'

Pearl stared at Bessie Penfold with amazement. There had been no censure, just advice, and now the offer of a room and job. Her eyes filled with tears again at such kindness. 'Oh, thank you. Thank you so much.'

'There's no need to thank me. If you remember, I told you that our paths would cross again and I was right. Now come on, I'll show you the

227

room and then I'd best open the shop again. I can't afford to lose customers.'

As Pearl rose to her feet she felt a surge of guilt. She had run out of the café, leaving them in the lurch, and she hoped Madge would be able to cope with the lunchtime rush. God – was she losing her mind? When Dolly found out she was carrying Kevin's child, she'd go mad. No, she couldn't go back, she couldn't face Dolly, and quaked with fear at the thought.

She followed Bessie upstairs, and as the woman led her into a small room, Pearl saw it as a refuge.

22

Pearl knew she had to go out, but couldn't face it. It was wonderful of Bessie to give her this room, but the feeling that it was a refuge soon wore off when she realised how close she was to the café and Derek's stall.

If she waited until the market closed before going to collect her things from Mo's, at least she'd be able to avoid Derek. But she still had to talk to Kevin, to tell him that he was the father of her baby.

She looked around the room, uncaring of the damp, peeling wallpaper and thick dust on every surface. Bessie had told her to make up the bed, but she was still sitting on the bare mattress, her mind twisting and turning.

An hour passed and Pearl's head was aching

with anxiety when she finally rose to her feet. Bessie had said there was linen in the hall cupboard, and in the back bedroom she would find some blankets or a quilt.

Pearl rummaged, finding a pair of old, yellowing sheets, but when she went into the back room her eyes rounded. It was piled high with clothes, old curtains and blankets, all giving off a musty, damp smell. She gingerly picked up a blanket, surprised to find that it was thick and in good condition. After rooting further, she found a home-made quilt with hexagons of pink and blue flowered material. It was beautiful, the stitching perfect, and someone had obviously spent many hours sewing it together.

With the quilt and another blanket under her arm, Pearl went back to her room. She needed to keep busy, needed something to do, and after making up her bed she tackled the dusting. Finally, with nothing else to do, Pearl nervously went downstairs.

'It's about time you showed your face,' Bessie said. 'You can't hide up there for ever and I've already had to get rid of Bernard Dolby.'

'Bernie! Bernie's been in here? But how did he know where to find me?'

'Wake up, love. You're not exactly invisible, and it seems several people saw you running from the café. A quick word with the market traders soon led him here.'

'What did he say?'

'Only that Madge hasn't come back from the doctor's and they need you back at the café.'

'I can't go back. I just can't.'

229

'After what you've told me, I don't blame you, but if you're determined to keep that bun in the oven you'll have to face them sooner or later. Blimey,' she added, cackling with pleasure, 'I'd like to be a fly on the wall when Dolly Dolby finds out she's gonna be a grandmother. The woman thinks she's a cut above the rest of us, but I can tell you something that'll give you a bit of ammunition when you face her.'

Pearl paled at the thought. 'I don't think I can ever face her.'

'Well, girl, you're gonna have to toughen up. If you show fear, Dolly will walk all over you. Anyway, if she gives you a hard time here's that bit of ammunition I mentioned. You can remind her that Kevin arrived only six months after her wedding.'

It took a while for the penny to drop, but when it did, Pearl gasped. 'You ... you mean...?'

'Yeah, she too was up the spout before she got married. It was common knowledge around here at the time, but there ain't many left in the area who'd dare remind Dolly of the facts. She scares the life out of most people, even her old man, and that's something she's cultivated over the years. If you manage to get Kevin Dolby to own up to his responsibilities, you're gonna have her as your mother-in-law, and as I said, the only way to stop her walking over you is to stand up for yourself from the start.'

Pearl knew she'd never have the courage to follow Bessie's advice, and hung heir head. 'I've got to tell Kevin first and somehow I've got to catch him on his own.'

'Even if he agrees to marry, you'd be mad to take him on. That young man will come to no good one day.'

'What do you mean?'

'I've got a funny feeling about Kevin Dolby. He might be a handsome bugger, but I reckon he's a bad 'un. Now then, don't look at me like that. I may be wrong, and anyway, I still think he'll try to squirm out of it.'

Pearl stared at Bessie, her heart sinking. Yes, she knew about Kevin's character and feared his reaction to the news too. But it was his baby, their child, the blame his as much as hers. Oh, surely he'd marry her, and once settled with a wife and child, surely he'd change. But what if Bessie was right? What if he tried to get out of it?'

Kevin Dolby heard the gossip as soon as he walked into the kitchen. His mother told him that Pearl was pregnant, and went on to say that it wasn't Derek's baby. He listened as she continued her tirade.

'I'm not happy that Pearl walked out and if Madge doesn't come back soon, we'll be in a right old fix. Pearl's staying with Bessie Penfold, but when your father went over there she refused to let him speak to the girl.'

Gertie pulled a face. 'Yeah, Bessie can be a right old dragon, but I wonder if she knows who the father is.'

'It's got to be someone from round here, and from what we've been hearing, Derek Lewis is out for blood.'

Kevin blanched. Christ, if Pearl said it wasn't

231

Derek's, it had to be his! So far it seemed that Pearl hadn't named him, but for how long? He shuddered. When Derek found out he'd be mincemeat.

'Are you all right, Kevin? You look a bit pale.'

'It's just a touch of asthma,' he lied, relieved when Madge came into the kitchen, diverting his mother's attention.

'Well, it's about time too,' she snapped. 'What did the doctor say?'

'Huh, it was a waste of time. He said I'm on the change and have to expect hot flushes. I ain't that old and couldn't believe it, but it seems that some women start early.'

'I hardly think this is a subject for my son to hear,' Dolly snapped, but then she exhaled loudly. 'Still, at least it's nothing to worry about. I should have guessed. After all, I seem to be surrounded by Mrs Neverwells. I'm glad you're back, Madge. As you can see, Pearl ain't here so you'll have to manage the lunchtime rush on your own.'

'Pearl ain't here. Why's that?'

'Mum, I'm going upstairs,' Kevin interrupted.

'Yeah, all right, son, and if your asthma is playing up, you'd best take it easy.'

Kevin nodded, leaving the kitchen before his mother told Madge about Pearl. Head down, he ignored his father as he headed upstairs. Christ, Derek would be out for blood soon. What was he going to do?

Kevin paced the room, finally deciding there was only one thing he could do, and that was to tell his mother.

He watched the clock, time ticking slowly until the café closed, and as she came upstairs, he blurted, 'Mum, I'm in trouble, big trouble.'

Her face blanched. 'What sort of trouble?'

'Derek Lewis will be after my blood. He'll make mincemeat out of me.'

Her broad forehead creased, the penny failing to drop. 'Huh, I'd like to see him try. It'd be over my dead body, but why is he after you?'

'Mum, do I have to spell it out? It's Pearl. When Derek finds out, he'll kill me.'

Dolly finally got it, her eyes rounding like saucers. 'What! Don't tell me that *you're* the father?'

He nodded, seeing his mother stagger across the room before flopping onto the sofa. For a moment she rubbed huge hands across her face, her voice a growl. 'I'll kill that bloody girl.'

'It isn't Pearl who's worrying me, Mum. It's Derek Lewis.'

'She's having your baby and all you can say is you're worried about Derek! Christ, son, get your priorities right.' She shook her head in disgust, pinched her bottom lip between forefinger and thumb, then said, 'Look, we need to think this through. How can you be sure you're the father?'

'Because I've had her and she's already said it ain't Derek.'

'Don't be crude. Anyway, she could have been with any number of men. If you ask me that girl has turned out to be nothing but a tart.'

He knew his mother was wrong, knew that Pearl was a virgin when he'd taken her. 'She ain't a tart, Mum. I was the first.' Even as the words left his mouth he cursed himself. Pearl couldn't prove he was the father and he should have kept his mouth shut. The trouble was he'd been too hung up about Derek Lewis to think straight, and now it was too late.

'It could still be Derek's.'

'Leave it out, Mum. If Derek was the father she'd have said so.'

'My God, this has come as such a shock and I can't get my head round it. I need time to think, to work out what we're going to do, and for that I need a bit of peace and quiet. Make me a cup of tea, and by the time you come back maybe I'll have sorted something out.'

With a small nod Kevin left the room, feeling somewhat safer now. His mother wouldn't let Derek Lewis touch him. He placed the kettle on the gas ring, thoughts now turning to Pearl and the baby. His mother said she'd sort something out, but would she make him marry the girl? No, surely not!

Dolly buried her head in her hands. Pearl was pregnant, Kevin was the father – and she was still struggling to accept it. The bloody girl had probably thrown herself at him and, like all men, when it was handed out on a plate he found it impossible to resist. Damage control, that's what she had to think about now, but the thought of losing her son to marriage made her groan in despair.

Dolly was desperate to find a solution, yet something Kevin said refused to go away. She tried to lock it behind a door in her mind, but it forced its way out. Kevin said he'd been the first, Pearl a virgin. Not only that, Pearl said with assurance that Derek wasn't the father, and that meant she hadn't slept with the man.

Dolly shook her head in despair again. She wanted to think the girl a tart, one who had set out to trap her son, but deep down knew it wasn't true. Yet could they still bluff it out? Maybe they could accuse the girl of lying – but even as the thought crossed her mind, Dolly doubted it would work. Pearl had only been in the area a short time, but she was well liked and the locals might not take kindly to a denial. Dolly wasn't stupid; she knew that, unlike Pearl, she wasn't liked and many would be glad to see her brought down.

As her mind continued to work, Dolly came to the sickening conclusion that they had no choice. When Pearl named Kevin, he would have to face up to his responsibilities.

Once again Dolly groaned, dreading the idea of losing her son, yet as she closed her eyes against the thought, she was struck by a way to keep him by her side. Kevin would have to marry Pearl, but she could see that they remained close by. In fact, there was no reason why they couldn't live here. Without a job, Kevin couldn't support a family, and Pearl could continue to work in the café.

Dolly exhaled loudly. It wasn't perfect, but it was a workable solution.

'Here you are, Mum,' Kevin said as he returned with a cup of tea.

'Right, sit down and let's talk. Firstly, I don't want people to think that you're to blame, so keep your mouth shut about Pearl being a virgin. It won't hurt to cultivate the idea that she threw herself at you.'

Kevin's face reddened. 'All right, Mum.'

'Now, like it or not, you're gonna have to marry the girl.'

'Marry her! But–'

'Shut up, Kevin. You'll do as I say, and this is how we are going to handle it...'

Bernie came into the room a little later, his face blanching when he heard that Kevin was the father of Pearl's baby.

'I'm ashamed of you,' he spat. 'How could you take down that nice, innocent girl?'

Dolly reared to her feet, face suffused with colour. 'Don't you dare say that! Pearl threw herself at Kevin, and when it was so easily offered, how was he supposed to resist?'

'Yeah, well, I didn't, that's for sure.' As soon as the words left his mouth, Bernie stepped back, but Dolly was already advancing towards him. Christ, he was so upset about Pearl that he'd spoken without thinking, but he was too late to avoid Dolly's huge hand, the slap across his face making his ears ring.

'Don't put me in the same class as Pearl Button,' she yelled.

'Sorry, love,' Bernie placated as he rubbed his cheek, knowing that if he didn't defuse the situation more of the same would follow. He should stand up to her, and should've done so from the start of their marriage, but she'd been pregnant with Kevin and, anyway, he couldn't hit a woman. Oh, there had been times when he'd been tempted over the years, but despite everything she'd laid on him, he just couldn't do it. Instead he found it easier to allow Dolly to rule, preferring the quiet life. 'I shouldn't have said that. You're nothing like Pearl Button.'

'Huh, I should think so too.'

Bernie exhaled with relief as his wife sat down again, secretly thinking that the girl's qualities were far superior to his wife's. In the short time Pearl had been working for them he had come to admire her soft, gentle nature. She'd had a rotten life so far but she wasn't bitter, yet as he listened to the plans that Dolly had made, his heart went out to the girl. Dolly would get her own way as usual, and Pearl didn't stand a chance.

Unable to resist, he said to Kevin, 'So, Pearl threw herself at you?'

'Well ... yeah. She fancies me and made it plain.'

Bernie eyed his son with distaste. Since childhood, Kevin blinked rapidly when lying, a dead giveaway, and he was doing it now. 'I wouldn't fancy being in your shoes when Derek Lewis finds out.'

'Mum's going to sort him out.'

'Yes, you leave him to me,' Dolly said. 'I'll go round to his place as soon as the market closes, but for now my head's splitting and I'm off to have a lie-down. In the meantime, Bernie, it's about time you dusted this room.'

As the door closed behind his wife, Bernie saw the look of scorn Kevin threw at him. 'Don't look at me like that, son. After all, this shows you ain't any better than me. Instead of facing Derek Lewis, you're letting your mother fight the battle for you. I reckon you're more a chip off the old block than you realise.'

'I'm nothing like you! I wouldn't let a woman lay a hand on me, and that's something Pearl Button will find out.'

Bernie swallowed the bile that rose in his throat. He didn't doubt that Pearl would suffer at Kevin's hands, and when she did, it would be his fault. Kevin had seen too much – witnessed him being beaten and humiliated, so much so that he was determined not to suffer the same fate. His eyes closed. *Oh, Pearl, what have I done?*

23

'What do you want?' Connie Lewis asked when she opened the door to see Dolly on her doorstep.

'I'd like a word with Derek.'

Connie's eyes narrowed suspiciously. Derek had come home from the market in an awful state, and she cursed Pearl Button. Just as she had feared, the girl had broken his heart, but even she'd been unprepared when he told her that Pearl was pregnant by another man. Now Dolly Dolby had turned up wanting to talk to Derek, and astutely she knew there could be only one reason.

'I can guess why you're here. Pearl's pregnant and I reckon your no-good son is the father.'

'Watch your mouth, Connie Lewis. That girl threw herself at my Kevin.'

A voice roared from behind Connie and she nearly jumped out of her skin.

'What did you say?' Derek demanded, thrusting his gran to one side.

'Look, I ain't having a slanging match on the doorstep,' Dolly said, imperiously pushing her way past Derek and into the small hall. She looked around swiftly before marching into the kitchen, Connie scurrying after her and Derek following with his fists clenched at his side.

'If Kevin's the one who got Pearl pregnant, I'll bloody kill him!'

'It takes two, Derek, and as I said, Pearl threw herself at my son.'

'I don't believe you.'

'Did she say he forced her?'

'She didn't tell me who the father is.'

'That isn't what I asked, Derek.'

His eyes glared, but then he sighed heavily. 'All right, Pearl said she wasn't forced.'

'Well, there you are then. If you ask me we've all been taken in by Pearl Button and she isn't the innocent she pretends to be. You should count yourself lucky.'

'Lucky?'

'Yes, lucky. After all, she could have named you as the father and then you'd be raising another man's child.'

'She's right, Derek,' Connie said.

'Leave it out, Gran. She couldn't have named me. We never...' His face reddened. 'Well, you know what I mean.'

Connie sighed with relief. 'Thank Gawd for that.'

'As I said, she fooled us all,' Dolly said bitterly. 'I think the girl was looking for a meal ticket and thought my Kevin would be a better catch. He soon sussed her out and told her he wasn't interested.'

'Huh, how come he got her pregnant then?'

'She invited him up to her room, threw herself at him,' the lies tripped off Dolly's tongue, 'and told him she intended to give you the elbow.'

Derek's face stretched with shock. 'Pearl said that?' He slumped onto a chair, face in his hands for a moment, but then his huge head rose, anger in his eyes. 'He still shouldn't have slept with her. It ain't right.'

'Oh, Derek, you can't blame Kevin. With Pearl saying she was going to break things off with you, he thought the coast was clear. He's a man and, all right, maybe a weak one, but now he's got to face the consequences and marry the girl.'

'Marry her! He's gonna marry her?'

'She's carrying his child so he doesn't have much choice. I came round here to explain the situation and hoped to allay any nastiness between you and Kevin. I would hate you to fall out over Pearl Button.'

'Huh! Well, I still think he deserves a slap.'

'Now what good would that do?' Connie said, laying a hand on Derek's shoulder. 'As Dolly said, the blame lies with Pearl.'

Derek rose to his feet, his voice strangled. 'I don't want to talk about it any more. I'm going upstairs.'

Connie waited until he was out of sight before speaking to Dolly. 'Like Derek, I reckon your son deserves a slap or two.'

'How dare you? It's Pearl who's to blame, not my son.'

'I'm not as gullible as my Derek and can read between the lines. How come you've just accepted that Kevin is the father? I mean, if Pearl is such a tart, it could have been any number of men.'

Dolly's face suffused with colour, but her stance was rigid. 'Just what are you accusing me of?'

'Bending the truth, but don't worry, I'll talk Derek round. I don't want him going down for giving your son a beating, even if Kevin deserves one.'

Dolly leaned forward, towering over Connie. 'Good, we understand each other then.'

'Yes, we do, and now I'd like you to leave.'

'Don't worry, I'm going,' was Dolly's parting shot as she sailed out, the street door slamming behind her.

Connie sat down, gripping the edge of the table, her mind cursing the lot of them – Pearl Button, Dolly Dolby, and her bloody no-good son. Bitter thoughts raged. What a mug she'd been, allowing herself to become fond of Pearl, the girl becoming like a daughter. She'd welcomed her into her home, made her a part of the family, when all the time the bitch was sleeping with Kevin on the side. Derek had been made a monkey of and, God, she'd like to get her hands on Pearl bloody Button.

Connie looked up as Derek came back into the room, his face looking haggard and drawn. 'I know you're hurt, love, but you'll get over it.'

'No I won't, Gran. I love Pearl ... still love her.'

'Derek, she ain't the girl we thought she was,' Connie said bitterly. 'She's just a tart.'

'I can't believe it, Gran. You know Pearl, and at any time did she strike you as a tart? Maybe I should talk to her again, hear her side of the story. She may not want to marry Kevin, and if she doesn't–'

'No, Derek,' Connie quickly interrupted, 'don't even think about it. She pulled the wool over my eyes and yours, but she's a slut all right. She was going out with you, but that didn't stop her from inviting Kevin up to her room and offering him sex. As Dolly said, Pearl thought he was a better catch and set out to trap him. I reckon she was hoping to get pregnant, but kept you on the side just in case her scheme didn't work. Christ, love, ain't the fact that she's carrying another man's child proof enough?'

Derek's eyes darkened. 'Yeah, you're right, but I'm off to find Kevin. No matter what Dolly said, he still slept with my girl and he deserves a slap.'

'No!' Connie cried, jumping to her feet and grasping Derek's arm. 'Think before you act. Kevin ain't to blame. Pearl made a mug of him, just as she did you, and now he's lumbered with marrying her.'

Derek's huge hands clenched into fists, veins bulging on his forehead. 'All right, I won't touch Kevin Dolby, but I'm going to the gym. I've got to take my anger out on something, so it had better be a punch bag.'

Connie sagged as the door slammed behind Derek. She'd done it, talked him out of attacking Kevin Dolby, and now she slumped onto the chair again. The room was quiet, with only the ticking of a clock breaking the silence as her thoughts raged. Yes, Dolly had bent the truth in some way, but she was trying to protect her son and it was understandable. Anyway, there was no getting away from the fact that Pearl had used Derek. Tears filled Connie's eyes. The girl had broken his heart and she dreaded how long it would take him to get over it.

24

It was seven o'clock that evening when Kevin sneaked out of the café. At first he'd balked at the idea of marrying Pearl, but his mother had been relentless – until he reluctantly accepted his fate.

He knocked on Bessie Penfold's door, just wanting to get this over with so he could go down the pub and drown his sorrows. The old woman glared at him, but he forced a tight smile. She was another one like his mother, a dominant, mouthy old woman, whom he usually kept well away from.

'Yeah, what do you want?'

'I'd like a word with Pearl.'

'You'd better come in then.'

Kevin stepped into the shop and through the back, following her upstairs. When they reached the first landing Bessie stood at the bottom of another flight of stairs, her voice loud for such a tiny woman. 'Pearl, you'd better come down here. There's someone to see you.'

'I'd like to speak to her alone.'

'Yeah, I bet you would, but that's up to her.'

It was obvious that Pearl was shocked to see Kevin. He forced a smile. 'You and me need to talk – and in private.'

'Yes, all right.'

Bessie pointed to the front room. 'You can talk in there. If you need me, girl, I won't be far away.'

They stepped into the room, Pearl immediately sitting on an old sofa, her body stiff with tension. She opened her mouth to speak, but Kevin interrupted.

'It's my baby, ain't it?' he said without preamble.

Her eyes widened. 'Yes, but how did you know?'

'You told my mother that it wasn't Derek's so it didn't take much working out. Anyway, that's why I'm here. She sent me to see you.'

'Your mother sent you? But why?'

'Because I owned up.'

'You told her! Oh, Kevin. What did she say?'

'What do you think? She ain't too pleased, but she says we've got to get married.'

'Oh, thank God.'

'Thank my mother. We're to make the arrangements straight away, and after the wedding we'll live with my parents.'

'Live with them! But–'

'You heard me. I ain't working so we've no choice. When I can raise some money we'll move out, but until then it's good of my mum to put us up. Oh, yes, and though you can have the week-end off, she wants you back at work on Monday morning.'

'No, please, I can't face her, or Derek, and–'

'Mum's had a word in Derek's ear,' Kevin cut in, 'and you've got to face her sooner or later.'

'She spoke to him? What did he say?'

'I dunno, I wasn't there, but he knows we're getting married.'

Pearl's eyes were moist. 'He'll never forgive me.' Her voice rose. 'Kevin, please, I can't face him yet. I don't want to work in the café, I ... I'd rather stay here.'

'Well, that's too bad. Mum said something about damage control and she wants you back – so that's that. Until we're married, you can kip down here, but there's no reason why you can't return to work.'

'No, please, Kevin.'

'Look, you know my mother. If you don't show up she'll come over here and drag you back.'

'She ... she'd do that?'

'I wouldn't put it past her. Anyway, after your shift on Monday, we're to go to the registry office in Wandsworth.'

'That soon?'

'Yeah, that soon. Pleased, are you?' Kevin asked, his voice dripping with sarcasm.

'I ... I wasn't sure that you'd marry me, so yes, but ... but you don't seem very happy about it.'

'I'm being forced to marry you, so what do you expect?'

Pearl's eyes widened. 'I ... I'm not forcing you.'

No, Kevin thought, she wasn't. It was his bloody mother. Pearl was leaning forward, arms wrapped around her body. Gazing at her, he realised that it might not be so bad after all. Pearl was a meek little thing, the antithesis of his mother, and he found himself looking forward to having her under his control. She'd be on hand whenever he wanted her, the sex free. He'd teach her a thing or two, show her what he liked and, now smiling, he said, 'Look, I know you're not forcing me. It's just come as a bit of a shock, that's all.'

'You ... you don't have to marry me if you don't want to.'

'Yeah, I know, but that's my baby that you're carrying so we'd better get spliced.'

She was obviously relieved, a sigh escaping her lips. 'Oh, Kevin, do you really mean that?'

'Yeah, of course I do, now come here and give me a kiss.'

Pearl stood up, about to walk into his arms, but then the door opened, Bessie Penfold coming into the room.

'Is everything all right, Pearl?'

'Oh, yes. Kevin knows about the baby and wants to marry me.'

'I should think so too.'

Kevin hid a scowl. The last thing he wanted was to be in the company of this smelly old cow. He'd wanted Pearl on her own, to have a little taster, but there was no chance of that. 'Right, Pearl, now that it's all sorted, I'm off. I'll see you on Monday.'

'What about tomorrow?'

'No can do, I'm busy,' Kevin said.

Pearl looked disappointed, but she nodded, but it was Bessie who moved surprisingly quickly to show him out. He clattered down the stairs, the old woman saying before she closed the door behind him, 'I'm glad you're doing the right thing by the girl, and I hope you treat her right.'

She was looking at him expectantly, but tight-lipped Kevin said nothing. Bessie Penfold was an interfering old cow, sticking her nose in when he had wanted to be alone with Pearl. Christ, he thought. It would be just as bad living with his parents. He and Pearl would have no privacy and with his mother close by, there'd be no chance to indulge his fantasies. He needed to raise money, big money, to find a place of their own, and as soon as possible.

Pearl was sitting on the sofa when Bessie walked back into the room. 'Well,' she asked, 'are you happy now?'

'Oh yes, except that Dolly's insisting that I return to work on Monday. Oh, Bessie, I dread facing her.'

'She doesn't own you and can't give you orders. You don't have to go back. There's work for you here.'

'I'd love that, Bessie, but it's impossible. After our marriage we're to live in Dolly's flat and if I don't do as she says, it will only make things worse. I have to go back. I don't have any choice.'

'There are always choices.'

'Not for me.'

'You don't have to marry him.'

'Oh, Bessie, I was an orphan and know what it's like to be without parents. I know I said I can bring up my baby alone, but I don't want to deprive it of a father.'

Bessie sighed. 'All right. I can see you've made up your mind so I'll say no more.'

As Bessie then took a seat, Pearl said, 'I should get my stuff from Mo's, but I dread seeing her.'

'Leave it for now. You can find a few bits in my stock to tide you over.'

'Thanks, Bessie,' Pearl said, glad of the reprieve. 'Shall I make us a drink first?'

'No, you go and sort yourself out. I'll see to it.'

Whilst Bessie went to the kitchen, Pearl went upstairs to the back room. It amazed her that Bessie kept so many clothes that were out of date, a lot now covered in mildew and unfit for anything but the dustbin. With careful sorting she managed to find a few things, her mind on the future now. She didn't like the idea of moving into Dolly's flat, but hopefully it wouldn't be for long. Once Kevin found work they could find a place of their own. Her heart lifted. They'd be a proper family, her baby with both a mother and father.

An hour later, Pearl and Bessie were sitting companionably in old, threadbare chairs by the fire. Though Pearl was happy, she still dreaded facing Dolly on Monday morning. She glanced across at Bessie, seeing that the old woman was staring into the flames.

Curious, she asked, 'Bessie, you said our paths would cross again and you were right. Can you really see into the future?'

Bessie turned, gazing at Pearl as though looking into her soul. 'Yes, but not at will.'

'But Derek's gran...'

'Go on, girl.'

'No, it's nothing.'

Bessie chucked. 'I can guess what Connie Lewis said. Like many bitter women, she thinks I've done her out of money. I suspect she said my powers are false too, but truth be known it's because I didn't tell her what she wanted to hear. Am I right?'

Pearl avoided Bessie's eyes. 'She didn't mention that, but she wasn't happy with the amount you gave her for her husband's clothes.'

'Christ, that was during the war. Connie must have a memory like an elephant. I can't remember how much I gave her, but times were hard then and a lot of men died in action. When that happened I was offered their clothes, but there was a glut and it was stuff I knew I wouldn't be able to shift. Still, I did the best I could to help out, even if I could only offer peanuts. Women's clothes were a different matter. There was a shortage and knowing I could sell them easily, I always gave a good price.'

Pearl digested Bessie's words, deciding that the old lady wasn't the skinflint that Connie had portrayed. The woman's psychic powers intrigued her and she asked, 'Do you make things up when you tell fortunes? I mean, you said we would help each other, and though you've helped me, I haven't been able to do anything for you.'

'The time will come, you can be sure of that, and somehow I know you and I will draw close.'

'But how?'

'Gawd, I don't know everything, girl, and sometimes I know nothing.'

'I don't understand.'

She looked deep into Pearl's eyes again. 'I rarely talk about my powers, but I feel I can trust you to keep your mouth shut. If you must know, I learned the art from my mother. She had the gift of second sight but, like with me, it didn't come at will. In fact it rarely does. My mother taught me how to read people, and you'd be surprised at what you can glean just by studying someone. When women sit in front of me they don't realise how much they give away, just by their actions. For instance, they sit up straighter when I hit on the subject that's worrying them, be it money, health, their husbands or children. There are things to look out for too: a wedding ring, or a white mark where there was one. Signs of illness can show up on the skin, eyes, and even the palms.'

'So you make it all up.'

'Don't look so disgusted, girl. The women who come to me are mostly desperate and looking for hope – sometimes searching for a reason to carry on. I give them that hope. When in despair they fail to realise that all things pass in time, be it sadness, pain or debt. The circle turns and, looking back later, they'll find that somehow they got through it.'

'Do you ever use second sight?'

'If it's given to me – yes, but even then it may

not be what the person wants to hear so I soften it as best I can. Sometimes I make mistakes, and when I do it isn't always pleasant. Let's get back to Connie Lewis as an example. Many years ago she came to me for a reading. When I mentioned her daughter she suddenly stiffened, giving me the clue. I'd heard on the grapevine that her daughter had left home, but not why, and thought perhaps Connie wanted to hear that she was coming back. Instead I had a sudden flash of intuition and knew she would never see her daughter again, but I also saw a child, one that would be living with Connie. Now there was the quandary. How could I tell the woman that she would never see her daughter again?'

'What did you do?'

'I just said that I saw a child and she might become a grandmother. Well, Connie went mad. She accused me of listening to gossip, said I had heard on the grapevine that her unmarried daughter was pregnant. She said I'm a fake, a shyster, one who takes money from people who can't afford it. With that she marched out, and has never spoken to me since.'

'So you saw into the future and knew her daughter was going to die?'

'Yes, but not the details. It doesn't work like that, but I saw the darkness.'

'Do you always see bad things?'

'No, thank goodness.'

'How often does it happen?'

'Blimey, I don't know. Sometimes every few days, but then it might be weeks before I get another one. Now enough. This is becoming like an inquisition. Put some milk on and we'll have a cup of cocoa before going to bed.'

Pearl made the drinks, thinking about Bessie and her fortune-telling. She wasn't sure that she approved of her methods, but surely it was all right to offer people hope when they were in despair.

Her mind gave her no answer, yet Pearl knew as she poured milk into two cups that she had clutched at this problem to avoid thinking about the café. It wasn't only Dolly she didn't want to face, it was the others too. There was Gertie, Madge, Mo, and worse, Derek. She would have to see him every day – see the hurt she had caused him – and it was going to be awful. The coster-mongers, the locals, had taken her to their heart, but what would they think of her now?

She and Kevin were to be married, and she was happy about that, but she wished Bessie could turn on her second sight to tell her what the future had in store.

25

Pearl still hadn't gone to Mo's to collect her things; instead she spent the whole of Sunday indoors. She felt ill with nerves, her stomach churning every time she thought about returning to the café and, after a restless night, woke heavy-eyed on Monday morning.

She forced herself to get ready, Bessie sympathetic and telling her she could still change her mind. Finally, with her head down, she emerged from the shop, feeling as though every coster-monger in the market was looking at her. She didn't look towards Derek's stall, couldn't bear to see his face, and was relieved to scuttle into the café.

'Morning, love,' Bernie said. 'Dolly wants to talk to you before the others arrive, but listen, there's something I want to ask you first. Kevin said that you threw yourself at him. Is that right?'

Pearl's eyes rounded. 'No, I ... I didn't throw myself at Kevin, but I do like him. When I was living in my bedsit, he came up to my room and and it just sort of happened.'

'Did he force you?'

She shook her head in denial, but then Dolly's head emerged from behind the kitchen door. 'Pearl, get in here!'

With a swift, frightened look at Bernie, Pearl hurried to do her bidding, but instead of yelling in anger, Dolly's voice was surprisingly calm. 'Right, to start with I've managed to talk Derek Lewis into keeping his hands off Kevin.'

'Oh, I hadn't thought of that, but I ... I didn't tell him the baby was Kevin's.'

'Well, he knows now, and if it wasn't for me he'd be looking for blood.'

'What ... what did you say to him?'

'I had to convince him that my son isn't to blame.'

'But–'

'If Derek thinks that Kevin took you down against your will, he'll give him a beating.

Anyway, the truth of the matter is that Kevin didn't force you, and you can't deny that.'

Pearl lowered her head. Dolly was right. She *had* allowed it to happen. She should have been more forceful in her protest, yet in reality she hadn't really wanted Kevin to stop. She had given in too easily, and what did that make her? Self-loathing made her stomach twist. 'No, Kevin didn't force me, and I don't want Derek to hurt him.'

'I should think not. Derek knows you weren't forced, but he still wants to give Kevin a hiding. I had to concoct a story, lay the blame on you, and if you want to keep Kevin safe, you'll just have to go along with it. It ain't gonna be easy for you. Derek is well liked around here and you'll probably face some aggravation, but for Kevin's sake, keep your mouth shut.'

'All right,' Pearl whispered, wondering what story Dolly had come up with. She was about to ask when the woman spoke again.

'Now, there are other things to sort out. A lot of people around here would like to see me brought low, so I don't want them thinking I'm against this marriage.' Her lips tightened. 'I ain't happy about it, but nevertheless we will *all* put on a happy front. Is that clear?'

Pearl bent her head in acquiescence, but then, hearing voices, Dolly spoke quickly. 'That sounds like Madge and, despite being my cousin, she's another one who would like to see me brought low. Mind you, I know how to put her straight. Now get that look off your face and replace it with a smile. We're about to put on the show of our lives and make sure you follow my lead.'

With that, Dolly beckoned Pearl to follow her, and together they emerged into the dining room. 'Morning, Madge. Have you heard the wonderful news?'

'What news is that?'

'Blimey, you must be the only one around here who hasn't heard that I'm to be a grandmother. I can't tell you how thrilled I am. Of course, it's a shame that Pearl and Kevin aren't married yet, but that's the way things seem to be happening nowadays and can soon be remedied.'

'What ... you're pleased?' Madge sputtered.

'Why shouldn't I be? I'm dead chuffed that Pearl is to be my daughter-in-law and, as I said, I can't wait to be a grandmother.'

'Well, stone the crows. I thought you'd go barmy.'

'Oh, so you *had* heard.'

'Well ... yeah ... and I can't believe you're taking so well. After all, Pearl's engaged to Derek Lewis.'

'Oh, that was just a fleeting thing,' Dolly said, beaming as she placed an arm around Pearl's shoulders, hugging her with affection as she told a few more lies. 'You see, Pearl went out with Kevin first – in fact she threw herself at him, but they had a falling out. She didn't think he'd take her back and that's why she agreed to go out with Derek. Isn't that right, Pearl?'

'Er ... yes.'

Madge frowned. 'Going out with him is one thing, but getting engaged is another. If you ask me, it was a bit quick.'

'Pearl tells me that she was heartbroken when

255

she and Kevin broke up and she agreed to marry Derek on the rebound.'

'Oh, yeah?' Madge said, her voice registering disbelief.

Dolly's face darkened. 'Madge, you of all people should understand. After all, when that bloke you were courting ran off, you married Eddie almost immediately.'

Madge reddened, but before she could say anything, Dolly spoke again. 'When Pearl found out she was carrying Kevin's baby, she told Derek and broke off the engagement. She didn't try to pass the child off as Derek's, unlike *someone* I could mention.'

Madge's colour deepened. 'I can't believe you're bringing that up after all these years. If you want to start mudslinging, I could say a few things about *your* hasty marriage too.'

Dolly gasped, eyes narrowing in anger, but thankfully Bernie stepped in. 'Now come on, you two, there's no need for this. We're all family and should stick together.'

Obviously fighting to stem her fury, Dolly heaved in a great gulp of air. 'Yes, Bernie's right. I shouldn't have said that, Madge, so let's forget it and start again. As my husband has pointed out, we *are* all family, and as your marriage worked out well I'm sure you wish the same for Kevin and Pearl.'

'Of course I do, but what you've told me is a different story to the one on the grapevine.'

'What have you heard?'

'Most people are saying that Pearl is a nice girl, and if Kevin got her pregnant it must have been against her will.'

'That's rubbish and I won't stand for my son being blamed! As I said before, Pearl threw herself at Kevin. All right, he shouldn't have taken things as far as he did, but you know what men are like, Madge. They're not going to turn it down when it's handed out on a plate.'

Pearl had listened quietly, but now gasped. She'd agreed to take the blame, but Dolly was making her sound awful.

Madge looked at her disdainfully, her lips curling. 'I'm surprised at you, Pearl.'

'Now then, Madge,' Dolly rebuked. 'Pearl is to be a part of this family and I don't want you being funny with her. All right, what she did was wrong, but what's done is done. From now on I want us all to put on a united front. I want everyone to see that we're happy about this baby, *and* the forthcoming marriage.'

'Right – if you say so, Dolly.'

'There's one other thing, Madge. You've heard what happened from the horse's mouth, so if you hear any further gossip that Kevin is to blame, I hope you'll put them straight.'

'Of course I will.'

'Good. Now then, the morning rush will be starting soon so I'd best get back to the kitchen.'

No sooner had Dolly disappeared than the first customers of the day walked into the café, taking a seat at one of Madge's tables. 'Well, here we go,' she said, 'time to tell them *Dolly's* version of the truth.'

Pearl watched from under her lashes, saw the men's quick glance in her direction, and then they began to speak earnestly to Madge. She shook her head emphatically, leaning forward as she spoke. Then, taking her pad, Madge took their order, pausing as she passed Pearl on her way to the kitchen.

'I've put them straight but it didn't go down well. Derek is well liked, and once the news spreads I reckon things are going to get tough for you. I wish you luck, girl, 'cos I think you're gonna need it.'

Surprisingly, when Pearl saw Gertie, the woman smiled. 'Dolly tells me that congratulations are in order.'

'Yes, Pearl, I've passed on the good news to Gertie,' Dolly said, 'and will do the same when Mo comes in. Have you been round to her place to pack up your stuff?'

'No, not yet.'

'You can go tonight, but she'd better not be funny with you. You'll be a part of this family soon and I'm not having her calling my future daughter-in-law a tart again. In fact, Kevin can go with you, and if Mo gives you any trouble she won't have a job to come back to.'

Despite being upset by the lies Dolly had told, Pearl felt a surge of gratitude and relief. Dolly was now standing up for her and her dread of living in the same flat lessened. Maybe, just maybe, it would all be all right.

The next hour was trying, with most coster-mongers making their displeasure obvious. Derek Lewis was one of their own, but when Frank Han-well came in, he gave her the first friendly greeting she had received that morning.

'Well, I can't say I wasn't shocked by the news and, as you can imagine, Derek ain't taking it too well.'

The fixed smile she had affected so far dropped, tears flooding her eyes. Frank touched her arm, his voice soft. 'Despite the rumours, I reckon the blame lies with Kevin, not you. I never did think much of that young man. You could do with someone in your corner and it's a shame that it's my last morning on the market.'

'Your last morning!'

'Yes, love, I'm handing my pitch over to the new bloke and we're moving to Shepherd's Bush tomorrow. There's a decent market there and I've managed to find a spot for my stall.'

Pearl lifted a hand to dash the tears away. 'Good luck, Frank.'

'Thanks, love. Now I don't know how it happened, but suddenly your name is mud around here. They're all gunning for you, but don't worry, I'll do my best to put them straight before I go.'

'No, Frank! Please, don't say anything.'

'Why not?'

Pearl hung her head. She had to protect Kevin, but dreaded saying the words. 'Because what you've been hearing is true. I am to blame.'

'Are you sure about that?'

'Yes, I'm sure. I ... I'm just sorry that Derek's been hurt.'

'Yeah, me too. He's a good bloke and thought the world of you. Well, love, despite how you've kicked Derek in the teeth, I wish you luck.

Marrying into this family, I reckon you'll need it.'

When Pearl went into the kitchen, she saw that Mo had arrived. The woman said nothing, her expression sour, but Dolly caught the look.

'Now listen to me, Mo,' she snapped. 'I've told you the truth of the matter and I won't stand for you being funny with Pearl. My son is a handsome young man and you can't blame her for throwing herself at him. She is to be a member of my family, my daughter-in-law, and I insist that you show her some respect.'

'Respect! You want me to show that tart respect?'

'Be careful, Mo. You're not irreplaceable, so either change your attitude or get out.'

Mo's body straightened and, hands on hips, she glared at her employer. 'I've stood a lot from you over the years, Dolly Dolby, but this is the last straw. On Saturday you agreed that Pearl was a tart, but now all of a sudden I'm supposed to believe that you're thrilled to bits that she's having Kevin's baby. You say she agreed to marry Derek on the rebound, but I ain't stupid. The dates don't work out so think on that before you spread your lies.'

'How dare you speak to me like that? Get out!'

'Don't worry, I'm going.' And turning to glare at Pearl she spat out more venom. 'Have you forgotten the night you went dancing with my daughter? Kevin was there and accused you of being a tart. He told my Emma that you were easy, but like fools we didn't believe him. Well, miss, he was right, and if you want your things, you'll find them outside by my dustbin. I don't want the likes of you putting a foot over my doorstep again.'

'Get out!' Dolly screamed again, her voice bouncing off the walls.

Mo grabbed her coat, brushing past Gertie as she almost ran out of the back door. For a moment there was silence, but then Dolly exhaled loudly. 'Now I'm stuck without a vegetable cook.' She closed her eyes for a moment. 'Right, Pearl, ask Madge to come in here. I might be able to persuade her to take over for the time being, but it'll mean you'll have to manage the tables on your own.'

'Please, can I do the vegetables? I'd rather be out here than in the dining room.'

'Are you having a hard time of it?'

Pearl nodded, her breath held as Dolly cocked her head to one side. 'Do you know how to cook?'

'No, not really, but you know I'm a fast learner.'

Dolly threw a glance at Gertie, speaking softly so the woman wouldn't hear, 'Yeah, you're fast all right,' she said sarcastically, 'and you're carrying Kevin's child to prove it.' She puffed loudly. 'All right, you can work out here, but I'll still need to talk to Madge. She might not take kindly to the extra tables. Go and get her.'

Madge agreed to do Pearl's tables, but only if she was given a pound a week more. Tutting her impatience, Dolly showed Pearl how to prepare the vegetables for the lunchtime rush.

Pearl didn't mind, she was just pleased to be

away from the customers. As she picked up yet another potato to peel, she tried to forget the snide remark Dolly had made. Dolly had said she was to be a part of the family, her daughter-in-law, and had stood up for her against Mo. Everything had happened so quickly and it must have been a terrible shock for Dolly. Once she and Kevin were married things would settle down, and surely then it would be all right.

Pearl had more to face when she finished her shift. Kevin was out, Dolly telling her to go back to Bessie's until he returned to take her to the registry office.

It was freezing as Pearl stepped outside. Hurriedly turning up the collar of her coat, she made to cross the street.

Connie Lewis suddenly loomed in front of her, blocking the path. 'I want a word a word with you, my girl,' she spat.

'Please, Connie, let me pass.'

'Not until I've had my say. You've ruined my Derek's life – made a laughing stock of him – and I hope I live to see you pay.'

'I ... I didn't mean to hurt him.'

'Don't give me that crap. You'd hardly been in the area for five minutes before you threw your-self at Derek. I had my suspicions from the start, but you took me in with your innocent act.'

'Honestly, Connie, I really didn't mean to hurt him.'

'Then why did you sleep with Kevin Dolby?'

'I ... I...' Pearl floundered.

'Don't bother looking for an excuse because

there isn't one. I've sussed you out and I know why. You're nothing but a user! You took up with my Derek, but only to keep him on the side in case you couldn't snare Kevin Dolby. If your little trap hadn't worked, you'd have married Derek as the second-best meal ticket, and no doubt made his life a misery. Well, miss, you've got Kevin, so it seems your scheme worked but, knowing that young man, I reckon you'll live to regret it.'

'No ... please, it wasn't like that,' Pearl protested, hardly recognising the woman who stood in front of her. Connie had been like a mother to her, a woman she had grown so fond of, but now all she saw in Connie's eyes was hate.

'Shut up, you bitch!' Connie screamed.

'Gran, come on, that's enough,' Derek called as he ran towards them.

'Enough?' Connie snapped. 'I ain't even started yet.'

'Yeah, go on, Connie, give her what for,' a costermonger called from the small crowd that had gathered.

Pearl looked around frantically, wanting only escape, but before she could move she felt the sting of Connie's hand across her face. She heard a small cheer, saw Derek staying his gran's hand as she lifted it again, and then, seeing a small gap, she ran through it, sobbing as she flew to Bessie's with Connie's words ringing in her ears.

Her steps faltered. It was true, she *had* used Derek, but not for the reason that Connie had spewed out. She looked back at her time in the orphanage and the way she'd always found some-

263

one to protect her. With deep shame Pearl realised she had done the same thing here. She had sought Derek out – sought his protection – and though not to keep him on the side, she had used him for her own ends. She ran into Bessie's, ignoring the old woman's shout as she fled to her room, throwing herself onto the bed as self-loathing swamped her.

Only fifteen minutes later, she heard Bessie calling, 'Come down, girl. Kevin's here to take you to the registry office.'

Lacklustre, Pearl rose from the bed, finding Kevin waiting impatiently when she walked into the shop.

'Come on, we ain't got much time before they close.'

'Pearl, are you sure about this?' Bessie asked.

'What's it to do with you?' Kevin snapped.

'Huh, take a look at her. Does she look like a girl who's happily going to arrange her wedding?'

'It's all right, Bessie, I'm fine, honestly,' Pearl said, managing a parody of a smile. She briefly touched the old woman's arm to reassure her, and then followed Kevin outside to his car.

'Look at that lot gawking,' Kevin said as they drove off. 'Anyway, why the long face?'

'It's nothing,' Pearl said.

'Well then, give us a smile.'

Pearl turned and as their eyes briefly met, she managed to force her lips into the semblance of one.

'That's better,' he said, his eyes back on the road. 'For a moment there you looked like a lamb going to slaughter.'

He concentrated on his driving then, speaking briefly about the arrangements, whilst Pearl hardly listened. She was an awful person, dreadful, hurting a man who had shown her only kindness. Oh, Derek – Derek, what have I done...?

'Sorry, what did you say?'

'For Christ's sake, Pearl, what's the matter with you?'

'Nothing, it's nothing.'

'Well, if you want to change your mind, now's the time to do it. We're almost at the registry office.'

For a moment Pearl was tempted. She wanted to run, to hide. To never have to face Derek, or Connie, again.

'Well, girl,' Kevin asked as he pulled into the kerb, 'what's it to be?'

She turned to look at him, her thoughts still racing. She couldn't do it, couldn't run. She was carrying Kevin's baby, he was the father and she needed him. Maybe there was a way out. When they were married, perhaps she could persuade Kevin to find a job out of the area. 'I don't want to change my mind.'

'Right, come on then, let's get this wedding booked.'

He smiled, and Pearl's stomach fluttered. He was so handsome, and he was being so nice, but things changed when they walked into the registry office.

The wedding proved difficult to arrange, neither of them anticipating that with Pearl being under-age, without a birth certificate, or parental permission, there'd be complications. Legal advice was suggested, and when they left the registry office Kevin was in a foul mood.

He flung open the car door. 'Christ, that was a complete waste of time and I don't see how a solicitor can help. He won't be able to conjure up a flaming birth certificate out of thin air.'

Pearl hung her head, thinking it was no more than she deserved. Derek's face returned to haunt her, the pain she had seen in his eyes. She had hurt him badly and still couldn't get Connie Lewis's words out of her mind.

They drove back to Battersea in silence, Kevin's mood still dark, and as they turned into the yard at the back of the café, he finally spoke.

'Come on, we'd better get this over with and tell my mother.'

They sat in the living room, Dolly saying after they explained what had happened, 'They must know what they're talking about if they suggested legal advice, but a solicitor's going to cost a pretty penny. Have you got any savings, Pearl?'

She shook her head. 'No, I'm afraid not.'

'Bloody hell, I ain't made of money, but I suppose I'll have to pay. You'd better make an appointment tomorrow and let's hope it doesn't take long to sort out.' She scowled. 'More bloody expense. Take her home, Kevin. I've had enough for one day.'

Pearl rose to her feet, her shoulders slumped as she left the room. They made their way downstairs and as Kevin unlocked the door a blast of cold air hit them.

'You don't need me to walk you home – there's

no point in both of us freezing – and I ain't too pleased about all this either. I was hoping to tap my mother for a few bob, but I ain't got a hope in hell now.'

She nodded, just wanting to get away from Kevin and his nasty mood. He was upset, and she couldn't blame him, but as he closed the door behind her, she almost ran back to Bessie's.

Bessie was sitting by the fire, one side of her face red from the heat.

'Blimey, what's up, love?'

There was concern and sympathy in the old woman's eyes and seeing this, Pearl flopped onto a chair. She then spilled her misery out in a torrent – the run-in with Connie Lewis, followed by what had happened at the registry office.

Bessie said nothing, letting her cry until there were just juddering sobs. She then leaned forward, saying softly, 'Come on now. A solicitor will soon sort things out.'

Pearl drew in another shuddering breath. 'If he doesn't, it's no more than I deserve.'

'Don't be silly. You can't beat yourself up over the things Connie Lewis said.'

'She's right. I ... I'm not a nice person.'

'Rubbish. You were only a child in that orphanage and did what you had to in order to survive. It doesn't make you a bad person.'

Pearl looked tiredly at Bessie. 'But I still carried on when I left. I wanted protection and Derek seemed an ideal choice.'

'Gawd, love, I wish you'd stop being so hard on yourself. When you left the orphanage you were still a youngster and had to strike out on your own. You came to a new area without any friends or family, and of course you were nervous. It's a bit rough around here and it ain't surprising that you felt the need for someone to look out for you.'

'But that doesn't make it right.'

'I'm not saying it does, I'm just saying it's understandable. Listen, girl, we all make mistakes, but hopefully we learn from them. You've had a hard lesson and you can let it sink you, or you can take it on board and grow.'

'How can I do that when I've ruined Derek's life?'

'Look, you can't change what's happened. Derek will get over it in time, and, who knows, eventually he might meet someone else.'

'Oh, I hope so, Bessie.'

'He's a nice bloke, and though not much to look at, I'm sure someone out there will appreciate his good nature. Now come on, buck yourself up. As I said, you've had a hard lesson, one to teach you that you can't hide behind someone else. You've got to stand on your own two feet.'

Pearl's nod of agreement was half-hearted. It was impossible – she'd never have the courage. It was women she feared now, especially the likes of Connie Lewis, Mo Price and her future mother-in-law. Oh, if only she could get Dolly to like her, to establish a good relationship. Nobody messed with Dolly and it would be wonderful to have the woman batting on her side.

Derek Lewis stepped out of the dark doorway,

the lamplight hitting his face as he threw a last glance up at Bessie's window before moving away. He was being stupid, he knew that, but was unable to stop himself from shadowing Pearl. She hadn't left Bessie's house during the whole weekend, but still he'd watched.

When Pearl emerged that morning, he'd only had a brief glimpse of her before she ran into the café. Then when she finished her shift he'd been horrified to see his gran attacking her. He'd stepped in to break it up, but Pearl hadn't even looked his way, and that had hurt. Christ, he was being a mug and he knew that, but he just couldn't get Pearl out of his mind.

Everyone was now saying that Pearl was a tart, and she was pregnant to prove it, but he still had doubts. He wanted a word with Kevin, to hear his side of the story, but the bastard was keeping his head down. Derek threw a look towards the café, and his shoulders lifted. There he was now, and moving swiftly Derek covered the distance between them.

'I want a word with you,' he growled.

'Look, Derek, none of this was my fault,' Kevin said hastily.

'Yeah, that's what I've been told, but I'd like to hear it from you. If you're so innocent, how come you've been avoiding me?'

'I haven't. I just didn't want to rub salt in the wound, that's all. Christ, mate, we go back years and I knew how cut up you'd be.'

'Yeah, right, so how come you had it off with my girl?'

''Cos, like you, I was taken for a mug. Pearl told

me that it was over between the two of you, and I believed her.'

'You could have checked that with me first.'

'Yeah, maybe, but at the time she was stripping off, and naked Pearl's hard to resist. She threw herself at me like a cat on heat.'

Derek pictured the scene, feeling sick to his stomach, but then shook his head in denial. 'That doesn't sound like Pearl.'

'I was shocked too. She looks such an innocent, but she ain't, mate, and if you must know, I wasn't the first either.'

'You ... you mean...?'

'Yeah, believe me, she was no virgin.'

Derek found himself gawking.

'Are you sure?'

'I've had enough women to know.'

Yeah, Derek thought, that was true enough. With his looks, Kevin had never been short of women. Everyone was right then: Pearl was a tart. He felt a wave of disgust. 'Christ, I could do with a drink.'

'Come on, I'll buy you a pint,' Kevin said. 'I could do with one too, and you should think yourself lucky. At least you ain't stuck with marrying her.'

'Yeah, I'm beginning to think you're right Derek said, deciding that Kevin was welcome to her, yet even as this thought crossed his mind he knew it would still take him a long time to get over Pearl Button.

26

When Pearl saw a solicitor, there had been no swift solution. He had written to the orphanage and was now awaiting their reply. He also advised that without a birth certificate, the only way forward was to swear an affidavit. When asking what this meant, he explained that it was a sworn oath, in his presence, that she was the person she claimed to be. It sounded a daft procedure to Pearl, but one that she complied with.

It was now the eve of Christmas and Pearl was on her way to work, something she dreaded every day. As she scuttled out of Bessie's door and into the market, she kept her head low, but as usual there were murmurs as soon as the costermongers saw her. She glanced up from under her lashes, saw Derek turn his back as she passed, the man beside him doing the same. Derek would never forgive her – Dolly's story had seen to that – but she missed him and his gran.

To keep Kevin safe she had gone along with Dolly's lies, but it didn't seem possible that only a short time ago she had felt a part of this community. Now she was an outcast. A costermonger hawked, the globule landing in front of Pearl's feet, and as she began to run, her stomach heaved.

'Yeah, that's it, do a runner, and keep going until you're out of Battersea,' the man shouted.

'Yeah, you tell her, Billy,' a woman customer cried.

Still fleeing, Pearl flung open the door of the café, almost falling inside. She didn't stop until she reached the kitchen, her breath coming in gasps as she pulled up in front of Dolly.

'Huh, judging by the state of you, I can see that the locals haven't stopped giving you a hard time.'

'Some of them are still spitting at me.'

Unsympathetic, Dolly shrugged her shoulders. 'As soon as they find another bit of gossip to titillate them, they'll lay off. In the meantime you'll just have to put up with it. Now I suggest you get on with the spuds.'

Pearl hung her coat up, after which she started to peel the potatoes. She had learned how to cook vegetables competently now and, glad to be out of the way, had no wish to return to the dining room. However, despite trying to please Dolly, she'd been unable to make any grounds. Her future mother-in-law continued to pretend that everything was fine when anyone else was in hearing range, but alone she dropped the act and made her feelings plain. Pearl knew she'd have to try harder, but despite always being polite and working hard, nothing she said or did seemed to please Dolly.

'Come on, Pearl, get a move on, and when you've finished the spuds, get on with the carrots.'

Pearl increased her efforts, surprised when Dolly spoke again, this time pleasantly. 'It'll be nice to have a couple of days off, and I'll expect you for Christmas dinner tomorrow. In fact, if

272

you come over at about eleven you can give me a hand.'

'I ... I won't be joining you for dinner.'

'Do what?'

'I can't leave Bessie. She's poorly.'

'If you're angling to bring her along, you can forget it. I can't stand the woman. Now as I said, I'll expect you at eleven.'

Pearl stomach quaked, dreading a confrontation but, worried about Bessie, she had no choice. 'I'm sorry, but I really can't come. Bessie's in bed and needs looking after. I can't leave her on her own.'

'She's on her own now, ain't she?'

'A neighbour is keeping an eye on her, but can't do it on Christmas Day.'

Dolly's face suffused with colour, but before she could say anything, Gertie came out of the washing-up room.

'I've finished all the breakfast dishes, Dolly. Can I have a break now?'

'Yes, of course you can. Get yourself a cup of tea and fetch one for me and Pearl while you're at it.'

Gertie hurried out, almost colliding with Kevin as he pushed through the doors. He swaggered up to Pearl, flinging an arm around her shoulders. 'Hello, love. Did you hear from the solicitor this morning?'

'There was nothing in the post.'

'Sod it. Well, that's that. We won't hear now until the New Year.'

'If this goes on much longer, she'll be huge by the time you get married,' Dolly snapped.

Pearl looked down at her stomach, seeing the

tiny mound. Kevin followed her gaze, a small frown creasing his forehead. 'I hope not, Mum.'

'Let's hope he gets a move on then. Now if you don't mind, Pearl's got work to do.'

'All right, I'm off out.' He gave Pearl another swift hug, ignoring his mother's scowl as he left by the back door.

Pearl, though, couldn't ignore Dolly's attitude. The woman hated Kevin to show her any affection and once again Pearl was filled with dread at the thought of living in the same flat as Dolly. If Kevin would find a job, they could move away, but he avoided the subject of work. Maybe she should talk to him again – but not in Dolly's hearing.

When the new administrator started work at the orphanage, she faced a pile of work on her desk, but was gradually ploughing through it. Today, in answer to a letter, she had to search the records. She had found a thin file on Pearl Button, but there was little to read. It was odd that the child had never been placed into foster care, and there'd been no applications to adopt. If she'd been mentally deficient it would have been understandable, these children always difficult to place, but looking at the sparse reports on Pearl's educational progress, this didn't seem to be the case.

In an endeavour to find out more about the girl, she had questioned members of staff, finding two who remembered her. Pearl Button had been described as nervous and quiet, but neither said she lacked intelligence.

The administrator picked up the letter from the solicitor again. It seemed that Pearl Button wanted to marry and he was enquiring if there were any relatives on record. There were none.

With a sigh she picked up her pen. There wasn't much she could tell the man. Pearl Button's records said that she'd been abandoned, the date, but that was all. The sparse letter completed, she blotted it, and after addressing the envelope she put it on one side for the post.

With a vast amount of paperwork in front of her, the administrator now put the girl's file to one side and tackled her next problem.

As Kevin drove along Falcon Road he was remembering how he'd been against the marriage at first, but it had been the thought of having Pearl in his bed every night that changed his mind. Now though, she was showing, her stomach starting to swell, and he doubted he'd fancy her for much longer. Christ, he hoped they'd hear from the solicitor soon, but when they married he'd see that his lifestyle didn't change. Unlike his father, he'd show his wife who was the boss from the start. His face darkened, realising there'd be little chance of that whilst they lived with his mother. She still treated him like a child, and ruled with a rod of iron. Not only that, if he showed Pearl any affection his mother acted like a jealous girlfriend, and it sickened him. He wanted away from her, to be the man of his own house, but without money it was impossible.

Once again he dreamed of one big job, one that would net him thousands instead of hundreds.

The last two he'd done with Nobby and Dick hadn't been bad, but by the time they fenced the gear through Vince and split the cash three ways, they'd each been left with peanuts. His lips tightened in anger. That bastard Vince had the borough sewn up. He didn't take the risks, leaving others to do that, but he was making a mint.

If he could find a job, and a good one, there was no way he'd fence the goods through Vince. It would solve his problems if he could find a cash haul, but needed an easy target. Small shops were useless, their takings hardly worth the risk, and of course robbing a bank would be impossible. His mind turned. If only he could find somewhere that held a lot of cash on premises, yet had little security. Huh, fat chance of that!

Fighting to suppress his frustration, Kevin's hands tightened on the steering wheel. He badly needed a trip to Soho, but his mother was keeping him short of money. He knew why. The cow. She was punishing him for getting Pearl pregnant.

When she finished her shift, Pearl was relieved to find the walk home from work trouble free, the market still buzzing with life as people rushed to do last-minute shopping. There were many unsold Christmas trees, men pursing their lips and vying for a bargain as they made their selections. It was freezing, a blustery wind blowing, but the costermongers were wrapped up warmly, their voices ringing out as they tried to sell the last of their Brussels sprouts, parsnips and carrots, each trying to shout louder than the others. Pearl would have liked to have stopped to buy a few things, but feared her reception as she hurried past.

She went straight upstairs to see Bessie, finding her huddled in bed with a scarf around her neck, and not looking much better.

'Thank the Lord you're back,' she croaked. Then fishing for her hot-water bottle, she held it out. 'I'm bleedin' freezing and her next door hasn't been in for hours.'

'I'll refill it,' Pearl said as she looked worriedly at the old lady.

'Make me a cup of tea while you're at it,' Bessie managed to choke out before a bout of coughing had her gasping for breath.

'I think you should see the doctor again.'

'No, I'll be all right. Pass me them fags.'

'I don't think you should be smoking.'

'Leave it out. It's a bit late to stop now, and anyway, a good cough helps to clear me chest.'

Pearl's eyebrows rose but, knowing it would be pointless to argue, she hurried to the kitchen. At least Bessie was showing some spirit, which was an improvement on yesterday.

If Bessie hadn't felt so ill, there was no way she'd have stayed in bed, and even now she complained constantly about the shop being shut and her loss of trade.

Pearl looked in the cupboards. She wanted to persuade Bessie to eat something, and pulled out a tin of soup.

In no time Pearl was on her way back upstairs with the hot-water bottle tucked under her arm as she carefully balanced a tray.

Bessie refused the soup, only taking the cup of tea. 'It's gonna be a bleak Christmas for you. I'd planned to cook us a nice dinner and maybe stick up a few decorations, but I just ain't been up to it.'

'It doesn't matter.'

'Still, I expect you've been invited to Dolly Dolby's.'

'Yes, but I'm staying with you.'

'There's no need for that. At least at Dolly's you'll get a decent Christmas dinner.'

'I'm staying with you,' Pearl repeated firmly.

Bessie sighed heavily. 'All right, and you're a good kid. I'm gonna miss you when you get married.'

'I'll miss you too, but don't worry, I'll pop over to see you as often as I can.'

Bessie patted the back of Pearl's hand. 'I know you will. As I told you, we were destined to meet.'

'Yes, but what else has your second sight shown you?'

'Nothing,' Bessie said, her rheumy eyes becoming veiled. 'Now bugger off and leave me in peace.'

'I will when you've had your medicine.'

The old lady's lips tightened with annoyance, causing Pearl to smile as she poured cough mixture into a teaspoon. Unmarried, with no living family, Bessie was fiercely independent and resented having to be nursed. She put on a hard and cantankerous front, but Pearl knew this was just a veneer that hid her kind, soft nature.

Pearl held the spoon to Bessie's lips. 'Here, drink this and I'll go, but I'll be up to check on you again.'

The old woman grimaced as she swallowed the medicine. 'Yuk.'

Pearl pulled the blankets over Bessie, saying as she left, 'I'll be back soon.'

Bessie just nodded, her eyes already drooping, and when Pearl went into the living room she found it freezing. She hurried to light a fire, screwing up old newspaper to place in the grate. After adding kindling, and a few nuggets of coal, she was pleased when it lit straight away.

After waiting a few minutes, Pearl piled on more coal, and then sank onto a fireside chair, holding her hands out to the warmth. The flames flickered and danced merrily, mesmerising Pearl as time ticking by.

Reluctantly Pearl finally stood up, her legs mottled and red with heat as she went to check on Bessie, finding the old woman asleep. She peeped in on her several times during the next few hours, and then just before seven a knock on the shop door had her hurrying downstairs to see who it was.

A smile lit her face. 'Kevin,' she cried, thrilled when he gave her a swift kiss as he stepped inside.

As Kevin walked into the living room he was surprised to find it empty. 'Where's Bessie?'

'She's in bed with bronchitis.'

'So – we have the place to ourselves.'

'Well, yes, I suppose so.'

Kevin smiled with satisfaction. He and Pearl had only been alone in his car, and in the small space it was unsatisfactory. When he called round to

Bessie's, she never left them alone, and his mother was the same. It maddened him. The silly bitches didn't seem to realise that they were bolting the stable door after the horse had bolted. He lowered himself onto the sofa, arms outstretched. 'Come here.'

As Pearl sat down, Kevin kissed her passionately, and as usual she melted against him. So far he had resisted revealing his preferences, deciding that he didn't want to frighten her off, but once they were married she'd learn a thing or two. He'd dominate, show what a man he was. With Pearl he always felt in control, but that wasn't enough. With his need to overpower, he wanted resistance, but she was always so soft and compliant.

'Kevin, have you had any luck finding a job? I really do want to move away from here.'

'I'm looking, but I ain't working for peanuts.'

'I can work too.'

'Oh, yeah? And what about when you drop the sprog?'

'Others manage.'

'Look, I've told you I'm trying to find a job, so just shut up about it.'

'All right. I'm sorry.'

Pleased that she didn't nag, he smiled. 'Come on, we're on our own so let's make the most of it.' His head dipped, once again kissing her passionately, nipping her lower lip and hoping to hear a yelp of pain.

There was no resistance and his frustration mounted. He paid the girl in Soho to fight, to beg for mercy, and God, he missed it.

Pearl snuggled up to him again, but he pushed

280

her roughly away. She was bloody useless! Her eyes widened, and on such a short fuse it was enough to set him off. He growled as he grabbed her, his teeth sinking brutally into her neck.

'Ouch! No, don't, you're hurting me!'

The fear in her voice drove away the last of his common sense. She had dared to protest and he loved it. 'Shut up and get on the floor,' he snarled.

'Wh ... what?'

'I said get on the floor.' Kevin shoved Pearl off the sofa and as she landed with a thump he swiftly knelt over her, laughing gleefully at the shocked expression on her face. Without preamble he yanked up her skirt, his eyes feasting for a moment on the bare skin that gleamed whitely where her stocking tops ended. Then, unable to wait, he tore at her underwear.

Pearl's hands fought to hold him off. 'Stop it – oh, please, Kevin, stop!'

Her white face staring at him wide-eyed with fear spurred him on. He raised a hand, slapping her across the mouth. 'Shut up – bitch!'

With another yank her knickers came apart, and as she cried out again he fumbled with his trousers. With a swift movement he thrust into her, grinning with delight at her yelp of pain.

She writhed in protest beneath him, increasing his enjoyment until he lost control. He was in a world of his own now, pounding into her without mercy, but it was quick – too quick. Disgusted, he flopped on top of her for a moment before rolling onto his side.

Pearl scrambled away, rising quickly to her feet, hands held over her mouth in horror as she stared at him. As he rose to his feet, she cried out in fear, 'No ... no, don't come near me!'

It was the terror in her voice that suddenly brought him to his senses. He wanted Pearl as his wife, a wife he could rule, but now he may have blown it. 'Christ, I'm sorry. I don't know what came over me.'

'That ... that was like rape.'

Kevin wanted to laugh, but fought to keep his face straight. Little did she know that it had been tame compared to what he got up to in Soho.

It was play-acting there, he knew that, but by paying for it he was able to resist his urges. Urges that made him want to rape women – to hurt them – to make them see that he was a man.

At seventeen years old he'd done it, attacked a girl, but he'd nearly been caught. After that he'd been too scared to try it again, yet deep inside he knew that if he hadn't discovered Soho, his needs would eventually have driven him to strike again.

Kevin now took a deep breath, forcing himself to look sheepish as his eyes met Pearl's. 'I'm sorry,' he said again.

'Why did you hurt me like that?' she sobbed, tears beginning to role down her cheeks.

His mind raced, struggling to find words, finally able to find a lie. 'I don't know, but I think it was suppressed anger. Anger that I'm being forced into marriage.'

Pearl's face was red and blotched, her clothes dishevelled, and her voice quavering as she spoke.

'But ... but we talked about this, and I said I'm not forcing you.'

'I know,' Kevin said, shaking his head as though in a quandary, 'and I don't know what came over me. It's just that we're never alone, and it's been driving me mad. If it ain't Bessie, it's my mother, and I'm sick of it.' He moved towards her, but she cowered away, her hands frantic as she straightened her skirt.

'Please,' she begged, 'don't touch me, and ... and I don't think I want to marry you now.'

He stepped forward again, feeling her flinch as he dragged her into his arms. 'Don't say that, Pearl.'

Her body was rigid as he held her. 'I ... I was so frightened.'

'I know you were, and I'm really sorry.' Kevin hid a scowl. He hated this, hated having to grovel.

'Please, let me go,' she begged.

Shit, he thought. Now what? Desperate times called for desperate measures and though loath to say the words, he forced them from his mouth. 'Pearl, please, I love you and don't want to lose you.'

She drew back, her eyes wide. 'You ... you love me?'

Unwilling to utter the words again, he just gave a slight nod, only saying, 'I really didn't mean to hurt you.'

At last he felt her body relax. 'Oh Kevin, I love you too, but you really frightened me. And ... and you could have hurt the baby.'

He blanched. Christ, hurting a woman was one thing, but a baby! He had hardly given the child she was carrying a thought but now, with sickening clarity, it hit him. The baby was his – his son

283

or daughter. 'Is it all right?' he asked.

'Yes, I think so.'

He gently ushered her towards the sofa. 'You'd better sit down. Are you in any pain?'

'No, well, I feel a bit bruised.'

'I hope I haven't hurt it. Maybe I should run you to hospital?'

'I ... I don't think there's any need for that.'

He paced the room, his hands raking through his hair, and moments later asked, 'Any pain yet?'

'No,' she said, touching her tummy.

He looked at the slight swell worriedly. 'Are you sure?'

'Yes.'

He stopped pacing to kneel at her side. 'Thank God for that! We must have a tough little bugger in there.'

For the first time a slight smile played across her lips and, seeing it, he enfolded her in his arms.

'Pearl, I really am sorry. Say you'll still marry me.'

'I ... I don't know. You're so changeable and it scares me.'

'I know I can be a moody bugger, but I can change. It's my mother, Pearl. You know what she's like and she drives me mad. Once we're in our own place, I'll be fine.'

'Do you really love me?'

'Yes,' he murmured, 'and I'll never do that again. I don't want to risk hurting our baby.'

She was quiet then and he held his breath, slumping with relief when she said, 'All right, I'll still marry you, but please, Kevin, find a job soon so we can move away from here.'

'Don't worry, I will.'

He held her gently, but hearing a thump on the ceiling, they drew apart. 'That's Bessie,' Pearl said. 'I'll have to see what she wants.'

'Are you sure you're up to it?'

'Yes, I'm fine. I expect she wants her hot-water bottle filled again.'

Kevin solicitously held her arm as she stood up, watching as she left the room. From now on he'd be gentle with Pearl, but to hold back the demons he'd somehow have to raise the money to go to Soho. Of course after the baby was born, it would be a different matter.

Pearl was still in a daze as she walked upstairs, her mind distracted as she went into Bessie's bedroom.

'Something woke me,' the old lady complained. 'I thought I heard voices. Is someone down there?'

'Yes, it's Kevin.'

'What's that on your cheek? It looks like a hand mark. Have you been crying?'

Pearl flushed, her hand rising to touch her face.

'Did he hit you?' Bessie demanded.

'We ... we had a bit of a row.'

'That's no excuse. I've got no time for men who lay into women. If he's hitting you now, I dread to think what he'll be like when you get married. If you've got any sense you'll call it off.'

'No, it's all right. He promised he won't do it again.'

'Huh, and pigs might fly. Listen, girl, you don't have to marry Kevin Dolby. Stay here with me and we'll manage all right. Who knows, with your fresh eyes we may be able to come up with a way to drum up a bit more business.'

'Don't worry, Bessie, I'll be all right. Kevin said he loves me and I love him too. If we can find a place of our own, I know we'll be happy.'

'Well, it's up to you, but I still think you're making a mistake.'

Pearl bent to straighten Bessie's blankets, her mind turning. It had been awful, the sex brutal, Kevin's face a mask of anger as he took her. Yet afterwards he had been so contrite and his explanation *was* plausible. She could understand that Dolly drove him mad, and once away from her he'd be fine. Kevin had been so worried about the baby, and not only that, he had said the words she'd been longing to hear. He loved her – he really did, and her heart soared. Soon she would have what she'd always dreamed of. A home and family of her own. She smiled. Three children would be nice…

Then Bessie coughed loudly and Pearl looked at her with concern. 'Your chest still sounds bad. Is there anything I can get you?'

'No, but I want that young man out of my house. It isn't right that you're alone down there, and I don't trust him.'

'Bessie, I'm having his baby and we'll be married soon. I think it's a bit late to worry about a chaperone.'

'That's as maybe, but I don't want him left on his own to nose about. He'd rob me as soon as look at me.'

'How can you say that? Of course he wouldn't

286

rob you.'

'I've heard rumours about him and what he gets up to with that Nobby Clark. Now do as I say and get him out of my house.'

Pearl wanted to argue, but Bessie's hacking cough started again and she didn't want to upset her any further. 'All right, calm down. I'll ask him to go.'

She hurried from the room, hoping that Kevin wouldn't be upset at having to leave, but the old lady's words played on her mind. Bessie had implied that Kevin was a thief. Pearl shook her head in denial. Of course he wasn't. Yet even as her mind dismissed it, she couldn't help thinking about the cartons of cigarettes she'd seen in Nobby Clark's shop. Had Kevin been involved?

Doubts about the marriage rose again, but as she walked into the living room, Kevin spoke anxiously.

'Are you all right? You're not in any pain, are you?'

Pearl grabbed at his words. Bessie wanted him to leave, and now a way lay open, one that she took. 'No, I'm not in any pain, but I am feeling a bit tired. Perhaps I should have an early night.'

'Yes, do that. I'll go now, but I'll be over first thing in the morning.'

'There's no need.'

'Yes there is,' he said, touching her tummy lightly. 'That's my son in there and I want to make sure he's all right.'

Pearl found herself smiling, pleased that he was showing such concern. 'Or your daughter.'

He grinned. 'A girl, eh? No, I reckon it's a boy.'

'We'll just have to wait and see.'

'Go on, go to bed,' he said, kissing her lightly on the tip of her nose. 'I'll see myself out.'

Pearl nodded, her heart melting as, for a moment, Kevin held her gently.

'We'll be all right, you'll see,' he said, giving her a final soft kiss before leaving.

She heard his footsteps on the stairs, the shop door closing, and smiled. Despite everything, she loved him, and now fought to dismiss the worries from her mind. Kevin said they'd be all right, and she believed him.

27

It was mid-February before all the legalities were sorted out, allowing Pearl and Kevin to marry. The registry office had originally said that she wasn't old enough to marry without permission, but without relatives the solicitor had finally sorted it out, presenting the affidavit and the reply from the orphanage to the registrar.

During this time, any doubts that Pearl had about Kevin were laid to rest. He was being so kind, so gentle, and on the rare occasions they were able to make love, he was careful and considerate. He was still looking for a job, he assured her, one out of the area, but so far hadn't found one with decent pay. She was disappointed, but he told her to be patient, saying that he didn't want her or the baby to want for anything and a well-paid job was sure to turn up soon.

Though most of the locals still refused to speak to her, the awful earlier animosity had eased, though Derek still turned his back when he saw her. She'd hurt him so much and it weighed heavily on her mind, but despite this, her love for Kevin deepened.

She hadn't made any headway with Dolly, but now that she was finally to marry Kevin, her worry eased. He would be her husband and was sure to stand up for her against his mother.

'Well, girl, are you ready?' Bessie asked on the morning of the wedding.

'Yes,' Pearl said, with a last look in the mirror. Although it was a registry office wedding, with only Dolly, Bernie and two witnesses in attendance, she still wanted to look nice. At five months pregnant she had been thrilled to find a cream swagger coat amongst Bessie's stock, one that hid her growing lump.

The marriage was to take place at ten thirty, but with Dolly refusing to close the café for more than a few hours, there would be no wedding breakfast. Instead, Dolly and Bernie were returning to the café, opening at twelve thirty for the lunchtime session.

Pearl's head was spinning. It had been a frantic morning. She'd been up at the crack of dawn, hurrying to work at five o'clock to prepare all the vegetables in advance. Gertie and Madge had been roped in to cook them, and with the rest of the menu partly prepared, they had only to put the trays in the oven ready for Dolly's return.

Pearl now put on a tiny pillbox hat before picking up her handbag. 'Do I look all right, Bessie?'

'Yeah, but if you ask me it's a funny sort of wedding. No reception, no honeymoon, and you ain't even carrying flowers.'

'I know, but it doesn't matter. Dolly has given me the rest of the day off and Kevin is taking me out to lunch.'

'Huh, big deal. Tell me, when you're back to work in the kitchen tomorrow, what will Kevin be doing?'

'Bessie, please, don't start again. I'm sure he'll find a job soon.'

There was a knock on the street door, the old lady speaking quickly as she grabbed Pearl's arm. 'It isn't too late to change your mind.'

Pearl saw the anxiety etched on Bessie's face and bent to kiss her on the cheek. 'Don't worry, I'll be fine. I know I thanked you last night for letting me stay with you, but I'm going to miss you so much.'

'I'll miss you too, but you never know – you may be back.'

'Back! What do you mean? Is it your second sight?'

'Now then, don't look at me like that. It's just wishful thinking from a silly old woman. I've grown fond of you, girl.'

The knock was louder this time. 'I'd best go, but I'll be over to see you as soon as I can.'

Kevin stood impatiently on the doorstep. 'Blimey, Pearl, you took your time. If we don't get a move on we'll be late.'

'Sorry, I was saying goodbye to Bessie. I wish

she was coming with us.'

'Mum didn't want any fuss, and once you start sending out invitations, where do you stop? It's better this way.'

He took her arm, leading her to his car, where she saw Dolly and Bernie sitting in the back. It was only Bernie who remarked on her appearance, saying kindly, 'You look nice, Pearl.'

Dolly was wearing a fitted, brown coat with a turban-style hat that hid every inch of her hair. She looked severe, grim, and nervously Pearl said, 'You look nice too, Dolly.'

She didn't respond, and as Pearl settled, Kevin closed the door. He walked round to the driver's side, saying as he climbed in and gunned the engine to life, 'Right, let's get this show on the road.'

As they drove through the market many eyes were watching. Pearl had a brief glimpse of Derek, thought he was hurrying towards them, but then they turned the corner. She looked over her shoulder, but couldn't see him, and decided she must have imagined it.

'What are you looking at Pearl?' Kevin asked.

'It's nothing. I just thought for a moment that Derek was chasing after us.'

'Why would he do that?' Dolly snapped.

Kevin chuckled. 'Perhaps he wanted to offer us his congratulations.'

'Huh, I doubt that,' Dolly said.

Pearl was quiet during the twenty-minute drive to the registry office. The atmosphere was strained, Bernie trying to lighten it, but Dolly hardly replied, except to complain about the business they were losing that morning. She looked grim as they climbed out of the vehicle, but Bernie tried to jolly her along. 'Come on, Dolly,' he cajoled. 'This is a wedding, not a flaming funeral.'

'Yeah, cheer up, Mum,' Kevin said.

'Shut up,' Dolly snapped. 'What's to be cheerful about? You're marrying a girl we know nothing about – well, except that she's a slut.'

'Now then, Mum, there's no need for that. Pearl ain't a slut.'

'Don't argue with me, Kevin. I won't stand for it.'

'Sorry, Mum,' Kevin said meekly.

'I should think so too,' she snapped. She then glared at Pearl, adding, 'Huh, well I suppose we had better get this farce over with.'

Pearl felt frozen to the pavement as she watched Dolly march into the building, her mind racing as all her doubts and fears rose to the surface. It was obvious now that Kevin couldn't stand up for her against his mother, and she shivered, unable to face the thought of living in the same flat. Kevin took her arm, but she turned wild eyes towards him. 'I ... I can't do it. I can't live with your mother.'

'Don't worry. It won't be for long,' he said, moving them forward.

Pearl clung on to that as they stepped into the building, but she barely took in her surroundings as once again Dolly glared at her. She saw the two witnesses, acquaintances of Bernie's, and tried to smile, but her lips quivered. Her eyes took in the large desk, the registrar, but as they stood in front of him, she barely heard his words, feeling as though Dolly's eyes were boring into her back.

In what felt like minutes it was over, the registrar announcing them man and wife, Pearl at last turning to look at Kevin.

He smiled. 'Well, that's it, love. We're married.'

As he leaned forward, their lips meeting, Pearl heard Dolly's grunt of disgust.

Bernie, though, came to their side. 'Congratulations,' he said, smiling warmly.

They had to sign the register then, Pearl unable to ignore Dolly, her hand trembling as she held the pen. It had been so quick that it felt unreal, and then the witnesses were called forward to add their signatures. They too offered their congratulations, but Dolly offered none, only saying impatiently, 'Right, now that's over with we can get back to the café.'

'Come on, Mrs Dolby,' Kevin said as he led Pearl outside.

She looked down at the narrow band on her finger. Instead of being Pearl Button, she was now Pearl Dolby, and it sounded strange to her ears.

'Thanks for coming,' Bernie said to the witnesses, shaking their hands. 'I'm sorry that we've got to go straight back to the café, but I'll buy you a drink later.'

The couple nodded, and after she had said goodbye to them, Pearl thought she saw sympathy in their faces as they walked away.

Dolly was still morose as they drove back to Battersea High Street, but her expression changed the minute she got out of the car. Many faces were turned their way, and now with a fixed smile she spoke loudly.

'Right, you two, have a nice lunch and we'll pop a bottle of champagne this evening.'

Bernie was out of the car too, but he leaned forward to speak to Pearl through the window. Unlike Dolly, his voice was soft. 'I'm sorry, love. It doesn't seem much of a wedding day. I still think we should've had a bit of a do.'

'It's all right, I don't mind,' Pearl said, and it was true, she didn't. There had been some discussion with Kevin about a wedding reception, but she'd been unable to think of anyone other than Bessie to invite. The Dolbys weren't a large family, and though she faced less animosity these days from the locals, she doubted any would want to attend. In the end it had been Dolly who vetoed the idea, saying that she'd spent enough money on the solicitor, and a reception was just a waste of money.

Bernie smiled sadly, but then Dolly pulled at his arm, saying that it was about time they opened the café. For a moment they both stood on the pavement, Dolly's smile still fixed as they waved the newlyweds off.

Derek Lewis surreptitiously watched the scene. He knew he was mad – that if anyone knew they'd tell him so to his face – but despite everything, he still loved Pearl. It was hell every time he saw her, her stomach growing with another man's baby. Kevin's baby. When he'd seen them leaving for the registry office, he'd reacted without thought, like an idiot running after the car. Christ, what was the matter with him? Pearl was a tart, yet he had actually wanted to stop the wedding.

The costermonger next to Derek sniffed loudly. 'Well at least you didn't chase after them this time, mate.'

'I know, but for a moment this morning I wanted to give the cow a slap,' Derek lied.

'Can't say I blame you,' the man said, turning as a customer came to his stall.

Derek nodded, relieved that the other coster-mongers had believed his excuse, but he was tired of putting on an act. It was this that had sealed his decision. He'd miss the market, but at least he wouldn't have to see Pearl every day. She was married now, and once and for all he had to put her out of his mind.

Kevin drove to Richmond. He'd booked a table at a pub/restaurant by the river, and as it was early they'd be able to have a couple of drinks before ordering their meal. His mother had stuffed some money in his hand that morning, but she had done so begrudgingly. Kevin was worried, really worried. He hadn't been to Soho for ages and was desperate for relief. In the past, he'd been able to manipulate his mother for extra money, but nowadays she was punishing him and was being as tight as a duck's arse.

It had been hell holding back with Pearl, but until she dropped the kid it would have to remain that way. 'What did you say?' he asked im-patiently when she spoke.

'I said I can't believe that we're really married.'

'Well, we are.'

'You seem upset. Are you regretting it already?'

'For Christ's sake! What do you want me to do – break out in song and dance? Now shut up and let me concentrate on the road.'

He glanced round to see that Pearl had lowered her head, and at last he smiled. At least the silly cow didn't answer him back and that made him feel better. He'd be the man in this relationship, and she might as well learn that from the start.

When they arrived at the pub Kevin pointed to a table, and as Pearl took a seat he went up to the bar. The landlord was a short, stocky man, looking harassed as he issued orders to several young women in waitress uniforms. It seemed that this wasn't only a restaurant, there was a function room too, one that had been booked for a wedding party.

Kevin listened with interest. The pub was in a prime riverside location, and the bloke must be raking it in. An inkling of an idea began to form, but one that would need careful planning – along with insider knowledge. Almost on cue a tall, plain-faced barmaid came to take his order.

'Hello, love,' he said, giving her his best smile.

She flushed, but her eyes lit up with interest. 'What can I get you, sir?'

'A pint of bitter and an orange juice,' he said, and by the time he was carrying the drinks to their table, he knew he'd cracked it. With her looks, the barmaid would be grateful for any attention, and he'd give her plenty of that whilst he fished for information.

Kevin sat drinking his pint, his eyes constantly scanning the pub, and then anxious to get to the bar again he turned to Pearl. 'Come on, drink up.'

'I don't want another one yet.'

'Please yourself,' he said, taking his own empty glass and smiling softly at the barmaid as she approached, ready with his favourite chat-up line.

'What can I get you?' she asked, smiling shyly.

'I'll have the same again, but I have a bit of a problem that you might be able to help me with.'

'A problem?'

'Yes. You see I've forgotten my telephone number, so could you give me yours?'

For a moment she looked bewildered, but then, pink-faced, she smiled. 'You ... you want my telephone number?'

'Yes, please.'

As her eyes flicked to Pearl he leaned a little closer over the bar. 'She's just a friend.'

'Mary, there's other customers waiting,' a voice said, and Kevin scowled as he saw the landlord approaching.

She quickly pulled on the pump, filling his glass with bitter, her manner brusque now. 'Sorry,' she mouthed as he took his money, and quickly scribbling on a scrap of paper, she passed him her telephone number.

'I'll ring you soon – *very* soon,' Kevin told her, smiling as he walked away. She was a good choice, one he was sure would spill the beans.

When they arrived back at the café, Kevin

unlocked the back door to find Nora sweeping the floor. He ignored the woman as he always did, his mind still distracted. He'd lingered over the meal, too preoccupied to take much notice of the food as he'd watched everything, taking mental notes, but knowing that this was only the start.

'Hello,' Nora said.

Kevin grunted, but Pearl smiled, returning the cleaner's greetings before Kevin ushered her up to the flat. His mother was sitting by the fire as they walked in, her smile tight as she spoke.

'You're back then.'

'Where's Dad?'

'He's putting the takings into the night safe at the bank.' She then turned to Pearl, her voice clipped. 'Put the kettle on.'

Pearl nodded, hurrying through to the kitchen, Dolly speaking again as the door closed. 'The girl can make herself useful and we might as well start as we mean to go on. For instance, she can help your father with the cleaning up here.'

'Hang on, Mum. She's already working in the café, and don't forget she's five months pregnant.'

'What's that got to do with anything? Pearl isn't ill. She's just having a baby and doesn't need treating like a china doll.'

Kevin shrugged, unwilling to get into an argument. If Pearl didn't want to take on the cleaning it would be up to her to say so but, knowing his mother, he doubted it would do any good. What she said went, both in the café and up here in their flat.

'Hello,' Bernie said as he returned. 'How was the meal?'

'Fine.'

'Where's Pearl?'

It was Dolly who answered. 'She's making a cup of tea, and I've told Kevin that she can take over cleaning the flat.'

'Blimey, don't you think that's a bit much? After all, the girl's having a baby.'

Dolly's face darkened. 'I worked like a dog when I was carrying Kevin, and I don't remember you protesting.'

Bernie lowered his eyes, and Kevin knew that, like him, his father was unwilling to argue with her. Once again his determination rose. There was no way Pearl was going to rule him. In fact, he would start right now, and this might be a way to earn a few Brownie points with his mother. If he could soften her up, she might be persuaded to give him a few quid.

When Pearl came back into the room, Kevin waited until she had put the tray down before speaking. 'Now that you've moved in with us, I think we need to sort out a few things. My mother's worn out after working in the café all day, and as she has agreed to let us live here rent free, I think you should take on the cleaning.'

Kevin threw a glance at his mother, pleased to see that she was positively beaming at him. He flushed with pleasure and then turned this attention to Pearl again, awaiting her reaction.

She was frowning, and for a moment he thought she'd protest, but then with a small nod she said, 'Of course I'll do the cleaning.'

'Don't worry, I'll give you a hand,' Bernie said, 'and why are we having tea? I thought you said we'd celebrate with champagne, Dolly.'

'Don't be stupid, and what's to celebrate? I only said that for the benefit of the locals. Champagne indeed! We're not made of money, you know.'

Kevin frowned, dreading an evening spent with his parents, something he usually avoided like the plague. Hang on! He'd decided that marriage wasn't going to change his lifestyle, hadn't he? There was nothing to stop him from going out later for a drink with the boys.

At eight o'clock Kevin was ready. Pearl looked surprised when he told her he was going out, but he'd told her in no uncertain terms that his mates wanted him to have a celebratory drink. She looked upset, but he ignored it, only flinging her a wave as he left.

Nobby and Dick looked surprised when they saw him walk into the pub, both offering to buy him a drink, but it was Dick who got them in.

'Where's your lovely wife?' Nobby asked.

'Indoors, where she's supposed to be.'

'And no doubt waiting for you to come home to bed,' Dick leered as he handed out the pints.

'Of course she is. Marriage has some compensations and I'll give her a good seeing to later.'

Nobby smirked. 'In that case you'd better go easy or you might get the brewer's droop.'

'No chance of that,' Kevin bragged.

'Have you heard the news about Derek Lewis?'

Kevin stiffened. 'No.'

'He's been offered a full-time job at the gym.'

'Oh yeah, doing what?'

'Old Jack Spencer is retiring and Derek's taking over. He'll be managing the gym, and is already talking about offering more kids boxing lessons.'

'What about his stall?'

'According to the jungle drums, he's keen to give it up, and you can't blame him.'

'What's that supposed to mean?'

'Come on, mate, it doesn't take much working out. Pearl made a fool of him, but I reckon he still ain't over her. I know she's your wife now, but a lot of people ain't got any time for her.'

Kevin relaxed. Yeah, Pearl had taken the fall, and as long as the locals continued to think that, he had nothing to worry about. He finished his beer, but with little money left he knew he only had enough for one round. 'Well, mate, if they ain't got any time for my wife, that's just too bad. Now me, I'm gonna have another drink.'

Kevin ordered three pints and the conversation turning to horse racing – a sure bet that Nobby was going to place the next day. 'This one's a cert,' he bragged.

'According to you they're all certs, but I reckon it's a mug's game.'

'No it ain't,' he protested. 'I won a few bob yesterday.'

'Yeah, and you'll lose it tomorrow.'

Nobby protested, and for a while went on about the virtues of the horse he'd been tipped would win.

'If you want to waste your money that's up to you, but right now, as you're so flush, when we've finished these, it's your round.'

Nobby got them in, and as they stood chatting a few people came up to congratulate Kevin, but he felt it was half-hearted. None offered to buy him a drink, and as he swallowed the last dregs in his glass, Kevin decided he'd have to leave before his turn came round again.

'Right, I'm off to service my lovely wife.'

The others laughed, and as Kevin walked outside, the cold air hit him. He wasn't drunk, it would take more than three pints to do that, but he felt mellow. It only took him a few minutes to walk home, and as he went upstairs to the flat he found it in darkness. With such an early morning start, his parents were rarely up after ten, and doing his best to tiptoe, he made for his bedroom.

Pearl was sitting up in bed when he walked in, the bedside light illuminating her wan face. She looked miserable, her huge eyes moist as she gazed at him.

'For Gawd's sake, what's the matter with you?'

At his tone she stiffened, her reply barely a whisper. 'N ... nothing.'

With a new double bed in it, the room was a bit cramped, and though Kevin knew he still had to go easy with Pearl, he consoled himself with the thought that any sex was better than nothing. With a grin he threw off his clothes, and scrambled in beside her. 'Good, glad to hear it. Now come here and give me a cuddle.'

As Pearl put her arms around him, Kevin became instantly aroused. Yes, he thought, marriage did have compensations. His hand lifted her nightdress and she groaned softly as he stroked her inner thigh.

Gently, he told himself as he positioned himself above her, fighting to control the need to hurt – to dominate.

'Kevin, did you lock up?' his mother's voice boomed as she barged into the room.

He froze above Pearl, his erection dying instantly. 'Christ, Mum, you could have knocked.'

'Huh, yes, I can see that,' she said, her voice and face showing her disgust as Pearl fought to pull the blankets over them. 'Now, as I said, did you lock up?'

'Of course I did.'

'Good,' she said, her lips curling with distaste, 'and if you don't mind, keep the noise down. Some of us are trying to sleep.'

Kevin felt sick as memories of his childhood rose to haunt him. As a little boy, if he so much as touched his penis, his mother reacted with disgust, the same look he was seeing on her face now. She would tell him that he was a dirty little boy, filthy, and if he touched himself again, she wouldn't love him.

She turned on her heels, leaving the room, and Kevin now felt Pearl trembling beside him. He forced the memories away, turning on his side to gather her in his arms. Softly he began to caress her.

'No, please, we can't,' she said, her body becoming rigid. 'Your ... your mother might hear us.'

'Not if we're quiet,' he whispered. Yet as he made to mount her again, he thought he heard a

303

noise outside their room, and tensed. Once again his erection died and he threw himself away with disgust.

'I ... I'm sorry,' Pearl whispered.

Kevin clutched at her apology. Yes, it was her fault, her bloody nerves putting him off. He turned on his side, whispered a curt good night, and then closed his eyes, the drink affecting him more than he realised as he almost immediately went to sleep.

28

Over a week passed, and Pearl's dream of a happy marriage was already fading. They still hadn't made love and she could sense Kevin's growing impatience. It was her fault, she knew that, but with her mother-in-law just across the landing she was unable to relax. Kevin would climb into bed now, immediately turning his back, whilst Pearl remained awake, just wishing that at least he would hold her in his arms.

Kevin went out most evenings and though Bernie tried to make Pearl feel at home when she joined them in the living room, Dolly kept her eyes glued to their small television and hardly spoke.

Now, as they closed the café on Saturday and she went upstairs, Pearl swallowed deeply, trying to pluck up the courage to speak to her mother-in-law about her wages.

She made them all a drink, wondering if she

should wait until Kevin came home to offer his support. Yet surely it was just an oversight, Dolly forgetting to pay her along with the others. As she handed her mother-in-law a cup of tea, it rattled in the saucer.

'Er ... Dolly, I think you've forgotten my wages.'

'Wages! Leave it out, girl. You're married to my son and whether I like it or not, you're part of this family now.'

'But–'

Dolly held up her hand, forestalling any argument. 'And, may I add, I don't take a penny for your keep. Pay indeed.'

'But I need to buy–'

'I can't see that you need anything,' Dolly interrupted. 'You live rent free, and all your meals are provided. I hope you don't think I'm providing money for you to waste on fripperies.'

'No, of course not, but my skirts won't fasten around my waist and I need a couple of maternity smocks.'

'Well, that's soon sorted. Gertie's good with a needle and she'll be able to add a bit to your skirts. She'll run you up a couple of maternity smocks too.' Dolly rose to her feet. 'I've got a length of material somewhere and I'll dig it out.'

Pearl watched her leave, her heart sinking. It wasn't just smocks she needed, there was underwear too. Bernie looked up from his newspaper, eyes sympathetic, and his voice barely above a whisper. 'I ain't got much, love, but I can give you five bob.'

'Oh, Bernie,' Pearl whispered gratefully, only to turn sharply as Dolly returned.

'There,' she said, holding up a piece of cream material, garishly patterned with bright pink chrysanthemums. 'It's been stuck in the cupboard for years, but I knew it would come in handy one day. I reckon there's enough here for at least two smocks.'

'Blimey, it looks like curtaining,' Bernie said.

'What does that matter? She'll only be wearing smocks for a few months and there's no sense in wasting money.'

'Well, if you say so,' Bernie said doubtfully, 'but I don't know what people are going to think if they see Pearl dressed in that. They'll think we can't afford anything better.'

Dolly frowned. 'Yeah, you may be right. I'll put this back in the cupboard and buy a new bit of material.'

Pearl could have hugged him. He'd obviously hit on the one thing that could make her mother-in-law change her mind: people's opinions.

As Dolly marched out of the room again, Bernie winked. 'You have to know how to handle her,' he whispered.

'Thanks,' Pearl mouthed, grateful that he was an ally in this strange household.

When Dolly returned, Bernie retreated into his newspaper again, and with a sigh Pearl found her fingers itching to paint, to bury her worries in art. Her supplies had run out, not only of paint, but sketching paper too, and with no money of her own, she'd be unable to buy any more. Art classes were a thing of the past now, her dream for the time being ending with her pregnancy. She missed the lessons, wishing she could still afford them, dreading the thought of another evening stuck indoors with her in-laws.

Kevin walked in at six o'clock, and for a moment Pearl brightened. It was Saturday night – perhaps he'd take her out. But her hopes were dashed when he spoke.

'I've got to go out again. Have you ironed my white shirt, Pearl?'

'Out again?' Bernie said, and, as though sensing how she felt, he added, 'Are you taking Pearl with you?'

'No. I've got a bit of business to sort out.'

'What – on a Saturday night?' Bernie asked, eyes narrowed as he gazed at his son.

'That's what I said, didn't I? Where's Mum?'

'She's having a bath.'

'Sod it. I need to talk to her. How long has she been in there?'

'A while. What do you want to talk to her about?'

'That's my business.'

'No doubt you're after money again. It's about time you found yourself a job.'

'I'm doing my best.'

Bernie shook his head in disgust. 'You're a married man now and should think about your wife and coming child.'

'He is looking, Bernie, really he is.'

'Oh yeah? Well, work ain't that hard to find.'

As Dolly walked into the room wrapped in a copious blue candlewick dressing gown, her eyes narrowed. 'Bernie, did I hear you having a go at Kevin?'

307

'I was just saying that he should get a job.'

'Keep your nose out of it, Bernie. I think I know what's best for my son and I don't want him working in some dead-end job without prospects. He has good qualifications and deserves a decent salary, not the pittances he's been offered so far.'

'Oh, so he's applied for some jobs then?'

'Of course he has,' Dolly snapped. 'Ain't that right, Kevin?'

Kevin blinked rapidly, his eyes avoiding his father's. 'Yes, but Mum, can I have a word with you in private?'

'Of course,' she said, beckoning him to her bedroom.

Kevin followed, but not before turning to Pearl. 'If you haven't ironed my white shirt, do it now.'

Pearl didn't move. Dolly had given her a stack of ironing yesterday, and she had done the lot, including Kevin's shirt.

Bernie said quietly, 'She'll give him money. She always does. I know what Dolly's game is. She doesn't want to lose her precious son, but she knows that if Kevin finds work the two of you will find a place of your own. Believe me, that's the last thing my wife wants and she'll do anything to keep him here.'

'But Kevin wants to leave as much as I do.'

'If you say so, love, but Dolly's crafty. She knows that as long as she provides Kevin with enough pocket money to keep him happy, the lazy bugger won't look for work.'

'But he *is* looking, he told me.'

'Huh, and pigs might fly. I don't believe him

308

and neither should you.'

Pearl shook her head, sure that Bernie was wrong. 'Do you think Kevin will speak to Dolly about my wages? I still need to buy a few things.'

'Leave it out, love. You've only been here a short while but you've seen how things stand. Kevin won't speak up for you, but maybe if you ask him, he'll drop you a few bob out of the money he gets out of his mother.'

'Oh, yes, I'll do that,' Pearl said, brightening now. When Kevin returned he went to their bedroom and Pearl followed. 'Kevin, your mother isn't paying me any wages now and I need some money.'

'Well, don't look at me.'

'But I need some new underwear and–'

Kevin paused in the act of throwing on his shirt, his eyes hard. 'If you want money, you'll have to sort it out with my mother. Now bugger off and leave me in peace.'

Pearl stared at him, her heart sinking. Since their marriage he had changed, his moods mostly foul. Nowadays, as she did with Dolly, Pearl tiptoed around him. She longed for his love, to be held in his arms, but he seemed so hard, so cold. *Oh, please let him get a job soon. Please let us find a place of our own.* Once away from his mother, Pearl was sure that she and Kevin would be fine.

Dolly's temper didn't improve, and a few days later another waitress walked out, leaving Madge to work the tables on her own.

Madge came through to the kitchen, puffing loudly to make her feelings plain. 'Why doesn't

Kevin help out a bit? If he did the counter, Bernie could give me a hand with the tables.'

'He's busy,' Dolly snapped.

'Doing what?'

'Madge,' Dolly said, her voice deceptively quiet, 'what my son does is no concern of yours. I said he's busy and that's an end to it. Until we find another waitress, I'll pay you a bit extra, but now I suggest you get back to work.'

'All right, but I ain't standing much more of this. In fact, I think I'll start looking around for another job.'

Pearl held her breath, waiting for her mother-in-law to explode, but Madge was at the end of her tether and if Dolly wasn't careful she'd walk out too, leaving them in a terrible fix.

For a moment the two women faced each other, but then Dolly heaved a great sigh. 'All right, Madge, if you want to get another job I can't stop you. However, if you stay I'll increase your wages permanently.'

Madge blinked rapidly, obviously as surprised as Pearl. 'By how much?'

'Another quid a week.'

She pursed her lips, her head cocked to one side as she thought it over. 'Yeah, all right, I'll stay.'

'Good, now as I said, get back to your work.'

No sooner had Madge left the kitchen than Dolly erupted. Her face red with anger, she banged a frying pan onto the cooker. 'Madge knew she had me over a barrel – the cow! Another quid a week! I must be mad. Huh, she thinks she's got one over me, but when we get another waitress, I might just give her the sack.'

With the potato peeler poised, Pearl glanced at the clock. It was ten o'clock, but she doubted Kevin was up. Since Bernie's comments, she too was beginning to doubt that he was looking for work. When he surfaced, Dolly would cook him a breakfast and he'd spend a leisurely hour eating it whilst reading the morning paper.

They'd only been married for two weeks, but Pearl was disillusioned. As long as Dolly kept Kevin provided with money, he seemed happy to remain there, virtually ignoring his new wife as he went about his own business. She no longer mentioned work to him, finding it put him in a nasty mood, and now she felt that he had lied to her about wanting a place of their own. Oh God, please let me be wrong, she prayed, dreading living permanently with her mother-in-law.

That evening Kevin cadged more money from his mother. She gave him a few quid, but not enough for a trip to Soho, and his frustration mounted. She was still keeping him short, and he couldn't get relief from Pearl – their lack of privacy had seen to that.

Pearl had stopped nagging him about a job at last, the silly cow unaware that he had plans in hand, ones he couldn't tell her about. Ones that hopefully would provide enough for a place of their own. He was going to rob the pub in Richmond, and to that end had given the barmaid a ring, pleased to find it was her night off and she was available.

Now he sat beside her, inwardly fuming. He'd

311

spent the last of his money inundating her with booze, but it had been a complete waste of time. New at the job, Mary had little information about the workings of the place.

At last he rose to his feet, snapping impatiently, 'Come on, I'll take you home.'

She looked up at him, eyes bleary and un-focused. 'Home? I don't want to go home yet.'

'Tough,' he said, grabbing her arm and heaving her up.

Kevin's jaw clenched, wishing now that he'd spent his money on a tart. How long had it been since he'd had a woman? Bloody ages. If he could get it up with Pearl it might have offered some release, but with his mother close by he found it impossible. Ashamed, he let Pearl think that she was to blame, turning his back on her every night.

Kevin walked out of the pub, his temper only just in check. The pub was remote, the car park, other than his car, empty. To ensure that nobody saw them together, he had arranged to pick Mary up at the end of her street, but his caution had been for nothing. Now he had to waste more petrol money driving the useless cow home again.

It was dark, woods surrounding them, but Kevin was uncaring of Mary as she swayed beside him. She tripped and he grabbed her arm, inadver-tently touching her breast.

She flapped her hand, saying with a silly giggle, 'Oh, you dirty boy.'

He stiffened. Dirty boy! Words his mother had used again and again when he was a child. He growled low in his throat, and in his angry and

312

frustrated state, Mary's comment set off a chain of action that overwhelmed Kevin.

Mindless now, his grip tightened on her arm as he dragged her towards the surrounding trees. Mary staggered beside him, hardly aware of what he was doing as he pulled her deeper into the woods.

Suddenly she halted. 'Where are we going?'

'Shut up, *bitch!*' Kevin hissed, forcing her forward again.

'Wh ... what?'

He ignored her as he looked wildly around. They were deep inside the woods now, fallen leaves crunching underfoot. It was perfect. There was hardly any light from the moon and, grinning with glee, Kevin threw Mary violently to the ground.

She landed heavily, crying out, but Kevin threw himself on top of her, his hands tearing at her clothes.

'No! No, don't!'

That was all Kevin needed, her cries like music to his ears. He smashed a fist into her face, and then began to tear at her clothes again, leering as she struggled beneath him.

She still resisted, arousing him, his actions becoming frantic as his fists beat again and again into her soft flesh. She was a woman, fighting him, and he punished her, his teeth sinking into her flesh.

At last she lay compliant and he loved it. He had won, she was helpless – his to control now as he forced her legs apart. He thrust inside her, groaning with pleasure, mindless as he sought the release he craved.

313

When had she become so still? Kevin had no idea, only aware, when he was finished, of Mary's motionless body beneath him. In the darkness he ran his hands over her, the breath leaving his body with relief when he felt her ribcage move. Christ, for a moment he thought he'd killed her.

His relief was short-lived as panic set in. Bloody hell, he was still in trouble. He'd raped her, beaten her. Staggering to his feet, he rushed blindly through the trees, thinking only of self-preservation.

Mary would go to the police, tell them she'd been raped, but what else could she tell them? Think, man! Think!

She didn't know his name; with the job in mind he'd been careful to give her a false one. Had he mentioned where he lived? No, of course he hadn't. His mind raced with his feet. How many people had seen them together? There had only been a couple of customers in the pub, old men playing cribbage, but the landlord might remember him and give a description.

Kevin's thoughts were still raging as he broke free of the woods, relieved to find himself close to the small car park. His car! Bloody hell, could they trace him through his car? He rushed towards it, diving into the passenger seat, at the same time realising that without them knowing the number plates, it would be unlikely.

He had to get away and quickly! Frantically gunning the engine to life, he roared out onto the narrow country road, sweat pouring down his face and almost blinding him as he screeched away around a corner.

29

Bessie locked the shop. She hadn't seen Pearl for a few days and was missing the girl. Pearl had been married for a few months now, and though she hadn't appeared happy at first, nowadays it seemed that everything in the garden was rosy.

They were still living with Dolly and, despite Pearl's protestations, Bessie thought Kevin was a lazy sod. He wasn't well, Pearl insisted, suffering from nerves, but Bessie didn't believe it. What did Kevin Dolby have to be nervous about? He'd been mollycoddled since childhood, spoiled rotten, and in her opinion it was just another excuse to avoid getting a job.

Bessie went upstairs, the empty living room cheerless as she walked in. Pearl had lived with her for only a short time, but since she'd left it emphasised her loneliness. Still, she had a card reading to do, and maybe Pearl would pop over to see her later.

She had barely made herself a cup of tea when the client arrived. Taking her into the living room, Bessie began to set the scene. She sat the woman opposite her at the table and then took out her cards, unwrapping them from a deep purple silk cloth. With a serious expression on her face she began to shuffle them, the cards old and worn after so much use. She then handed them to the client, the woman looking deeply worried as she took them. Bessie studied her, and judging by her age felt the consultation might be due to marital problems.

When the cards were returned she laid them out, glancing at the woman as she said, 'Ah, I see a dark-haired man, one you may have worries about.'

'Yes, that'd be my husband,' the woman replied eagerly, her back straightening in the chair.

Bessie hid a smile. She had hit on the problem almost immediately, making this reading easy. 'You care deeply for this man,' she offered.

'Yeah, I do,' she said sadly.

Bessie fished again, hoping she was right. 'You're suspicious about something, perhaps an affair?'

The woman's eyes filled with tears and, nodding, she sobbed, pulling a handkerchief out of her pocket. 'Yes,' she whispered.

Bessie turned another card, surprised to feel a sudden flash of intuition. 'You're wrong, he isn't having an affair.'

'But ... but he hasn't been himself lately. Are you sure?'

'Yes, I'm sure. I think it's his health that's worrying him, and maybe you should talk to him about it.'

'Oh, no! It ain't anything serious, is it?'

'The cards aren't clear, but I don't think so.' She placed a card across the last one, smiling softly. 'I see a good marriage, a strong marriage, and if your husband hasn't mentioned his concerns, it's because he wants to protect you from worry.'

'Oh God,' the woman said, 'and here I am thinking that just because he ain't touched me lately, he's having it off on the side.' She rose swiftly to her feet. 'Thanks, Bessie, but I don't want to hear any more. I just want to go home and talk to him. I've been giving the poor sod a rough time, and now I know that he doesn't deserve it I feel awful.'

As the woman opened her purse, Bessie held up a palm. 'No, love, it was only a short reading and there's no need to pay.'

'Thanks, it's kind of you,' the woman said.

She hurried from the room and Bessie had a job to keep up with her as she ran downstairs. She let her out, calling goodbye and then, puffing, returned to the living room. With a sigh she picked up the cards, shuffling them as her mind moved. The flash of intuition had come in handy, making the reading an easy one, but she couldn't help feeling a little concerned about the woman's husband. She hoped his illness wasn't serious, her intuition unclear about that, but at least now he would have his wife's support.

Bessie glanced at the clock, once again wondering if Pearl would pop over, and then, as she absentmindedly laid a card on the table, intuition flashed again. Her face stretched in horrified surprise as she stared at the card. She didn't want to see it, wanted to shut it out, hastily returning the card to the pack.

Pearl smiled as Kevin stretched out beside her. He had changed so much during the last few months, hardly ever going out now, and since he'd persuaded his mother to buy another television for their bedroom, they spent every evening together.

They still hadn't made love, but Pearl didn't mind. In her eighth month of pregnancy her stomach was huge and she found it difficult to sit or lay comfortably.

She still worked in the kitchen but for the first time there was a common consensus between Pearl and her mother-in-law, and that was their concern over Kevin's nerves. She still felt Dolly's animosity towards her, but at least she was used to it now and mostly able to ignore it.

Kevin was a little better, but there was a marked change in his personality that worried them. His swagger had gone, his confidence, and he was far too quiet. Not only that, his car, once his pride and joy, sat dirty and unused in the yard.

Pearl turned carefully onto her side, snuggling closer, her tummy pressed against him. *'Emergency – Ward Ten* is on in a minute.'

He moved away as if repulsed by her stomach. 'Huh, it's a load of old claptrap. I prefer *The Adventures of Robin Hood.*'

'Richard Greene is a bit of all right.'

'If you say so,' he said, swinging his feet to the floor and surprising her when he added, 'I'm popping out to buy a packet of fags. I won't be long.'

As Kevin left the room, Pearl turned onto her back again, feeling a twinge of pain. It soon passed and for while she was able to concentrate on her favourite programme, but then another small pain had her squirming uncomfortably. She'd had this before, and Dolly had told her the baby was probably pressing on a nerve. Thankfully the episodes were short-lived, and as she shifted into another position, Pearl's hands unconsciously stroking her tummy, whilst her eyes once again focused on the television.

When *Emergency – Ward Ten* came to an end, Pearl struggled to her feet. She was thirsty and slowly made her way to the kitchen.

'Are you all right, love?' Bernie said as she passed through the living room.

'I'm having a few twinges of pain again, but I expect they'll pass.'

'The baby isn't coming, is it?'

'Don't be daft,' Dolly snapped. 'She's got another month to go yet. Anyway, where's Kevin? He said he was only going out to buy cigarettes and I expected him back by now.'

'Me too,' Pearl agreed, gasping as she bent forward.

'You'd best sit down,' Bernie urged as he rose to his feet.

'It's only a small pain.' But even so, she sank thankfully onto the sofa.

Bernie hovered anxiously by her side. 'Do you want a glass of water or something?'

'For goodness' sake, stop mollycoddling the girl,' Dolly snapped.

Relieved that the small twinge had passed and anxious to placate her mother-in-law, Pearl struggled to her feet. 'I'm fine now and I'll make a cup of tea. Would you both like one?'

'I'll make it,' Bernie said, 'and if you ask me I think it's about time you stopped work.'

'Leave it out! I haven't found someone to stand

in for her yet, and until I do she'll have to carry on.'

'Have you seen her feet? They're swollen up like balloons.'

'That's nothing. Mine were the same when was carrying Kevin, but I don't remember you showing *me* any concern.'

'Honestly, Bernie, I don't mind working,' Pearl said, knowing that this could soon escalate into a violent row. She knew what her mother-in-law was capable of and had seen her laying into Bernie on several occasions. 'I've got a chair in the kitchen and can sit down whilst preparing the vegetables.'

Bernie shook his head doubtfully, but said no more as he headed for the kitchen.

Dolly stood up and, walking to the window, she drew the curtains aside. 'I can't imagine what's keeping Kevin.'

'Maybe he's met up with his friends and is having a drink–' Pearl suggested, breaking off with a gasp as another pain shot through her.

Dolly swung round at Pearl's gasp, her brow creased.

'If that's another pain you may be having contractions.'

'But the baby isn't due yet.'

'It could be coming early. We'll time them, and for Christ's sake sit down again before you fall down.' Dolly showed no sympathy as she added, 'And don't look at me like a frightened rabbit. You're only having a baby and there's no need to make a fuss.'

Kevin's eyes had flicked up and down the High Street before he stepped outside. It had been months now and surely he was safe? After it happened he'd scoured the newspapers, but there had been nothing, no report of a rape, and he was beginning to think that Mary hadn't reported it.

Maybe he could risk raising his head a little. With that thought in mind he made for the local pub. If he sat indoors with Pearl for much longer he'd go mad, the silly cow driving him daft with her inane chatter. At one time all he'd thought about was moving out, of finding a place of their own, but that had been put on the back burner now. They'd do it one day, but in the meantime they were fine where they were. With Pearl as big as a house he had no interest in her body, and his mother kept him supplied with pocket money.

He pulled open the bar door, a cloud of cigarette smoke engulfing him as he walked inside.

'Well, bugger me, look what the cat's dragged in,' Nobby said, his smile tight. 'Has your old woman let you off the leash at last?'

'Pearl hasn't got me on a leash. I've been a bit under the weather, that's all.'

'Don't take us for mugs, Kevin. We've seen you scuttling around on the odd occasion and you looked all right.'

'My asthma's been playing me up.'

'If you say so, but you've surfaced just in time. We're on to a nice little earner and need a driver.'

'No, thanks, mate. I want to keep my nose clean for a while.'

Nobby's eyes narrowed. 'I thought so, and I

ain't too pleased that you left us out of the loop.'

'What are you talking about?'

'There's only one reason why you'd keep your head down for this long and it ain't got anything to do with asthma. I reckon you did a job without us and nearly got caught.'

'That's rubbish. I told you I ain't been well and I came in here for a drink, not a cross-examination. Now if you don't mind I'm going to get myself a pint.' He glanced at the glasses in Nobby and Dick's hands. 'Are you ready for another?'

'Yeah, I wouldn't say no,' Dick Smedley said, speaking for the first time.

Nobby nodded an affirmative, but his voice was hard as he said, 'and once you've got them in, we'll talk again about the little scam we've got planned.'

'You can talk all you like, mate, but I ain't interested.'

Despite all the cajoling, Kevin refused the job. Nobby was angry, but he didn't care. As far as he was concerned the bloke was all mouth and he wasn't intimidated.

At ten thirty, after a good few whisky chasers, Kevin left the pub and staggered across the road. An ambulance was parked outside the café, but his eyes were barely able to focus. He halted in his tracks, swaying, but before he could gather his addled thoughts, it drove off.

With unsteady hands, Kevin let himself in, almost falling up the stairs to the living room, and as soon as his father saw him, he jumped to his feet.

'It's about time you turned up. Pearl's in labour

and she's been taken to hospital.'

'Where's Mum?'

'You weren't here so she's gone with Pearl and she ain't too pleased about it. Well, don't just stand there, get yourself to the hospital.'

Kevin grinned inanely, trying to focus on his father as he spoke again.

'Look at the state of you and you ain't fit to drive, that's for sure. I'll call you a taxi.'

With a bemused expression Kevin sank onto the sofa, closed his eyes and knew no more as he fell into a drunken sleep.

'Kevin! Kevin, wake up!'

'Wh ... what?'

'I said wake up.'

His mother's voice sounded loud in his ears and, managing to open one eye, Kevin saw her looming over him.

'You've got a son.'

'Wh ... what?'

'Christ, you sound like a parrot. Wake up, for Gawd's sake.'

'What's the time?'

'It's four o'clock. Now did you hear what I said? You've got a son!'

Kevin's head was thumping and he groaned, trying to pull himself upright, surprised to find himself on the sofa. His mouth was dry, and he grimaced at the bitter acrid taste on his tongue. 'Any chance of a cup of tea, Mum?'

'Bloody hell, Kevin. I can't believe you. I've just told you that you're a father and all you can do is ask for a cup of flaming tea.'

Kevin knuckled his eyes and saw his father coming into the room, his expression showing concern.

'How is she, Dolly?' Bernie asked.

'She's fine, but it was a long labour. Well, Bernie, you're a grandfather. Pearl gave birth to a lovely, bouncing boy.'

At last Kevin's brain began to function. 'Pearl's had the baby?'

Dolly exhaled loudly. 'So, you've come to life at last. You picked a fine time to go missing and I've been stuck at that flaming hospital all night.'

'She's actually had the baby?'

'Am I talking to myself? Yes, she's had the baby and you have a son.'

'Christ,' Kevin said, sinking back with shock.

'Make us all a drink, Bernie. I'm fair worn out and without any sleep I don't know how I'm gonna cope with the café today. Bloody hell, who's gonna do the vegetables?'

'I can't believe this, Mum,' Kevin said as his father scuttled from the room. 'The baby wasn't due yet.'

'He came a bit early, but he's fine and you can see him later.'

'And Pearl's all right?'

'Yes, of course she is.'

'Bloody hell, I'm a dad,' Kevin whispered in awe.

'I've been trying to get that through your thick skull for the last fifteen minutes.' His mother's words sounded harsh at first, but now she smiled softly. 'He's a lovely baby and the spitting image of you.'

'Is he?' Kevin said eagerly. *His son!* And he couldn't wait to see him.

'Here you are,' Bernie said, passing a cup of tea to Dolly and then handing one to Kevin.

Dolly yawned widely. 'Trust that girl to go into labour at such an awkward time, and now we're well and truly stuck.'

'You could ask Madge to do the vegetables. The new waitress will just have to manage on her own.'

'I suppose it's a possibility, but she ain't gonna be too happy about it. Still, it'll only be for just over a week. Pearl will be home again then and we can get back to normal.'

'I don't see why Kevin can't give us a hand. If he takes over the counter, I can cover for Madge while she's working in the kitchen.'

'Leave it out, Dad. I'm going to the hospital to see my son.'

'You can't go yet,' Dolly said. 'Visiting time isn't until one o'clock and there's nothing to stop you giving us a hand. That goes for every day until Pearl comes home.'

'But, Mum–'

'No arguments, Kevin,' she said, her voice firm. 'It won't hurt you to help out. After all, it's your wife that's putting us to all this inconvenience, and until she can get back to work we'll have to pull together.'

Kevin gazed up at his mother, wanting to argue, but this time he could see that she was in no mood for cajoling. She looked tired, dark rings under her eyes.

Suddenly he was struck by a thought. 'Hold on,

325

Mum. Pearl won't be able to work in the café when she comes home. She'll have the baby to see to and I don't fancy taking Dad's place behind the counter permanently.'

'Don't worry, son, there'll be no need for that. I've got it all worked out but I'm too tired to talk about it now. I'm gonna have a bath and hopefully it will freshen me up.'

Kevin frowned, wondering what his mother had in mind, but then his mouth tightened. Christ, he dreaded working in the café and, like his mother, he'd be glad when Pearl came home.

30

Dolly was pacing up and down, the baby held firmly in her arms. 'One more day off, Pearl, and then you can get back to work.'

'But how? I can't leave Johnny.'

'We just need a routine, that's all, and I've worked it all out.'

'But–'

'It's simple,' Dolly interrupted. 'You can start work extra early and I'll look after the baby while you prepare the vegetables. As long as I'm downstairs by six o'clock it'll be fine, and you won't need to be in the kitchen again until it's time to cook them.'

'Who'll look after Johnny while I'm doing that?'

'Kevin can watch him for an hour or so or, failing that, we can have him with us in the kitchen.'

Pearl ruminated on Dolly's words. Yes, she could start work early, but would she be able to drag herself out of bed? 'I'm hardly getting any sleep. Johnny only lasts an hour before he wants another feed.'

Dolly smiled fondly at the baby. 'Yes, I heard him last night. He's a hungry little bugger, that's for sure. The best solution would be to put him on a bottle and then any of us can feed him.'

'Oh, no, I don't want to do that!'

'If he wants feeding that often, it's probably because you haven't enough milk to satisfy him. Surely you don't want to starve the poor little mite?'

'Not enough milk? But he only woke up once a night when I was in hospital.'

'While he was in the nursery they probably topped him up with a bottle. After all, they wouldn't want to disturb all the other mothers in the ward by bringing him to you every hour.'

'But surely my milk is best for him.'

'Not if he's hungry. A bottle would be the best thing. Wait and see, he'll thrive.'

'I'm still not sure.'

'Well I am, so that's an end to it. Now take Johnny for a minute while I find my purse. I'll give you the money for all the paraphernalia. You'll need to buy bottles, teats, and powdered milk. Then in the morning, we can start the new routine.'

Pearl wanted to protest, but was too scared of Dolly to argue. 'I'll take Johnny with me to the chemist. It'll do him good to get a bit of fresh air.'

'No, it'll be quicker to go on your own. You can

leave him with me,' Dolly insisted, laying the money on the table and taking Johnny from Pearl's arms.

With a sigh Pearl did as she was told, and was soon outside, heading for the chemist. She turned the corner, almost colliding with Derek.

'Oh!'

'Well, well, I didn't expect you to be out and about so soon.'

'Oh ... you've heard that I've had my baby.'

'Yeah, I heard. I may not be working my stall, but gossip still reaches me. How are you doing?'

Pearl was relieved that Derek wasn't showing any animosity. His expression was mild. 'I'm all right, and Dolly insists that I start work again tomorrow.'

'That soon?'

'Yes, well, you know Dolly. My mother-in-law rules the roost and we all have to do as she says. Mind you, Kevin won't be too pleased about having to look after the baby while I'm working in the kitchen.'

His face immediately hardened, mouth grim as he replied, 'Yeah, somehow I can't see Kevin as a babysitter. Still, you knew what he was like – Dolly too – before you schemed to marry him. As the saying goes, you made your bed and now you've got to lie on it.'

Pearl knew she deserved this, deserved all that Derek threw at her. 'I hurt you, and I'm sorry, but I didn't mean to. Really I didn't.'

'It's a bit late for apologies now, Pearl,' Derek said, and as her eyes met his, he gazed into them for a moment. 'When I look at you like this, I can't believe what happened. Dolly told her story, Kevin too, but somehow, along with yours, they don't ring true. If you want to open up, I'll listen, and if you're unhappy, you only have to say the word.'

Pearl tore her eyes away. Time had passed, but even if Derek found out the truth, he might still go for Kevin. No, she had to keep her mouth shut – for both their sakes. 'It *was* the truth, Derek, and if you hate me, I don't blame you.'

He opened his mouth to speak, but she interrupted. 'I'm sorry. I must go now. 'Bye, Derek,' she blurted, hurrying away.

Pearl rushed to the chemist, saddened by her encounter with Derek. She had opened up old wounds for him, seen his pain. Oh, if only they didn't have to see each other, if only she and Kevin could move from this area. Kevin's nerves had been bad and he had given up looking for work, but he was recovering, and now maybe she could broach the subject again.

Another week passed. Pearl had been home for over two weeks now and disturbed by her's movements, Kevin turned over in bed. He forced his eyes open to glance at the clock. Bloody hell, it wasn't even four in the morning and he didn't know how she got up this early to start work.

'Kevin! Kevin, where's the baby?'

He ignored the panic in her voice, saying impatiently, 'In his bleeding cot. Where do you think?'

'He isn't. It's empty.'

'What!' He swung his legs over the side of the

329

bed, his mind jumbled before he had a coherent thought. 'Maybe Mum's got him.'

Their eyes met, and without another word they made for Dolly's room.

As Kevin opened the door, all he could see were two humps in the bed and his heart began to thump in panic.

'Mum, wake up!' he shouted. 'Johnny isn't in his cot.'

'Bloody hell, where's the fire,' Dolly grumbled as she turned onto her back. 'I heard him crying in the night again so I brought him in with me.' She moved the blankets to reveal Johnny snuggled by her side.

'Christ, Mum, you frightened the life out of us.'

'Well, that's nice, ain't it? I thought I'd give Pearl the chance of a good night's sleep and this is the thanks I get.'

'Yeah, sorry, Mum,' Kevin said his heart calming down. 'It was good of you.'

'I'd better give him his bottle before I start work,' Pearl said as she stepped forward.

'He's already had it, *and* I've changed his nappy. The poor little mite was soaking wet,' Dolly said reproachfully, and then her tone broaching no argument she added, 'he can stay with me and you can put the kettle on.' Kevin glared at his wife, his voice equally harsh. 'You daft cow Pearl. I'm going back to bed and I don't appreciate being woken up for nothing.'

Pearl saw her husband storm off, and chastened by both him and his mother, she headed for the kitchen. Whilst waiting for the kettle to boil, she had a quick wash, finding her breasts hard and painful, engorged with milk as she gingerly took off her nightdress. Tears filled her eyes as a feeling of helplessness washed over her. In the short time she'd been home from the hospital, Dolly had taken over her son, so much so that she hardly felt that Johnny was hers. Even his name had been Dolly's choice, Kevin happily falling in with his mother's suggestion.

The kettle began to whistle, and hurriedly throwing on her dressing gown, Pearl rushed to make the tea, carrying two cups through to Dolly's bedroom as soon as it had brewed.

'About time too,' her mother-in-law complained.

'Morning, Pearl,' Bernie said, but his eyes were on the baby snuggled between them. 'Look at him, he's spark out, but how come he's in with us every morning?'

It was Dolly who answered, 'The poor little nipper was screaming his lungs out, but as usual Pearl didn't hear him. Honestly, I don't know how she sleeps through it. I always heard Kevin when he was a baby.'

Unable to believe that she'd failed to hear Johnny crying again, Pearl's eyes filled with tears. What sort of mother was she?

'Get going, girl,' Dolly snapped. 'There's work to be done, but you're standing there like a tit in a trance.'

Pearl nodded, throwing one last glance at her son before leaving the room. He looked so snug and cute sandwiched between her in-laws, but her arms ached to hold him, to console him for not hearing his cries. Pearl dashed her tears away.

The sooner she prepared the vegetables, the sooner she'd be back again and for a while she'd have Johnny to herself. She hurriedly dressed and, without bothering to drink her tea, dashed downstairs.

That afternoon, when she finished cooking the vegetables, and despite Dolly's scowl, Pearl went across to see Bessie, the woman smiling as she went into the shop.

'Hello, love,' she said, moving to look into the pram, her face soft as she gazed at Johnny. 'He's thriving.'

'Yes, and it seems Dolly was right about putting him on the bottle.'

'If you say so. Anyway, what's up, love? You seem a bit down in the mouth.'

'Nothing really.'

'Don't give me that. Now come on, tell me what the problem is.'

Pearl sighed. 'It's just that I don't hear Johnny crying in the night and I feel like a useless mother.'

'Considering that you have to be up at four in the morning, it ain't surprising.'

'Dolly said she never failed to hear Kevin when he was a baby.'

'Huh, I can see she's still holding herself up as a saint.'

'She wakes for Johnny, and I don't.'

'If you ask me, you shouldn't have to work in the café. When is Kevin going to get a job?'

'I don't know. I mentioned it yesterday, but he said his nerves are still bad.'

'Huh, nerves my arse.'

'Oh, Bessie, don't be like that. I'm sure as soon as he's able, he'll find work.'

The door opened, a woman coming in.

'Hello, Tessa,' Bessie said. 'What have you got for me?'

'A really nice coat,' she said, laying a parcel on the counter.

Bessie opened the package, the smell arising awful. She held it up, her nose wrinkling. 'Sorry, love, but I can only give you a tanner for it.'

'All right, and thanks,' Tessa said, her hand held out.

Bessie gave her the money, and Pearl shook her head as the woman left the shop. 'That coat's only fit for the dustbin. Why on earth did you buy it?'

'Tessa's struggling. Her son used to look after her, but he's just been sent down for six months.'

'What did he do?'

'A bit of petty thieving. He'll see me all right when he comes out again and, in the meantime, us locals will keep an eye on Tessa.'

Pearl nodded, used now to the ways of the area. She still felt like an outcast, and missed the easy camaraderie she used to have with the coster-mongers. They didn't cut her dead now, and some stopped her to have a look at the baby, but others still refused to speak.

Pearl glanced at the clock. 'I'd best get back or Dolly will go on the warpath.'

'Christ, girl, you've hardly been here for five minutes.'

'I know, but when the café closes she likes to

333

spend time with Johnny.'

'Whose baby is he? Yours or Dolly Dolby's?'

'He's mine, of course, but I don't want to get on her bad side.'

'Pearl, when are you going to stand up for yourself?'

'Stop worrying, I'm fine,' Pearl lied. 'I'll see you soon, but I must go.'

Bessie didn't look convinced, but Pearl ignored this as she hurried back to the café. It was all right for Bessie to say she should stand up for herself, but she didn't live with Dolly.

This thought was affirmed when Pearl walked into the living room.

'It's about time too,' Dolly snapped, immediately rising to her feet and taking Johnny from her arms. 'Bloody hell, what sort of mother are you? His nappy is soaking wet.'

'Is he?' Pearl said, her eyes widening with surprise. Johnny had felt fine to her and she was sure he didn't want changing. 'I ... I'll change his nappy.'

'No, I'll do it,' Dolly snapped. 'I've shown you time and time again, but you never do it right and one of these days you'll stick him with the bloody nappy pin.'

Pearl knew that when Dolly was around she was fumbling and awkward, the constant criticism making her nervous. 'I wouldn't do that. I'd never stick the pin in him.'

'Huh, so you say. Anyway I could do with a cup of tea. Leave Johnny to me and get to the kitchen. I'm peckish too, so make me a sandwich while you're at it.'

'I'll do it,' Bernie offered, throwing Pearl a sympathetic glance.

'No you won't,' Dolly snapped. 'I told Pearl to do it and don't need your interference. There ain't much she can do, especially when it comes to looking after this poor little bugger, but at least she's learned to make a decent brew.'

Pearl felt her eyes filling with tears, but hurriedly left the room, at least making sure that Dolly didn't have the satisfaction of seeing them, something she obviously enjoyed.

Oh, if only Kevin would get a job, Pearl thought for the thousandth time. If only they had a place of their own.

31

A month passed and at five one Saturday afternoon, Kevin was sitting on the side of their bed, Pearl beside him. She was looking scrawny and miserable, and he tensed, fed up with her constant complaints.

'I'm at the end of my tether, Kevin. I don't feel that Johnny is our baby. Your parents seem to have him all the time, and every morning when I wake up I find him in their bed.'

'Whose fault is that? You still don't hear him crying in the night, and you should thank God that my mother does. She looks awful lately, with dark circles under her eyes from lack of sleep, but you don't hear her complaining.'

'I can't understand why I don't hear him. I wasn't a heavy sleeper before Johnny was born, so why now?'

'How should I know?' Kevin shifted on the bed, hoping that Pearl had said her piece, but no, she was off again.

'I'm grateful that she hears Johnny, but it's getting me down that she undermines everything I do. I'm fine with Johnny when we're on our own, but when your mother's around she acts as though I'm incapable of looking after him and it's turning me into a bundle of nerves.'

'Don't exaggerate, and I'm sure she only telling you what's best for the boy.'

'What's best in *her* opinion. But Johnny's our son, not hers. As soon as the café closes your mother shoots up here to take him over. Where is he now? He's not in here, with us, that's for sure. He's in the living room with your parents.'

'He's their first grandson and they're bound to be a bit doting.'

'Please, Kevin, go and get him.'

'Why me?'

'Your mother won't give him to me. Please, love, she won't say no to you.'

With a sigh Kevin rose from the bed. 'All right, anything for a quiet life.'

As Kevin stepped into the living room it was to see Johnny on the floor, his mother changing his nappy. He grinned as his son's fists waved, but then his chubby little hands moved down, one of them touching his tiny penis.

'Stop that,' Dolly admonished as she slapped his hand away. 'You're a dirty little boy.'

Kevin's face darkened and, rushing over, he snatched his son up into his arms. 'Don't say that, Mum. It ain't right.'

'Say what?'

'That he's dirty when he touches himself. He's only a baby, for Christ's sake, and doesn't understand.'

'It's best to start as you mean to go on, and I intend to break *that* nasty habit as soon as I can.'

Kevin's anger mounted, words spilling out of his mouth without thought. 'It's perfectly natural – something that grown men do too. What's wrong with giving ourselves a bit of pleasure?'

'Kevin, don't speak to me like that – it's disgusting!'

Johnny started to cry and Kevin heaved a deep breath in an effort to calm down, his voice now registering controlled anger. 'Mum, there's nothing disgusting about masturbation. In future, if my son wants to play with himself, he can. You made me feel dirty as a child – even going so far as to tell me you wouldn't love me if I touched myself. Well, you ain't doing the same to Johnny.'

He saw his mother's jaw gape, but before she had time to speak he turned to leave, managing a mocking smile as he added, 'And anyway, you needn't worry. I think it'll be some time before Johnny manages to toss himself off.'

'You filthy boy! How dare you speak to me like that? Get out of my sight.'

'Don't worry, I'm going,' Kevin snarled as he stomped from the room.

Pearl took Johnny from his arms, comforting the squalling child, whilst Kevin flopped down beside her. The baby quietened and Kevin watched as Pearl expertly folded a nappy, laying their son across her lap as she fastened the triangular shape in place with a pin.

Kevin was still seething. Deciding that he was safe, that the coast was clear now, he was filled with renewed determination. 'It's about time we found a place of our own, Pearl.'

Her head swung round, her eyes wide with delight. 'Oh, I'd love that.'

'Right, and to raise some money I'd better see about finding a job.'

'The local paper is due out tomorrow. There's bound to be something advertised.'

Kevin smiled faintly. It wasn't employment he was seeking, but Pearl didn't know that. What he needed was to raise money quickly and that would be impossible, working in a sodding engineering factory.

He stretched out on the bed, already formulating a plan. He'd considered this job ages ago but, thinking it too risky, had discarded the idea. Now, though, the need to get away from his mother overcame his doubts.

Sleep eluded Pearl. At last Kevin was going to get a job. Excited about the future, unusually she was still awake after midnight.

She turned onto her side, but had just snuggled under the blankets when the bedroom door swung slowly open. In the dim light Pearl saw her mother-in-law creeping into the room, moving stealthily to the cot, her hands reaching inside.

Pearl swiftly turned on the bedside light. 'What

are you doing?'

Dolly visibly jumped, her voice blustering as she said, 'I thought I heard Johnny crying.'

'He hasn't made a sound.'

'How would *you* know? When was the last time *you* heard him crying in the night?'

'What's going on?' Kevin asked as he pushed himself up on one elbow. 'Can't a bloke get a bit of sleep?'

'Your mother said she heard Johnny crying, but I've been awake all this time and can assure you he didn't make a sound.'

'Well, I must have been mistaken,' Dolly snapped. 'Anyway, now I'm here I might as well take him. No doubt he'll want a bottle soon.'

Anger gave Pearl the courage to speak, her voice quiet but firm. 'There's no need. I'll see to him, but thank you anyway.'

To her surprise, Dolly said no more, just throwing Pearl a dark look as she turned on her heels to storm from the room.

Pearl didn't speak until the bedroom door closed. 'Kevin, have you ever heard Johnny in the night?'

'No,' he said shortly, plumping up his pillow.

'Don't you think it's a bit strange that neither of us have heard him crying?'

'Let it rest, Pearl. I want some sleep.'

'I can't. Your mother came to take Johnny, but he wasn't making a sound. I think she's being doing it every night.'

He turned onto his back, yawning widely. 'Yeah, you could be right.'

'Kevin, don't you see what this means? She's

339

been accusing me of being an awful mother, but I'm not,' Pearl cried, her voice high with indignation. 'I didn't hear Johnny because he wasn't in his cot.'

'Yeah, and I'm sorry, love. I don't know what my mother's game is, but I should have listened to you before. Well, we know what she's up to now, and don't worry – we'll be out of here soon.'

Pearl smiled as she flung back the blankets, hurrying to the cot. Despite the noise, Johnny remained undisturbed and it seemed a shame to wake him. Sure now that she would hear him if he cried, Pearl climbed back into bed. 'Oh, I can't wait for us to have a place of our own,' she whispered as she flung an arm round Kevin, only to find that he had already gone back to sleep.

It didn't matter, Kevin was on her side now, and for once she felt him an ally against her mother-in-law's games.

Johnny had woken once during the rest of the night and Pearl was immediately roused. Her eyes were bleary as she fed him, changed him, and then settled him down again. She wanted to confront Dolly, but fear still held her back. Kevin had assured her that they'd be in their own home soon and, dreading a face-to-face argument with her formidable mother-in-law, she decided it would be best to say nothing.

Pearl climbed wearily back into bed, relieved that it was Sunday and she didn't have to get up early. Kevin turned over and, though asleep, his arms enfolded her. She smiled softly, enjoying the closeness as she snuggled in. With Dolly

340

around, she was still tense, and Kevin had given up trying to make love to her. She didn't blame him, but things would be different in their own home. They'd have a normal love life – a normal marriage – and she couldn't wait.

Warm and snug, Pearl closed her eyes, immediately drifting off to sleep and was surprised to find when she woke again that it was after seven.

She went to the cot but Johnny was still asleep, one little hand tucked under his chin. Kevin moaned softly, stretched his arms and then pushed himself up on to one elbow. His hair was tousled, his face relaxed and she couldn't miss the growing resemblance. 'Do you know, Johnny is getting more and more like you.'

'Is he? Then he must be a handsome little devil.'

'Oh, he is,' Pearl said, adding with a smile, 'but his head isn't as big as yours.'

Kevin grinned and Pearl's heart swelled with love. Johnny stirred and she picked him up, placing him in Kevin's arms. He gazed at their son, his affection obvious, and once again Pearl's heart soared. He was a good father, and now their future together looked rosy.

'Yuk, he's bloody soaking.'

'Well, you'd better change his nappy then. I'm off to make his bottle.'

'Leave it out, Pearl. That's women's work.'

She shook her head, feigning exasperation. Some things would never change and sorting out their son's nappy was always going to be down to her.

32

After changing Johnny, Pearl went to the kitchen, relieved to find that her in-laws weren't up. She made the baby's bottle and a cup of tea, returning to the bedroom with everything balanced on a tray.

Johnny was squalling and Kevin held him out. 'He wants his grub.'

Pearl placed the tray on the chest of drawers and, perching on the side of the bed, she gave the baby his bottle, watching as he pulled on the teat.

'Kevin, if you don't mind, I think I'll pop over to see Bessie later.'

'Why you bother with that old ragbag is beyond me, but I'm going out too so please yourself.'

'Bessie's been good to me and I'm fond of her. Where are you going?'

'I've got someone to see – a bit of business to sort out.'

'Oh, is it to do with a job?'

'Yeah, you could say that,' Kevin said, smiling enigmatically as he threw back the blankets, heading for the bathroom.

Johnny finished his feed, and after Pearl had winded him he contentedly drifted off to sleep. She gently placed him in the cot, smiling down at him for a moment before leaving to rinse out his bottle. Dolly was in the kitchen now, making a fresh brew, but she totally ignored Pearl. The atmosphere was awful, tense, and when Kevin finally showed his face, he received the same treatment.

Dolly continued to bang around, slamming doors, driving them out of the kitchen and, soon after, the house, earlier than they'd anticipated.

'We might be in for a bit of a rough ride,' Kevin said as they left the café. 'My mother can sulk for England, but she can stew in her own juice as far as I'm concerned.'

Pearl grinned. 'Any more metaphors before we part company?'

'You cheeky bitch,' Kevin said, but his smile took the sting out of his words. He leaned over to give her a swift kiss on the cheek, gave Johnny the same, calling, 'See you later,' as he sauntered off.

Pearl pushed the pram across the road, feeling that something had shifted in their relationship. Kevin seemed warmer, more relaxed, his nerves completely gone and a swagger back in his step.

'Hello, ducks,' Bessie said as she opened the door. 'Come on in.'

Pearl lifted Johnny from his pram and followed the old woman upstairs, but her nose wrinkled as she walked into the living room.

'Get that sour look off your face,' Bessie said. 'I know the place is a mess, but after running the shop all week, I'm too knackered on my day off to worry about housework.'

Pearl took at good look at the old woman and didn't like what she saw. Bessie looked pasty, her eyes hooded with tiredness. 'You look awful.'

'Thanks and it's nice to see you too,' she retorted, flopping onto a chair and holding out her arms. 'Blimey, he gets bigger every time I see him.'

When Pearl laid Johnny in Bessie's arms, the old woman tickled him under the chin, but he remained undisturbed, sleeping soundly. 'He sure likes his kip.'

'Yes, he's a contented baby,' Pearl replied before turning on her heels to head for the scullery. 'I'll make us a drink.'

The room was in an awful state, dishes piled in the sink, all her work when she had lived with Bessie undone. She shook her head and set to, but it was some time before she returned to the living room.

'Here,' she said, placing a cup of tea beside Bessie.

'Blimey, it's about time. What have you been doing out there?' Before Pearl had time to reply she sailed on, 'Huh, I can guess. You've been cleaning up. It's good of you, but I'd have got round to it eventually.'

'You said you're worn out, and I think a rest is more important.' She took Johnny from Bessie's arms, laying him gently on the sofa. 'While he's sleeping, I'll tidy up in here.'

'Leave it, love. Other than the occasional card reading, you're the only person who visits me, so what does a bit of mess matter?'

'It won't take long.'

'What is it with you and housework? I'd rather you sat down for a chat.'

'We can talk while I'm working.'

'How are things over in the café?'

Pearl paused, a pile of old newspapers in her

arms. 'You wouldn't believe it if I told you.'

'For Gawd's sake, you're making my neck ache. Leave the bloody tidying up and sit down.'

Returning the newspapers to where she had found them, Pearl flopped beside Johnny. 'I don't know where to start really but, as you know, I haven't been hearing the baby at night.'

'Yeah, and I know it's upsetting you.'

'It was, but not now. I couldn't sleep last night, and Johnny wasn't crying, but it didn't stop Dolly from sneaking into our room to take him.'

Bessie straightened in her chair. 'Bloody hell, and do you think she's been doing that every night?'

'Yes, I'm sure she has.'

'Huh, with the way she's been trying to take him over, I should have guessed.' Bessie chuckled. 'Blimey, you've got Dolly well and truly scuppered now and I bet she doesn't like that. I hope you gave her what for.'

'Er ... not really, but I didn't let her take Johnny and she wasn't too happy about that.'

Bessie's brow lifted. 'In other words, you're letting her get away with it.'

'Oh, Bessie, the atmosphere is awful now and there's no point in making it worse, especially as Kevin is getting a job and we'll be in our own place soon.'

'Huh, I wouldn't count your chickens before they're hatched.'

'What do you mean?'

'Look, it's nothing. Forget I said anything. I'm just annoyed that you've let Dolly get away with it but I should have kept my mouth shut.'

The old woman had her head down, and Pearl looked at her worriedly. She'd heard metaphors from Kevin, but Bessie's felt somehow prophetic. 'I can't just forget it. You inferred that something is going to stop us from getting a place of our own. Have you had another vision?'

'I told you, it's nothing. It happened a while ago, after I gave someone a reading, but it was just a flash.'

Bessie was still avoiding eye contact so Pearl didn't believe her. She had seen something bad, Pearl was sure of it, and her heart began to thump.

'Bessie,' she begged, 'you can't leave me up in the air like this. Please, please, tell me what you saw.'

A sigh escaped Bessie's lips and finally she turned her head. 'Christ, me and my big mouth, but I can see you ain't gonna leave me in peace until I tell you. All right, if you must know, I saw Kevin in some sort of trouble.'

'What sort of trouble?'

'I told you it was only a flash. All I saw was Kevin surrounded by policemen.'

'Oh God! Was it an accident or something? Was Kevin all right?'

'*I don't know!* It was unclear and, if you ask me, best left alone.'

'You don't know!' Pearl shrieked. 'But you must have seen if he was all right.'

'Bloody hell, why do you think I didn't want to tell you? I knew this would happen and that you'd want answers I can't give you.'

Pearl's cries had disturbed Johnny and he awoke,

squalling. She picked him up, rocking him in her arms. 'When is this going to happen?'

'I don't know, but I think soon.'

Pearl closed her eyes. Bessie had seen Kevin surrounded by policemen. What did it mean? Oh God, she prayed, please let him be all right.

The road was quiet, few people around early on a Sunday morning. Kevin stood in the opposite doorway, gazing across at the shop. When he'd first considered this job, he'd thought about ambushing the old man when he took his takings to the bank, but after following him a few times he'd seen there were always a lot of people about, making it far too risky.

His eyes took in the alarm box above the jeweller's. He'd foolishly hoped to get in that night, but the system was state of the art and too hard for him to crack. Kevin scowled. He didn't want to bring Nobby and Dick in on the job, but what was the alternative?

Kevin emerged from the doorway and walked across the road. The only alternative would be to hit the shop when it was open, a risky move but, thinking of the mass of gems inside – which he didn't want to share with Nobby and Dick – he licked his lips. If he covered his face and got in and out quickly, maybe he could get away with it.

Kevin peered through security grids on the windows, seeing large displays of jewellery, and knew that even if he managed to get only the stuff on show, it would fetch a pretty penny. He moved into the deep entrance now, taking in the side windows. To the right he saw watches and clocks, and to the left more fine jewellery. The door was covered by another thick grid and, hearing a key turning in the lock, Kevin's eyes widened as it slid back. The door then opened, an old man emerging.

As their eyes met, both froze for a moment, but it was Kevin who moved first. Bloody hell, it was fate, it had to be. He shoved the old man back into the interior, kicking the door closed with his heel. Christ, who'd have thought the jeweller would be in the premises on a Sunday. Talk about luck!

Kevin took in the shop, seeing that, like outside, the internal windows were covered by security grids. He pointed at them, voice thick with menace as he growled, 'Give me the keys.'

The old man was trembling. 'I'll get them for you, but please, don't hurt me.'

'If you do as I say, you'll be fine. However...' Kevin left the threat hanging in the air.

'Th ... they're behind the counter,' the jeweller muttered, and Kevin pushed him roughly forward.

The old man shuffled behind the counter, fumbling underneath whilst Kevin's thoughts raced, his adrenalin high. This was great and he still couldn't believe his luck. It was so easy, the geezer obviously terrified and under his control.

At that moment an alarm sounded, jangling loudly in Kevin's ears. He looked around in panic, his eyes wild as they turned to the jeweller.

'You bastard! You set off the alarm!'

'I ... I know you. I've seen you somewhere before,' the old man spluttered, unaware that his words sealed his fate.

With a cry of rage Kevin swept up the only thing to hand, a heavy chair in front of the counter. He lifted it high before swinging it down with all his might, smashing it on to the old man's head.

The bastard had recognised him! His rage now out of control, Kevin ran behind the counter, hitting the man again with the only thick piece of wood left in his hand.

The alarm still sounded, jangling loudly, but Kevin hardly heard it now. He couldn't leave the man alive – he had to silence him – and seeing only a wall of red before his eyes, he smashed into the jeweller's skull over and over again.

Blood spurted from the old man's head, but mindlessly Kevin carried on, only stopping when a hand seized his arm from behind.

The grip was vicelike and, looking over his shoulder with sweat pouring down his face, Kevin saw the hand belonged to a policeman.

33

Dolly was in deep shock – Pearl too, but somehow she had to keep going for Johnny's sake. For the first time in the living memory of most locals, the café was closed, and had been for a week.

Bernie threw yesterday's newspaper to one side with disgust. 'I don't know how they got hold of Kevin's photo, but his face is plastered all over the front page again.'

'I don't care what they say. It was self-defence, it had to be. My son would never do something like that.'

'I don't think the jeweller could have put up a fight. He's an old man and lucky to be alive.'

'There must have been someone else with Kevin and he did it.'

'Not according to the police. Christ, Dolly, he was caught in the act, and he was the only one there.'

'Shut up, Bernie! Instead of standing up for Kevin, it sounds like you've already decided he's guilty.'

'I'm just facing the facts.'

'I'm telling you he didn't do it!' Dolly cried, but she remained seated, for once not lashing out at her husband.

Pearl had been surprised by her father-in-law's reaction to the news. He'd shown no sympathy for his son, his thoughts for the poor old jeweller, whom Kevin had bludgeoned almost to death. She shuddered, still hardly able to believe that her husband was capable of doing such a thing.

Someone was banging on the front door. Seeing that both her in-laws were ignoring it, Pearl made her way downstairs. Tentatively she opened the door.

'Mrs Dolby?' a man said. 'I'm a reporter from the *Sketch* and–'

'Go away!' Pearl screamed, cutting off the man's words as she slammed the door in his face.

The letterbox lifted. 'Have you any comment about the new accusations against your husband?'

New accusations! What new accusations? For a

moment Pearl stood rooted to the spot, but then she turned, racing back upstairs. 'Bernie! There's a reporter outside and he said something about Kevin facing new accusations.'

'Christ, that can only mean the jeweller's snuffed it. Kevin must be facing a murder charge now.'

'No. Oh, no!' Dolly sobbed.

They soon found out when, following another loud banging on the door, Pearl went to the window to see a costermonger walking away. She crept downstairs to find that today's newspaper had been shoved through the letterbox.

After reading it they were all stunned. A young woman had seen Kevin's photograph in the paper, coming forward to accuse him of rape and battery.

'I don't believe it,' Dolly cried. 'She's telling lies, she must be, and how come we're the last to hear of it?'

'Why would she lie about something like that?'

'I don't know, Bernie, but it ain't true. Maybe she's jumped at a chance to make money by selling a trumped-up story to the newspapers.'

'That seems a bit unlikely.'

'My son is *not* a rapist,' Dolly snapped. Her eyes flicked to Pearl and she added venomously, 'Kevin was all right before he married *you*.'

Pearl had been reading the report again, but now she dropped the newspaper before rushing, gagging, from the room.

It wasn't long before Bernie heard Pearl being sick and looked at his wife with disgust. Dolly

351

was grasping at straws, and rather than face the truth about Kevin, she was using Pearl as a scapegoat. She had to find an excuse for her precious son's behaviour, but to lay the blame on Pearl was bloody ridiculous. With a small shake of his head, Bernie went after his daughter-in-law, finding her just leaving the bathroom. The poor kid looked awful, ashen, as she dragged a hand across her mouth. 'Are you all right love?'

'I ... I've been sick.'

'Yeah, I know, but listen, don't take any notice of Dolly.'

Pearl nodded sadly and he saw a tear rolling down her cheek. 'I ... I think I'll go to my bedroom for a while.'

Bernie returned to the living room, his mouth set in a grim line. 'Dolly, I don't think it's fair to blame Pearl. She's really upset.'

'It's no more than she deserves. Kevin changed when he married her. He became a nervous wreck and hardly left the flat. God knows what that girl's been doing to him.'

'You're mad, woman! Read the newspaper report again and check the dates. Huh, Kevin's nerves! It all makes sense now. He did it, Dolly. He raped that woman, and was scared of being caught. That's why he's been staying in so much. He was too bloody frightened to show his face!'

Dolly reared to her feet and Bernie stiffened, expecting a clout. 'Why do you always think the worst of him?' she yelled. 'He didn't do it! That woman's lying. I know she is.'

Bernie kicked off his slippers and reached for his shoes. 'All right, I'll go down to the station

352

and we'll see what they've got to say about it.'

'We're going to see Kevin tomorrow and we'll hear the truth from him.'

As Bernie finished tying his laces he felt something snapping inside. Kevin had been caught almost beating an old man to death and he had no doubts about these latest accusations. 'No, Dolly, *you're* going to see him, not me. I never want to set eyes on him again.'

'But he's your son!'

'I was only there at the conception. I've had no hand in bringing him up. You saw to that.'

Dolly raised her hand but this time Bernie didn't flinch. For the first time in years he felt no fear, and uncaring of the consequences his voice rose. 'I'll tell you something else. Pearl has just been sick and if you ask me that girl deserves an apology.' And on that note he strode from the room.

When Bernie left the café he saw that the market was thronging with life, and there was no way he could avoid being seen. Someone shouted his name but he ignored it, keeping his head down until he was out of sight. Christ, he'd known his son had a weak character, but had never dreamed he was capable of such violence. If anything, he had thought him a coward, a mummy's boy, and his stomach twisted. Had his home environment caused it? Had Kevin seen too much and it had somehow turned his mind? Bernie shook his head, refusing to believe it. He'd heard of worse parents, ones that neglected, starved or beat their children, yet none had turned out like Kevin. No, the boy must have been born like it, he and Dolly bringing a monster into the world.

Pearl heard Bernie going out, but remained sitting on the side of the bed, her hands clutched between her knees. It wasn't her mother-in-law's accusation that had made her sick. Like Dolly, she couldn't believe that Kevin had raped and beaten a woman, but as she read the newspaper report, a memory surfaced. Before their marriage, when Bessie had been ill in bed and they were alone, Kevin had virtually attacked her too, the sex violent. She remembered how frightened she'd been, Kevin calming her fears with excuses, ones that she had believed ... until now.

She groaned, rocking back and forth. It was as if her eyes had opened and she was seeing Kevin for the first time. The man she thought herself in love with didn't exist. Yet even as these thoughts crossed her mind, Pearl knew she was fooling herself. There had been many times when she had worried about his Jekyll and Hyde character but, loving him, she had chosen to dismiss her fears.

Pearl had no idea how long she sat there, her thoughts twisting and turning, but then Bernie poked his head around the door.

'Come into the living room, Pearl. I've been down to the police station and I've got some news.'

She rose to her feet, following Bernie into the living room.

Dolly's head snapped up as soon as she saw her husband. 'What did the police say?'

354

'They wouldn't tell me much, but one copper was a nice bloke and took me to one side. He said that so far there's lack of evidence to support the young woman's story.'

'See, I told you my boy wouldn't do such a thing.'

'He's not out of the woods yet. They're still making enquiries and are bringing a few people in for an identity parade.'

'They're wasting their time.'

'Don't be so sure. And are you forgetting what he did to that old man? He's lucky he hasn't been charged with attempted murder.'

'How many times have I got to tell you that he didn't do it?'

'And how many times have I got to say that he was caught red-handed? If that copper hadn't turned up when he did, Kevin would have killed that old man. There's no getting away from it, Dolly. Even if Kevin gets off a charge of raping that young woman, he'll still go down for robbery with violence.'

'He can't ... he won't,' Dolly cried, tears filling her eyes. She leaned forward, her sobs turning to wails as she rocked back and forth.

Pearl and Bernie looked at each other, both floundering. This wasn't the Dolly Dolby they knew. The once-strong woman was almost choking on her own tears, and neither knew how to react.

'Oh, Bernie, Bernie,' she sobbed.

With a small shake of his head, he sat beside her, placing an arm around her shoulder. 'Come on, old girl. If you carry on like this you'll make yourself ill.'

She fell against him and, feeling like an intruder, Pearl quietly left the room.

Johnny was still asleep, but she lifted him from his cot. She needed comfort too, someone to talk to, and only one person came to mind: Bessie.

She'd only managed to see the old lady a couple of times since Kevin's arrest, and now wondered if she'd heard about the latest charges. It didn't take Pearl long to get Johnny ready and, popping her head around the living-room door, she was surprised to find Bernie alone.

'Dolly's in an awful state. I should have kept my mouth shut. She's gone to lie down, but I can't get her to stop crying.'

'Maybe you should call the doctor.'

'You could be right, but I know Dolly and she won't thank me. Instead she'd probably go potty. It might be safer to wait and see how she is in a couple of hours. Where are you off to?'

'I'm just popping out to see Bessie.'

'All right, but before this you've only been to see her when the market was closed for the day. Tongues are wagging and it might be a bit rough for you.'

Bernie was right. It was awful walking through the market. Heads turned, murmurs could be heard, but Pearl ignored them all until a hand touched her arm. She raised her eyes, stunned to see Derek by her side.

'I'm so sorry, Pearl. You're having a rotten time of it and I can't imagine what you're going through. Mind you, in the light of this latest news

356

I've got more doubts about how you got pregnant. I think you took the blame, but you can tell the truth now. Did Kevin rape you too?'

Tears filled her eyes. She had badly hurt this man, but here he was, offering her sympathy. 'No, Derek, he didn't.'

'Are you sure about that?'

'Yes, I'm sure.' And, unable to bear his kindness, she moved quickly away from him, almost running to the second-hand shop.

'Oh, Bessie,' she cried as she rushed inside, relieved to find that there weren't any customers. 'Derek just offered me his sympathies. Wasn't that nice of him?'

'Yeah, he's a good bloke.'

Pearl sank onto an old chair. 'I suppose you've heard that Kevin's been accused of rape as well now?'

'Yes. It doesn't take long for bad news to spread around here.'

'You knew it was going to happen, didn't you?'

'No, love.'

'You told me you saw Kevin surrounded by police, but you saw more than that, didn't you?'

Bessie heaved a sigh. 'There wasn't much more, and I once told you that I'd misinterpreted a vision I had about Connie Lewis. Since then I'm loath to say anything unless I'm a hundred per cent sure.'

'What did you see, Bessie? It's happened now so there's no harm in telling me now.'

'All I missed out was that I had a bad feeling about it. I felt that Kevin was up to no good and would be caught, but I don't think it had anything to do with rape. I think I saw the robbery.'

'Oh, Bessie, it's bad enough that Kevin attacked that old man, but now there's a woman too. When he's found guilty of either offence he'll probably go to prison for years.'

'I notice that you said *when* he's found guilty – not *if*.'

'He was caught red-handed at the jeweller's, and somehow I just know he attacked that girl.'

'I warned you against Kevin from the start. I told you he'd come to no good, but you wouldn't listen.'

'I know, but I loved him, Bessie, and I didn't take any notice of your warning.'

'Well, you ain't the only one. As I've told you before, people only hear what they want to. Anyway, if you're right and Kevin goes down for a long time, what are you going to do? Have you given any thought to your future?'

'Well, no, but all this has been such a shock.' For a moment Pearl was quiet, pondering the old woman's words. 'I'd like to get out of this area. It would be awful for Johnny to grow up hearing his father talked about as a man who nearly killed someone and, not only that, raped a woman too.'

'Yeah, I can understand that, but where will you go?'

Pearl stared at Bessie, her mind racing. There was no doubt that Kevin would go to prison, and for many years. She'd be alone again, and even if she could get out of Battersea, how was she going to survive on her own?

34

In an effort to identify Kevin, the police had brought a few people to an identity parade. There was a publican from a country pub, along with a customer, and also the girl's employer, but as the attack had happened some time ago, none had been able to positively identify him. There was no forensic evidence either, and now the charges had been dropped.

Hearing this news, Dolly had rallied a little, but Kevin remained on remand for the charge of robbery with violence. Nearly three weeks had passed, but still the café remained closed, Dolly's thoughts only for her son.

Then, at six o'clock that evening, they heard a banging on the café door.

'I'll see who it is,' Bernie said. Soon he returned upstairs with Gertie and Madge.

Without preamble, it was Madge who spoke. 'Dolly, we're worried about our jobs. I know you've got a lot on your plate, but when are you going to open the café again?'

'I can't think about that now, Madge.'

'Look, I can understand how you feel, but me and Gertie can't afford to wait around much longer. If you ain't gonna open up soon, we'll have to start looking for something else.'

Dolly at last reacted, her neck stretching as though on a stalk. 'Neither of you have shown your faces until now, and *you*, Madge, are family. Your lot could have called round to offer us a bit of support, but we haven't seen hide nor hair of you.'

'We knew you'd be going through hell and didn't like to bother you,' Madge blustered.

'Nor me,' Gertie agreed. 'I mean, from what we've heard, the jeweller's in an awful state and I can't understand how Kevin could do something like that.'

'What! My God, it sounds like you've tried and convicted him already.'

'Of course we ain't,' Gertie said, 'but seeing as he was caught red-handed, there can't be much doubt about it.'

'Get out! And as for getting another job, go ahead. You're both sacked.'

'Well, that suits me,' Madge bristled, 'but the least you can do it pay our wages for the time we've been hanging around.'

Bernie's voice was quiet, but there was an undertone of anger. 'Don't worry, you'll get your wages, and I'm only sorry that we didn't think about it before. But we've been through a lot, and as Dolly said, you took your time coming to see us.'

'I'm here now, ain't I?'

'And me,' Gertie agreed.

'Yes, but only because you're worried about money. As for you, Gertie, well, you've been with us for years and should have known that you'd get paid. Now come on, I'll show you both out.'

It was only a short time before he returned, shaking his head as he walked into the room.

360

'Well, Dolly, I can understand why you sacked them, but now we're in a right old fix. We'll have no staff when we open up again.'

'I don't give a damn about the café. You heard them, Bernie. If those two are anything to go by, everyone around here must think that Kevin is guilty.'

'Yes, love, I'm afraid they do.'

Dolly stared at him for a moment. Then, jumping up, she fled to her bedroom.

As the door slammed behind her, Bernie shook his head, 'Christ, Pearl, I've put my foot in it again, but when is she going to face the truth?'

'I don't know, but perhaps deep down, she already has.'

'I doubt that.' He sighed heavily. 'Dolly ain't liked around here, and that's her own fault, but I didn't expect Madge and Gertie to behave like that. I should have thought to pay them until we open up again, but there was no need for that attitude. Instead of sympathy, they rubbed salt in the wound.'

Pearl nodded her head in agreement, but in truth she wasn't surprised. Dolly had ruled the roost, enjoying her dominance over the women, and though she'd been shocked by Gertie's behaviour, she knew that Madge was glad to see Dolly brought low. Family or not, Madge had no love for her cousin.

It was visiting day and Pearl sat opposite Kevin, listening as her mother-in-law monopolised the conversation as usual. Was he all right? Was he getting enough to eat? On and on she went whilst

361

Kevin sat morosely, only answering in mono-syllables.

'I knew that girl was lying, Kevin, and now I've been proved right.'

Pearl watched the range of emotions that chased across her husband's face, but she was seeing him clearly now, the veil lifted. Guilt was the one expression that stood out. He had nearly killed a man, raped a woman, and she was sick-ened. Had she ever really loved him? In truth she had never really known him. She'd fallen for his handsome face, and had chosen to ignore the side of his personality that she feared. He really was like Jekyll and Hyde. On one side, charming, but the other side, a monster.

Kevin spoke to her now, his voice hoarse. 'How's my boy, Pearl?'

'He's fine.'

With shock, Pearl saw tears forming in Kevin's eyes. 'Johnny will be an adult before I get out of here.'

'Don't say that,' Dolly cried. 'You may get off the other charges too.'

'No, Mum. I'll be going down for years.'

'Oh, Kevin...'

He ignored her, his eyes still on Pearl. 'I've had a lot of time to think while I've been on remand, and I don't want Johnny to see me while I'm in prison. In fact, you can stay away too.'

Pearl couldn't help it: she felt only a sense of relief. She had felt it her duty to visit Kevin, but now he had freed her. 'Why don't you want me to visit you?'

'It's obvious. As I said, I'll be going down for a

long time, and you ain't likely to wait for me.'

'Of course she will, Kevin.'

'Leave it out, Mum. Ours wasn't exactly a love match and I only married her because she was having my kid. Yes, and that was your idea too. Christ, it's all your fault.'

'My fault! How can it be my fault?'

His look darkened. 'I only robbed that jeweller because I wanted enough money to get away from you.'

'Get away from me! But why?'

Kevin's voice was as hard as his expression. 'You need to take a good look at yourself and then you'd know.'

'What's that supposed to mean?'

'All right, Mum, you've asked for it. You're a sick, narrow-minded bully.'

'What!'

'You heard me. You've ruled the roost, made Dad's life a misery, and because I've had to watch it, mine too.' His eyes flicked to Pearl before continuing, 'When Pearl was unfortunate enough to marry into the family, look how you treated her, and I'm sorry to say I wasn't much better.'

'You were fine before you married her.'

Kevin's laugh was derisive. 'No, Mum, you can't blame Pearl for the way I turned out. It's all down to you, and I'll tell you something else, I don't want you ruining my son.'

'Kevin, how dare you talk to me like this? Of course I won't ruin Johnny.'

'Oh, I dare.' And then his eyes turned to Pearl, his voice hissing and urgent as visiting time drew to an end. 'My mother made sex a dirty word, and I want you to get Johnny away from her. Find somewhere else to live, and don't come here again.'

Pearl stared at him in confusion, but then a guard came to lead him away. Dolly reared to her feet, calling, 'I know you don't mean it, son. You're under a lot of strain, that's all. I'll be back to see you as soon as I can.'

'Don't bother,' he shouted, 'and, Pearl, do as I say. Get Johnny away from her.'

Dolly's face was white as she turned to Pearl. 'He's upset, and you mustn't take any notice of what he said.'

'Please, I just want to get out of here.'

Dolly nodded, becoming quiet, and she hardly spoke on the way home. Pearl too was deep in thought. Kevin has said some strange things. He said that Dolly was sick, that she had made sex into a dirty word. What did he mean? Had Dolly interfered with him in some way? Oh God, it was awful. He had told her to get Johnny away from his mother and, somehow, she intended to do just that.

The following day Dolly was morose, hardly speaking and, wanting to get out of the flat, Pearl got Johnny ready, wheeling him across to Bessie's shop. She wanted to talk to the old lady, to tell her what Kevin had said.

'Hello, love,' Bessie said as Pearl pushed the pram inside, her head cocking to one side. 'What's up?'

Pearl took a seat by the counter. 'It's Kevin. I had a bit of a shock when we went to see him.'

She went on to tell Bessie what had happened, finally saying, 'He told me to move out, to get Johnny away from Dolly.'

'Well, love, I must admit I don't like the sound of it. Are you going to take his advice?'

'Yes, of course I am, and I want to move out as soon as possible.'

'Can't say I blame you, but before we work out what you're going to do, I must tell you about another vision.'

'Was it about Kevin again?'

'No, this time it was about you.'

'Me! What did you see?'

Bessie's forehead creased. 'It was odd. All I saw was a woman sitting in bed looking at a newspaper, and your face was on the front page.'

'But I've never been in the newspaper, and who was this woman?'

'I have no idea. All I can say is that she looked ill, but happy.'

'Is that all?'

'Yes, but I have a feeling she'll come into your life.'

Pearl rubbed a hand across her forehead. Why would a strange woman be happy to see her? 'Maybe I'll meet her when I move out of this area?'

'Have you any money, Pearl?'

'No.'

'So how do you think you can move away? You'd need to find a home, a job, and you can't work with a baby to look after.'

Pearl knew Bessie was right. She'd been stupid, living in a dream world, and now she was facing reality, tears stung her eyes.

'Don't get upset, love. Why don't you come back here? I know it's only a stone's throw from Dolly, but it's a start.'

'I can't expect you to keep me.'

'Keep you! Leave it out. There's work for you in the shop and it'll be nice to put me feet up for a while.'

Pearl's heart surged with gratitude. This lovely old lady was offering her a way out, and she grabbed it. 'All right Bessie, I'll come back, and thank you.'

Things didn't work out as Pearl expected, her happiness short-lived. During her absence Dolly had collapsed and Pearl returned to find Bernie in a dreadful state.

'She's hardly said a word since seeing Kevin yesterday and when you went out she just sort of folded. It was weird, Pearl, and she won't stop crying.'

'Have you called the doctor?'

'Yes, and he should be here shortly, but what happened to bring this on?'

She told him that Kevin had said he didn't want to see his mother again, blaming her for all that had happened. Her face reddened, too embarrassed to tell Bernie the bit about Dolly being sick and making sex a dirty word.

'I can't believe that he doesn't want to see his mother again, and no wonder she's upset.' There was a knock on the door. 'That'll be the doctor,' Bernie said. 'Would you let him in, Pearl?'

She went downstairs, returning to wait with

Bernie whilst the doctor examined Dolly.

Bernie scratched his head. 'I reckon that, like Dolly, Kevin is looking for a scapegoat. He's done wrong, but it's easier to blame someone else than face his own actions. Dolly spoiled him rotten, but that doesn't mean she's responsible for what he did.'

Before Pearl could respond, the doctor emerged, Bernie jumping to his feet. 'Is she all right?'

'I think your wife is suffering from nervous exhaustion.'

'What the hell is that?'

'It's caused by stress. Has she been sleeping?'

'No, not really, but she's a strong woman and always has been.'

'Everyone has a breaking point, Mr Dolby, and I think your wife has reached hers. I've given her a sedative, and if you keep her free of any further worries, I'm sure she'll be fine.'

'Gawd, how am I supposed to do that? She still has our son's trial to face.'

'Don't let her go. Keep her at home.'

'Huh, if she wants to go there'll be no stopping her.'

The doctor sighed. 'You can tell her it's against my advice, and until then keep her as quiet as possible. Call me if you have any worries.'

When the man left, Bernie went in to see Dolly, but he soon returned. 'She's asleep, but what about when she wakes up? I don't know how I'm going to cope with her, Pearl.'

Bernie looked sick with worry and, with a sinking heart, Pearl realised she'd have to remain. Bernie had always shown her kindness and she was fond of her father-in-law. She couldn't abandon him now. She'd stay for a while, just until Dolly recovered, and then she'd be out of there like a shot.

Dolly was up in less than a week, but she still looked awful and hardly spoke. Bernie seemed lost, creeping around his wife as though she was made of china. However, later that morning both he and Pearl were surprised when she suddenly surged to her feet, her voice strong and assertive again.

'I'm going to see Kevin.'

'You're not up to it, love,' Bernie protested.

'I have to see him. He's my son.'

'All right, if it means so much to you, I'll come along.'

'No, Bernie, I want to see him on my own.'

Nothing Bernie could say would prevent her, and when she left they felt as if they were holding their breath until she returned.

One look at Dolly's face was enough for them to realise her visit had been a mistake. She looked almost on the point of collapse, her eyes red and swollen from crying.

'What happened, love?' Bernie asked.

'Kevin agreed to see me, but said it was for the last time.'

'He said what?'

'Oh, Bernie, he still blames me for everything and I ... I think he's right.'

'Don't be daft, Dolly. He tried to rob that jeweller – not you.'

'Yes, but he only did it to get away from me.'

'He's just making excuses. If he wanted money to move out there was nothing to stop him from getting a job.'

'Maybe, but he said I'm a dominant and interfering mother.'

'Well, you certainly ain't mouselike,' Bernie chuckled, trying to inject a bit of humour.

Dolly didn't smile; instead her voice rose. 'Kevin's right then. I drove him to it!'

'Leave it out, Dolly. You weren't that bad and, if anything, you spoiled the lad.'

'Didn't I do *anything* right?' she cried, running from the room.

Bernie looked at Pearl, shaking his head in bewilderment. 'I seem to be making a habit of putting my foot in it. I'll go and see if she's all right.'

It wasn't long before he came back. 'She's in a right old state and I think I'll have to call the doctor again.'

Pearl nodded, but her heart was heavy. She had hoped that Dolly was getting better, but now the woman had taken a step backwards. Oh, if only she could move out, but she still couldn't bring herself to abandon her father-in-law.

35

It was mid-September and Pearl still hadn't moved in with Bessie. She had no love for Dolly, but Bernie seemed incapable of looking after her. The doctor had put Dolly on medication and mostly she just sat, seeming to draw great comfort from just holding Johnny in her arms. Strangely, though, she always asked permission now before picking him up, and with all the housework, the washing, ironing and cooking to do, Pearl was sometimes pleased to hand him over to her mother-in-law. She had watched carefully, but hadn't seen anything to make sense of Kevin's accusations. Nevertheless, she remained vigilant, making sure that Bernie was always around before leaving Johnny in her mother-in-law's care.

Then, after all the waiting, Kevin was at last brought to trial, Dolly insisting that she was going to attend. As though it had brought her a new lease of life, she bustled around getting ready, only stopping her preparation when Bernie spoke.

'The doctor has advised against this, but you just won't listen. All right, go then, but you needn't think I'm coming with you.'

She hardly reacted, only closing her eyes for a moment before turning to Pearl. 'What about you?'

'Yes, I'd like to go, but I don't want to take

Johnny. Would you mind looking after him, Bernie?'

'Of course I will – well, as long as you make sure you have his bottles made up.'

Pearl smiled her thanks and went to get ready, afterwards preparing everything for the baby.

Bernie insisted that she call a cab. Dolly hardly spoke during the journey, and when they entered the courtroom it was to find it packed, many locals showing an avid interest in the case.

The chamber buzzed with voices, and a sea of faces looked at them as they sat down. Dolly kept her head low, Pearl surprised when she reached out to grip her hand.

There was a hush as Kevin appeared in the dock, which continued when the judge entered the courtroom.

The trial began, but after all Pearl's nervous anticipation, it was quickly over. On his lawyer's advice Kevin had pleaded guilty, and now the judge was looking at the medical evidence. The jeweller had recovered, but only just, the report revealing brain damage.

Pearl's found her eyes were fixed on the bench and the stern-faced judge. He looked grim as Kevin stood before him, and she gasped as he passed a sentence of fifteen years imprisonment.

The courtroom came alive, buzzing with voices again, but Dolly slumped in her seat. Pearl thought she had passed out, and bent anxiously over her mother-in-law, but as Kevin was led away Dolly rallied enough to rise to her feet.

'Oh, son,' she cried.

Kevin's eyes flicked towards them, but then he

was urged downstairs and out of their sight. Dolly stood transfixed, but Pearl took her arm, pulling her mother-in-law towards the exit.

They emerged into bright sunlight, but it was the flash of a camera going off in Pearl's face that made her blink. She hadn't expected reporters, new headlines taking up the front pages, and now looked frantically for a taxi. One was coming and she raised an arm to hail it, almost bundling Dolly inside before slamming the door behind them.

'Battersea High Street,' she told the driver.

'Oh, Pearl, I can't believe it,' Dolly whispered. 'Why did Kevin plead guilty?'

'With the amount of evidence against him, I don't think he had any choice. If Kevin tried to plead not guilty and then lost the case, the judgement would have been harsher.'

Dolly sunk low in her seat, dabbing at her eyes, and as the taxi drove off Pearl didn't look back. Kevin was going to prison, he didn't want to see her again, and that meant her marriage was over. Suddenly she felt a surge of freedom again, followed by another of shame. How could she feel like this when her husband had just been sentenced to fifteen years in prison? Yet as she closed her eyes against her guilt, Pearl found that nothing could mar her feelings of relief.

Bernie was giving Johnny his bottle as they walked in, his eyebrows rising in enquiry. 'Fifteen years,' Pearl told him.

'It's what I expected,' he said, but then as Dolly suddenly staggered he rose to his feet. 'Pearl, take the nipper. I'll see to Dolly.'

She took her son, surprised when Bernie spoke firmly to his wife. 'See, I told you not to go, and in future perhaps you'll listen to me.'

'Oh, Bernie...' Dolly groaned.

'Come on, let's get you to bed,' he said.

As her father-in-law led Dolly from the room, Pearl saw that he was growing in stature. He seemed the leader now, Dolly clinging and the follower, but Pearl couldn't help wondering how long this situation would last.

As they left the room, Pearl sat down, popping the teat into Johnny's mouth. She gazed at his face, seeing Kevin in his features. Her marriage was over, but he had given her Johnny and she would always thank him for that.

When Bernie returned, his face was etched with worry. 'Dolly's taken the sentence really badly. I think she was clinging to the misguided hope that Kevin would get off.'

'Maybe it would help if you get back to a routine again. Perhaps open the café.'

'Dolly refuses to talk about the business and I'm really worried about her. She's becoming almost a recluse, only leaving the flat when she went to see Kevin. If we continue to live and work around here, I can't see her ever getting back to her old self.'

'Given time, she'll bounce back.'

'No, I don't think so. She's been brought too low, and I've been giving it some thought. I reckon we should sell up and move out of the area.'

'Sell up! But where will you go?'

'I ain't thought that far ahead, but a nice little teashop in Devon or Cornwall would suit me. That nipper seems Dolly's only comfort now, and as long as you're with us, I reckon she'll be happy to move anywhere.'

Pearl drew in a breath. It was time to tell him, but she dreaded his reaction. 'No, I'm sorry, Bernie, but I won't be coming with you. My marriage is over, and though I feel sorry for Dolly, it wouldn't be right to go on living with you.'

'Don't be daft. You're family, and how can you bring Johnny up on your own? You'd need to earn enough to support you both, and you can't work with a baby to take care of.'

'I wouldn't be on my own. Bessie has asked me to live with her.'

'Well, yeah, you could do that, but do you really want to stay in this area? If you come with us it would be a fresh start, and nobody need know about the past.'

'I admit I'd like to get out of Battersea, but I can't face living with Dolly.'

'Look, I know she gave you a rough time of it, but she's different now. Please, Pearl, I need you. Until Dolly gets back to normal, I don't think I can cope with her.'

'Yes you can. You're doing fine, but what about when she is back to her old self? She'll try to take Johnny over again, undermining everything I do.'

'I'll see that she doesn't,' Bernie said, and, seeing Pearl's expression, he smiled faintly. 'There's no need to shake your head in doubt. Things have changed, Pearl. I let Dolly get away with dominating me in the past, but I don't intend to let it happen again.'

'I'm sorry, Bernie, but Kevin urged me to get Johnny away from his mother, and though I don't know what made him say that, he must have had his reasons. I don't want my son hurt.'

'Leave it out. Dolly loves the nipper – we both do – and neither of us would do anything to harm a hair on his head.'

'I know you wouldn't, Bernie, but when it comes to Dolly I can't take that chance.'

He shook his head sadly. 'It's madness, if you ask me, but it seems you've made up your mind. I just hope that I can still persuade Dolly to move.'

Dolly didn't surface until the following morning, her long hair hanging lacklustre down her back, and her complexion wan.

'How are you feeling, love?' Bernie asked as he lowered his newspaper.

'I'm all right.'

'Did you take your pill?'

'Not yet.'

'Well then, how about having a cup of tea and a couple of slices of toast first?'

'I'll do it,' Pearl offered, rising to her feet with the baby in her arms.

'Can I hold him?' Dolly asked.

With Bernie in the room, Pearl didn't mind, 'Of course you can.'

Bernie waited until Pearl left the room and then leaned forward, speaking earnestly. 'Dolly, how do you feel about moving out of the area? We could sell up and buy a little tearoom in the West

Country. Nobody would know about us and it'd be a fresh start.'

'But that's miles away! No, I need to be near Kevin.'

'Dolly, he's in prison and doesn't want to see you.'

'I know that, but he's sure to come round. When he does, I'll be able to visit him.'

'Maybe, but even so, you won't be able to see him every day. I'm only talking about moving to Devon or Cornwall, not Timbuktu.'

With infinite gentleness Dolly stroked the baby's cheek. 'It might be nice for Johnny to grow up in the country.'

Bernie knew there was no putting it off. Pearl had made up her mind to leave and he couldn't see her staying for much longer. 'No, love, Pearl won't be coming with us. She's moving in with Bessie.'

A spark returned to Dolly's eyes, her voice indignant, 'She can't take Johnny away from us. We're his grandparents.'

'She can, love. Now that the marriage is over, Pearl can do what she likes.'

'Who said it's over? Pearl is still Kevin's wife and it's her duty to wait for him until he comes out of prison.'

'Dolly, for Gawd's sake, you're talking rot! He beat up a man, raped a woman and, if you ask me, Pearl's better off without him.'

Before his eyes, Bernie saw the transformation in his wife's demeanour. The spark in her eyes turned to fire as she spat, 'He didn't rape that woman, and I am *not* talking rot. Like it or not,

Pearl must stay with us. I've already lost my son, and I don't intend to lose my grandson too.'

'It's Pearl's decision,' Bernie said.

'She'll move in with Bessie over my dead body.'

'Dolly...'

'Enough! I don't want to hear another word about it.' Dolly stood up and, finding a clean nappy, she laid the baby on the rug to change him.

Pearl came back into the room, carefully balancing a tray, smiling at her son's antics. He loved being free of the binding, his chubby legs kicking, and hands waving before going down to pull on his little penis. Dolly slapped it away, her voice loud. 'Stop that, you dirty little boy,' she cried. 'Bad boy, it's nasty to do that.' Then, seeing Pearl, she added, 'What's this about you moving in with Bessie Penfold?'

Dolly looked surprised when Pearl slammed the tray down before moving swiftly to her side. She picked the baby up, her face and voice tight, 'Yes, that's right.'

'Well you can forget it.'

'But—'

'No buts. You're Kevin's wife and your place is with us. Bernie has suggested that we move out of the area and I think it's a good idea. Mind you, Devon or Cornwall is a bit far, but Dorset would be all right. It'll be lovely for Johnny to grow up in the country and while we're waiting for Kevin to come home, we can all work together in a nice little tearoom.'

Bernie held his breath, but Pearl didn't argue, just saying, 'Johnny needs a wash and then I'll get

377

him dressed.'

Dolly, he saw, had a smile of satisfaction on her face. 'See, I soon sorted her out. Right, Bernie, let's see about getting this place on the market.'

Bernie heaved a sigh. He should have stood up for Pearl but, like Dolly, he didn't want to leave their grandson behind. 'So, you fancy Dorset then?'

'Yes, and the more I think about it, the better it sounds. We can offer sandwiches and homemade cakes, served on pretty china. There'll be no more getting up at the crack of dawn to cook flaming breakfasts. Oh, I can just see it, Bernie. Lovely fresh white linen tablecloths and small vases of flowers on the tables.'

'Sounds good to me, love.'

'I'll be able to spend a lot more time with Johnny.'

Whilst they happily made plans, unbeknown to them, Pearl was rapidly making her own. She was stuffing clothes into bags before hiding them in the bottom of the wardrobe. She'd wait until that night, wait until her in-laws were asleep, and then she was getting out of there.

36

The house was silent. Pearl's nerves were jumping as she crept downstairs. She had taken all she could carry, stuffing bags into the pram, and now, fully loaded, she carefully opened the street door. With infinite care she closed it behind her, stepping outside into the dark night. She was leaving, her shoulders stiff with resolution. Dolly was back to normal, laying down the law, but Kevin had told her to keep Johnny away from his mother, and she intended to do just that. She was going to Bessie's, and there was no way Dolly Dolby was going to drag her back.

Pearl banged on Bessie's door again and again, relieved when at last she opened it.

'Bloody hell, love, what are you doing here at this time of night?'

'I'm sorry, Bessie, but I had to get away.'

'All right, come on in, but why didn't you wait until the morning?'

'Dolly's back to normal and if I hadn't sneaked out now, there's no way she would let me leave.'

'She couldn't have kept you a prisoner.'

'Dolly's capable of anything,' Pearl said as she put the brake on the pram, leaving Johnny asleep as she lugged her things upstairs. She then went down again to get her son, laying him gently on the sofa.

'Right,' Bessie said. 'Start at the beginning.'

'They're going to sell up and move out of the area, and it's as though the decision has given Dolly a new lease of life. Only yesterday she was a wreck, but now she's back to laying down the law. She won't accept that my marriage is over and insisted that I go with them to Devon or Cornwall.'

'For goodness' sake, Pearl, you're not a child. You're a grown woman and she can't force you to go.'

'I ... I just didn't want an argument.'

'If I know Dolly, you won't have much choice. As soon as she finds you've gone, she'll be over here.'

'Oh, Bessie, what am I going to do?'

'For starters you can get that frightened rabbit look off your face and stand up for yourself. As I said, Dolly can't force you to go, and you'll just have to tell her that.'

Pearl shook her head doubtfully, her head drooping.

'Come on,' Bessie said. 'Let's get to bed and we'll worry about Dolly bloody Dolby in the morning.'

With a nod of agreement, Pearl rose to her feet and lifted Johnny into her arms. She followed Bessie upstairs, her tired eyes widening when she saw her old room and the cot in the corner. 'Oh, Bessie.'

'Now then, don't start the waterworks. I knew you'd be moving in eventually and the cot didn't cost me anything. It was in the back room, but cleaned up nicely.'

Pearl took in the clean white sheets, the soft blankets and choked, her eyes watery as she said, 'I don't know how to thank you.'

'Leave it out, girl. Now get yourself and Johnny to bed and we'll talk again in the morning.'

Bessie left then and, after settling Johnny, Pearl climbed into her own bed. She had done it; she had got away from Dolly. But now she shivered. Bessie was right: as soon as Dolly found her gone, she'd come looking for her and she dreaded it.

Pearl wanted to remain hidden, but Bessie wouldn't stand for it. 'You can't stay up here for ever, love. If Dolly comes over here, stand your ground. She doesn't own you and can't drag you back.'

Reluctantly Pearl followed the woman downstairs, but as she settled Johnny in his pram and glanced out of the window, her heart skipped with fear.

'Oh God, Dolly's already on her way over.'

'Now then, don't run away. As I told you, stand your ground, girl.'

Pearl wanted nothing more than to flee, but moments later the door flew open, crashing back against the wall. Ramrod straight, her hair still loose and flying wildly around her shoulders, Dolly marched into the shop.

'I don't know what your game is, but you can bring that child back to the café.'

The noise woke Johnny up and he began to cry, but as Dolly moved towards the pram, Pearl barred her path. 'Keep away from him.'

'You must be mad, girl. I'm not having my grandson living in this dump!'

'Oy, watch your mouth, Dolly Dolby,' Bessie said, moving from behind the counter.

'Shut up!' Dolly shouted, her hand coming out as though Bessie was a fly to swat away.

'Don't you dare touch her!' Pearl screamed.

Dolly stayed her hand, saying with a scowl, 'Huh, I wouldn't touch her with a bleedin' bargepole.'

She made for the pram again, but Pearl bent swiftly, snatching Johnny up and holding him tightly to her. 'Stay away from my son!'

'I'll do no such thing! He's *my* grandson and his place is with me.'

Pearl felt her body swelling, stretching, and from somewhere inside she felt imbued with strength. 'No, Dolly, his place is with me, *his mother!* I'll decide where he lives, not you, and we're staying here.'

'You heard her. I want you out of my shop, Dolly Dolby, and now.'

'I told you to shut your mouth, Bessie Penfold! I ain't going anywhere without my grandson and if you get in my way I'll smash your bleedin' face in.'

When Pearl heard the threat it was the final straw. She had lived in fear of this woman, allowed herself to be ordered about like a servant, but she wasn't going to let Dolly take her son. Johnny was still wailing, but her voice rose above his cries. 'You lay one finger on Bessie, or my son, and I'll call the police.'

'You wouldn't dare!'

'Oh yes I would.' And playing what she hoped was a trump card, she added, 'And I'm sure the locals would love to see another Dolby being carted off to gaol.'

'You little bitch,' Dolly spat. 'All right, I'm going, but I ain't finished with you yet!'

The breath left Pearl's body in a rush as Dolly marched out of the shop, slamming the door behind her.

'There, there, it's all right,' she soothed, patting Johnny on his back. His cries turned to little hic-cuping sobs, and then finally stopped.

'Well done, love,' Bessie said. 'She was like a bleedin' Amazon, but you sorted her out.'

'Yes, but for how long?'

'You've got the upper hand now, and it won't take her long to realise that if she wants to see her grandson, she'll have to behave.'

Pearl smiled at last. She had done it. She had stood up to Dolly and from now on, nobody was going to walk all over her again.

Dolly was fuming as she marched across the road, but saw many eyes looking at her, and heard sniggers of laughter. Her hand flew up, touching her hair, and she suddenly realised that she had dashed out without giving any thought to her appearance. Christ, she still had her slippers on! Head down she surged forward, almost running to the sanctuary of the café.

The postman had been and a few letters lay on the floor. She swept them up, still sick with shame as she flicked through them, but then stayed her hand as one caught her eye. It was addressed to Pearl, the writing spidery, and she frowned, wondering who it was from.

Well, sod the girl. She had run off, taking Johnny with her. Without hesitation, Dolly tore the envelope open. Her mouth gaped in disbelief as she read the contents. She then smiled slyly. She'd keep this bit of information to herself and it would serve Pearl right. Dolly stuffed the letter into her pocket and went upstairs.

'She wouldn't come back then?' Bernie said.

'No, and she even had the cheek to threaten me with the police.'

'Blimey! Why did she do that?'

'Oh, I dunno. Probably because I threatened to give Bessie Penfold a clout.'

'Bloody hell – what did you do that for?'

'Cos the old cow told me to get out of her shop.'

Bernie shook his head. 'Dolly, it sounds to me like you went in there like a bull into a china shop.'

'Yeah, well, maybe I did, but Pearl can't keep me away from my grandson.'

'Dolly, she can, and we can't do anything about it.'

'Huh, we'll see about that. I'll go to a bloody solicitor if I have to.'

'It won't do any good. We have no legal rights over Johnny.'

'Don't be daft. We're his grandparents.'

'As the law stands at the moment, it doesn't make any difference.'

Dolly sunk onto a chair, her mind turning. So, they had no legal rights, but she wasn't going to give in. 'I'll tidy myself up and go over there again.'

'It might be better if I speak to her.'

'No, I'll sort her out.'

'Dolly, if you aren't careful, you'll frighten her off. There's nothing to stop her leaving Bessie's, and if she does we'd lose track of her.'

Dolly frowned. Bernie was right. She didn't want the girl bolting and needed time to think, to plan. In the meantime, Bernie might be able to calm things down.

'All right, you talk to her. She always did have a

soft spot for you.'

Bernie left half an hour later. Awaiting his return, Dolly paced the floor. She wanted out of this area, but had no intention of leaving without her grandson. A plan began to form, and as she went over it, Dolly decided it could work. But would Bernie agree?

A lot depended on how quickly they could sell the business, but then, struck by a thought, she stopped pacing. The letter that had been delivered for Pearl might put a fly in the ointment. Grabbing her coat from the back of the chair, she pulled the crumpled envelope out of the pocket.

As she read the contents again, a small smile of satisfaction crossed her face. The woman was ill, too ill to travel, and that suited Dolly fine. There was no chance of her turning up for the time being, no chance of any interference, and with any luck they would be long gone before she showed her face.

She went over the plan again, a little unsure if Kevin had any legal rights. He must have, he was Johnny's father! It might be for the best if Bernie approached him. He could tell Kevin that Pearl was an unfit mother and that Johnny was in danger. It was rubbish, of course, but Kevin loved his son and would want to protect him.

Dolly frowned, unsure of this stage of her plan, but then her back straightened. Even if Kevin wouldn't co-operate, it could still work. They'd have to change their names, of course, but just in case Bernie baulked at the idea, she'd wait until they had a buyer for the café before telling him. He might not like it, but she'd get round him, and if not, well, sod him. She'd do it on her own.

Bernie sat in Bessie's living room, relieved that Pearl had agreed to speak to him in private, his eyes soft as he gazed at his grandson. The lad was growing fast, sitting up now and a happy baby, with chubby arms and legs that waved with excitement at the sight of his toy.

'Dolly is really sorry, Pearl, but when you went off without telling us, she nearly went out of her mind.'

'That's no excuse for coming over here and threatening Bessie.'

'I know, but she's come to her senses now. All she wants is to be allowed to see the nipper now and then.'

Pearl shook her head. 'I've already told you. Kevin warned me to move out and to keep Johnny away from his mother.'

'That doesn't make any sense, love. Dolly may not be perfect, but who is? And she loves Johnny. It would be cruel to stop her seeing him.'

'You'll be moving out of the area as soon as you've sold the café.'

'If you're not coming with us, I doubt she'll go.'

Pearl was quiet for a while, her head down, Bernie unaware of her thoughts. She wanted Dolly to leave, to be free of the woman, yet it would be Johnny who kept her here. 'Do you think she'll agree to go if I allow her access to Johnny?'

'Well, she might, but living in the West Country it won't be easy.' He scratched his head. 'It's too far to drive down for the day. We'd no sooner get here than it would be time to return. If you'd let us have him for weekends it might work.'

'No, I can't allow that.'

'It's that or we stay here.'

Pearl once again became quiet as her mind turned. She didn't want Dolly near her son, sure that somehow she had turned Kevin's mind. Maybe she could pretend to agree. Once gone they couldn't do anything about it when she changed her mind. 'All right, Bernie, you can have him for the occasional weekend.'

'Thanks, love. Dolly's sure to agree now and, in the meantime, until we move, can we see the lad?'

'Yes, I suppose so, but I don't want Dolly left alone with him.'

'Blimey, I think you're taking this a bit far.'

'It's that or nothing, Bernie. I want you there with them the whole time, and you can only have him for a couple of hours. If you agree, you can pick him up tomorrow afternoon and then maybe again in a day or two.'

He exhaled loudly. 'All right, I'll make sure I don't leave the nipper alone with Dolly, but it still doesn't make any sense.' He rose to his feet, leaning over to kiss Johnny on his cheek. 'I'll see you tomorrow, bruiser.'

Johnny waved a chubby fist, and Bernie's eyes saddened. Christ, he was going to miss the boy, but at least he'd talked Pearl into giving them access.

When Bernie went downstairs he found Bessie standing behind the counter, her arms folded across her chest.

'Now you listen to me, Bernard Dolby. I ain't having your wife marching in here again, shouting like a bloody fishwife, and you can tell her that from me.'

'It's all right, Bessie. Pearl has agreed to let us see the baby and it won't happen again.'

'The girl's too soft for her own good.'

'He is our grandson, Bessie.'

As the old woman gazed at him, Bernie shivered. Her eyes looked strange, unfocused, almost as though she was seeing through him and into the distance.

Her head cocked to one side as she spoke. 'Pearl tells me that you're leaving the area. Is that right?'

'Yes, as soon as we sell the business.'

'She's up to something,' Bessie murmured.

'Who's up to something?'

'Your wife.'

'What are you talking about?'

'I saw something, a vision, but it was just a flash. Yeah, she's planning something.'

Bernie shook his head impatiently. Visions. What a load of rot. He wasn't going to stand around listening to this nonsense. ''Bye,' he said shortly.

As he left the shop, Bernie's eyes took in the market, and a couple of costermongers lifted their arms to wave. Would he miss the area? With a shake of his head he realised he wouldn't. The only thing he'd miss would be his grandson. Without him and Dolly, he hoped to God that Pearl would be able to cope – financially.

His thoughts continued to turn. The café was in

388

a prime location and should fetch a pretty penny. When they brought a small tearoom they'd have plenty left over and maybe he'd be able to persuade Dolly to drop Pearl a few bob. After what she'd been through she deserved it, and maybe they could put some money in trust for Johnny.

Bernie went into the café, locking the door behind him and then gazed around the dining room. For a moment it seemed to echo with memories – the customers, the waitresses that had come and gone – and seeing that the room looked dusty and unused, he smiled sadly as he thought about their cleaner, Nora. Like Madge and Gertie, they hadn't given a thought to the poor woman and her wages, something he was ashamed of but had now put right.

With a shake of his head he headed for the stairs, hoping they had all managed to find jobs. Dolly was waiting, and he smiled, glad that he was able to give her some good news.

'Pearl is letting us have Johnny for a couple of hours tomorrow afternoon.'

'Well done, love,' she said, and Bernie's chest swelled. 'In the meantime, let's get this place on the market.'

37

Pearl was enjoying herself as she reorganised the shop. Bessie was happy to give her a free rein, and with Johnny in his pram behind the counter, he got most of the old woman's attention.

She had given the place a good clean, afterwards putting the stock into sections: clothes racks in one area, furniture in the other, arranged to resemble a room. Most had been improved with a good polish, and already they had managed to shift a dining-room table and a sideboard.

The clothes got her attention next, and Pearl made sure that everything on offer was clean and pressed. Bessie had moaned at the garments spread over lines in the upstairs flat to dry, but it resulted in more sales.

Pearl's nose wrinkled. There was still a musty smell in the air and she knew it came from the piles of old blankets and quilts, but washing such large items presented a problem.

She turned to Bessie. 'Maybe we should get rid of this lot. They won't sell in this state.'

'Get rid of them! Leave it out, girl. Not everyone is as fussy as you, and the blankets are worth a few bob each.'

'In the two weeks I've been here they haven't sold. Is there any way to wash them?'

'I suppose you could take them to the laundry baths, but if you ask me it's a waste of time.'

'You said that about the clothes.'

'Yeah, well, I must admit we've shifted a lot since you sorted them out, but look at you. All this washing is wearing you out and you're up half the night ironing.'

'It's been worth it, and I've nearly finished now.' Pearl frowned. 'I suppose the laundry is the answer for these blankets, but I'd be stuck down there for hours.'

'Well, I ain't taking them. That place is full of gossiping old biddies and–'

The door opened, cutting Bessie off in mid sentence, and both smiled as Nora came in.

'Hello,' Pearl said.

'Hello,' she replied, her eyes puzzled. 'What you doing here?'

'I work here now. What about you? Have you found another job?'

'No,' she said, her eyes flicking to the pram. 'That your baby?'

'Yes, and his name is Johnny.'

Nora leaned over the counter, and as she pulled faces at him, he chuckled, dribble running from the corner of his mouth. 'He likes you, Nora.'

'What can we do for you, love?' Bessie asked.

'Want new coat. Mummy gave me this,' she answered, holding out two shillings.

Involuntarily Pearl glanced out of the window. September was drawing to an end, but thankfully it was still mild. They didn't have many winter coats, and with just two shillings Nora's mother must be expecting a miracle. Moving across to the racks, she flicked through them, finding only one that might fit the short, chubby woman.

Now that everything was priced, she checked the tag, but it was too expensive. 'I'm sorry, Nora, but at the moment we've only got one that will fit you and you haven't got enough money. We may get more in later.'

'Mummy said get coat now.'

Pearl glanced at Bessie but, obviously reading her mind, the woman shook her head.

'We can't reduce it. I paid good money for that coat and there'd be no profit if we let it go for two bob.'

With an appeal in her eyes Pearl continued to look at Bessie, but to no avail.

'Now don't look at me like that. We're not a charity and we've got to eat.'

With a sigh, Pearl put the coat back on the rack, but was then struck by an idea. 'Nora, do you know how to use the machines at the laundry?'

'Yes. I does our washing.'

'Bessie, she could take the blankets. Freshly laundered, they're sure to sell and we could let her have the coat for two shillings as payment.'

'Oh, all right then. Gawd, if I ain't careful I'll end up as soft as you.'

'I tell Mummy, then come back,' Nora said.

'What have you got us into now?' Bessie complained as the door closed behind Nora. 'If those blankets don't shift we'll have wasted money having them laundered, let alone letting Nora have that coat for two bob.'

'Don't worry, they'll sell,' Pearl assured her, praying she was right as she bent to the pile, selecting those in the best condition. 'Poor Nora, it's a shame she hasn't found another job. Do you know her mother?'

'Yes. Lily's a nice woman. She had Nora late, when she was in her forties and must be getting on a bit now. Let me see, I'm sixty-six, so Lily must be coming up to seventy.'

Pearl looked at Bessie in surprise. Somehow she had thought her older, the woman's skin lined and her hair grey. 'What about Nora's father?'

'He died a few years ago.' Her eyes took on a thoughtful look. 'Lily was often in the market, but I ain't seen her lately.'

'Perhaps she's ill.'

'Yeah, that could be it. I'll ask Nora when she comes back.'

Pearl tied the blankets into a bundle, and when Nora returned Bessie was quick to ask the question.

'I haven't seen your mum for a while, Nora. Is she all right?'

'Yes,' the woman said, taking the blankets from Pearl's arms.

'She's not ill?'

'No,' she said brusquely.

With a sigh Bessie took some money from the till and, shoving it into her pocket, Nora bustled off.

'Well, that was short and sweet. She ain't one for conversation, that's for sure. If Lily isn't ill, I wonder why I haven't seen her lately.'

Pearl shook her head. 'I've no idea, but maybe you've been too busy to notice.'

'I suppose so.' But there was doubt in Bessie's expression.

Pearl was right and, two weeks later, the last of the laundered blankets had sold. There were still loads more unlaundered items, let alone those in the back bedroom so, feeling confident, she suggested that they use Nora again.

'These quilts would come up a treat, and even if we pay Nora for the hours she spends at the laundry, we'd still make a profit.'

'I'm not arguing. You've achieved wonders in just a month. It was a good idea to display some of our choice pieces in the window and I've never had so many customers.'

Pearl smiled with satisfaction, glad that she was earning her keep. She glanced at the clock. Bernie would be arriving to pick Johnny up soon and she wondered if there would be any news. He'd said on Monday that a man might buy the café, but wanted to look at the account books first. She looked out of the window, seeking Derek passing the shop, and as their eyes met he lifted his hand to wave. Living in such close proximity, she often saw him out and about, reminded every time of how much she had hurt him. He looked nice, Pearl thought, smart, and thankfully there was no animosity in his manner. She missed his friendship, missed Connie, and as he moved out of sight, she turned away.

When Bernie arrived a few minutes later he held out a bag and her portfolio. 'We've been sorting out the bedrooms and you left this stuff behind.'

'Thanks, Bernie.'

'We've got a buyer for the café, Pearl.'

'Is it the chap you mentioned on Monday?'

'Yes, and he's keen to get the purchase through as soon as possible. We could be moving out in less than a month.'

'Have you found a place in Dorset?'

'No, and to tell you the truth we haven't been looking. Dolly thinks we shouldn't rush into anything so we're going to rent a little house for a while. It'll give us a chance to find the sort of premises we're looking for, and who knows, we might just find an established business.'

Pearl wheeled the pram from behind the counter. 'Johnny's had his bottle and he's taking solids too. He scoffed a bit of rusk mashed down with milk, and then went to sleep.'

Bernie smiled fondly. 'He likes his kip, that's for sure. I'll fetch him back in a couple of hours as usual.'

He called a goodbye and as soon as the door closed behind him, Bessie nodded at the portfolio. 'What's that?'

'I went to art classes for a while and they're my efforts.'

'Can I have a look?'

At Pearl's nod, Bessie began to flick through them. 'Blimey, girl, these are really good. If you stick them in the window you could make a few bob. They'd look even better in frames and if you have a rummage round, I think you'll find some.'

'I miss art classes, and one day I hope to get back to them. I'm not good enough yet and I can't see anyone wanting to buy these.'

'Don't be daft. I reckon the ones of the market will fly out.'

'I could give it a try, but I won't be able to sell the portraits.'

'Why not?'

'Can you imagine what they'd say? Take Dolly, for instance. I don't think she'd be happy to see her face displayed in the window.'

'Yeah, I suppose you have a point, but...'

The door opened, Nora poking her head inside. 'You got job for me?'

Bessie and Pearl exchanged looks, both wide-eyed with surprise.

'Blimey,' Bessie asked, 'how did you know that?'

'Just do,' Nora replied.

'Pearl, we only just decided to give her some work. Don't you think her turning up on cue is a bit strange?'

'After living with you for a month, I don't find anything strange.'

'You cheeky moo.' But Bessie's eyes narrowed as she looked at Nora. 'Maybe she's a bit psychic.'

'Goodness, I hope not. I don't think I could cope with two of you.' Pearl then bundled up some quilts. 'Here you are, Nora, you can take these to the washing baths, but I hope they aren't too heavy for you.'

'Hang on, I think I've got an old pushchair in the yard,' Bessie said, heading for the back door.

'She nice,' Nora said.

'Yes, she is,' Pearl agreed. She was happy – happier than she'd been in a long time – and it was all thanks to Bessie.

Bernie carefully lifted Johnny from his pram and, though he stirred a little, he didn't wake. As he walked into the living room, Dolly indicated the sofa, and as he laid the child down, she looked at her grandson fondly.

'Bernie, we need to talk. There's a lot to sort out before we move.'

'I know that, love. You've got so much stuff piled in cupboards that we'll probably need two removals vans.'

'No, it's not that. We need to talk about Johnny. He shouldn't be stuck in that bloody dump of a shop. If he came with us we could offer him a decent home and he'd want for nothing.'

'Now then, we've been over this before and you know that Pearl won't come with us.'

'If Kevin knew what was going on, I reckon he'd agree with me. He'd want the best for Johnny.'

'Maybe, but Pearl has made up her mind and we can't do anything about it. At least we'll be having the lad for the occasional weekend.'

'Huh, that's big of Pearl,' Dolly said, her voice dripping with sarcasm. 'I've been thinking, Bernie, and I reckon you should go to see Kevin. Tell him what's going on and persuade him that Johnny would be better off with us. He must have some say in his son's upbringing and could sign something to give us guardianship until he comes out of prison.'

'Dolly, surely you're not suggesting that we take him away from Pearl?'

'I am, and what's wrong with that?'

'Christ, I don't believe this. We can't take the

child away from his mother!'

'Yes we can.'

'Don't be daft. Pearl would never agree to it.'

'She won't be able to do anything about it.'

'You're living in cloud-cuckoo-land. Kevin's in prison, and even if he agreed to this daft idea, it wouldn't be legal.'

'Sod the law then. We'll just take the boy. We won't go to Dorset. Instead we'll go north and go somewhere that Pearl won't be able to find us.'

'Bloody hell, Dolly. Now you're talking about kidnapping!'

'No I'm not. He's Kevin's son, we're his grandparents, and despite what you say, it isn't kidnapping.'

'I think you've taken leave of your senses and—'

'No I haven't,' Dolly interrupted. 'And anyway, if we change our names nobody will be able to find us.'

'You're mad, woman!'

Bernie watched her rear up, but stood his ground. 'Now listen, Dolly, I love the boy as much as you, but I can't agree to this.'

Red-faced with anger, she glared at him, but then Johnny stirred. Dolly heaved in a great gulp of air, fighting to calm down before picking him up. 'Shush, Gran's here,' she said, rocking him for a minute or two.

At last Dolly looked up at Bernie, her voice quiet now. 'All right, you win. It was a daft idea, but I'm going to miss him so much.'

'Me too, love,' he said.

Bernie slumped with relief. For a moment he thought she'd lost her mind. To take the lad with them was an insane idea, one that could have landed them both in prison. Thank God he'd been able to talk her out of it.

38

By the time another three weeks had passed, Nora had become almost a fixture in the shop. She turned up every afternoon, and though most of the time they had nothing for the laundry, she stayed until closing time.

At first Bessie had grumbled, but gradually Pearl saw a growing fondness for Nora in the old woman's eyes. Nora was always cheerful, making herself useful, and Pearl often saw Bessie slipping her a couple of bob.

Luckily the business was continuing to do well, and Pearl had been pleasantly surprised when her paintings sold. Now there was only one left. Cocking her head on one side, she looked at it critically. It was a winter scene and perhaps too bleak. The market stalls were also a little out of proportion, but if she reduced the price someone might buy it.

Nora came in, and Bessie smiled a welcome.

'Hello, love. We haven't got anything for the laundry today.'

'Mummy cross. She chucked me out.'

'Lily wouldn't do that.'

'Kicked me.'

'What did she do that for?'

Nora shrugged. 'Dunno.'

Bessie came out from behind the counter. 'Pearl, there's something fishy about this. I think I'll pop round to see Lily.'

Nora headed for Johnny, distracted by the baby as Bessie left the shop. A happy baby who rarely cried, and growing rapidly, he chuckled when he saw her. Bernie would be here shortly, and then on Saturday, he and Dolly would be leaving.

'Hello,' Bernie said as he pushed open the door. 'And how's my grandson?'

'He's fine.'

'Well, Pearl, only two days to go now before we move. It's been a bit chaotic sorting all our stuff out, but Dolly's on top of it now. Once we're settled, maybe by the following Friday, can we have Johnny for the weekend? In fact, why don't you come too? A bit of country air would do you both good.'

'Oh, no,' Pearl blurted, covering her rudeness with a tight smile as she added, 'but thanks for asking.'

'Pearl, I know you're worried about Dolly, but there's no need. She's accepted that your marriage is over now, and I'm sure she'll make you welcome.'

Pearl doubted that was true and fobbed Bernie off. 'I'll think about it.'

'Right, see you later,' he said, wheeling the pram from the shop.

No sooner had the door closed, than Nora asked, 'Where Johnny going?'

'Bernie's taken him to see Dolly.'

'No like her.'

'Nor me,' Pearl agreed. She still didn't trust Dolly and had no intention of letting her have Johnny for the weekend. When Dolly found out, there was no doubt that she'd kick up an almighty fuss, and Pearl's stomach flipped at the thought. She stiffened her back. She could stand her ground with Dolly now, and would cross that bridge when she came to it.

Bessie returned, frowning worriedly as she drew Pearl to one side. 'Lily's gone a bit strange. At first I don't think she recognised me, and she got a bit aggressive. She stank rotten too and I reckon she's wetting herself.'

'Oh dear. What are you going to do?'

'I think I'll get the doctor to take a look at her. In fact, I'll go to the surgery now.'

As Bessie made to go out again, Nora ran to her side. 'Where you going?'

'I'm just popping along to the doctor's, love. I won't be long.'

'Take Mummy away.'

Bessie's eyebrows rose. 'Of course not. Now I won't be long, and when I come back we'll have a nice cup of tea and some biscuits.'

'Yes, biscuits,' Nora agreed, and, placated, she didn't protest when Bessie hurried out again.

Dolly was jiggling Johnny up and down on her lap, singing a little ditty that made him giggle. Oh, he was gorgeous, just like Kevin at this age. When she stood him up, strong little legs pummelled her lap. 'Look at that, Bernie. He's less than six months old and is trying to walk already. Did Pearl say we can have him next weekend?'

'Yes, and I invited her too.'

'That's nice,' Dolly said, playing her game and pretending she was pleased. She grimaced then as Johnny grabbed a chunk of her hair – 'Oh, you little bruiser'– and whilst doing her best to disentangle his hands she asked, 'What time are you picking him up on Saturday?'

'At nine o'clock, but it'll be chaotic with the removal men here too. Still, it's our last chance to see him before we go.'

Dolly hid a smile. It was all going to plan, everything in place, and both Pearl and Bernie had a shock coming. As far as she was concerned it served her husband right. He should have gone along with her plans, but he'd always been a weak, soft and useless bugger.

Come to think of it, he and Pearl were two of a kind, neither of them capable of bringing up Johnny. Children needed discipline, and that had been her mistake with Kevin. She'd spoiled him, been too soft, but she wouldn't make the same mistake with her grandson. Oh, she'd love him, but she'd be strict too. Johnny was her second chance, and for Kevin's sake she'd make sure that his son turned out right.

The doctor had examined Nora's mother, and now Bessie looked at him worriedly as she answered his question.

'I don't know if she's got any family. Why do you ask?'

'I've given her a thorough examination and in my opinion she has dementia.'

Dr Baxter's expression was grave. He'd been

Bessie's doctor for many, many years and she trusted him – but dementia...? 'Christ, poor Lily. Are you sure?'

'Yes, Bessie, I'm sure. Not only does she seem confused and agitated, there's memory loss. She also has difficulty with reasoning and communication. There are signs of malnourishment too.'

'Gawd, no wonder Nora always seems hungry.'

'Yes, well, her mother is incapable of looking after her now. In the circumstances, and until other relatives can be found, I'll make arrangement for Mrs Dobbs to be admitted to hospital immediately.'

'But what about Nora?'

'A home will have to be found for her too. I'll get on to the health authorities.'

'No, don't do that. She can stay with me for a while.'

'Are you sure, Bessie?'

'Yes. She'll be better off with me than stuck with a load of strangers.'

'I'll still need to inform the health authorities.'

'You do that, and no doubt the nosy buggers will be round to check me out.'

'Yes, they'll have to, but don't worry, I'll vouch for you.'

'You can do that?'

'Yes, Bessie, and I'll tell them that despite your grumpy nature, you have a heart of gold.'

'Grumpy! I ain't grum–' She saw the amused smile on his face and halted. 'Oh, you...'

'I'll go and make the arrangements. Will you stay with Mrs Dobbs until the ambulance arrives?'

'I'll suppose I'll have to,' Bessie complained.

'See, I told you – grumpy,' he said, still smiling with amusement as he left.

When Bessie was finally able to return to the shop, she spoke to Pearl out of Nora's hearing.

'The doctor's had Lily admitted.'

'Admitted! But why?'

'She's got dementia.'

'Oh dear. What about Nora?'

'I said she could stay with us while they trace any relatives. I just hope they find someone to take her on.'

Pearl stood back as Bessie approached Nora, gently breaking the news. Surprisingly, Nora didn't seem upset, only throwing her arms around Bessie. 'I stay with you?'

'Yes, love, and I tell you what, how do you fancy a nice plate of pie and mash?'

Nora nodded vigorously and Bessie took some money out of the till. 'What about you, Pearl?'

'No thanks,' she said, unable to understand what the local people saw in it. She could stomach the pie, and the mash, but the thick, green and sickly-looking liquor that was poured over the meal made her stomach turn.

Nora went off eagerly and Pearl found out why when the door closed behind her.

Bessie said, 'She's half starved, her mother too. There was hardly any food in the cupboards and goodness knows when they last had a square meal.'

'But Nora doesn't look to have lost any weight.'

'Well, there was a bag of broken biscuits and a loaf of bread. They must have been living on stuff

404

like that.'

'It's just as well you went round there.'

'Yes, but it's odd when you come to think of it. It was the end of September when Nora first turned up looking for a winter coat, and still mild. Seeing Lily, I doubt she was capable of thinking about Nora's clothes. In fact the woman hardly knew what day it was.'

'Yes, it is strange, but it's just as well she came in. If she hadn't, I dread to think what would have happened.'

'Me too, love and you should have seen the state of the place. Still, Nora will be all right now. We'll take good care of her until someone in her family turns up.'

'Huh, and you call me soft. You're just as bad.'

'Yeah, well, keep it to yourself. I don't want the customers to think I'm an easy touch.'

'There's no chance of that,' Pearl said, yet smiling fondly at Bessie.

It was only a little later when the door opened with a ping, and Pearl saw that Bernie had returned. 'Has Johnny been good?'

'He always is. Talk about a placid nipper. As agreed, I'll pick him up at nine on Saturday and that will give us a couple of hours with him before we go.' His eyes saddened. 'Dolly's gonna be heartbroken to leave him – me too.'

Bernie leaned over the pram, gently kissing Johnny on the cheek, and he gurgled with pleasure. ''Bye, lad. Grandpa will see you on Saturday.'

Johnny's chubby hands reached out to touch Bernie's face, and suddenly Pearl felt selfish.

Bernie and Dolly were Johnny's grandparents and, other than her, the only family he had. She'd been an orphan, with no relatives of her own, and now she was depriving her son of his only family. She still couldn't bear the thought of letting them have Johnny for the weekend, but maybe she could take him to see them occasionally? In the meantime, she still had to carry on with the charade.

'The rental on the cottage has been finalised now so we're all sorted,' Bernie said. 'It's a nice little place and we'll be fine there for a while. We'll be going down in Kevin's car. There's no sense in leaving it to rot.'

'I didn't know you could drive, Bernie.'

'Of course I can, love, but it's been years since I had a car.'

'Oh dear, are you sure you're not out of practice?'

He grinned. 'Don't worry, I'll be fine, and when he comes to stay Johnny won't come to any harm with me.'

Pearl lowered her eyes. Yes, Johnny might be safe with Bernie, but after Kevin's warning, she still couldn't say the same about Dolly.

39

On Friday morning, Pearl was rearranging the window display when she saw Derek Lewis talking to a costermonger. Across the distance he saw her, and then, crossing the road, he stood outside, looking at the picture in the window that hadn't sold. For a moment he studied it, and then he came into the shop.

'Is that painting of the market one of yours, Pearl?'

'Yes, but it isn't one of my best.'

'I can see my old stall, and I'd like to buy it.'

'You don't have to do that. You can have it for nothing.'

'Thanks, but I'd rather pay.' His eyes flicked around the shop. 'Where's Bessie?'

'She's upstairs. Nora's staying with us for a while and they're sorting her room out.'

'What, nutty Nora? Oh, sorry, I know you don't like to hear her called that, but why is she staying here?'

Pearl briefly explained and Derek said, 'I don't think she's got any other relatives.'

'Not even distant ones?'

'Not as far as I know.'

Johnny jiggled in his pram, arms waving as he gurgled happily. Derek smiled. 'Bit of a bruiser you've got there, Pearl.'

'Yes, that's what everyone says.'

'How are you coping?'

'I'm fine. What about you? Are you enjoying your job at the gym?'

'Yes, but I still miss the market at times.' He paused, licked his lips and then said, 'Like me, Gran thinks there's more to your story than meets the eye. Are you still sticking to it, Pearl?'

'Well, it wasn't quite like Dolly presented it, but it doesn't matter. It's all water under the bridge now.'

'It wasn't just Dolly, there was Kevin too. He told me that he wasn't the first to ... well, sleep with you.'

'What!'

'It's all right, Pearl. I know now that he was lying.'

'Oh, Derek ... how could he?'

'Self-preservation, love, and, knowing what I'd do to him, I ain't surprised. I'm just annoyed that I believed him. Despite your denial, I still reckon that like that other girl, he raped you.'

Pearl shook her head. There had been enough lies and Derek deserved the truth. 'No, as I told you before, he didn't rape me. Like a fool, I was flattered by Kevin's attention and couldn't believe he was interested in someone like me. I should have stopped him, I know that, but I didn't. I'll never forgive myself for hurting you, and hope one day you'll find happiness with someone else.'

He was quiet for a moment, but then said, 'All right, Pearl, and thanks for being honest. As for finding someone else, well, I've got a date tonight.'

'Have you? Oh, that's wonderful.' Pearl kicked

herself. She sounded over-enthusiastic, but finding that Derek had moved on lifted her spirits. 'Do I know her?'

'I don't think so. Her name's Jessica Bailey and she brought her son to the gym to ask about boxing lessons.'

'Her son?'

He smiled faintly. 'She's a widow. But enough about me. How much is the painting?'

'Please, Derek, let me give it to you as a gift.'

For a moment she thought he was going to refuse, but then he said quietly, 'All right, and thanks.'

She lifted it down. Derek took it from her hands and held it up. 'Yes, look, that's my stall, and I can even see china on display.'

Pearl looked at it too, but critically, once again thinking that she hadn't got the proportions right. Oh, she missed art classes, missed sketching. Bessie had insisted that she keep any money from the sale of her pictures, and she was so grateful, saving hard for a few materials.

'I hear on the grapevine that Bernie and Dolly are moving tomorrow,' Derek said as he lowered the painting to his side.

'Yes, they're going to Dorset.'

'So much is changing around here, but I never thought I'd see the day when Dolly didn't run the café. Still, there's quite a few that won't be sad to see the back of her – you included, I should think.'

Pearl offered no comment, and then Derek spoke again.

'Do you visit Kevin?'

'No, and anyway, *he* doesn't want to see me. As soon as I can afford it I'm getting a divorce.'

'Can't say I blame you, and are you going to stay here permanently?'

'I'd like to move away before Johnny's old enough to hear his father talked about, but it won't be easy. For the time being I'll have to stay – well, that's if Bessie's prepared to put up with me.'

'Anyone would put up with you, Pearl.'

She saw the fondness in Derek's eyes, and looked away. She had hurt him so badly, used him, and yet still he cared. For a moment she remembered how safe he made her feel and was tempted. She could have married this man. He would have treated her like a queen, but instead she'd been Dolly's servant and Kevin's doormat. If she went out with Derek again, she wouldn't have to fear Dolly's reaction when she backed out of the weekend visits. Instead she'd have this man's protection, her son too. Stop it, she berated herself. Yes, she'd been fond of Derek, but it hadn't been love, and here she was thinking about using him again. Derek deserved someone better than her, someone who could truly love him. He had to forget her, to walk away, and maybe the woman he was taking out that night could bring him happiness.

Brusquely she said, 'Well, I had better get on with some work.'

'All right, Pearl, and thanks for the painting.'

'You're welcome.'

He shuffled on his feet for a moment, but when she refused to meet his eyes, he turned swiftly, saying no more as he left the shop.

Pearl was sickened by where her thoughts had been taking her. Connie Lewis was right, she was a user, but it had to stop, and now. Somehow, no matter what she faced in the future, she had to stand on her own two feet.

It was ten minutes later when Bessie and Nora appeared and by that time Pearl had managed to pull herself together. Johnny threw a toy out of his pram, something he did umpteen times a day, and whilst Nora bent to pick it up, Pearl went to speak to Bessie.

'Derek's just been in and he said that Nora hasn't got any other relatives.'

'No, I didn't think so.'

'But that means she'll have to go into a home.'

'Not if I have anything to say about it. If they'll allow it she can stay with us, and you must admit she's turned out to be handy to have around. She cleans the place like a demon and, other than feeding her, she ain't gonna cost much to keep.'

'So, you knew there wasn't anyone else when you brought her here?'

'Well, yeah.'

'Do you know something, Bessie Penfold, you're a lovely woman. First you took me in, and now Nora.' With a grin she added, 'Are there any more waifs and strays that you've got your eye on?'

'No I bleedin' ain't,' she said, obviously trying to hide her pleasure at the compliment as she added brusquely, 'Anyway, you can both earn your keep. I've put Nora in the back bedroom, but we had to move piles of stuff. The pair of you can sort it out, while I keep an eye on Johnny.'

'Yes, ma'am,' Pearl said with a mock salute, and calling Nora, they went upstairs, to start on their work.

40

On Saturday morning, Pearl was getting Johnny dressed. Bernie would be here soon and she was easing her son's arms into his coat when Bessie spoke.

'Don't let them have the lad today.'

'Not have him? But why?'

'I dunno, it's just a feeling.'

'Oh God! Have you had another vision?'

'Only a small one and it was some time ago now, but I don't think you should let Johnny out of your sight.'

Pearl's eyes were wide as she gazed at Bessie, her thoughts still racing when Bernie turned up. It was then that she came to a decision. 'Do you mind if I come with you today?'

'No, love, but what's brought this on?'

Pearl forced the parody of a smile. 'Well, er ... I think I should say goodbye to Dolly. It would be nice to part without bad feelings.'

'I'm sure she'll be dead chuffed.'

Pearl doubted it, but with Bessie's warning in her ears she wasn't going to let her son out of her sight.

The furniture was already being loaded when they arrived at the café, and though Dolly gawked when she saw Pearl, she soon recovered, her smile pleasant.

'Hello, Pearl, how nice that you've come to say goodbye.' She took Johnny from her arms, kissing him on the cheek. 'I'm going to miss him so much, but thank you for letting us have him for weekends. You'd be welcome too, Pearl.'

Finding this Dolly unrecognisable, Pearl said, 'That's kind of you. I ... I'll think about it.'

'Bernie, keep an eye on the removal men,' Dolly ordered, and then her attention was once again focused on Johnny.

During the next half an hour, Dolly struggled to remain pleasant. Christ, Pearl turning up had ruined everything. She'd had it all worked out, right to the last detail, even a bag of stuff stashed away for Johnny to get them through the first twenty-four hours. After that she'd planned to buy everything they'd need.

Her lips tightened. Now it was all going wrong, but she refused to give up. There had to be a way – and almost immediately she found it.

When Bernie came back into the room, Dolly handed Johnny to him. 'Here, you have him for a while. I'd best ring the solicitor to see if the money has come through. We can't leave until we know the sale has been properly completed.'

Bernie lifted Johnny high into the air, laughing up at him. 'It's about time your granny gave me a look in.'

Dolly went into the hall to ring the solicitor.

The call was short, the money cleared, and after making sure it would be transferred to her private bank account she replaced the receiver. She'd planned to use this excuse with Bernie, pretending that she needed to see the solicitor, taking Johnny with her whilst he remained to supervise the loading. Of course she had no intention of returning, her route planned, and despite Pearl turning up, it could still work.

Fixing an indignant look on her face, she returned to the living room, taking Johnny from Bernie as she formed the lie. 'Huh, I thought it was expecting too much that things would go through without a hitch. Apparently there's a document that needs signing and I've got to go to their offices immediately.'

'I thought you'd already signed everything.'

'So did I, but it's to do with the fixtures and fittings. Sod it, if I go out now I won't have much time with Johnny. Can I take him with me, Pearl? The solicitor is only in Falcon Road and I won't be long.'

'Er ... er, I'll come with you.'

'There's no need and–'

One of the removal men poked his head into the room, 'Excuse me, missus, we'll need to load the stuff in here soon and there's a woman downstairs asking to see someone called Pearl.'

'Send her up,' Dolly said, thinking that the gods were smiling on her. She didn't know who this woman was, but with any luck she'd be able to slip out with Johnny whilst Pearl was distracted. She moved closer to the door, saying, 'I wonder who it is, Pearl?'

A youngish woman appeared, but she looked frail, breathing heavily as she climbed the last stair. It wasn't anyone Dolly recognised, but she gestured her into the room. As long as this woman held Pearl's attention for a minute, it would be enough.

When Pearl saw the woman walking into the room, her voice came out in a squeak.

'Miss Rosen!'

'I'm so sorry, my dear, but when you didn't respond to my letter, I just had to come.'

'Letter ... what letter?'

'I wrote to you over a month ago.'

Pearl shook her head in confusion. She hadn't received it, and though it was lovely to see her old art teacher, what was she doing here? The woman suddenly paled, swaying on her feet, and Pearl moved quickly forward.

'Are you all right?'

Bernie moved at the same time, grasping the woman's arm. 'Here, sit down.'

Miss Rosen's upper lip was beaded with perspiration. She looked ill, her skin holding a greyish tinge as she sunk onto a chair.

'Can I get you anything? A drink of water?' Pearl asked.

'Yes, please.'

'I'll get it,' Bernie said, hurrying through to the kitchen.

Pearl continued to gaze at Miss Rosen, glad to see that she was looking a little better and then Bernie returned, holding out an old cup. 'I'm sorry, but all our stuff has been packed and this is all I could find.'

Miss Rosen waved his apology away before sipping the water. A little colour returned to her cheeks, but her expression was anxious as she looked at Pearl.

'As you didn't get my letter, this is going to be a little difficult. Would it be possible to speak to you alone?'

Pearl's eyes flicked to her father-in-law first, and then she looked towards the door, suddenly tensing. 'Bernie, where's Dolly?'

'Blimey, she was standing over there a moment ago.' He scratched his head. 'I expect she's gone to see the solicitor.'

Bessie's warning rang in Pearl's mind, her voice holding panic, 'Bernie, she's taken Johnny with her.'

'Yeah, but she'll be back soon.'

'But what if she isn't?'

'Don't be daft, love. She'll be here in a minu...'

Pearl heard no more as she headed for the door, stumbling down the stairs in her haste to find her son. Oh, no, God! Oh, please God! The words were a chant in her head as she dashed outside.

She ran across to Falcon Road, her eyes frantically searching, but there was no sign of Dolly. How far along was the solicitor's office? She continued to run, legs pumping and heart thumping in her chest. Where was she? *Oh, please, let me find her.*

Pearl was mindless with fear when she stopped, leaning forward as she gasped for air. Had she passed the solicitor's office?

Once again her eyes flicked frantically up and down the road, but then with sickening clarity the truth dawned. Dolly hadn't gone to see the solicitor. It was a ruse, and by now she could be anywhere!

Bernie stared at Pearl's back as she flew from the room, wondering what all the fuss was about Dolly would be back soon and in another hour or so they'd be on their way. Pearl's panic would have been understandable if she'd known about Dolly's insane idea to take the boy with them, but thankfully he'd talked her out of that.

He froze. He had talked Dolly out of it – hadn't he? Bernie felt a moment of doubt. Had Dolly given in too easily? With a sick feeling in his stomach he made for the telephone.

'What's going on? Why did Pearl run out like that?' Miss Rosen asked.

'I'll explain later,' he said, scurrying into the hall.

After speaking to the solicitor and hearing that there weren't any papers to sign, Bernie found his hands shaking as he replaced the receiver. Dolly had lied, and he guessed why. She'd done a runner with the lad.

Christ, she'd been cunning, clever, and must have planned this, fooling them with her amiable act. He had to stop her, do something, and quickly. For a moment his mind raced, but then he exhaled loudly. There was no choice, he knew that, and, picking up the receiver again, Bernie dialled 999.

It took some time, but at last he was taken seriously, the police on alert now and saying they'd be round to take a statement. When the call was finished he became galvanised, rushing into the living room to give Miss Rosen a potted explanation before going to find Pearl. A removals man halted him in his tracks, but Bernie dismissed his query, only saying, 'Look, we've got a bit of a problem so why don't you have a break? Leave the rest of the loading until I come back.'

As he stepped outside, another thought crossed Bernie's mind. It might not be a bad idea to spread the news. Someone might have seen which direction Dolly had taken.

'I didn't see her,' the first stallholder said. 'She's taken Pearl's kid, you say. Blimey, I'll put the word out.'

Bernie thanked the man and then crossed the road, almost immediately seeing Pearl. She was running back along Falcon Road, her face set in panic.

'I can't find her, Bernie!'

'It's all right, love, calm down. She can't have gone far and I've called the police. They'll find her.'

Pearl began to cry then, tears flooding down her cheeks. 'But what if they don't? Oh, Johnny ... Johnny.'

Bernie ineffectually patted her back, his voice coaxing. 'Don't cry, love. I've given the police a good description and, let's face it, Dolly ain't easy to miss. Now come on, let's get back to the café. The old bill will be arriving soon to take a statement, and that woman is still waiting to talk to you.'

'I've put the word about, Bernie, but so far nobody's seen your missus,' the stallholder said when he saw them.

'But someone must have seen her leaving!' Pearl cried.

'No, sorry, love.'

Pearl pushed the heels of her hands into her eyes and Bernie could see that she was close to collapse.

'Come on,' he urged, 'let's get you indoors.'

'I can't just sit and wait. I have to do something to find Johnny.'

She made to run off, but Bernie held her arm. 'Wait, Pearl. We have no idea which direction Dolly took and all we'd be doing is running around like headless chickens. Leave it to the police. They'll find her.'

Her huge eyes were wide, her face drained of colour, and suddenly her knees gave way. Holding her up now, Bernie urged her into the café, mentally cursing his wife.

They hadn't been upstairs for long, Pearl verging on hysteria, when the police arrived. She tried to answer their questions, but had to leave most of them to Bernie. When they left she was unable to sit still, pacing the room, and when Miss Rosen tried to comfort her, she was barely aware of her as she shrugged the woman off, her mind only on her son.

Miss Rosen's expression was sad, but she sat down again, talking to Bernie now. 'I seem to have come at a bad time, but surely your wife wouldn't run off with the baby?'

419

'Huh, you don't know Dolly. When she gets an idea in her head there's no stopping her. I should have realised that.'

Pearl continued to pace, stopping only to look out of the window every now and then. Eventually she saw Bessie, with Nora by her side, heading for the café. 'Bessie's on her way over,' Pearl told Bernie, glad when he went to let her in.

'Don't worry, my dear,' Miss Rosen said, standing up and moving to Pearl's side again. 'I'm sure you'll have your baby back soon.'

Pearl's brow creased, wondering again why Miss Rosen had come to see her, but then Bessie came into the room, the thought forgotten as she flew across the space, throwing herself into the old woman's arms. 'Oh, Bessie, Dolly's taken Johnny.'

'I know, love, but don't worry, I'm sure the police will find her.'

'But it's been over an hour now!'

'Train,' Nora said.

'What did you say?' Bessie demanded, unravelling Pearl from her arms.

'Train,' Nora said again. 'Dolly get train.'

'How do you know?'

Nora shrugged. 'Just do.'

'Do you know what station she's gone to?'

'Big one.'

'Bernie, call the police, tell them what Nora said. I've a feeling she could be right.'

He shook his head. 'I should think they're already checking the stations.'

'I'll call them,' Pearl cried as she ran from the room.

420

'It'll be a waste of time,' Bernie said. 'The old bill know that Dolly has done a runner, that she's taken Johnny, and are taking it very seriously. They're on full alert, and are hopefully checking train stations as we speak.'

'Bernie, I warned you that Dolly was planning something and I've been proved right!' Bessie said.

Bernie ignored her, his face white with strain, and deciding this wasn't the time to rub salt in the wound, Bessie turned to Miss Rosen, saying, 'Do I know you?'

'Pearl knows me as Emily Rosen, but I don't think we've met.'

'Do you live around here?'

'No, I've travelled down from Winchester.'

'Winchester. Blimey, you've come a long way.'

Pearl came back into the room again. 'I told them,' she said, before starting to pace again. Was Nora right? Was Dolly headed for a railway station? Tears filled her eyes again. It would take ages to check them all, and Dolly could be long gone before they got there. She stopped her pacing for a moment to look out of the window, tears running down her cheeks. Arms wrapped around her, and she turned into them, Miss Rosen holding her close.

Derek Lewis had been on his way to the market when he saw Dolly Dolby. She looked furtive, harassed, and as a taxi drew into the kerb, she climbed inside. Derek was puzzled. She and Bernie were supposed to be moving today, but Dolly was going off on her own. No, not on her

421

own – she had Pearl's baby with her.

He saw another taxi and, acting on impulse, Derek hailed it, feeling foolish as he urged the driver to follow the one in front. The man's eyebrows lifted, and he grinned. 'In all my years as a cabbie, I've been waiting to hear that.'

'Just do it,' Derek growled.

With a shrug the driver pulled off, Derek leaning forward anxiously, and relieved to see that they hadn't lost the other cab. They crossed the Thames, driving through London, Derek's thoughts racing. He could be making a fool of himself and should have checked things out with Pearl before chasing after Dolly. Maybe there was a reason for all this, but if so, why was Dolly acting so suspiciously?

They finally turned into Euston station and in his haste to keep track of Dolly, Derek almost threw his fare at the driver, hurrying into the station in time to see her heading for the ticket office. This wasn't right, he was sure of it, and increasing his pace, Derek grabbed her arm.

She jumped like a startled rabbit, her eyes wide. 'Derek, what are you doing here?'

'I'm trailing you, Mrs D, and I'd like to know where you're taking Pearl's baby.'

'Er ... well ... it's like this,' Dolly said, her eyes now darting from side to side as she obviously fought for words. 'Pearl has decided to come with us, and ... and she stayed behind to supervise the removals. I ... I'm going on ahead, and taking Johnny with me. Pearl and Bernie will travel later.'

Derek cocked his head. She was lying, he was

sure of it. 'Do you mind if I ring the café to check this out?'

'Don't be ridiculous. Now get out of my way. I have a train to catch.'

'No, Mrs D, until I've had a word with Pearl, you ain't going anywhere.'

'How dare you? Let go of my arm!'

Her yell startled Johnny and he began to squall, but still Derek held on. There was a shout, the sound of running footsteps, Derek still refusing to let go as three policemen surrounded them. He had no idea how they had come to Dolly's rescue so quickly, but as he loosened his grip on her arm, she tugged it away. Dolly then turned to run, but one of the constables barred her path.

'Mrs Dolby?' he asked.

'No, I'm not Mrs Dolby,' she protested.

'Yes she is,' Derek said loudly.

Another officer appeared, this one female and, moving to Dolly, she said firmly, 'Give me the child.'

'No,' Dolly snapped.

The policewoman endeavoured to pull Johnny from Dolly's arms, but she shrieked, clutching him to her. 'No! No, leave him alone. He's my baby, my son! You can't take him!'

A tussle ensued, a male officer joining in, and soon they were surrounded by a crowd, all watching the scene with avid interest. 'Help me,' Dolly yelled, her eyes frantic with appeal. 'They're trying to take my baby.'

No-one moved forward to help, and at last the male officer was able to pull Johnny, kicking and screaming, from her grasp. Her arms empty,

423

Dolly went mad. She reared like an angry bull, lashing out at the policeman, her fist connecting with his nose. Derek heard his 'oomph' of pain, but the man had the presence of mind to turn away, shielding Johnny in his arms before passing him to the policewoman.

'That's enough, missus!' another officer shouted, trying to pin Dolly's arms.

'Get off me!' she screamed, her strength amazing as she shook him off.

With the help of his colleagues, the policeman tried again, this time managing to cuff her, yet still she fought, kicking out with her legs.

Derek's legs had felt glued to the spot, but at last he moved. 'Mrs D! Stop! This isn't doing any good.'

Maybe it was his voice that penetrated Dolly's fury – Derek didn't know, – but suddenly her struggles ceased. Johnny was still screaming, his face red, nose running, but seeing his grandmother, he held out his arms towards her in appeal.

Sobbing, Dolly tried to move forward, but was held tightly, one of the officers calling, 'Get that kid out of here.'

The policewoman nodded, hurrying away. 'Kevin! Kevin!' Dolly screamed in anguish, but as they went out of sight, her legs folded and she collapsed.

Why had Dolly said the baby was her son? Why had she called him Kevin? Derek moved forward, appalled to see her suddenly convulsing, foam forming on her lips. She looked mad, rabid. 'She's having a fit – she needs help.'

The constables were kneeling by her side, but one looked up, 'Don't worry, sir, she'll be taken care of.' He then rose to his feet, leaving his colleagues to attend to Dolly. 'We'll need to take a statement from you.'

'What about the baby?'

'He'll be returned to his mother.'

Derek nodded. Yes he'd give a statement, but judging by the look of Dolly, they wouldn't get much out of her.

When the telephone rang, Bernie hurried out to the hall to answer it, returning with a wide smile on his face.

'It's good news, love,' he said, moving to wrap an arm around Pearl's shoulder. 'They've found Dolly. She was at Euston station, and Derek was with her.'

'Derek! What was he doing there?'

'I dunno, love.'

'And Johnny?'

'He's been seen by a doctor and he's fine. He's being driven here as we speak. Dolly had some sort of fit, and I've got to go and see her. Oh yes, and the police want to know if you're going to press charges.'

Pearl flew from the room, dashing downstairs and outside to wait for the police car. Her eyes flicked the street anxiously, just wanting it to arrive, to hold Johnny in her arms.

After a few minutes a costermonger came to her side. 'Have they found him, love?' he asked.

'Yes,' Pearl said, but her eyes were still on the road.

'That's good.'

Pearl hardly heard the man as she saw a police car approaching. She dashed forward as it drew into the kerb, a policewoman climbing out. She was holding Johnny, and Pearl's heart soared. He'd been crying, his eyes red and his nose caked with mucus, but his arms went out when he saw her, a smile now lighting his face. Pearl took him, holding her son closely, her eyes once again filling with tears, but this time of joy.

Johnny lay against her for a moment, but then struggled, pushing back, his eyes now darting curiously around the market and the crowd that had gathered. One of the costermongers stepped forward, patting the boy on the head. 'I'm glad you've got him back, love.'

Pearl smiled her thanks, but then the policewoman said, 'We'll need to talk to you.'

As they went inside, Pearl asked, 'Please, can you tell me how Derek Lewis was involved in this?'

'From what he told us, it appears that he followed your mother-in-law, and it was lucky he did. He was able to hold her up until we got there, preventing her from catching a train.'

'He did! Oh, I must thank him.'

They stepped into the living room, everyone crowding around Pearl.

'Mrs Dolby, we need to know if you intend to press charges against your mother-in-law,' the officer said.

'Please, I've only just got my son back. Can it wait?'

The policewoman looked doubtful for a

moment, but with so many people in the room she nodded. 'All right, we'll come back in an hour.'

As the constable left, the others all made a fuss of Johnny for a while, but as they moved away Pearl saw Miss Rosen hovering in the background. She again wondered what had brought the woman here, but at the moment all she wanted was to hold her son, to keep him close and never let him out of her sight again.

'Look, I've got to go, love. What they said about Dolly is worrying me and I need to see how she is,' Bernie said.

Pearl's lips tightened, but Bessie broke in and didn't give her a chance to speak. 'And we'll go back to the shop,' she said. 'Come on, Pearl, you don't want to stay here. What about you, Miss Rosen, would you like to join us?'

'Emily, please call me Emily, and thank you, but no. I think that Pearl has been through enough today. If it's all right, I'll come back tomorrow.'

'Yeah, do that, love,' Bessie said.

She moved to Pearl. 'We'll talk tomorrow, my dear.'

'Yes, all right.' But then Johnny started to cry, Pearl distracted as she comforted him.

When he quietened, there was only one thing uppermost in Pearl's mind. The police would be back for her decision. Did she want to prosecute Dolly?'

41

When they arrived at the shop, all trooped up-
stairs, Pearl immediately asking Bessie's opinion.
'Do you think I should press charges against
Dolly?'

'From what Bernie said, it seems that Dolly's
had some sort of fit. She must have been mad to
think she'd get away with kidnapping your baby,
but I can't advise you, love. It's got to be your
decision.'

Pearl chewed on her bottom lip. Dolly had tried
to kidnap her son. Now her relief at getting
Johnny back was replaced by anger. Fit or not,
Dolly would recover. She'd bounce back as she
always did. 'If I let her get away with it I'll have
to spend years looking over my shoulder in case
she tries it again.'

'I don't think even Dolly would be daft enough
to do that. Come on, you've been through
enough and let's forget it for now. I'll make us all
a cup of tea and, by the look of you, you could do
with one.'

Bessie bustled off, and Nora began to amuse
Johnny, pulling her usual faces whilst Pearl's
mind continued to churn. She couldn't forget it.
The police would be back soon for her answer.
She couldn't let Dolly get away with it. She'd
have to press charges.

In the end it was Bernie who stayed Pearl's hand. Dolly was ill, he said, when he came to see them. Her mind was unhinged. Pearl saw the deep sadness in her father-in-law's eyes as he spoke.

'I should have realised she wasn't quite right, Pearl, but now she seems to have lost it completely. Maybe those tranquilliser pills the doctor prescribed held it off, but she must have stopped taking them. She's raving, Pearl. She thinks that Johnny is Kevin and that the police were taking him away from her.'

Confused, Pearl shook her head, but Bernie continued, 'I had to speak to a psychiatrist and he asked me lots of questions. I told him about Kevin and then he spouted bloody theories that Dolly couldn't face up to what Kevin had done, or losing him to a prison sentence. He said the catalyst must have occurred when the police snatched Johnny. His theory was that Dolly slipped back to a time when Kevin was a baby, and that her mind couldn't cope with losing him twice.'

Pearl sighed heavily. 'I suppose it makes some sort of weird sense. Did you have to give permission for her to be sectioned?'

'Yes, but even if I'd refused, it would have been taken out of my hands. Anyway, seeing the state Dolly's in, it wasn't a hard decision. She needs help, a lot of help, and at the moment a psychiatric hospital is the best place for her.'

'What will you do now, Bernie?'

'I dunno, love. With the café being in Dolly's name, I couldn't halt the sale, but I'll stay around here. The psychiatric unit is in Tooting, and I want to be close by.' He rose to his feet. 'Anyway, I'd best be off to sort to find myself a bed for the night. Can I pop in to see the nipper now and again?'

'Yes, of course you can,' Pearl said, her heart going out to Bernie. He looked awful. With his shoulders stooped, suddenly he was like an old, old man.

'Thanks, Pearl.'

As Bernie left, she slumped back and closed her eyes, feeling mentally drained.

'Are you all right, Pearl?' Bessie asked.

'I'm just tired,' Pearl said, forcing her eyes open again. It was only five o'clock, but felt much later.

There was another knock on the door.

'Bloody hell, what now?' Bessie said as she went to answer it.

Bessie returned with Derek behind her and Pearl rose swiftly to her feet. 'Oh, Derek, I was going to come to see you, to thank you. How did you know what Dolly was up to?'

'I didn't, but it seemed odd that she was going off with your baby. I followed her, and I'm glad I did.'

'Me too,' Pearl said, impulsively giving him a hug.

His arms tightened around her and she leaned against him, feeling his strength. This man had stopped Dolly from kidnapping her son. Tears of gratitude filled her eyes. 'I ... I can't thank you enough.'

'It was nothing, love, and anyway, the police weren't far behind me.'

'Hark at him, playing it down,' Bessie chuckled. 'From what we heard you held on to Dolly until they arrived. I reckon you deserve a medal.'

Pearl was still in his arms, but before drawing away she heard words said almost under his breath: 'Sod a medal, I'd rather have Pearl.'

She pretended she hadn't heard, but her mind reeled with confusion. Derek still loved her, still wanted her, and as she looked up at his face she realised that she cared for him too, maybe more than cared.

'I've got to go, Pearl,' he said. 'I'm due at the gym.'

'Yes, of course. I ... I'll show you out.'

Derek called goodbye to the others, and then Pearl led him downstairs. She paused before opening the door. 'Are ... are you still seeing that woman?'

'No, love, it didn't work out.'

'Oh, I'm sorry.'

'Is there any chance for me, Pearl?'

She wanted to say yes, but held back. She felt something for Derek, but was it love? He held none of the passion that she had felt for Kevin, but there was something, like a seed that had been planted yet needed water to flourish. 'I don't know, Derek. Maybe, but so much has happened and I don't think I'm ready for another relationship. Perhaps if you give me a little more time and then ask again...'

'I'll wait, Pearl,' he said eagerly. 'You can have all the time in the world, and I'll still be waiting.'

He looked like a big, soft bear and Pearl had to smile. She stood on tiptoe, giving him a swift

431

kiss. 'Thanks, Derek.' Then impulsively she added, 'And … and I don't think I'll keep you waiting for long.'

It was as though a light had switched on inside Derek's eyes and they glowed with happiness as he looked at her. He grinned, and Pearl found herself grinning back. His wasn't a handsome face, but suddenly Pearl loved it.

'When things have calmed down, come round to see me. Maybe in a week or two.'

'Wild horses couldn't keep me away,' Derek smiled, and as Pearl finally opened the door he stepped outside. 'Take care, love, and if you need me before then, you know where I am.'

Pearl was smiling as she closed the door, walked back upstairs and into the living room.

Bessie said, 'Right, let's hope that's the last caller. I can't face cooking a meal so me and Nora are off to get some fish and chips.'

'I'll get them,' Pearl said.

'No, love, we'll go, but it's nice to see you smiling again. That Derek's a smashing bloke.'

'Yes, he is,' Pearl agreed.

'You could do worse.'

'I know,' Pearl said, but this time she wasn't going to rush it. She had learned her lesson, and would take things slowly. Yes, she cared for Derek, but didn't know if it would grow into love. It wouldn't be fair to give him false hope, and she'd have to tell him that from the start, but it would be nice to go out with him again.

When Bessie and Nora returned, they sat around the table to eat, Nora's portion the first to disappear from her plate. She then got up, moving across to play with Johnny, whilst Bessie said, 'That woman who turned up today – it's a bit strange really, but with so much going on I've only just realised where I've seen her before.'

'Miss Rosen was my art teacher during my last year in the orphanage. I must admit I was surprised to see her.'

'She's the one I saw in my vision, the one I told you about, who was sitting up in bed looking at your face in the newspaper.'

Pearl frowned. 'I wonder what she wanted to talk to me about?'

'Well love, you'll find out when she comes back tomorrow.'

Pearl found herself puzzling about Miss Rosen for the rest of the evening, but it had been a fraught day and she was yawning widely by nine thirty.

'I think I'll have an early night,' she said.

'Yeah, you do that, love,' Bessie agreed. 'Me and Nora won't be far behind you.'

Pearl took Johnny upstairs and, after changing his nappy, laid him gently in his cot. He gurgled, his smile wide as he held his arms up. Unable to resist, she picked him up again. She held him against her fiercely for a moment, thanking God that Dolly had been caught, but then, yawning again, she put him back. He protested, so Pearl sat on the side of her bed with a hand through the bars, holding his until he went to sleep. She then lay down but, tired as she was, her mind was still restless, her thoughts again turning to Miss Rosen as she wondered why her old art teacher wanted to talk to her.

42

When Pearl got up the next morning, she found Johnny soaking. He didn't seem to mind as he gurgled happily to see her.

She tickled him under the chin. 'Come on, darling, I think you need a bath.'

Bessie was up, but there was no sign of Nora when Pearl finally got her son bathed and dressed. He was starting to cry now, obviously hungry, so Bessie took him while Pearl went to prepare his bottle and rusk, something her son had taken to with relish.

'Blimey, Pearl, he's getting to weigh a ton,' Bessie said when Pearl returned.

'Yes, I know,' she said, smiling fondly as Johnny's mouth opened like a baby bird waiting to be fed.

'Thank Gawd it's Sunday,' Bessie said, ''cos I don't know about you, but I still feel worn out.'

'I'm fine now, and just glad that Dolly didn't get away with it.'

Nora appeared, hair sticking up like a brush, but she made straight for Johnny. 'Me hold him, Pearl?'

'Yes, when he's finished his breakfast.'

It was a leisurely morning, but at eleven o'clock someone knocked on the door. 'I'll get it,' Pearl said.

When she opened the door, Miss Rosen smiled, 'Hello, my dear.'

'Please come in,' Pearl invited, thinking that the woman looked frail.

Emily Rosen followed Pearl upstairs, but after saying hello to Bessie and Nora, she said, 'I'm sorry to sound rude, but would it be possible to talk to Pearl alone?'

Bessie stood up. 'Of course it would. Come on, Nora, we'll make ourselves scarce for a while.'

'Please, sit down,' Pearl said as the door closed behind them. 'It's lovely to see you again, but I must admit I'm puzzled. What do you want to talk to me about?'

'Oh, my dear, I'm afraid this is going to be another shock for you, but when you didn't respond to my letter I began to think the worst, that ... that you didn't want to see me.'

'I can't imagine why I wouldn't want to see you. I left the café just over a month ago, and maybe the letter arrived after that. If Dolly found it I'm not surprised she didn't pass it on.'

'Never mind, I'm here now, and only sorry I couldn't come sooner. I've been rather ill and until now, unable to travel. Anyway, my dear, I don't know how to break this gently, so I'll just tell you. You see, I'm your mother.'

Pearl's jaw dropped. 'What! But you can't be!'

'I am, my dear, and I can't tell you how wonderful it is to find you again.'

'But ... but I don't understand. If you're my mother, why didn't you tell me when you came to work at the orphanage?'

'I'm afraid it wasn't that simple.'

Johnny awoke, crying loudly. Pearl picked him up and, as she comforted him, bitterness rose like bile in her throat. No matter what, she could never abandon her son. She would die first. She glared at the woman who claimed to be her mother. Emily Rosen had dumped her on the steps of the orphanage, but now had the cheek to turn up all these years later. Where had she been when she had felt so alone? Where had she been when she needed her?

Taking a seat again with Johnny perched on her lap, she voiced her thoughts. 'Do you know I grew up dreaming about my mother, wondering why she had left me. The only comfort I could find was in thinking that she was ill, too ill to keep me and that she'd died. What other excuse could there be for abandoning me?'

'Oh Pearl, I didn't, really I didn't. Please let me explain.'

'No,' Pearl cried. 'You can't be my mother! You just can't.' And, holding Johnny closely, she ran sobbing from the room.

'What's going on?' Bessie demanded, but Pearl ignored her shout as she reached her bedroom, shutting the door behind her.

Bessie frowned and, marching into the sitting room, she demanded, 'What the hell's going on? Don't you think that girl's been through enough without you turning up to upset her?'

'Please, I didn't know she'd take it like this. Like me, I thought Pearl would be overjoyed.'

'She didn't look overjoyed to me. What did you say to her?'

For a moment Emily hesitated, but then said quietly, 'I told Pearl that I'm her mother.'

Bessie's face stretched in shock. 'What?'

'I said I'm Pearl's mother.'

For a moment Bessie just stared at Emily. Then, heaving a deep sigh, she pulled out a chair. 'Come on, tell me about it, and start at the beginning.'

Nora came into the room, Bessie snapping, 'Go and make your bed.'

The tone in Bessie's voice was enough to have Nora scuttling out again, and for a moment Emily said nothing. She then looked deeply into Bessie's eyes, and as though seeing someone she could trust, she began, 'It's a long story.'

Bessie listened, thinking that the woman still showed signs of illness, and didn't interrupt until her story came to an end. Then she said kindly, 'Well, love, it's a sad tale, but once Pearl has heard it I'm sure she'll come round.'

'Oh, I do hope so. Now that I've found her, I couldn't bear to lose her again. I can't offer her much, but I have a small cottage and hoped to offer her a home.'

'As I said, she can't fail to come round, but if she moves in with you, I'm gonna miss the girl. Anyway, Emily, I should think she'll have calmed down by now. Go and talk to her. You'll find her on the top floor, the room at the end of the landing.'

When Emily left, Bessie sat thinking. She had no doubt that Pearl would leave to be with her mother, and she felt a wave of sadness. It seemed that some people came into your life and remained, yet others came only briefly. Yet as paths crossed, each person brought a new experience, a new lesson to learn. Sometimes it would be a bad experience and you'd hurt someone, or be hurt – others were good – but no matter what, it brought the opportunity for spiritual growth.

She'd known that she and Pearl were destined to meet, that for a short while the girl would need her, just as she now knew it was time for her to move on.

Bessie sighed heavily. It had been a two-way thing, of course. She had let the shop, and herself, go, but when Pearl turned up it had given her a new lease of life. That was the lesson: a reminder that there was always a reason to carry on.

Nora came into the room, her expression nervous, but Bessie smiled at her and, visibly relaxing, Nora smiled back. Bessie was fond of Nora and knew she shouldn't have snapped at her. As with Pearl, the two of them needed each other. The circle was turning, and as one door was closing, another had opened. She had Nora now. Thanks to Pearl the shop was doing well, and between them they'd keep up the good work.

Yes, she and Nora would rub along well together, and somehow Bessie knew it would be for many, many years.

When Emily Rosen knocked softly on the door before walking into the room, Pearl cried, 'Leave me alone. We have nothing to say to each other.'

'Oh, Pearl, I didn't abandon you. Please let me explain.'

Part of Pearl wanted to know, to hear the story, but the other still held bitterness. Yet the woman looked so sad, so frail, and something touched Pearl's heart. 'All right, I'm listening.'

'This is going to be a long story, and I'm afraid not a pretty one, but I hope you won't judge me too harshly.' Emily walked towards the bed, wringing her hands. 'I think I had better start at the beginning. You see, I'm afraid I was unmarried when I fell pregnant with you, and my father almost threw me out of the house. I had disgraced him, had a love affair with a gardener, and I think that was more unforgivable to him than the pregnancy. It was only my mother who stayed his hand, but I was kept virtually a prisoner until you were born.'

Pearl stiffened. It sounded ridiculous, like something out of a Victorian melodrama. If this was her mother, she was making it up, trying to make excuses. 'You say my father was a gardener. What happened to him?'

'Oh, my dear, I'm afraid he was sacked. He never knew that I was pregnant, and it was many years later before I had news of him. By then it was too late. He ... he had died in a farming accident.'

Pearl closed her eyes momentarily. So, her father was dead – well, that was if this story was true. 'What was his name?'

'Jack – Jack Peterson.'

Unable to help herself, Pearl blurted, 'What was he like?'

'Oh, he was a fine man, and I can see something of him in your features.'

Pearl's voice still held bitterness. 'If you really are my mother, how come I ended up in an orphanage?'

'I was told you were stillborn, Pearl, and I find it unforgivable that I was lied to. I had no idea what a devious man my father was, and it seems he paid someone in the orphanage to keep you there.'

'This all sounds a bit far-fetched. I mean, if you thought I was stillborn, how did you find out I was alive?'

'I only found out when my father became seriously ill and, I think, wanted to make his peace with God. He said he'd planned to tell me one day, but not until you had left the orphanage, making it impossible for me to find you. Oh, it was so cruel, Pearl. He wanted me to suffer twice – to grieve when I thought you were stillborn, and then to suffer all over again when he told me you were alive. I can't tell you how I felt. I was angry, yes, but full of joy too.'

'So why did you come to the orphanage as a teacher? Why didn't you just claim me, tell me who you were?'

'Pearl, it wasn't that simple. My father arranged for you to be taken into the orphanage without identification, and claimed he didn't know what name you'd been given. I wrote to the orphanage, giving your date of birth, but they denied any knowledge of you. I found this very odd, but because I knew you only had a year left before leaving, I was desperate. I used another name and applied for the post of art teacher.'

'Another name. Why?'

'Because I had already written to the orphanage for information using my own name, and didn't want to arouse suspicion. My real name, our name, is Harmsworth.'

Pearl looked away. The story still sounded too fantastic to be true, but if this woman wanted to make excuses, wouldn't she have found a simpler explanation? Emily then gasped and Pearl blurted, 'Are you all right?'

'Yes, don't worry, it was just a spasm.'

'What's wrong with you?'

'I have a slight heart condition, angina, but don't worry, I've had treatment and I'm recovering. Now, where was I?' she continued, precluding any further questions about her health. 'As I said, I was told you were stillborn and you were whisked away before I got even a glimpse of your face. It was a foolish dream to think I'd begin work in the orphanage and recognise you straight away as my daughter. There were so many children, so many of the right age, and though I looked at all their faces, I was still unsure. I tried asking questions, but Miss Unsworth was always evasive, keeping her records under lock and key.'

She paused again, shaking her head. 'In the end, I knew that time had run out. I had waited a year, until all the children of the right age had gone, and with no longer any reason to stay, I handed in my resignation.'

'So how did you find me?'

She smiled softly. 'For the first time it seemed that God was smiling on me. When I went to Miss Unsworth's office, she was in the throes of leaving too, and had a pile of files on her desk. She was in the process of tearing something up from one of them when I walked in, and thrust it back into the file. As luck would have it she was called away, and I'll never know what made me do it, but I looked in that file. It was yours, Pearl, and inside I saw my letter, along with another that I recognised was in my father's handwriting.'

'What did Miss Unsworth have to say?'

'I didn't wait to confront her, Pearl. I had found you, saw where you had been placed, and that was all that mattered.'

Pearl gazed at Miss Rosen – no, Miss Harmsworth – wanting to believe her, but still she hesitated. 'Why have you waited this long before coming to see me?'

'Oh, Pearl, you disappeared. You left the laundry, the hostel, and nobody knew where you'd gone. I was desperate to find you, and if I'd had money I would have hired a private detective, but my father must still have wanted to punish me, leaving me nothing in his will. I refused to give up, I kept looking but, shortly after, I was taken ill.'

'How how did you find me?'

'It was like a miracle, Pearl. I saw your picture in a newspaper, along with a story about your husband.'

'Bessie was right,' Pearl murmured.

'What do you mean?'

Pearl told her about Bessie's vision. Emily gasped, 'My goodness, that's amazing.'

Johnny stirred and Emily moved to the cot, leaning forward to cup his face gently in her hand. 'He's lovely, and ... and I can't believe I have a grandson. Oh Pearl, I mourned you for so many years. How could my father do such a thing?' Her composure broke and tears began to roll down her cheeks. 'I missed so much, Pearl. Your first smile, your first step, and I've never even held you in my arms.'

Something jolted inside Pearl. It was true. This woman was her mother! Johnny's grandmother! 'Please, don't cry.'

Emily dashed the tears from her face. 'Oh, my precious girl, they are partly tears of joy. I've found you. After all these years, I've found you!'

Pearl saw the love in her eyes, and suddenly nothing else mattered. With a small cry she rose to her feet, running straight into her mother's arms.

They clung together, swaying, both now sobbing. Pearl could feel how thin her mother was and as they drew apart she said, 'Are you sure you're all right?'

'Yes, I'm on medication now and there's nothing to worry about.'

She then took Pearl's arm, drew her to the bed and they sat down. 'We have so much to talk about, so much to catch up on.'

'Yes, I know. Do you still teach art?'

'Yes, my dear. I left a local school to come to the orphanage to look for you, but they were kind enough to take me back.'

'I love art too, and until I fell pregnant, I took lessons.'

'Yes, I recognised your talent, and even dared to hope for a while. But when you were one of the first to leave, I thought your date of birth must have been earlier in the year. Too early for you to be my daughter. Oh, Pearl, we have lost so many years and I can't bear to be parted from you again. I ... I have a cottage in Winchester. Please, will you come to live with me?'

'With you?'

'Yes, Pearl,' she said, animated with excitement now. 'It isn't large, but there's a spare room. I'd love you to live with me, to see my grandson growing up. Please say yes.'

Pearl gazed at her mother, saw the appeal in her eyes and felt her heart fill with joy. This woman, this frail but beautiful woman, was her mother and was offering her a home. For a moment her face straightened and she hung her head. It would mean leaving Battersea, and though this was something she had longed to do, it would mean leaving Bessie – Derek too.

As though reading her mind, Emily spoke. 'I realise there are people here that you'll miss, but you can still see them.'

'Winchester is so far away and it wouldn't be easy.'

'Nonsense. It isn't that far and there are trains. If you want to see Bessie, you could visit at weekends, and I'm sure she'll always offer you a bed.'

'Yes, she would,' Pearl agreed, yet still she hesitated.

'Oh, my darling girl, I'll understand if you want to stay, but will you come with me, if only for little while? I love you, my dear, will always love you, but I want so much for us to get to know each other.'

Hearing her mother's words, Pearl's heart once again surged with joy. It was as if her dreams had come true. She had a mother. A mother who loved her. It would be hard to leave Bessie, but she had Nora now and wouldn't be alone. She could talk to Derek, explain that she'd come to see him as often as she could. He said he'd wait, but it would be a long time before she was divorced – free. Would he wait that long?

Pearl sighed. There was no way of knowing, the future not hers to see. She and Derek would have to take it one step at a time, but for now, her mother was right. They needed to get to know each other.

She turned, smiling widely. 'Oh, yes please, I'd love to come to stay with you.'

The publishers hope that this book has given you enjoyable reading. Large Print Books are especially designed to be as easy to see and hold as possible. If you wish a complete list of our books please ask at your local library or write directly to:

Magna Large Print Books
Magna House, Long Preston,
Skipton, North Yorkshire.
BD23 4ND

This Large Print Book for the partially sighted, who cannot read normal print, is published under the auspices of

THE ULVERSCROFT FOUNDATION